STORMY WEATHER

Faith stood in the darkness, her sadness suffocating her and making her breaths come in short, harsh gasps. The rain beat down on her, but it couldn't drown the memories or quench the fire that raged inside, destroying the apathy she'd fought so hard to maintain.

"Faith." The voice came from everywhere and nowhere. At first, she thought she'd imagined it, but then she saw large hands close over hers, felt a massive chest pressed to her back, and heard Jesse's familiar voice.

"Leave me alone," she cried, her voice fierce, raw with a hurt she yearned to ignore. "Just leave me the hell alone!"

She wrenched her hands from his. Whirling, she lashed out at him, anger and pain and fear making her fight when she wanted nothing more than to sink to the ground and dissolve into the mud puddle beneath her feet. Anything to escape the emotions that she swore she'd never feel again.

Something flickered in Jesse's dark eyes; then he whispered, the sound barely audible above the rain, "I know what you're feeling, Faith. I know." And then his mouth swooped down and his lips captured hers.

FAITHLESS ANGEL

KIMBERLY RAYE

LOVE SPELL BOOKS   NEW YORK CITY

LOVE SPELL®

February 1999

 Published by

Dorchester Publishing Co., Inc.
276 Fifth Avenue
New York, NY 10001

ISBN 0-505-52296-9

The name "Love Spell" and its logo are trademarks of Dorchester
Publishing Co., Inc.

Printed in the United States of America.

For Bonnie Tucker, Jan Freed and Kathleen McKeague,
for all the red ink and inspiring trust.
You guys pushed me to the next level
and I'm forever in your debt!

And for Gerry Bartlett, who lends her help and advice
and willingly inconveniences herself time after time.
You're the best!

And special thanks to Carol Gooden
with Children's Protective Services in Houston, Texas,
for lending her expertise and answering all my questions,
no matter how trivial.

FAITHLESS ANGEL

Be not afraid to have strangers in your house,
for some thereby have entertained angels unawares.
—Hebrews 13:2

Chapter One

This had to be a mistake.

Stepping back, Jesse Savage glanced up, his gaze slicing through the drizzle to study the bold black numbers mounted above the porch doorway. No mistake. He studied the front of the house. The place looked too clean for this neighborhood and too well cared for, especially since the woman who lived inside had supposedly given up caring for anyone or anything. Only the black iron burglar bars covering the windows and the front door gave any indication that this was far from the best part of town.

Jesse moved back onto the porch and pulled his fist from his pocket to press the doorbell. Just shy of pushing the button, he stared at the deep pink scar that zigzagged its way across his hand, from his tattered coat sleeve clear to his thumb.

He closed his eyes to the rush of memories—the pain, the voices. . . .

Lookee what we got here.

This ain't none of your business.

Get lost, Savage. Your brother's who we want.

His brother. But Jesse had been the one to go down first. The one who'd smashed into the floor. The one who'd landed in a heap, hurt and bleeding. Dying . . .

No more! He forced his eyes open. It was almost over, he reminded himself. After he finished with the woman inside the immaculate, whitewashed duplex with the neatly trimmed hedges and the jungle of half-dead hanging plants swinging beneath the porch eve, it truly would be over. He would have his chance to ask forgiveness. One last chance. Then no more scars, and no more regrets. Nothing but peace.

Ignoring the sting of pain as his jacket cuff chafed the tender flesh around the scar, he pressed his finger to the doorbell. A chime sounded, then quiet. Only the swoosh of passing cars on the busy intersection a block away disturbed the drizzly afternoon's silence.

He stabbed the button again and flexed his fingers, the pain in his hand aggravated by the cold that had swept into Houston that morning. The wind battered him, lifting his hair to creep beneath the collar of his jacket and spread over his skin. He'd almost forgotten how erratic the weather could be in Texas, even in May. Summer one day, lingering winter the next.

A string of high-pitched barks scattered his thoughts. The muffled voice of a woman came from somewhere in the house, and the barking quickly died down. The slow creak of a door followed seconds later and he found himself gazing past the bars, into a questioning pair of green eyes—wide, gold-flecked green eyes that seemed to stare straight through him. Eyes that would have made him think of sunshine and picnics if there hadn't been rain clouds lurking in their depths.

She wouldn't want to open the door to a man like him. He knew it even before he saw her hesitation. With his worn clothes, his hair long and unkempt, and his face in sore need of a shave, he looked like nothing more than a bum. Street trash. Scum.

The words filtered through her head to his, as if a current flowed between them, connected them. . . . Hell, they *were* connected. That had been part of the deal. But he'd never imagined the feelings would be so strong. So fierce.

He had the insane urge to reach out and reassure her that he meant no harm. Then again, she lived and worked in this neighborhood. She'd sure as hell seen far worse, and Jesse had never been one to comfort. Or to speak his feelings. That was why he was in this damned mess in the first place.

"Yes?" Her question was little more than a sigh. Her bottom lip trembled so slightly that anyone else might not have noticed. But he did. He noticed everything about her. Her scent—a sweet mingling of roses and warm female—filled his nostrils. Her heart beat a frenzied tempo in his head. Her breathing followed the rise and fall of his own chest.

Connected. Linked.

"Faith Jansen?" he asked.

Her eyes, red-rimmed and slightly swollen, narrowed considerably. "Do I know you?"

"Not yet. I'm Jesse Savage." He extended his hand, fingertips brushing one iron bar. She made no move to accept his gesture, not that he blamed her. Not the way he looked. She continued to stare at him, suspicion swimming in those incredible eyes of hers.

"Is your name supposed to mean something to me?" She looked thoughtful, then shook her head. "I'm afraid it doesn't."

It will. Soon. Very soon . . .

"I'm here about the job," he told her.

"What job?"

"The one listed in the *Houston Chronicle*." He fished inside his coat pocket and pulled out the crumpled piece of newspaper. Uncurling the edges, he held up the want ad. "You own Faith's House, right? That foster home for troubled kids a block off San Jacinto?"

"Maybe." One slender arm shot out between the burglar bars to take the paper from his outstretched hand. Her fingertips brushed the scar and he jerked back. Not from pain, but from a sizzle of current that went through him at the hint of contact with her.

Her gaze zeroed in on his hand and her eyes went wide. "I'm so sorry. Did I hurt you?"

"It's nothing." He didn't mean to sound so harsh, especially since he heard the open concern in her voice, felt it in the sudden stall of her heartbeat.

Concern, when she'd supposedly given up on emotion.

It was gone with her next words, however. The sting of his reply had undoubtedly zapped her back to reality. To her grief.

Damn, but he was stupid.

And determined, he reminded himself. And where there was concern, there was more. Hope. Compassion. Faith. And that was why he was here.

"The job," he said again, indicating the ad. "I'm here about the job."

14

She studied the paper for a few seconds, while Jesse studied her.

She was nothing like he'd expected. With light brown hair pulled back in a simple ponytail, her face devoid of makeup, she looked a lot younger than her twenty-eight years, and way too innocent. Not hardened or jaded like a woman who'd been around the block one too many times. Nothing like he'd imagined.

He shifted uncomfortably and she turned those green eyes on him again. That was when he saw the truth. A slow-burning hurt simmered just below the surface of those green-gold depths, beneath the suspicion and the anger. She was someone who'd seen too much, felt too much, and he knew then that she was the one.

"I didn't place that ad," she told him.

"But you do own Faith's House?"

"Yes, but my assistant is running things now."

"I could really use the job, Ms. Jansen."

"Then you'll have to contact Bradley Winters." She shook her head, obviously puzzled. "How did you get this address in the first place? The ad gives the phone number for Faith's House, not my home listing."

"This is a small neighborhood. You do a lot for the community. Everyone around here knows you. They all appreciate what you're doing."

"Sure they do. Is that why my garbage cans are stolen on a weekly basis?" Her words dripped with a cynicism that Jesse knew all too well. "Garbage cans, of all things. If it isn't chained down, kids will run off with anything in this neighborhood."

"I really do need the job," he pressed.

"Look—"

"I've had some college," he cut in. "I don't have a

degree or anything. I didn't quite make it that far, but I worked with an outreach program that mentored troubled teens, and I know kids. I had a brother and sister, both younger than me. I'm good with children. Practically raised my brother and sister myself."

"That's commendable, Mr.—" She caught her full bottom lip for a thoughtful second. "What did you say your name was?"

"Savage. Jesse Savage, and I'm a reliable worker, too."

"I'm sure you are, Mr. Savage. But the kids are in Bradley's hands right now. You want to answer his ad, call the phone number printed there. I'm on leave."

"For how long?"

Her gaze narrowed at his bold question. "Are you sure I don't know you from somewhere? I mean, your name isn't familiar, but something about you is."

His body tingled beneath her lingering stare. Heat pulsed through veins that had known only cold contempt for so long. Too long.

He forced the notion aside and shook his head. "No, but I really need this job."

"Sorry. I can't help you." She went to close the door, but Jesse reached past the bars and grasped the door frame, his hand so close to her face that he could feel the heat that colored her cheeks.

"Maybe you could at least put in a good word for me," he said, wanting so much to touch her. Just one slow sweep of his hand. Her skin would be warm and supple beneath his fingertip—

"And maybe you could move your hand."

Annoyance laced her words, but he heard something else, as well. Desperation.

Yes, she was the one.

Unspoken challenge charged the air between them for several long moments before he finally let go of the door frame. His knuckles brushed her cheek then, a bold move he regretted instantly. She was warmer than he'd expected, and softer.

He watched her stiffen. Fear fought a battle with the anger that blazed in her eyes.

Then again, she was right to fear a man who looked the way he did. She'd be stupid otherwise, and careless. She might have lost her hope, but she hadn't lost her smarts. Not completely, anyway, despite the fact that she'd answered the doorbell in the first place.

"You said the guy to contact is Bradley Winters?" he asked as she moved to close the door.

She stopped just two inches shy of completely closing it and stared at him through the small space. "He's the acting administrator right now. Hiring and firing are in his hands."

"That's a shame. I hear you've got quite a reputation with the kids."

"Don't believe everything you hear, Mr. Savage." An unmistakable bitterness fueled her voice.

"I don't," he replied. "And I don't talk just to talk, Ms. Jansen. Those kids need you."

He saw something flicker deep in her eyes. Then the shrill ring of a phone sounded somewhere in the house, followed by a quick succession of barks mimicking those he'd heard when he'd first rung her doorbell. Her lips pursed, and her eyes narrowed. "And I need to be left alone, if you don't mind."

"But I do mind."

She stared at him for the space of two heartbeats, a puzzled expression on her face. Then the door shut, the lock clicked, and Jesse found himself standing alone, the cold swirling around him, *inside* him.

Turning, he stepped off the porch into the steady drizzle that quickly grew to a frenzied shower. He lifted the collar on his jacket and thrust his hands deep in his pockets, his fingers tight around the scrap of newspaper.

Maybe Faith Jansen wanted to be left alone, but that was the last thing she needed. The last thing Jesse intended to allow. He needed her, and she needed him, though she didn't realize it.

Yet.

"Just drop the papers off here, Bradley," Faith said into the phone seconds after she closed the front door. She stared past the lace curtains covering her front window.

Her gaze followed the stranger as he headed down the driveway toward the street, the rain pelting him, his faded jeans now drenched. The material clung to his thighs, like a denim skin that outlined the lean perfection of every muscle.

"No can do," the man on the other end of the phone said. "Megan eloped with that bagel guy last night and I can't leave a house full of kids unchaperoned. She won't be back until after the honeymoon. Three weeks minimum."

"So bring the papers over after she gets back." She forced her attention higher, to Jesse Savage's broad shoulders outlined by a faded high school letterman's jacket. He moved through the downpour, head held high, his body swift and sure, even when the rain came harder. The fiercer the storm grew, the more purposeful his step, until he seemed to blend in with the elements and become one with them.

". . . you there?" Bradley's voice penetrated her thoughts.

"I'm here." She let the lace curtain fall back into place and bent down to scoop up the tiny puppy she'd unwillingly adopted last week when she'd found him abandoned in a cardboard box behind a nearby trash Dumpster. "What were you saying?"

"I said Children's Protective Services is bringing the kid today. If you're not here to sign, CPS will keep him in protective custody for God knows how long. You have to come over here."

She stroked the puppy's head, the gesture rewarded with a barrage of ticklish licks to her fingers. "I can't, Bradley."

"Dammit, Faith! You leave me high and dry, working my tail end off for the past two weeks while you hibernate at home—"

"I'm sorry. I really am. I wish you could understand." She held the dog close, absorbing the warmth of his small body, wishing with everything she had that it was enough to penetrate the ice surrounding her heart.

"I understand perfectly. You're the one out in left field, Faith. You've turned into a hermit lady."

"I have not."

Silence stretched between them for several seconds before Bradley finally spoke, his voice soft, pleading. "Face reality, Faith. Jane's gone, but there's a whole houseful of kids who still need you."

Those kids need you. Jesse Savage's words echoed in her head, and oddly enough she felt a small pang of guilt. Strange, considering she'd been numb for the past two weeks—ever since she'd watched them lower the coffin into the ground, heard the first plop of dirt hit the lid.

"Aren't you advertising for someone to help out?"

She put the puppy on the carpeted floor and watched him waddle toward the pallet of blankets in the corner. She glanced at her fingertips and saw they were still smudged with newsprint from Jesse's soggy want ad.

"Yeah, but that won't solve today's dilemma. CPS won't release a child to anyone's custody but yours. I'm your official assistant, but you're the foster mother. Unless you want to send this kid back where he came from—and I hear he's been living the past few weeks at that hellhole Booker Hall—then you'd better pull yourself together and come down here."

"Okay," she said after a hesitant moment. "I'll be there, but just to sign the papers. In and out of my office; then I'm gone. And . . . don't tell the kids."

"Thank heavens, there is a God," Bradley said, letting loose a relieved sigh.

"I wouldn't bet on it."

"Try to cheer up, honey. What happened to Jane was no one's fault." Bradley's voice filled with sympathy. "It was a tragic accident, Faith. These things happen."

"That's the problem. What happened to—" Her throat closed around the name and she swallowed, but there was no ache in her chest. Nothing. She wouldn't let herself feel anything.

"It wasn't your fault."

"Forget it, Bradley. What time should I be there?"

"Around three. I'll leave your office unlocked, the papers on your desk."

"Where will you be?"

"Neck-deep in kids, as usual, and hunting like hell for an assistant of my own, since you haven't decided to come back to the land of the living."

But how could she live when she'd already died inside?

The question stuck in her brain as she placed the receiver in its cradle. Shoving aside a pile of throw pillows, she sank down onto her cream-colored sofa and stared at the chaos that had once been her living room.

Newspapers blanketed most of the champagne-colored carpet. Old pizza boxes cluttered the coffee table. Balls of wadded tissue overflowed from the brass trash can near one end table. Silver bits and pieces of what had once been her prized CD collection littered the corner of the room near a virtual forest of dying ferns.

Grubby waddled across the floor from his pallet, nudging papers and trash with his nose. Cocoa-colored with white speckles sprinkled across his fat tummy, he was the only redeeming thing in the entire room, and she almost smiled.

Instead, she closed her eyes and concentrated on the rain that beat a steady tattoo on the roof, the sound almost deafening, numbing. . . .

Yes, numb was much better. Easier. Much easier than those few days she'd spent at the hospital, crying and praying and urging Jane to fight for her life. Her words had been wasted, her tears for nothing, her prayers meaningless. Like everything now.

Those kids need you.

Little did Jesse Savage know that those kids were better off without her. What could she possibly offer them?

A roof over their heads. Food in their stomachs. Someone to care for them, her conscience answered for an instant before her cynicism kicked in.

So what? In the end, none of that mattered. It hadn't mattered that Jane had been like her own daughter, that Faith had nursed her through nightmares, fed her, clothed her, loved her. It hadn't mattered a bit. Jane was dead, despite everything.

Shoving a strand of hair back from her face, she let her fingers linger at her cheek. She could still feel the brush of warm male skin, the sudden heat that had spread through her and thawed her insides for the split second when Jesse Savage had touched her.

Dangerous. That was what she'd first thought the moment she'd pulled open the front door and seen him standing there, filling the empty space of her porch.

With an overgrowth of stubble, dark, piercing brown eyes, and even darker hair brushing his collar, he'd looked more than simply dangerous. He'd looked downright deadly. She'd been a fool to open the door to someone like him, especially in this neighborhood, even with the burglar bars she'd installed last year.

Then again, cautious people died as quickly, as easily as fools did. Everyone died. Dumb and not so dumb. Rich and poor. Young and old. Everyone. No reason, no rhyme.

As dangerous as he'd looked, he'd also struck her as oddly familiar, as if she'd seen him somewhere before. But where—

The crash of trash-can lids brought her eyes wide open. She bolted from the couch and rushed to the kitchen, reaching the back door in time to see one large silver trash can, newly purchased just last week, take a tumble off her back steps. At the same time, a grungy teen wearing a tattered pair of jeans and a shabby T-shirt snatched up the other gleaming can.

Instead of pulling open the door as she used to, and giving the thieving adolescent a piece of her mind, she simply turned away. She shut out the noise and the sight of garbage littering her back steps and headed for the bedroom to change.

She wouldn't care.

The firm vow didn't bring a smile to her lips, or tears to her eyes. There was no freedom, or even guilt. Nothing except the image of a dark and dangerous and disturbingly familiar stranger, his deep voice echoing, *Those kids need you....*

And for a fraction of a heartbeat, Faith wanted to believe him. But her beliefs, her faith, were now as dead as her dear, sweet Jane.

"Take it easy, Emily."

The boy's familiar voice stopped Faith's hand in midair. She glanced up from the stack of papers she'd been signing, her gaze sweeping from the back door of Faith's House, which she'd entered only minutes ago, to the closed door that led to the rest of the building. Her attention riveted to the knob and she silently damned herself for not thinking to lock the door when she'd first come inside.

But she'd never locked her door. She'd never shut it, even when the house had been full of noise and chaos. But she'd never slipped in the back way, either.

"It isn't your CD, you pighead," another voice, this one female, replied. "Bradley told you to keep your slimy paws off my stuff. Now give it back!"

A loud thud and the door trembled.

"Hey, watch it," Ricky grumbled. "That hurt."

"Good. Touch my stuff again and I'll do more than that, understand?"

Ricky grumbled a "Geez, Em"; then rubber soles squeaked against the polished hardwood floor. Everything fell silent again.

Kimberly Raye

Faith breathed a sigh of relief and went back to signing the stack of documents on her cluttered desk. As she stared at the pile of work, she almost felt sorry for Bradley. She hoped he could find a proficient assistant, because she meant today to be her last day at Faith's House.

She took a small sip of black coffee and stared at the folded blue-bound set of legal papers protruding from the outside pocket of her purse. Once she signed and presented the forms to Bradley and he signed on the dotted line, he would be the official foster parent—CPS had already approved him—and she would be free and clear to "hibernate" at home, as he'd called it. Faith's House would no longer be Faith's House, but Bradley's House.

You're home, Jane. Home—

Faith slammed her mind shut to that memory. This wasn't a home. Home was where the heart was, and Faith had lost hers.

The sound of voices penetrated her thoughts. Voices turned to shouts, and she reasoned that Emily and Pighead were going at it. Then she heard it—a vicious bellow of anger that brought her out of her chair.

Her Styrofoam cup of coffee tipped over. Steaming black liquid spread across her desktop. She shoved her papers aside so they wouldn't get soaked and flew to the door. Yanking it open, she rushed down the hallway. That was when she saw him.

"I ain't staying here!" cried a skinny, teenage boy who headed straight for her. Long, tangled blond hair hung past his shoulders. His pale blue eyes were slightly swollen, as if he'd been crying, or was coming off the wagon, the second being more likely.

"Calm down, Daniel," said the woman behind him. Estelle Adams, the foster-home development

24

worker from CPS, held a small, battered suitcase in one hand, and her black imitation alligator purse in the other. "This is the only place that will take you—"

"Come on, man. Give us a chance," Bradley cut in, following on Estelle's heels. "You'll like it here. Promise."

"Go to hell," Daniel said in a hiss, his skinny frame shooting past Faith, making her cling to the wall to avoid being trampled. "I ain't staying in this hell-hole, do you hear? I ain't." But instead of heading for the back hallway, he whirled and reached for Faith. One wiry arm wrapped around her neck, while the other hauled her up hard against him.

"Anyone comes near me and I'll cut her," he said.

And with his words came the feel of cold steel at Faith's neck. The blade bit into her skin and chased the air from her lungs, and Death himself breathed down her neck.

Chapter Two

Faith watched, the knife at her throat, as Estelle and Bradley stopped short, along with the cluster of kids who now followed them.

"He's got a blade, Mr. Winters," one small voice said.

"He's got Ms. Jansen!" came Emily's shocked cry.

"He's gonna cut her!"

"Somebody do something!"

"Quiet!" Bradley held up his hand. "Everyone quiet." His attention went to the boy holding Faith prisoner. "Don't do this, Daniel. Please."

"He was searched before he left Booker Hall. I can't imagine how he got that. . . ." Estelle's words faded into the shocked murmurs echoing through the group crammed into the hallway.

"Think, Daniel," Bradley said in the calm voice he used with all the kids, but he looked anything but calm. Panic flashed in his eyes, and the hand he held out shook noticeably. "You do this right here, right now, in front of everyone, and you'll be headed for jail. *Jail*, do you understand?"

"This dump ain't much better, and if you take one more step, I'll gut her like a fish."

Oddly enough, it wasn't fear that made Faith gasp for a breath. It was the force of the boy's grip. He was unusually strong for his age and weight; Faith knew, for she'd tackled the best of them during the past five years running Faith's House. Ricky, "Pighead," played high school football, and she'd even wrestled him down once when he'd been uncooperative and a bit too sassy for his own good.

She had faced knives before, too. She'd even stared down the barrel of a gun when Emily had been dead-set on running away the first week she'd come to the house. And always before, Faith had been scared. Terrified.

Not this time. Jane's image flashed in her mind—mousy brown hair, big, wide brown eyes—and Faith's heartbeat remained steady, as if her life didn't hang in the balance. But it did, she reminded herself. It did!

She stayed calm.

The frail chest pressed against her back heaved frantically, and she knew her attacker was anything but calm. He was frightened, as frightened as she should be, and he was all the more dangerous because of it.

She raised one hand and gripped the wrist near her throat.

"Don't even think it, lady," Daniel said, his voice shaky despite his threat.

Still, Faith's fingers wrapped about his wrist. The blade pressed deeper into her throat. She felt his pulse race beneath her fingertips.

"Move another muscle and I'll cut you," Daniel threatened. "I swear it." The knife edged deeper.

Bradley turned stark white, his eyes pleading with her captor. "Let her go, Daniel! Don't do this, man. You'll be shipped off to a place a hundred times worse than this."

"Do it," Faith whispered. "Stop talking and do it—" Her voice caught as the blade pressed deeper.

"Shut up!"

"You think you're scaring me? she rasped while Bradley shot her a warning look. He thought she was trying to psyche Daniel out, make him blow his cool and lose his nerve. A bitter laugh rose to her lips. She was saying exactly what she would have said a month ago. The difference was, now she meant it.

"You're not," she went on. "You don't scare me, and neither does that knife, and death couldn't be much worse than the past two weeks. So go on and put me out of my misery."

"I said *shut up!*" he ground out. Knuckles dug into her throat as Daniel adjusted his hold on the knife. "You wanna die? Well, you just might get your chance. Keep talking and you'll get it good—" His words were cut off, followed by a yelp.

The knife clattered to the floor and Faith found herself free. She stumbled forward, her fingers going to her throat. She landed on her knees, the room spinning around her for a dangerous second.

Then a large, strong hand came from behind, gripped her arm, and helped her to her feet.

Faith stared up into the face of Jesse Savage. Apparently, he'd come through the back door, approached from behind, and grabbed Daniel by the shirt collar. Jesse's lips formed a deep scowl, his dark eyes alight with anger and worry and something else—something she might have mistaken for fear if she hadn't known better.

But she'd known men like Jesse Savage. They came from the streets; they fought their way through poverty, most ending up behind bars or six feet under. Fear wasn't a weakness they indulged in. But neither was kindness, yet here he was, her hero—whether he looked the part or not.

"What the hell is wrong with you?" he demanded. "Are you crazy, testing a kid like this?" He glanced at the sullen-looking Daniel dangling by his collar. Jesse's grip tightened on the boy's shirt. "He could have killed you! A second more and he would have." Those intense dark eyes riveted on her throat. "And I can't say as I would have blamed him, with you running your mouth like that. You were asking for it."

"He was bluffing."

"But you weren't." Jesse's fingertips burned into her arm, stirring a strange heat that made her body tingle. "Were you?"

"No."

His fingers tightened considerably and she wondered who posed the bigger threat: this dark stranger who wore a look as menacing as thunder, or the frightened teenager who'd nearly sliced open her jugular?

She knew the answer as she stared deep into Jesse's eyes and saw a lifetime of pain and hatred and misery. Fear rippled through her, along with an unmistakable pang of sympathy that crumbled her control. She took an unsteady step back, leaning against the wall as the floor took a dangerous tilt.

"Faith, are you all right?" Bradley was beside her, concern wrinkling his forehead. A visibly shaken Estelle followed him.

"I'm so sorry, dear," Estelle chimed in. "Daniel was searched at Booker Hall. I can't understand how—"

"It's all right," Faith rasped. Her throat burned like the devil, distracting her from the strange feeling Jesse Savage had stirred.

"The show's over," Bradley said, turning to the group of kids clustered behind him. "Everybody back to your chores." His words met with several grumbles, but after a fierce look from him and a nod from Faith, the crowd started to thin. The sound of a vacuum cleaner resumed. The chatter of voices drifted from the kitchen. Dishes clattered, and Faith's House returned to its usual buzz of normal activity.

"We owe you, mister." Bradley shook Jesse's hand. "And it's back to Booker Hall for you," he told Daniel, who still dangled from Jesse's right hand.

"No." Faith shook her head. "He's staying here."

"You can't be serious?" Estelle gripped Faith's hand. "It's too dangerous to have him at a place like this. The other kids—"

"—were just as bad when they first got here," Faith finished for her. "Richard attacked me with a baseball bat, and Drew set the living room drapes on fire. But look at them now." Her gaze shot to the two boys barely visible down the hall. One had a can of furniture polish and a rag in his hand. The other boy sprawled on the sofa, his nose buried in a library book.

"Besides, that was the whole purpose of this, wasn't it, Daniel? To get out of staying?" Faith fixed her gaze on Daniel, whose pale blue eyes widened considerably beneath her inspection. "You don't get your way around here by bullying people. Cooperation and hard work are the only things that pull any weight."

Daniel dropped his head, and studied his worn tennis shoes. He tried to shrug away from Jesse, whose grip seemed to tighten.

"We'll pair him up with Mike," Faith told Bradley. "Mike!" A few seconds later a young man in his early twenties filled the hallway. Wearing a flannel shirt and jeans, he looked like a lumberjack—big, brawny, intimidating. . . . A definite badass, the kids called him.

"Daniel's our newest arrival," Faith told him, doing her damnedest to block out Jesse's presence. But her body seemed insistent on paying attention to him. Her skin still prickled with awareness where he'd touched her.

He'd felt strong. And warm. And so—

"Yeah, it sounded like quite a show." Mike's voice derailed her train of thought. "I was in the shower when it started, so I only heard the tail end, or I would have been here a heck of a lot sooner. You all right?" he asked Faith.

"I'm fine, but I think Daniel needs a little one-on-one until he gets used to the routine here. Think you can keep an eye on him and show him the ropes?"

The young man, a deep frown on his face, his brown eyes solemn, studied Daniel for a long moment. The boy actually swallowed beneath the careful scrutiny, and a smile tugged at Faith's lips. He wasn't so hard beneath that tough-as-nails exterior. He was just a kid. A scared, lonely kid.

"You want me to go with *him?*" Daniel stared at her as if she'd just sentenced him to the electric chair.

"Think of him as your shadow for the next few weeks." Faith stared pointedly at Daniel. "And don't even think about taking advantage of him. He's got a black belt in karate and he'll eat you for breakfast if you give him a reason."

"Oh, yeah?" Daniel tried to shrug away from Jesse's grip again, but the effort was useless. "Well, I guess he can't be much worse than Hercules here." He cast a resentful glance at Jesse.

"Don't count on it," Mike said, and Daniel visibly paled.

Faith fought back the urge to laugh. Most everyone had the same reaction to Mike. He was huge, all muscle and menace, but he had a kind heart and a way with troubled kids. But then, Mike could relate. He'd been one of them not so long ago.

"Come on, Daniel," Mike said, holding out one beefy hand. Daniel took another step back, coming up hard against Jesse, who scowled at him.

Despite Jesse's expression, Faith didn't miss the amusement dancing in his dark eyes. The look drew an unwilling smile to her own lips.

"Go on, Daniel. He won't bite," Faith said. "Unless you try another stunt like the one you pulled on me." At Faith's nod, Jesse released Daniel, who straightened his T-shirt and glared at everyone around him, as if to say *stand back*.

Mike wasn't intimidated. "Come on, buddy. You and I have a little talking to do." Immediately, Mike grabbed the boy's arm and pulled him down the hallway, despite a string of heated curses that burned through the air and made Bradley blush.

When the two had rounded the corner, Daniel's voice fading to an indistinguishable grumble, Faith turned to Estelle. "Let me finish signing Daniel's paperwork—it's in my office—and we'll get him settled in."

"I hate that this happened, but I'm glad you're

back," Bradley told Faith as he followed her into the small, cramped room.

"I'm not back."

His smile died. "Geez, Faith. You can't leave me here with that kid. You might have a death wish, but I like my neck in one piece, thank you very much."

"I'm not leaving you here all by yourself. Megan will be back after the honeymoon. You've got Mike to supervise the not-so-cooperative ones." She glanced past Bradley to the man who'd followed him into the office.

Jesse's intense dark eyes locked with hers, and she had the sudden urge to cover herself. He didn't simply stare at her; he looked *inside* her to probe her thoughts.

"Mr. Savage here can help you out with the rest of the kids." She reached for a stack of files to keep from folding her arms in front of her, as if it would do any good. Jesse could give Superman a run for his kryptonite when it came to X-ray vision. "You're still interested in a job, aren't you, Jesse?"

"That's what I came for."

"Good timing," Bradley said. "What do you say, Estelle?" he asked the woman the minute she walked through the doorway, her tattered briefcase in hand. "Think you can run this man's application through your office ASAP so he can start right away?"

The older woman gave Jesse an assessing stare. He smiled at her, and her expression quickly relaxed, easing the deep crow's-feet near her eyes. "Why, I'm sure I can get the approval, provided your background checks out, Mr. Savage. That should take two to three weeks. Then we'll get all the paperwork in order." Had he looked nervous when she mentioned a background check, or was it Faith's imagination.

"We need him sooner than that," Bradley said. "Faith is bailing out on me."

"A leave of absence," Faith corrected. "Indefinite."

"A shame," Estelle replied. "But I don't see a way around the time stipulation. We're always short-handed, and background checks have to be thorough. . . ." A thoughtful frown settled on her face; then an idea seemed to strike her. "You can't officially hire him without department approval, but he could start right away as a volunteer." Her thin red lips spread into a smile. "Once the paperwork goes through, you can pay him back salary."

"Sounds good to me if it works for you," Bradley said, turning to Jesse. "I'll float you an advance on your salary. The job includes room and board. Mike bunks out in a small efficiency apartment over the garage when he's not supervising a problem case. With Daniel here, he'll be keeping the boy company upstairs, so you can have the efficiency until Daniel gets settled. We'll see to something more permanent after that. What do you say, Savage?" Bradley held out a hand to seal the deal with a shake. "Pay ain't that hot, but I make a mean lasagna. And Faith here—" His words ground to a halt as he glanced at her. "Well, she did make a great omelette, but we'll have to make do without it. For now."

Jesse looked hesitant. Then he pulled his hand from his pocket, slowly, almost reluctantly. Strong, lean fingers clasped Bradley's stubby ones for a brief moment.

Faith's gaze riveted on the jagged pink scar that marred Jesse's otherwise tanned flesh. The urge to reach out and trace the line, to share his pain and ease the suffering she saw deep in his eyes, was incredible. She pushed the thought away, grabbed her pen, and accepted the papers Estelle handed her. She wasn't some silly bleeding heart. Not anymore.

"All done," she said, standing up a few minutes later.

Estelle took the papers and glanced at her watch. "Oh, I really must go. I've got a meeting in half an hour."

"I'll walk you out." Bradley took her briefcase and followed her through the doorway. "Be back in a sec," he said over his shoulder.

The moment the two of them disappeared, Faith reached for her purse. All she needed was Bradley's signature; then she could get out of here before the kids finished their chores and came looking for her, particularly Emily. Faith and the girl had grown very close over the past two years.

No more, Faith told herself.

She reached for the papers. The moment her fingertips brushed one folded corner, a strange numbness gripped her hand. The documents sailed to the floor.

Odd. She flexed her fingers. They felt fine now. A ripple of apprehension seeped through her, but she quickly shook it away and reached again.

A large, scarred hand beat her to the task.

"What are these?"

"Just some papers." She held out her hand.

"Important?"

"Very." She swallowed against the sudden tightening of her throat. "Can I have them back?"

He hesitated a moment before placing them in her palm. "Thanks for the job."

"No thanks necessary. You earned it."

"And you nearly got yourself killed. Do you always

live so dangerously?" His voice was rich, deep, unsettling.

She swallowed. "It's what I do." *Did*, she silently corrected. Being a foster mother to a group of troubled teens brought a fair share of danger, but that had never put Faith off. Sure, there were dangerous instances, but she'd always believed that you get out of life what you give, and she'd always given love, hope, help.

How foolish. The world didn't work that way. Tragedy struck in the blink of an eye, no rhyme or reason to it, and no number of good deeds could prevent it.

No more, she told herself. *No more*.

She went to unfold the papers, but they slipped again from her suddenly trembling fingers to land in the puddle of coffee she'd spilled earlier.

"Damn it." She wiped at the liquid on the pages, but the ink had already started to run. "Great. Now I'll have to wait until Monday for another copy." She closed her eyes in frustration. She wanted out, yet she found herself more trapped at every turn.

"Copy of what?"

"I'm sure Bradley has a ton of work for you." She folded the soggy papers and stuffed them into her bag. "Tell him I'll talk to him later."

"You're leaving?"

"Yes." With her response came the tiniest spasm of guilt, so small she immediately pushed it aside.

She inched past Jesse, ignoring the strange heat that shot through her when she brushed against one lean, muscled arm. She moved toward the back door, but a large hand closed over her shoulder and brought her to an abrupt stop.

"Thanks again," he said, the words enough to send

a tremor along her nerve endings. "You won't regret giving me this job."

She stared at the toes of her worn flats, resisting the urge to turn, to look into his eyes. "I already do," she whispered, her voice so low she wondered if he could even hear it.

If he did, he gave no indication. He murmured a quick, "I appreciate the chance," then let his hand fall away.

She forced her feet forward, fleeing the office into an afternoon that had turned even bleaker since the early morning. More rain, more rumbling thunder, and the ever-present feeling that somehow, in some way, Jesse Savage was responsible, not only for the storm that raged around her, but for the faint stirring of emotion within.

Nothing had changed, Jesse thought as he wiped a hand over his rain-slick face and squinted into the darkness. With the sky thick with clouds, dusk seemed more like midnight. But even the darkness couldn't hide the dilapidated structure that stood at the corner of Walter and Carpenter, smack-dab in the middle of the Third Ward, one of Houston's high-crime slum areas.

The condemned building had only three stories, but they seemed to tower over him. Grafitti covered most of the fading brick. Nothing but empty black holes existed where windows had once been what seemed like ages ago, though it hadn't quite been a year.

Funny how things could change in the blink of an eye. One minute the building had been modest but clean, home to several families with tight incomes, but now a bitter desolation surrounded the entire place, as if the end of the world had come and this building was all that remained. No people. No life, just a vacant, intimidating shell.

Only the faint gleam of a candle from an upstairs window gave any indication that somebody still lived there. Illegally, of course. The neighborhood had taken a nosedive from bad to worse, and the few tenants who stayed inside were here because they had noplace else to go.

But Jesse had someplace to go. He had something better waiting for him, a chance to ask forgiveness and ease his guilt, and Faith was his ticket to peace.

He pushed her image aside—her pain-filled green eyes, her delicate features that reminded him of a china doll he'd found in an old Dumpster in back of Restoration, Texas's only five-and-dime.

He was far away from his hometown now, from those days when he'd still had a little faith of his own. It didn't seem right to think of someone like Faith in a place like this. This was Jesse's own private hell, where his demons lived and breathed. Where the past called to him and beckoned him inside.

Even as reason screamed for him to leave, to walk on by and go back to the foster home, he couldn't make his feet move. He knew why he'd come back, and he couldn't resist the lure of this place. Maybe if he saw the inside one last time, just once, he could quiet the demons and get on with his business at Faith's House. Maybe . . .

He climbed over the board that read KEEP OUT and blocked the main doorway. Inside, the hallway was pitch black. The heavy scent of rotten food and urine overwhelmed him as he moved into the darkness toward the staircase at the far end of the corridor. His boots echoed in a steady rhythm, in tempo with the rain that pounded down outside.

Jesse climbed three flights of stairs, feeling eyes peer at him from darkened doorways. No one said a word, but he sensed their presence. These were the people with nowhere else to go. Society ignored them. The city wanted them out of sight, and so they came to places like this, to escape the rain and the cold of the streets. Only, inside wasn't much better, with its filth and the rats and the awful smell.

The faint glow of a streetlight spilled through an open window, illuminating the faded yellow tape that blocked the doorway to apartment 3B. He stopped and simply stared for a long moment, wondering why he'd come back. Why, when he'd wanted only to leave the past behind and get on with eternity. With forgiveness.

His hand shook as he snatched the tape aside and walked into the all-too-familiar room. Debris littered the floor. The wind gusted through the windows, the edges jagged with broken glass. Rain drip-dropped in one corner from the leaky ceiling Jesse had patched at least a dozen times in the short three months he and his brother and sister had lived here. As soon as he'd sealed one leak, another had sprung.

He almost smiled; then he caught sight of the dark stains that covered the rotting floor near the far corner of the room. He didn't want to look, but something deep inside—the rage, the fury he'd felt that night—refused to allow him to look away.

Funny. The stains didn't even resemble blood anymore. His own blood that had soaked the floor in this very spot. His own life that soiled the rotting wood.

Well, lookee what we got here!

The voice exploded inside his head, and he clamped his hands over his ears. But it came again, vicious and relentless and determined to make him remember.

Jason, what's going on? Who are these guys? Jesse heard his own voice, remembered the confusion when he'd rushed inside the apartment. The agonizing scene he'd stumbled upon.

"Jess, please just turn around and leave," his younger brother, Jason, pleaded. *"You don't want any part of this."*

"That's right, pig," the man muttered to Jesse, his face hidden beneath a heavy black beard, his lips twisted in a cruel smile. *"This is private business, my business, which means it ain't none of yours, cop."*

"Like hell. I want to know what this is about. Now!"

"Now," the man scoffed. *"The pig wants to know now, so I guess we better tell him."* He motioned to Jason. *"Your brother here has been moving a little merchandise for us,"* the man said. The knife in his hand flashed like silver fire in the dim apartment light. *"But he ain't been what you might call a model employee. He's been holding out, ain't that right, Jason? And now he owes us."* The man advanced, moving the knife closer to Jason, who took a step backward, fear filling his deep brown eyes.

"No!" Jesse pushed in front of his brother at the same time that his younger sister walked out of her bedroom.

"Jesse!" Her frightened scream pierced his ears.

He whirled, gun drawn, but the warning came too late. The knife plunged down. Again and again and again . . .

Chapter Three

Jesse sank to his knees, gripping his hand, which throbbed unmercifully. He stared down, expecting to see the blood again. There'd been so much. Spilling from his hand, his chest, his neck . . .

There was nothing now. Only newly healed skin and the pain of those few moments as his life had slipped away. He'd listened to his sister's dying screams, his brother's final gasps, breathed his own and wished with all his heart he could do something, say something.

The words had been there on the tip of his tongue, yet he hadn't been able to speak them, no matter how he'd tried. The pain had swamped him, paralyzing his vocal cords. Then he'd taken that last, final breath, and the opportunity had been lost.

Jesse gasped for air. Heat surged through his body. He slammed his fist against the floor and threw his head back, staring at the collection of shadows that blackened the ceiling. He wanted to scream, to shout, to cry, but he couldn't. Not in this place. Here, rage dominated his emotions, refusing to let him feel anything except the hatred of that night.

The bearded man's face filled Jesse's thoughts, his eyes black and cold and glassy. Even a year hadn't dulled the picture, eased the anger, or soothed the regret.

What about an eternity? The words whispered in his head like a cool wind easing the blistering heat inside, and Jesse opened his eyes to stare up at the sagging ceiling, at the pinpoint of light that pushed its way through, like a moonbeam directed at his kneeling form.

The light grew brighter, swirling around him, comforting him, along with the voice.

An eternity, Jesse. Remember that. We're offering you an eternity.

Jesse fixed his gaze on the light and prayed for strength.

Like a wave of peaceful serenity, the sensation washed through him, from the tips of his fingers to his toes. He opened his eyes in time to see the light fade into nothing more than a crack in the sagging ceiling. Then came complete darkness.

A second chance. The voice drifted through his head, calming him and keeping his emotions from boiling over.

And though Jesse didn't want to think of her, Faith Jansen's image pushed its way into his mind, reminding him of his purpose. The one and only reason he'd come back in the first place.

Not for vengeance. But for forgiveness. For Faith.

He managed to climb to his feet.

"You all right, mister?" The small voice came

from one darkened corner of the room.

Jesse's thoughts disintegrated as he stared at the young girl, no more than thirteen or fourteen, who materialized from the shadows. A street lamp sent jagged shafts of light through a nearby window, illuminating her emaciated form. Concern sparkled in wide eyes that should have been wary when gazing at a man like him.

But he wasn't an average man. He was more, and perhaps she knew that, though he knew she hadn't seen the light. That vision had been his alone, a link to the other side. Still, she sensed something different about him, and it kept her rooted to the spot when otherwise she might have bolted.

She wore a tattered sweater, oversize jeans with holes at the knees, and boys' hightop gym shoes that looked at least three sizes too big. A smudge of dirt marred the otherwise smooth features of her tanned complexion. Tangled shoulder-length blond hair surrounded her small face.

"What are you doing here?" Jesse's voice sounded harsh even to his own ears. She didn't seem the least put off, however.

"Keeping dry," she said. "And staying away from the rats. They don't like it much up here, and that suits me just fine." She pulled an object up in front of her, and Jesse noticed the battered guitar she held.

"You all by yourself?" he asked.

She shrugged. "Got a few friends downstairs, but they don't like to come up here much. They say it's kinda creepy, considering what happened and all. You heard the story?" She took a step closer and added, "Some people got murdered up here, least that's what they say."

"No kidding." The words were more of a comment than a question.

"Honest. One guy got sliced up right there where you're standing. Lot of folks say his ghost lives up here. Can't believe even a ghost would live in this run-down hole. Maybe one of them fine houses over in River Oaks, but not in a gutter like this. You ain't a ghost, are you?" she asked, her face hinting at a grin, the expression making her look much younger, much more innocent than he'd first thought.

"No." Jesse flexed his fingers, the cold biting into his skin—living skin. He was all too real, a predicament he was about to do his damnedest to rectify.

"I didn't think so. Ain't no such thing anyway. That's what my ma used to say. Ghosts live in your head. Ain't nothing to be frightened of in the world 'cept what you can see and touch. People are who you got to watch out for."

"Sounds like good advice."

"Yeah, my ma was good at giving advice. It was staying around she had a hard time with." Pain flashed in her eyes—eyes that contrasted with the innocence of her face and made her look old again. Old and used. She shook her head, as if to shake away the memories. "It doesn't matter anyway. I get along just fine without her."

"Fine, huh?" Jesse glanced around the room. "Living up here with the filth and the ghosts is fine?"

"It ain't that dirty, and like I told you, there ain't no ghosts," she pointed out, gripping her guitar.

No ghosts. Just memories.

"Besides, nobody comes up here much, what with the story and all. It's private, and the sound is pretty good." She pulled the guitar up into her arms and strummed a chord. "So what's your name, mister?"

"Jesse."

"Name's Trudy," she said, strumming another chord. "So tell me what you were doing a few seconds ago. You looked kind of out of it. You sick?"

"No," Jesse replied. "Can you do more than just strum that thing?"

She smiled for a split second before launching into a melody that was so slow, sad, and heartbreakingly sweet that Jesse actually felt the residual anger from earlier slip away.

The music filled his ears and made him want to cry at the injustice of life, that something so vibrant, so alive, could exist amid such poverty and heartache. It was downright cruel. As if God were giving him a little taste of beauty that only made him hunger for more, when there wasn't any. Not in this life, anyway. He knew that firsthand.

When Trudy had played the last note, quiet settled around them, only the sound of the rain reminding Jesse that the world still existed outside. The world and all its ugliness.

"Not bad, huh?" Trudy asked, giving him a grin and a glimpse of innocence again. "Taught myself, you know."

"No lessons?"

"If I had money for lessons, you think I'd be here?"

A pang of awareness shot through him and he shook his head, suddenly feeling colder, more alone than he ever had before. "You shouldn't be here anyway. Didn't your mother ever warn you about talking to strangers when she was giving all that good advice?"

"Sure she did."

He stared at her as if to say, *Then why aren't you hustling yourself downstairs?*

"But you ain't no stranger. Your name's Jesse. Hey, where'd you get that jacket?" She eased her guitar to the floor and hugged her stomach. "Looks awful warm."

"You like it?" he asked. At her nod, he pulled off his letterman's jacket, faded and worn and fifteen years old, and handed it to her, much to her obvious astonishment.

"What about you? The days are warm but the nights have been awful chilly, and the weatherman on the TV down at the pawnshop is predicting another cold front. You'll catch your death."

"It's too late for that," Jesse replied; then he turned and walked from the room. As he hit the stairs, the sound of the girl's slow melody followed him, along with images from his past.

The bearded man's face flashed in his mind, and Jesse walked faster, taking the stairs two at a time as he headed for the first floor. It wouldn't be too hard to find that man, to give him a taste of what he'd been so quick to give Jesse that night.

Forgiveness, a voice whispered as he exited the building.

The rain pelted him as viciously as his rage pushed and pulled at his determination. After an indecisive moment, he turned and walked toward the corner. A quick left, and he headed for Faith's House. His desire for forgiveness had won. This time.

But what about the next time?

The question haunted him as he covered several blocks. He found himself wondering if he was strong enough to put aside his hurt and accomplish his mission with Faith Jansen. He had to be. Otherwise he'd forfeit his second chance and be stuck here in this abysmal world for another lifetime. It wasn't a case of heaven or hell. No, he'd died too soon, which meant he had one early shot at heaven.

If he completed his mission in two weeks—the anniversary of the date of his death—he would find his reward and be reunited with his brother and sister. If not, he would stay here. It was a fate worse than the memories, as far as Jesse was concerned.

". . . the Southside slaying of a teen gang member brings the total deaths related to gang violence to fifty-eight. Stay tuned for more news after this commercial break." The newscaster's voice faded into a lively commercial jingle that pounded through Faith's head with the fury of one of Ricky's Metallica CDs.

Groping for the mute button on her remote control, she turned over to snuggle into one sofa pillow. Grubby stirred next to her and she stroked his back, lulling him back to sleep with the gentle motion. As she sank back into oblivion, the crash of metal yanked her back to reality.

Grubby started to bark. She rolled onto her back and forced her eyes open. The bright morning sun streamed through her living room windows. The blinds . . . Why had she left the blinds open last night?

For the same reason she'd left the television set blaring, her plastic TV dinner tray in the middle of the coffee table, and a load of clean, unfolded laundry piled on one end of the couch. She didn't care. She didn't want to care—

The thought ground to a halt at the sound of garbage cans being manipulated on her back porch.

Shielding her eyes with one hand, she glanced at the clock that ticked away, keeping tempo with the heavy-metal drum solo beating away inside her skull. Six A.M. The neighborhood delinquents couldn't even wait for a decent hour to start vandalizing her property.

Now she had to buy another set of trash cans—

But she had no trash cans, she quickly remembered as yesterday's scene replayed in her head. She crawled from the couch, pulled her T-shirt down over her bare midriff, and wondered what the little devils could be after this time. She kept nothing on her back porch except a couple of wrought-iron chairs and a small table. Surely they weren't trying to make off with her half-rusted patio furniture.

Shoving the curtains aside, she stared out at her back porch. The lid of one shiny new trash can caught the sun's rays and blinded her for a split second. Then a shadow obliterated the light. The sound of clanging metal resumed, along with a steady grinding and a slight tremble of the door frame.

"What in the world are you doing?" she asked as she threw open the back door. She stared through the burglar bars at Jesse Savage, who was stooped on her back porch, a drill in one hand, a small metal chain in the other.

He tilted his face toward her. His lips hinted at a grin. "Making sure these cans don't get ripped off again. You did say that was a problem, didn't you? Your cans getting stolen?"

"Well, yes, but . . ." She stared at the shiny new cans. "These aren't mine. The new ones I bought last week were ripped off yesterday." Her gaze traveled past him, toward the stone steps and her small backyard. Not a piece of trash littered the dew-covered grass, as if the chaos she'd seen yesterday had never existed.

"And whoever ripped them off made one helluva mess."

"I know." Her gaze met his. "You cleaned all of it up," she said accusingly.

He touched his heart in an overly dramatic gesture. "Your gratitude is overwhelming."

"I'm sorry, I guess I'm just used to cleaning up my own trash. I should have said thanks."

His grin turned into a full-fledged smile—a smile that warmed her a great deal more than the morning sun that showered the porch and outlined Jesse's powerful frame. Without the rain making him hunch down, he looked larger, his shoulders broader in the faded sleeveless sweatshirt he now wore. The worn jeans still clung to his thighs, outlining the bunched muscles as he knelt.

He indicated the white trash bag beside him. "I also brought over a couple of new cans."

She shook her head. "But how did you know mine were stolen yesterday?"

"Actually, I just came by this morning to secure the ones you already had to the wall here." He tugged on the small chain that ran from the door frame to the bottom of one can. "Makes them much harder to swipe if they're attached. When I got here, I saw yours were missing, so I went back to Faith's House, and Bradley let me have a couple of extra cans. Thought I'd save you the trouble of getting new ones. You don't look like you enjoy going out much."

"Don't say it."

"Say what?"

"That I'm a hermit lady. That's what Bradley says, but he's wrong. I just like being alone."

"Whatever makes you happy." His dark eyes swept from her head, down past her rumpled white T-shirt and fleece pants, to her toes encased in bright red tube socks.

A tingle crept up Faith's spine and she shifted, putting one hip behind the kitchen door to escape some of his scrutiny.

"So, does it?" he persisted.

"Does what?"

"Does hiding make you happy?" The words were soft, a question he might have been murmuring to himself, except that she heard all too clearly.

She stiffened, her fingers tightening on the door-knob. "I'm not hiding, Mr. Savage."

"Jesse," he corrected.

"I'm not hiding, *Jesse*."

"Then why is it that Bradley's swamped with work, and you're here lazing around, doing nothing?"

Oddly enough, with the words came the same stab of guilt she'd experienced when she'd left Faith's House yesterday. Guilt, of all things, when she didn't want to feel anything.

Her fingers tightened considerably until the door-knob bit into her palm, and the pain was enough to silence her conscience.

"You know something? You're right. Bradley is swamped, which makes me wonder what you're doing here instead of at Faith's House. I don't recall you being hired to be my personal handyman."

"No, but it looks as if you could use one." His attention shot past her to the kitchen table, which was stacked with empty food containers and old newspapers. "Or at least a housekeeper."

Heat crept up her neck and she actually felt herself blush. The realization made her stiffen. "How I keep house is none of your business, and neither are my trash cans."

"I just thought I'd lend a hand." The sincerity in his voice brought another wave of heat to her face.

This time it wasn't embarrassment. No, it was shame, damn him.

"I don't need a hand."

"Consider it a favor."

"I don't need any favors."

"Then payback."

"Payback? For what?"

"I owe you for yesterday. For helping me get the job."

"You managed that all by yourself. You disarmed Daniel and forced him to let me go."

He considered her words. "Then I guess *you* owe *me*."

She stared at him, those dark, intense eyes holding her captive for a brief, heart-stopping moment. A moment where she should have felt nothing, least of all the slight tremor that danced up her spine.

"So maybe I did give Bradley the okay to hire you."

"And maybe I've fixed it so your cans won't get ripped off anymore." He tugged on the chain, then stood. His silhouette obliterated the morning sun, and a shiver worked through her. But she wasn't sure whether the sensation was from the sudden cold that came from standing in the shadows, or from the way he stared at her.

"You still owe me," he went on. "Fix me a cup of coffee and we'll call it even."

"I—I'm busy."

"Cleaning up?" His gaze swept past her again. She glanced over her shoulder, following the same direction to the dishes piled high in the sink. Empty potato-chip bags and cereal boxes cluttered the counter. She inched from behind the door to block his view.

"Don't you have to get to work?" she asked again,

eager for an excuse to get him off her porch. Out of
her life, and quick. Before she had to analyze her
body's reaction to this scruffy stranger. *He's a
stranger!* reason screamed.

A disturbingly familiar stranger who'd saved her
life, another voice reminded her. Not that she'd forgotten. She couldn't forget. That was the trouble.
With him staring so intently at her, she could do
nothing but remember. The pain deep in his eyes,
the desperation, drew on those old feelings she'd
tried so hard to bury. Caring, trust, concern . . .

Feelings she had buried with Jane.

Until he'd shown up and unearthed what she
wanted desperately to forget: the way things had
been before—the way she'd been before. But Jesse
stirred more than just that. He made her feel new
things, as well. Attraction, excitement, desire.

"Bradley said he wants me bright and early at
seven. That leaves a little under an hour. Enough
time for that coffee." He held her gaze, daring her
to look away, yet at the same time refusing to let
her. He compelled her to look. To remember.

That was the real trouble. He reminded her of too
much, which was why she needed to get rid of him.
Fast.

If coffee would do the trick . . . Surely she could
find some in the mess that had once been her neatly
arranged cupboards.

"I can't promise cream or sugar." She made one
last attempt to dissuade him.

"Black's fine."

"Or even a clean cup."

"I'll wash my own."

Reluctantly, she twisted the lock on the burglar
bars and swung the iron gate open.

After wiping his boots on her floor mat, Jesse Savage walked into her kitchen, and for a brief moment, Faith got the inexplicable feeling she'd not only let him into her kitchen, but into her life. He was definitely trouble.

"Nice place," he said after he'd glanced around at his surroundings. "You live here alone?"

"Yes." She turned her back to him and walked to the sink. A familiar whimper sounded and she turned to see Grubby waddle into the kitchen, his black nose shining. "Well, almost alone."

Jesse smiled, bent down, and scooped the dog into his powerful arms. "Hey, fella." He rubbed Grubby's head with his fingertip. "Are you hungry?" When the dog started licking madly at his thumb, Jesse shot her a knowing glance. "I think that's a definite yes."

Faith snatched a can of dog food from the cupboard, then hunted in a drawer until she found a can opener. After opening the food and dishing it into a bowl, she set it on the floor.

Jesse placed Grubby on the tile and they both watched as the puppy sniffed his way over to breakfast. He batted one small paw at the edge of the bowl a few times, scooting it around to just the right position before his small snout plunged inside. A few gobbles later he chanced a glance at Faith, licked his chops, and wagged his tail.

Faith was smiling when she felt Jesse's gaze on her. Their eyes locked, and she saw his smugness, as if he'd caught her with her guard down and was immensely pleased. She turned back to the counter.

Heat burned her cheeks as she rummaged around in a drawer, found the last clean dishtowel, and tossed it to him.

"You really want me to wash my own cup?" he asked, laughter in his voice.

"I'll wash and you can dry." Nervous energy

53

rushed through her, and she turned the faucet on full-force. "And I can't promise how long it will take us to find a cup. We'll have to get through some of this first." She eyed the stack of plates, then shot him a quick glance. "Second thoughts?"

"Not on your life," he replied, coming up beside her.

She forced her attention from the scarred hand gripping the dishtowel and concentrated on the present task. Shoving a loose strand of hair behind her ear, she squeezed a river of dishwashing liquid onto the dirty dishes and grabbed a dishrag.

Silence settled around them as Faith attacked the sinkful of dishes, her movements quick, frenzied. Before Jesse could finish drying one plate, she had at least two more for him.

"If I didn't know better, I'd say you're in a hurry to get rid of me," he said after they'd washed nearly half the dishes.

"Smart man."

"You don't like people much anymore, do you?"

"Anymore?" She shot him a quick sideways glance, and immediately regretted it. Her gaze caught his for a brief moment, and she felt that same feeling, as if he poked and prodded at her thoughts with nothing more than those dark eyes of his. She forced her attention back to the soapy saucer in her hand. "And what makes you so sure I've ever liked anyone?"

"A woman who invests her time and money in playing foster mother to a houseful of delinquent kids? I'd say somewhere along the line you cared about people. Otherwise you would never have taken up your present line of work."

"Correction—my former line of work. I'm through with Faith's House. It's Bradley's burden now." She shoved the saucer beneath the hot water.

"Why?"

"Do you make it a habit of prying into other people's business?" She shoved the saucer at him and gave him a freezing glare.

"No. You're the lucky one." He smiled, lips curving to reveal a straight row of white teeth and a deep dimple that cut into his left cheek.

A tingle of warmth spiraled through her and she attacked another dish. "I like my privacy, Mr. Savage, and you're invading it."

"It's Jesse, and I was only trying to find out where you went wrong so I can avoid that route."

"Meaning?"

"I'm new at Faith's House and I aim to stick around a while. I don't want to burn out, so I thought you could give me a few pointers, maybe steer me away from the road you traveled."

She'd cared too much. Tried too hard. Thought too deeply. "You want some advice about your new job, Mr.—Jesse?"

"Shoot."

"Remember it's only a job."

"What's that supposed to mean?"

"It means that in the end, it's only a job. Those kids are your job, nothing else. Nothing personal. You keep that in mind and you won't end up like me."

"An old hermit lady?"

A grin tugged at her lips despite the ache in her chest. "Exactly."

She reached for a cup and the air lodged in her throat. With trembling fingers she traced the Houston Rockets logo emblazoned on the outside of the white mug, an authentic Hakeem "the Dream" Olajuwon autograph on the opposite side. Her eyes burned as she remembered the teenage girl who'd sat in her kitchen day after day, drinking cocoa or iced tea or something from the cherished cup an English teacher had given as first prize in a school poetry contest. *Jane . . .*

"The pain," she whispered, the words raw.

"What did you say?"

"The pain," she repeated, forcing her fingers to let go of the cup. She sat it on the drainboard and gathered her control. "Getting involved isn't worth the pain. Why try so hard when, in the end, it doesn't make a damn bit of difference how many times you held them while they cried, how many lunches you packed, how much homework you coached them through? Those things mean nothing in the face of death."

He opened his mouth, as if he wanted to say something. Then his jaw clamped shut and he raked a hand through his hair almost angrily. As if he felt the fury heating her blood, the pain gripping her heart. As if he *felt* as intensely as she did.

The realization made her clutch the counter. Jane's favorite cup filled her peripheral vision. It sat there in red and black and white glory, mocking her, reminding her, calling out to her. . . .

The numbness she'd fought so hard to hold on to was slipping away. Instead her throat burned, as fiercely as the tears that threatened to spill past her lashes. *Tears . . .*

"I—I think you'd better go," she managed to whisper.

She expected him to shake his head, to argue with her. Instead he nodded, his eyes flashing a message she couldn't comprehend. Instead of looking away, however, she caught his gaze. As she stared long and hard and deep, she wondered how he could make her feel anything again when she'd managed to cut herself off. *The hermit lady*.

She saw the compassion flash in his eyes; then his expression closed.

"Yeah, I think I'd better." He turned and headed for the back door.

She opened her mouth, the urge to beg him to stay nearly overwhelming. Stay? No, he had to leave, just as she had to forget the past.

The door slammed and she flinched. A coldness swirled around her, and panic skittered across her nerve endings. Logic fled as she rushed after him and grabbed the doorknob.

Stop!

The voice blared in Faith's head, and she closed her eyes, pressing her forehead against the door, her hands clenched around the knob as the past unearthed itself and played through her mind.

"Stop!" The frantic cry drew Faith off the couch and up the darkened stairs at Faith's House. Her desperate steps ate up the distance down the hallway, to the room at the far end.

The room was pitch black without even a sliver of moonlight to cut the darkness. The girl appeared little more than a shadow huddled on one corner of the bed. Soft sobs reached across the room to draw Faith inside.

"Jane? What's wrong, honey?" But Faith already knew. The girl had been at Faith's House less than a week since she'd been dismissed from the hospital after recovering from her chest wounds, but each night had been the same.

"I—I had a bad dream," came the small, faceless voice.

57

"It's okay." Faith sank down on the edge of the bed. *She'd known her own share of nightmares, the fear of being in a new place, of being alone. So alone.*

But Jane's situation was even worse. She didn't even have memories to keep her company, just a blank void where the past should have been.

Gathering the girl's body in her arms, Faith held her close. Shudders shook the thin form. Warm tears spilled onto Faith's hands.

"I'm scared," the small voice whispered, and Faith felt a tear trickle down her own cheek.

"I know, sweetie. I know." And she did. She knew all too well because she'd faced her own tragedy, her own nightmares. "But you don't have to be. You're not alone anymore. I'm here, honey. I'm here."

Jesse opened his eyes and stared down at his hand, which still gripped the doorknob to Faith's back door. He knew she touched the exact same spot on the inside. He felt her warmth. And he saw her thoughts as if they were his own.

We are linked. Connected.

He sensed it when she turned and walked away. He felt her slip out of his grasp, her warmth fading from the cold metal of the knob. But the sound of Faith's voice echoed in his head; the image of her reaching out in the darkness was still vivid in his mind.

He could certainly see why she'd been chosen to receive a miracle. Now if he could get past the wall she'd built up around herself, maybe he could give her one.

After Jesse left, Faith finished up the dishes and sank down onto the sofa in front of the TV. She stabbed a button on the remote control. A television preacher filled the screen, carrying on about fire and brimstone. She punched to the next channel and found the morning news.

". . . the fire broke out and eight people were killed."

She stabbed the button again until she found nothing but snow. No voices ranting about death and destruction. Just blessed, unintelligible snow.

Leaning her head back, she closed her eyes, willing her hands to stop trembling, her body to stop feeling, her mind to stop remembering Jesse Savage and the fleeting pain she'd glimpsed in his eyes the moment before he'd left. He'd wanted to say something to her, as if somehow, some way, he'd known what she'd been feeling. The loss, the grief—*No!*

Bolting to her feet, Faith rushed into her bedroom and changed into a pair of jeans, a sweater, and worn hiking boots. She paused at her dresser, her gaze going to the antique jewelry box that sat atop a lace doily.

The sudden urge to look inside nearly overwhelmed her. She'd stashed the precious piece of jewelry away right after the funeral. She'd wanted no mementos of Jane. No memories. Only now a part of her wanted to remember. Needed to—

She jerked her hand away just shy of the latch. With trembling fingers, she grabbed her house keys and hurried outside into the brightly lit morning. But even the sun in all its glory didn't bring any warmth to her surroundings.

The tiny houses dotting her street looked all the more worn, with their peeling paint and rusted burglar bars. The lot for sale directly across from her, still filled with concrete debris from the building torn down last year, was as ugly as ever. Even more so with no shadows to hide the leftovers from the demolition team. She breathed in the stench of garbage and filth and headed for the corner, and Montrose Boulevard. She needed numbness, and there was no place better to find it.

The bright morning sunlight heated her cheeks as she walked, but reality iced her heart as she drank in her surroundings. An old homeless man picked through an overflowing Dumpster. A drunk sat dozing in the doorway of an abandoned building. The graffitied walls of what had once been the entrance to Crackhead Central, a park now closed after two homicides and a mess of drug trafficking, glared back at her. Ugly. It was all so ugly.

Faith walked endlessly, staring at every tenement, every drug addict, every group of delinquents clustered on the street corners, until she was numb again. But no matter how dark and depressing her surroundings, she still glimpsed beauty. Life . . . In the smile of a mother as she lifted her small child from his stroller, the sparkle of sun off a serene duck pond, the smiles of a group of kids as they played tag.

Frustrated, she returned home late into the evening and collapsed on the sofa. Depression sapped her strength until she was limp with it. The darkness wrapped around her, but sleep didn't come. Instead, Jesse Savage came to her, his face crystal clear in her mind—his full lips, strong jaw, piercing, pain-filled brown eyes that tugged at too many emotions she wanted to bury forever.

Grubby licked at her ankles. His thin whine shattered the silence surrounding her. Faith opened her eyes and stared at the half circle of moonlight that bathed the carpet near her feet. The wail of a distant siren mingled with the buzz of the refrigerator, the hum of the television in the far corner, the screen still a snowy blur.

Reaching down, she scooped up the puppy and held him close. Still, loneliness crept through Faith, filling the emptiness inside her, making her chest ache and her eyes burn. She forced a deep breath and swallowed against the tightness in her throat. She wouldn't cry. Crying was useless.

Clamping her eyes shut, she held the puppy and willed away the tears. But she could no more will away Jesse's image, alive and vivid in her mind, than she could have saved Jane that fateful night. And the more her thoughts centered on him, the more the dreaded loneliness clutched at her, refusing to be ignored or forgotten like everything else.

Like him.

Chapter Four

Jesse cast a quick glance at the locked kitchen door before he flicked off the light. He walked down the darkened hallway of Faith's House, his boots making a steady thump on the hardwood floor. Rock music drifted from upstairs, along with a steady chatter of voices. He eased his exhausted body down into an armchair in the living room and stared at the muted television screen. Images flashed there sending a dance of shadows across the otherwise darkened room.

He longed to close his eyes. The day had been exhausting. There were eleven kids at Faith's House, twelve including Daniel, and only two full-time employees—Mike the black belt and Bradley—and Megan, a part-timer who'd eloped with the counter clerk at Bagelrama, home of Texas's hottest jalapeño bagels. The work at the foster home was endless, overwhelming with so much cooking, cleaning, paperwork, and a million other things. He couldn't blame Faith for calling it quits.

That was the problem. He couldn't blame her because he understood exactly where she was coming from. It was easier to stay aloof, emotionless. Jesse had done the same for too many years to count. By the time he'd realized his mistake, it had been too late.

But he had another chance now. If he fulfilled his mission by the deadline he'd get the opportunity to make restitution, to ask forgiveness and soothe the guilt and regret eating him up inside.

First, however, he had to renew Faith's hope in herself, in life, in living. The spark was still there inside her, whether she recognized it or not. He'd heard it in her voice when she'd mentioned the kids, seen it in the brief flash of pain that had quickened her lifeless green eyes. That was why Jesse had to work fast. She wasn't completely hardened yet, though she fought like the devil to be just that.

Faith's picture pushed into his mind—her eyes wide, filled with the tears she'd fought so hard not to shed when she'd touched the Houston Rockets mug. He could see the slight quiver of her lips, almost feel their softness against his own—

He forced the image away. No use dwelling on what he couldn't have. He had no future here other than the next two weeks, and to get close to Faith, then abandon her, would do neither of them any good.

He had only one purpose—to renew Faith's hope in life. Jesse had to forget the pain in her eyes, the lure of her soft, full, trembling lips, and convince her living and caring and sharing were all worth the effort.

He couldn't walk out on her again as he'd done

this morning. He had to get close to her, win her trust, make her feel.

A sudden sense of loneliness swept through him, not his own, but Faith's. He stiffened.

Linked. Connected.

"You all right?" Bradley's voice cut through Jesse's thoughts. He glanced up to see the man standing in the doorway, a clipboard in one hand, a pair of wire spectacles in the other.

Jesse nodded. "Do you need me for anything?"

Bradley shook his head. "No. Everybody's upstairs getting ready for bed." He walked into the room and sank down into a chair opposite Jesse. "I hope you aren't having second thoughts about staying on here. The kids really took to you today. I haven't ever seen Ricky do dishes without putting up at least fifteen minutes of griping."

Jesse smiled. "He owed me. I beat him at arm wrestling, and he wanted a rematch. No dishes, no rematch. The kid hates to lose."

"You got that right." The other man grinned; then his face took on a serious expression. "He pounded another boy last month for tackling him during football practice. Gave the boy a black eye and a bloody lip. The school rewarded him with one month of detention for fighting." Bradley shook his head. "But now is a cakewalk compared to the way things used to be. Just last year Ricky was a walking pharmacy and armed to the hilt. He'd already been ditching school regularly for three years. CPS got him when he shot one of his connections because the guy ripped off five bucks' worth of drugs." Bradley wiped a hand over his eyes. "Nothing compared to detention, huh?"

"Sounds like he was pretty bad news."

"He was. He's still a little violent, but he takes

most of his aggression out on the football field. Except, of course, for last month. But with a past like his, you can't complain about a little fighting. Way back when, Ricky would have shot that boy instead of laying into him with his fists."

"This place must be doing him some good."

"It is—not only Ricky but the others, as well. Last year we even received a recognition award from the mayor."

"How long has Faith's House been around?"

"Faith started off about five years ago, right after she graduated from college. At least a dozen agencies contacted her about a job, but she wanted to start her own group foster home. She'd volunteered at a shelter in Austin while she went to University of Texas, and that's where she came up with the plan for Faith's House."

"Who provides the funding?"

"The state gives a monthly reimbursement for each child, but it isn't nearly enough to provide for them like this." Bradley's gaze swept around the room, the comfortable sofa and chairs, the thick carpeting. The furnishings were low-key, tasteful, but high quality. "It's not the Hilton, but it ain't Motel 6 either. Anyhow, Faith pumps a lot of her own money into this place. Payback, she always tells me."

"How's that?"

"She was orphaned herself when she was a teenager, though she never had to go through the welfare system. She had a guardian, but he was little more than a stranger. I guess that's why she relates so well to the kids. I hate to think where they'd be if not for Faith. She takes on even the worst. Or she did." Bradley rubbed at his tired eyes. "I just hope things run smoothly while she's off trying to get herself together."

"What happened?"

"One of our kids was killed a little over two weeks ago by a drunk driver. It devastated Faith. She was really close to this particular girl. Jane—that's what we called her—wasn't like the other kids. Before she came to Faith's House, she went through some terrible incident where she was severely wounded. The trauma caused amnesia. Nobody knew who she was. Somebody had wheeled her into the emergency room and left her there. It was about this time last year, and school had just let out for the summer, so there were no reported absences, nobody calling in about a missing child. Nothing. CPS didn't have a clue as to her name, so they started calling her Jane Doe.

"I don't know what it was about her, but Faith took to her right away," Bradley went on. "Maybe it's because the girl was just about the same age as Faith when she'd been orphaned. Anyhow, Faith helped her through some pretty rough nightmares those first few months." He shook his head. "To nurse Jane through such a hard time, then lose her in the blink of an eye devastated her. She hasn't been the same since. Yesterday was the first time she's set foot here since the funeral, and I was surprised she even did that. I was hoping that seeing the kids might make her stay, but I guess not."

"It's only been a couple of weeks. Maybe she just needs a little time to come around."

"And maybe Ricky will win the good citizenship award."

Jesse smiled. "Miracles do happen."

"I hope you're right." Bradley got to his feet and headed for the doorway. "You don't know Faith. She eats and sleeps this place. For her to give it up for over this long is a terrible sign. It'll take nothing short of a miracle to bring her around after what happened to Jane."

That it would, Jesse thought as he listened to Bradley's fading footsteps. A door creaked shut, and silence closed in.

It would take a miracle, but then that was why Jesse was here. Tomorrow he would go back to Faith's and resume his mission. Nothing, not even the lingering memories of his untimely death, would spoil what he had to do. He wouldn't let them.

Jesse closed his eyes and tried to ignore the image that lurked at the far edges of his mind—the brilliant green eyes, the full, kissable lips. He had to think of her in purely professional terms. This was business. A means to an end.

Linked. Connected.

If only the pull of her wasn't so strong. So potent. If only . . .

Jesse shifted his thoughts away from Faith and concentrated on the sound of raised voices that came from upstairs.

"I've got five minutes more bathroom time, you pighead, so stop bothering me."

"You've been in there thirty minutes, Em. I've got to go."

"You'll just have to hold it."

"And you'll just have to hurry up. . . ."

A smile tugged at his lips as his memory stirred a similar scene. The voices faded as time pulled Jesse back until he found himself in apartment 3B.

He stared across the living room to the teenage girl and boy playing tug-of-war with a black leather jacket emblazoned with a Harley Davidson logo on the back.

"It's mine, Jason," the girl said in a hiss, pulling and tugging, her soft brown hair slapping against her pale cheeks.

"Jess gave it to me," Jason fired back, his eyes blazing the same midnight fire as the girl in front of him. "Didn't ya, Jess?"

"What's the fuss over? There's a windbreaker hanging in the closet, and two blue-jean jackets," Jesse told them, buttoning up the shirt to his uniform. He wiped at his sleepy eyes, wishing he'd had at least a few more winks. But he had to get a move on or he'd be late for his shift. He stuffed the ends of the shirt into his pants, checked his gun, then reached for his badge.

"A windbreaker is for geeks."

"And the blue-jean jackets?" Jesse asked.

"Not total geekdom, but way too old to be cool," Rachel, his younger sister, informed him. "Everybody's wearing the Harley jackets, and I called it first, and you owe me for baking you that cake last week. You'll just have to stay home," she told her brother. "Or go à la geek. But then your new buddies don't really go for the nerd look."

"Shut up," Jason replied. "Now give it up. They're waiting for me."

"Who?" Rachel challenged. "Ask him where he's going, Jess. I bet it ain't to the library."

"It isn't," Jesse corrected, sitting down to pull his boots on. "I bet it isn't to the library."

Jason laughed in his sister's face, and she tightened her grip on the "cool" jacket, as Jessie had heard over and over before he'd given in and forked over nearly a hundred bucks to get one for Jason's last birthday. Money he would have been better off saving. Finances had been tight for the past few months since they'd made the move to Houston. Tighter than tight. Hell, he'd nearly gone under a time or two. But not much longer, he promised himself.

"You can stay home tonight," Rachel informed Jason. "It won't kill you, you know."

"Enough," Jesse said, getting to his feet. "Give Rachel the jacket."

"But it's my jacket."

"You should have thought of that when you were eating that chocolate cake."

Jason ground his teeth, but he let go. A triumphant Rachel hugged the jacket, then threw her arms around Jesse's waist.

"Thanks. I wish you didn't have to work all night."

"I have to." He patted her shoulder, ignoring the urge to slide his arms around her and pull her even closer.

"I know, but I still wish you didn't. I love you," she said fiercely, giving him another hug.

The words hovered on the tip of his tongue, but he couldn't open his mouth. Years of holding back, of bottling up his feelings, barricading them behind a hard wall of strength, had taken their toll.

He simply stroked his sister's smooth hair for a long moment, relishing the feel, like silk against his palms. Then she pulled away and disappeared into an adjoining bedroom, the coveted jacket clutched tight in her hands.

"I don't need a stinking jacket just to go out," Jason muttered, arms folded, a frown on his face. "It's not that cold." He folded his arms in a belligerent pose. "I can't believe she thinks that stunt is gonna keep me cooped up here. I can look cool without that stupid jacket."

"Where is it you have to go that's so urgent?" Jesse asked.

"Just to hang out at Mitch's."

"And who's Mitch?"

"This guy I met. He's in one of my classes at school."

"And you can't skip one night?"

"I can, but I don't want to."

"You sure there isn't more to it?"

"Scout's honor."

"You're not a scout."

"I swear." Jason crossed his heart.

Jesse gave his brother a searching glance, then let his expression soften. He retraced his steps to the bedroom, rummaged inside the closet, and pulled out a worn jacket that hadn't seen light in at least fifteen years.

He ran a hand over the football patch embroidered just under his name, before tossing it at his surprised brother. "This cool enough for you?"

"You're letting me borrow your letterman's jacket?" *The boy's eyes lit with surprise, then excitement.*

"Don't get it dirty, and be home by ten. And Jason," *Jesse said, drawing the teenage boy's full attention.* "If you aren't on the level with me, you'll regret it. Understand?"

Jason nodded.

Then the scene started to blur, turning to a kaleidoscope of shapes and images that made Jesse's head hurt.

This ain't none of your business . . .

Jesse's eyes snapped open. His gaze swept the room, from the lifeless fireplace to the patchwork quilt draped over the back of a beige sofa. No dirty floors or leaky ceilings. He was at Faith's House, and Jason and Rachel were gone.

Gone. The word beat through his head, making

him bolt to his feet. He rubbed his fingers over the scar covering his hand, felt again the cut of the knife.

Heat swirled around him, choking him, and he headed for the back door. The night pulled him outside, into the fresh air for some blessed relief. Only there was no relief. Just the heat and the rage and the hatred that still pulled at Jesse's conscience, turning his intentions to mush.

He glanced up at the garage apartment where he was to stay. A light burned brightly in the window, calling to him, his body urging him toward the stairs. He needed to sleep so he could try again tomorrow with Faith. So he could forget Jason and Rachel, and everyone else. For now. Everything except what he had to do.

This ain't none of your business . . .

It wasn't. Not anymore, he told himself, but the voice grew loud, demanding. *None of your business . . .*

Instead of mounting the apartment steps, Jesse headed for the street.

Final payback, he told himself. Then he could get on with his mission. Then the past would be laid to rest. Then Jesse could rid himself of the damned voice in his head. . . .

He'd barely taken two steps when a scream split the night. He whirled, and as loudly as his past called to him, the scream was louder. More insistent. More heartbreaking.

And it came from Faith's House.

"Go away," Faith grumbled, covering her head with the sofa pillow. But the pounding on her front door persisted. Louder, louder . . .

"Dammit, Faith! Open the door!"

The sofa pillow slipped to the floor and she jerked her head up. Peering through the midnight shadows filling her living room, she fixed her blurry gaze on the front door. The porch light burned brightly, illuminating the dark figure that loomed outside. Jesse Savage's voice thundered in her head.

"Open up!"

It wasn't so much the command itself that had her climbing from the couch. No, it was the urgency lacing each syllable. She threw open the door just as he was about to pound again.

"It's about time." He wore faded jeans and a plain white T-shirt. The soft cotton stretched across the broad expanse of his chest and accented each carved muscle.

"What took you so long?" His voice, deep and rich and aggravated, brought her unconscious inspection of him to a dead halt. She stiffened, squelching the strange tingling in her stomach.

"I was sleeping," she murmured, hoping her voice didn't sound as shaky as she felt. Shaky? What was wrong with her? Flipping the lock on the burglar bars, she swung the iron gate open. "It's after two A.M., for Pete's sake—"

"There's been an accident."

An accident. The car came from nowhere and—

She slammed her mind shut on the memory and tried to focus on the words spilling past Jesse's lips.

". . . Daniel tried to go out the upstairs window. Bradley's already at the emergency room. Get some street clothes on. They're waiting for us."

"Us?"

"You're Daniel's foster mother. You have to sign the admission papers, insurance forms—all that stuff. Bradley took the Suburban to the hospital. I've got his Celica. I'll drive you—"

72

"Hold on." She held up one hand and gripped the door frame with her other. Wood bit into her palm. The pain should have been enough to dispel the fuzziness from her brain. It wasn't. Jesse's form blurred and Faith rubbed at her eyes—not only to erase the last remnants of sleep, but to wipe away the images pounding through her head. The memories.

An accident . . . Massive internal injuries . . . Head trauma . . . You'll have to give permission for us to operate—

"You okay?" Jesse's voice cut through the sudden drumming in her ears.

"I . . ." The words fell short, stuck in the knot in her throat. She swayed for a split second; then Jesse was beside her, holding her.

She should have welcomed the support. She would have, but he was too warm, and she'd been cold for much too long. And worse, he saw too damned much with those eyes of his.

"It's okay." Gentle fingers threaded through the hair at the nape of her neck, his palm moving in a gentle massaging motion that sapped her strength even as she summoned it. His touch lulled her; his words were so soft, filled with such conviction, she actually thought it might be okay. But the memories persisted.

Massive injuries . . . The prognosis isn't good. We're sorry, Ms. Jansen. So sorry . . .

She went rigid, her hands pushing at him, as if putting some distance between them would stop the flow of memories.

Inches, then feet separated them as she backed toward the wall. The night air was warm, humid, with only an occasional breeze. Still, she was ice cold. She hugged her arms about her, desperate to

73

ease the chill that gripped her from the inside out.

Jesse studied her for a long moment. Something flashed in his dark eyes, and she got the inexplicable feeling that he wanted to reach out to her. Something held him back, though. Some indefinable emotion that etched severe lines in his face and held his large body stiff.

The clock in the hall ticked away the seconds, the sound louder somehow in the sudden hush that settled around them.

Finally, Jesse shoved his hands into his pockets and said, "We have to get to the hospital."

"No." She shook her head. "I have papers that will sign over Faith's House to Bradley. You can take them to him, get his signature, and he'll be the foster parent for all the kids." She rushed toward the couch, frantically searching the darkness for her purse. "They got a little messed up yesterday. I was going to have them redone, but maybe they'll suffice. Just let me get them—"

Jesse's hands closed over her shoulders as she pulled the stained legal papers from the pocket of her bag. "They're ruined, Faith. There's no way the hospital will accept those. They aren't in the habit of setting themselves up for any kind of lawsuit."

"So call Estelle. She's the foster rep. She can sign any papers—"

"Bradley tried. He couldn't reach her. You have to come with me."

We did all we could. We're sorry. Sorry . . . Sorry . . .

But even as the words beat through her head, reminding her of the past, the warmth of Jesse's hands proved calming. Heat spread through her, giving her the courage to nod her head when she wanted only to sink to the couch and bury her face in the pillows.

"What happened to him?" Her lips trembled with each word.

"He broke his arm."

Unconsciously, she rubbed at her arms, her chest tightening as she imagined Daniel's pain. The poor kid—

She fought against the budding concern and concentrated on the goose bumps prickling her flesh.

". . . need your permission to treat him," Jesse was saying. "They want to keep him for a few days."

She turned a questioning gaze on him. "For a broken arm?" The bud of concern blossomed into panic.

Jesse hesitated as if gauging her reaction. His dark eyes studied her with a thoroughness that made her swallow nervously. Then one lean finger came up to push a strand of hair from her cheek. A tingle sizzled down her spine. "The arm was a result of a suicide attempt, Faith. He didn't try to crawl out the window at Faith's House. He jumped."

"Jumped?" The word was little more than a gasp, her brain refusing the truth even as Jesse's voice rang loud and clear in her ears.

"His medical records from Booker Hall show three suicide attempts in the past two years. The doctor who's in charge of his care has to give him a thorough evaluation, make sure he's out of danger before he releases him to your custody. In the meantime, you've got a stack of paperwork waiting for you."

She wanted to tell Jesse to leave. That she didn't care about Daniel or his suicide attempt, or if the whole town were to catch fire with her smack-dab in the middle. But strangely enough, as she stared deep into his brown eyes that were so disturbingly

75

familiar, she couldn't make herself say the words.

"I'll just be a few seconds." She pulled away from him and rushed into her bedroom. Minutes later she was back, dressed in black leggings and an oversize T-shirt, her hair pulled back in a loose ponytail. She grabbed her purse and followed Jesse to the door.

"You don't have a car," he remarked several seconds later as they pulled out of her driveway in Bradley's prized cherry red Celica.

"The Suburban is mine," Faith told him. "I left it at Faith's House because Bradley needed it for the kids. It has a lot more room than this little car. Besides, it took me a few months just to get him to park this thing at Faith's House. He was afraid it would get vandalized."

"He doesn't seem like the flashy sports car type."

"He really isn't, but there's just something about this car. His link to his wanna-be lawyer years, he calls it. And nothing short of an act of Congress could get him to tote any of the kids around in it." She knew she was chattering on, but she couldn't stop herself. Talking kept her from thinking, from acknowledging the deep-seated dread seeping through her body. "I'm surprised he let you drive it. What did you promise him? Your firstborn?"

Jesse smiled, a lazy tilt to his lips that made Faith regret her words. She caught her bottom lip and focused on the road ahead, her purse gripped tight in her arms.

He was so close . . . just the slightest shift in her seat and her arm would brush his.

"So what have you been doing for transportation?" His words cut into her thoughts.

"I don't go out much, and when I do, walking suits me just fine." Her words were short, clipped, harsher than she meant them. She stared at the blaze of lights that streaked by them as they drove toward St. Joseph's Hospital.

"Walking is dangerous in this neighborhood. Aren't you scared?"

"Of what? After what I've been through—" She bit her lip to stop the flow of words, but they came anyway. "There isn't much that would scare me right now." *Except you*, a voice added silently.

As if he heard, his fingers tightened on the steering wheel. Faith's gaze was drawn to his scarred hand, barely visible in the shadows. As bad as the scar was, she knew the cut must have been deep. Painful. Her fingers itched to reach out and soothe that pain. She dug her nails into the soft black leather of her purse and forced her attention back to the road.

"Everybody's scared of something."

"Not me. Not anymore." She gave him a pointed stare. "And what do you care, anyway?"

"I care, that's all."

"Well, don't," she retorted. *Please don't*, her mind echoed.

"Dammit, I don't want to," he started, "but it's not that simple—" The rest of his words were lost in the wail of an ambulance that raced by them and hung a sharp right just a few feet ahead at a blazing neon sign that read EMERGENCY.

Faith wanted to ask Jesse what he meant, but he was already maneuvering the Celica into the hospital drive.

Minutes later, Faith, with Jesse at her side, his hand warm beneath her elbow, walked into the brightly lit emergency room. Her heart clenched at the sight of the nurses' station.

An accident, Ms. Jansen . . . Massive trauma . . .

She pushed the thoughts away and summoned her courage. "I'm Faith Jansen," she said to the woman behind the desk. "I'm here about Daniel Michaels."

"Just the woman we've been waiting for." The nurse smiled and handed Faith a clipboard stacked with forms. "Just return these when you're done."

"Told you so," Jesse murmured when Faith cast an incredulous look at the nurse.

An enormous amount of paperwork later, Faith sat in the ER waiting room and sipped a cup of strong black coffee. Bradley came through a pair of swinging double doors and dropped down beside her. His eyes were bloodshot, his expression tired. She quickly stifled the pang of guilt that went through her.

"I swear, that boy gave me the scare of my life," Bradley muttered, rubbing his palms on his navy blue sweatpants.

"Exactly what happened?"

"Emily leaned out her own window a couple of rooms over just in time to see Daniel take a dive. I heard her scream and raced upstairs to find out what was going on. By the time I got outside, Jesse was already there loading Daniel into the Suburban, despite the boy's cussing and screaming. That man sure can handle the rough ones. Even Mike was a little white when he saw Daniel's arm. But Jesse came through in a pinch. Where is he?"

"He went to move your Celica. We had to park in a loading zone."

"Loading zone?" Bradley's face lit with worry, and Faith almost smiled.

"Calm down. You didn't get towed. How's Daniel?"

"He's settled down, finally." With a shake of his head, he added, "For the life of me, I can't figure out how this happened. Mike had just climbed into bed. He didn't even have time to close his eyes before Daniel made a beeline for the bathroom. Mike started to get up to go after him. He swears the boy didn't have time to unzip his pants, much less unlock the window, pull a chair over, and climb through, but I'll be damned if he didn't."

"But how—" Faith started, her words drowned out by the voice of the nurse who suddenly appeared at her side.

"Ms. Jansen?" the nurse asked.

"Yes?"

"The doctor said it's all right for you to see Daniel now. He thinks the boy should hear that we're keeping him for a few extra days from someone other than our staff. Since you're his foster mother . . ."

Faith shook her head and started to protest, but before a syllable could pass her lips, Bradley nudged her arm. "Go on, Faith." He pushed her up from her seat. When she turned pleading eyes on him, he shook his head. "I'd do this for you in a heartbeat. You know that. I love those kids, even the Daniels of the bunch. But I'm tired." He rubbed his eyes and shook his head firmly. "I'm not used to doing this by myself."

She opened her mouth to argue with him, but the words wouldn't come. Instead, she nodded.

The nurse led Faith down the ER hallway, the bright lights nearly blinding her. Not that she needed anyone to lead her around. She was all too familiar with the main floor and the trauma unit.

They stopped just short of the elevators and turned right, then proceeded down an unfamiliar hallway.

"Where are we going?" Faith asked.

"Psychiatric unit." But Faith had already read the bold red letters emblazoned across a set of white double doors that loomed up ahead. These doors didn't open automatically like all the rest in the hospital. Instead, the nurse punched a black button and identified herself into a speaker box just to the right. A beep sounded and the doors swung wide.

The nurse ushered her down another hallway, past a row of closed doors that Faith would have bet were locked. At the far end of the hall sat a nurses' station filled with TV monitors of each room in the ward. Before they reached the station, the nurse stopped in front of one closed door. She pressed a black button and the door opened.

"Here you go," she said, turning to Faith. She waved her inside. "When you're done, just press the button and Vivian over there"—the nurse pointed to a gray-haired woman who sat in front of the monitors—"will let you out."

Faith took two steps forward and the door shut behind her. She found herself alone in a dimly lit hospital room that looked like any other, with the exception of bars built into the thick window glass and the padded furniture—what little there was. The sparse furnishings consisted of a single chair and a hospital bed.

Her attention went to Daniel, who lay so calm and serene in the small bed that for a fleeting second, an image rushed to her mind of a young girl huddled in the darkness, haunted by nightmares, by her loneliness. . . .

I'm scared.

She shook the memory away. This wasn't Jane. It didn't matter that this boy was just as needy, just as scared. Daniel wasn't Jane.

With that firmly in mind, Faith fixed her attention on the boy, his arm hidden in a thick white cast that covered from mid-bicep to wrist. The smell of disinfectant filled her nostrils and she closed her eyes to another wave of memories.

Sorry, Ms. Jansen. Sorry.

She forced her eyes open and concentrated on Daniel. She would look in on him, make sure everything was okay; then her duty would be done. Tomorrow she would have new papers drawn up and sign the whole responsibility of Faith's House over to Bradley. First thing tomorrow.

As she drew closer, she realized Daniel looked much smaller than she remembered. Younger, with his fine blond hair and his pale, almost sickly looking skin. Before she could stop herself, she reached out and traced a finger along his cheekbone. Dark circles rimmed his eyes. Her gaze traveled farther down his body. Fresh bruises covered the upper half of his chest, the marks disappearing beneath the thick white cast on his left arm.

So young, and so undeserving . . .

She closed her eyes to the thought, her mind filled with another image—a young girl with dark hair and lightly tanned skin and an entire future ahead of her.

Sorry we can't do more.

Severe trauma . . .

Sorry . . .

Faith's eyes snapped open to the sudden lash of rain against the hospital window. Water began running in thick rivers down the tinted glass. Her gaze went to the nasty abrasion on Daniel's cheek, obviously from the fall.

Correction—jump. Suicide. Daniel had *wanted* to hurt himself. To kill himself. *Three suicide attempts.*

He wanted to die, and Jane had desperately wanted to live.

The realization brought a bitter smile to Faith's lips. It was so unfair. Every day people took their lives, wasted them, while others yearned to live—

"What the hell are you doing here?" Daniel's voice, a hoarse whisper, shattered the silence.

A wave of doubt swamped her and she tried to move, to back up. But his hand closed around her wrist with surprising strength and she froze.

Trapped.

Chapter Five

"I . . ." Faith swallowed against the sudden panic.

Panic, and he was only holding her wrist. Where had the feeling been yesterday when he'd held a knife to her throat?

She took a deep breath, gathered her courage, and disengaged her hand. Unconsciously, her fingers stroked the spot on her wrist where he'd held her. "I was just looking in on you. How are you feeling?"

"Alive, unfortunately." Accusing blue eyes glared up at her. "Couldn't mind your own business, could you?"

"Why did you do it?" As if he could answer, she thought. As if any explanation could help her understand why he was so eager to give up what Jane had fought so desperately for.

"Why not?" he countered, the question flip, cold, and Faith felt the irony gripping her harder. "You think living in some hellhole with strangers is better?" He shook his head, his words dripping with venom. "Go on back to your kids, lady. I don't need your pity, or your help. Just leave me alone."

She would have gone, but something—something wrought from years of pushing and fighting and helping—prodded her on. And, of course, his eyes— they were so wide and belligerent and . . . *needy*.

"I'm here, Daniel, and I want to help you." The words flew from her mouth before she could stop them. "But you have to want that help. You have to meet me halfway. You have to reach out." She touched him, a gentle hand on his good arm.

He jerked away as if she'd zapped him with a cattle prod, and the concern that had spread through Faith evaporated.

"I don't want your help," he said in a growl, the words like a stinging slap in the face. "I can do what I want, and you can't stop me." Those pale blue eyes burned into her, stoking her frustration. Her anger.

He was right. She couldn't stop him, even if she did want to. The raw truth sawed through her like a dull blade, Daniel's pain stirring her anger at an unseen God who could snatch a life from someone with a passion for living, all the while letting someone else throw their precious existence away. Most of all, she felt hatred for herself because she couldn't stop it. She couldn't keep Daniel from throwing his life away, any more than she'd been able to keep Jane's from slipping away.

"Get the hell out of here, Miss Do-gooder," Daniel sneered. "Just leave. . . ."

She whirled and raced for the door. His voice followed her "You ain't wanted here, lady. Go on and run, and keep running. Keep away from me."

It isn't fair! The cry echoed from deep in her soul

and she stabbed the security button with trembling fingers. A split second later, the door opened.

Faith rushed past the nurses' station, down the hallway, oblivious to the gray-haired nurse who called her name. The double doors buzzed open, and she left the psychiatric unit behind, fleeing through the hospital like a woman being chased by the devil himself.

But there was no devil. No God. No heaven.

Ah, but there was a hell. And she was caught in it.

She couldn't hold on any longer. I'm sorry, Ms. Jansen. Sorry . . . Sorry . . . Sorry . . .

She ran out an emergency exit and into the wet night, frantically searching for a place to run, to hide. Her boots slapped the pavement, splashing water and drenching her leggings. The darkness pressed in, suffocating her and making her breath come in short, harsh gasps. The rain beat down at her, but it couldn't drown the memories, or quench the fire that raged inside, burning up the numbness she'd fought so hard for.

Fight, Jane! she'd begged and pleaded. All for nothing. Nothing . . . in the face of death.

Or rejection.

She'd failed before. She'd reached out to problem children only to have them turn away, run away, go back onto the streets. The lost ones haunted her, preyed on her conscience, chipped away at her determination to make a difference; then death had dealt the final blow to her stamina.

"Why?" she cried, skidding to a halt. She slammed her fists against an abandoned storefront. The wood boarding up what was left of the front window cut into her clenched fists, scraped at her skin. Still, she pounded again and again and again until her hands were throbbing and bleeding. But the pain wasn't enough to block out reality.

Jane was gone, and there was nothing Faith could do. *Nothing* . . .

"Faith." The voice came from everywhere and nowhere. At first she thought she'd imagined it, but then she saw large hands close over her fists, felt a massive chest pressed to her back, and heard Jesse's familiar voice. "Accept it, Faith. Accept it and let go or it'll eat you alive."

"Leave me alone," she cried, echoing Daniel's words, her voice fierce, raw with a hurt she yearned to ignore. "Just leave me the hell alone!"

"You need to grieve and get on with your life. She's gone. Admit it and let her go. Just let her go."

She shook her head frantically and wrenched her hands from his. Whirling, she lashed out at him, anger and pain and fear making her fight when she wanted nothing more than to sink to the ground and dissolve into the mud puddle beneath her feet. Anything to escape the damned compassion that gleamed in the dark depths of Jesse Savage's eyes.

"Let her go?" Her tears came harder, faster, pouring down her cheeks as forcefully as the rain that hammered down around them. "I shouldn't have to let her go! Don't you understand that? Her body healed and she made it through the nightmares, even though she couldn't remember anything. She deserved to live, to have a second chance. It's not fair that she made it through all that and now she's gone!"

He caught her fists again and yanked her up hard against him. For a fraction of a moment, he stared down at her. He stared long and hard and deep, the compassion gone, replaced by a pain so intense it made Faith want to scream. She knew that pain. It was her own.

Something flickered in his dark eyes; then he whispered, the sound barely audible above the rain, "I know what you're feeling. I know what it's like to lose somebody close to you. To love them and lose them. I know." And then his mouth swooped down and his lips captured hers.

She froze in shocked silence for the space of a heartbeat as his mouth searched hers. Then she felt something pass between them, like a jolt of electricity from two live wires that touched, sparked, fused.

Her lips parted, but it wasn't an act of surrender to his plundering mouth. No, it was one of desperation. She'd been so cold inside since Jane's death, so dead, and now she wanted to feel warm, alive, vital, and Jesse Savage made her feel all those things, and more.

It was as if he knew just how to soothe her grief and draw her past the invisible wall she'd built around herself, as if he knew what haunted her, as if he'd faced the same demons himself and had found a way to fight them.

His tongue slipped past her lips, tangling with hers, sucking and stroking until heat shot from her nipples to her belly, and lower still. She could feel the powerful muscles of his chest beneath her palms. His scent—raw male and the sharp smell of danger—filled her senses, intoxicated her. His body's warmth seeped through the cotton of his T-shirt to scorch her as fiercely as his mouth.

His breath became her breath, his strength her strength, his sadness—

The thought shattered as he jerked away from her, his chest heaving, his dark eyes wild with passion and something else. Disbelief? Regret?

"It's raining," he said, his voice gruff. "We'd better get out of here." He thrust his hands into his pockets.

She nodded, not trusting herself to speak. She felt too strange. Shaky. Unsure of herself. Like nothing she'd ever felt because of one measly kiss.

She'd kissed men before. She'd gone even further than that with Max, her college boyfriend. But nothing, not Max's kisses, or even his lovemaking, had made her feel the way she felt now. As if she'd been standing in the middle of a train crossing and come within inches of being crushed. Her entire body felt exhilarated. Alive!

Her heart beat rapidly. A tingling rush of warmth covered her skin despite the rain that slashed at her. She touched her hands to her cheeks, her palms seared by the heat in her face. Yes, definitely alive.

"Come on. I'll take you home." Jesse didn't touch her again. Instead, he turned and walked up the block toward the Suburban parked near the curb. He didn't even glance back to see if she followed. He knew. She could tell by the stiff way he moved, his shoulders hunched beneath his jacket. He felt her presence as keenly as she felt his.

The ride home was silent. The streets passed in a blaze of lights that Faith barely noticed. She tried to keep her eyes on the road in front of her, but her gaze kept straying to him.

He sat like a stone statue, the only movement that of a tiny muscle that jumped in his jaw. His dark hair hung in wet tendrils past his shoulders. Raindrops fell from his hair to run in tiny rivulets down his forehead, the chiseled slope of his cheek, until they disappeared in the overgrowth of stubble that covered his jaw. The moisture caught the passing lights, sculpting his features in a colorful dance of shadows that made him look all the more dangerous.

Dangerously attractive she admitted to herself. He really was good-looking, in a rebellious, bad-boy sort of way. She'd never been drawn to men like him. The few times she'd actually been attracted to anyone, they'd been the three-piece-suit types, with college degrees and nice substantial bank accounts. Men like her father had been.

Jesse Savage certainly didn't wear a suit. And she'd be willing to bet he'd didn't have enough money to fill a piggy bank, much less a bank account.

Still, there was something about him. Something that demanded her attention. A connection between them, as if they related on a different level, one that went below the superficial clothes, looks, and wealth society used as criteria to label people. Yes, Jesse touched something far beneath the surface.

"Why did you come after me?"

"I was worried," he said without sparing her a glance.

"But *why?* You don't even know me, and I don't know you." She held up her hand when he started to protest. "I know your name and I know you like kids. That's it. I don't know where you're from, what you did before coming to Faith's House, whether or not you're married. . . ." She cut him a sideways glance. "You're not married, are you?"

He shook his head and relief swept through her.

"Where are you from?"

"Restoration."

"Restoration?"

"A small town on the other side of Fort Worth. I moved to Houston last year." The words were so low she almost didn't hear him. It was as if he hesitated to talk, to reveal anything about himself.

"And?"

"That's it." He frowned and Faith could practically feel the tension pouring off him. "I'm not really much of a talker."

"It's not that difficult. You just open your mouth and let the words go. So you have a brother and sister, right?"

He shot her another glance, his grip tightening on the steering wheel. "Had," he finally said. "They were killed shortly after we moved here. I've spent the past year . . . wandering, I guess you could say. I needed a job and I saw your ad in the paper. That's it," he finished, yet his words had softened, his expression was not as severe, as if talking about himself hadn't been as difficult as he'd anticipated.

"Did you ever work with kids before?"

He shrugged. "A little volunteer work, but I stayed pretty busy supporting my brother and sister. Our mom died when they were barely out of diapers. I was a senior in high school at the time."

"What about your dad?"

"He was never really in the picture." His jaw tightened again and Faith had the insane urge to reach out and touch him, to soothe away the expression. The pain . . .

Her fingers dug into the folds of a sweater she'd picked up as she sought a distraction. "So what did you do after high school?"

Her question seemed to distract him from his troubling thoughts. The lines of his face eased. "I went on to another job, and part-time college classes at a small community college in Fort Worth. I worked during the day, went to school at night."

"That must have been hard."

"It never seemed that hard. Whenever I started to

burn out or give up, all I had to do was look at my brother and sister. They pretty much kept me going. I was all they had and they were all I had."

"What happened to them?"

Her question met with the screech of brakes as Jesse swung into her driveway and brought them to a jolting halt.

"We're here." He drummed his fingers on the steering wheel, the motor idling as he waited, rather impatiently, she guessed, when the twitch of the muscle in his jaw seemed to speed up. The tension was back, twining around him, pushing everything else away.

"Looks like we are." She pulled at the door handle, her fingers suddenly clumsy. After three attempts, she finally shoved the door open.

"I could walk you inside—" he started, but the "No!" she blurted out killed the rest of his sentence.

"I can see myself in." She climbed from the car. "Thanks for the ride and . . . everything."

She let herself meet his gaze then, and the reality of what had happened between them crashed around her. There was no mistaking the regret swimming in the dark depths of his eyes. Regret, when all she felt was . . .

Guilt, shame, embarrassment. The emotions washed through her with the intensity of a tidal wave. She slammed the car door shut and pivoted toward the house. God help her, but she'd let him kiss her. Worse, she'd kissed him back, and she'd thrown all caution, all thoughts about anything else to the wind.

She forced her eyes wide, fighting back a sudden surge of misery as she fumbled with the lock on the front door. No guilt, she told herself. No anger. No embarrassment. Nothing. Nothing was better. Safer.

But Jesse Savage made her feel anything but safe. He made her *feel*, period, and she knew then that her first instincts about him had been right. He was much too dangerous, and better forgotten.

But inside, as she peeked past the curtains and watched him pull out of the driveway, she couldn't deny the loneliness surrounding her. It followed her through the dark house and crept into bed with her later that night.

Loneliness, and oddly enough, relief. She'd released her anger over Jane's death, and when she closed her eyes, the nightmares didn't come. Only sweet dreams of a young, vibrant girl with brilliant brown eyes.

Jesse's eyes . . .

Jesse stripped off his clothes and stepped into a cold shower, eager to wash Faith's scent from his body, the feel of her from his hands, the taste of her from his lips.

He'd kissed her. Of all the stupid, ridiculous, insane things he could have done, he'd kissed her.

He slammed a fist into the tiled wall. Pain splintered through him, but it wasn't enough to erase the memory of her. So close. So warm. So damned responsive.

What the hell had he been thinking?

He hadn't been thinking. He'd acted on impulse, gut reaction, sheer desperation.

The anger had been eating her up, the rage destroying her, and something had shifted inside him. Faith was a woman who knew what it meant to hurt, to ache, to hate so badly there was nothing else left inside.

Nothing but burning vengeance.

But it hadn't been vengeance that had passed between them for those few seconds. Jesse had realized that the moment he'd stepped up behind Faith, reached for her. . . .

A wild current of feeling had flowed between them. Desire, lust, want, understanding. Jesse had never felt so connected to someone, or been so damned aroused.

He turned the water up full-force and took several deep breaths. Okay, so he was aroused. He'd been without a woman a long time. There'd been many before that fateful night. Nameless, faceless women, no one he could actually recall.

It was only natural that when he finally touched a female again after all this time, all he'd been through, he would want to do a hell of a lot more. It was raw need, pure and simple.

That he could handle. Control. He wasn't a teenager hard up for anything in a skirt. He was a man— for now, anyway.

Jesse soaped his arms, his shoulders, relishing the feel of water sluicing over him. It had been so long since he'd had even this simple pleasure. He inhaled the soap's fragrance and turned his full attention to the slippery wetness gliding over his skin.

A shower was good. A definite distraction.

Or was it?

He slid the soap over his pounding heart, down his belly and lower. . . .

His eyes closed and he sucked in a sharp, ragged breath.

It couldn't be. . . . Even as the thought echoed in his head, he felt Faith's fingers trailing over his aching length, touching him. He grew harder, hotter, damned near ready to explode.

His gaze snapped to attention and he stared into the small shaving mirror hanging from the showerhead. The brown of his eyes fired a brilliant, iridescent white. Like twin beams from a pair of headlights, only brighter. Light skimmed over his skin, outlining his body in a pulsing glimmer.

You shouldn't have poked your nose into this, Savage. We ain't got no beef with you, cop. It's your brother we want.

Reality pelted him as fiercely as the icy pellets of the cold shower. The light faded as quickly as it had come, his eyes deepened to their usual brown, and Jesse looked to be a man again.

For the time being.

But he wasn't a man to indulge in a man's fantasies, much less act on them. He should have only three goals when it came to Faith Jansen: Get close to her, find out her heart's desire, and see that she saw firsthand what true faith could do.

Miracles do happen.

Faith, with her kind heart and her lifetime of do-gooding, had earned herself one, and Jesse was the delivery man.

Then he could kiss this place good-bye forever. There was nothing for him here. Everyone he'd ever loved was gone, and he wanted to follow, to say the words that burned inside him.

A second chance to ask forgiveness. To gain peace.

He rinsed himself off and reached for a towel. As much as he might want to bed Faith—and he did—it wasn't part of the deal, and he wouldn't jeopardize an eternity of heaven in the hereafter for a fleeting glimpse of it here on earth. Not no, but sure as hell *no*.

His mind knew all the reasons why not, all the

obstacles that stood between them, the stakes riding on the success of his mission.

If only his damned body understood, as well.

When Jesse finally climbed into bed, he didn't get the good night's sleep he'd expected after almost a year spent floating in oblivion. No, he tossed and turned, and ached and burned, and the feelings had nothing to do with the hate swirling inside him.

They had everything to do with a fresh-faced woman with pain-filled eyes, who tasted of hope and innocence and kept him throbbing and aroused and feeling like nothing more than a man desperate for a woman. *His* woman.

"I've been living under a rock," Faith told Grubby the next morning. She sat at the kitchen table, nibbled a stale piece of toast, and watched the puppy gobble up the last can of dog food. "A really big rock."

He looked up at her with anxious eyes and licked his chops.

"Sorry, buddy. That's it for you." She tossed the empty can into the nearest trash, along with an old bread wrapper. "For both of us if I don't get to the grocery store."

She glanced around at the chaos of her kitchen. At least she'd done the dishes yesterday, thanks to Jesse. Otherwise the entire room looked like it had been hit by a tornado—

The thought ground to a halt as she caught her reflection in the toaster. A gasp stalled in her throat. Staring back at her was a stranger. A lost, lonely stranger.

A tangled mass of brown hair framed the thin, wan face, the complexion pale from lack of proper nourishment and sunshine. The green eyes were smudged with shadows, the lips drawn and color-less.

She'd seen her reflection many times over the past two weeks when she'd chanced a glance in the mirror. She'd seen the same face, yet she'd never felt this way before. . . .

Bitterness and grief, yes. But no regret. She'd been too angry to care how she looked, too lost to try to find herself again.

She stiffened, tugging at her wrinkled T-shirt. She looked awful. Her clothes were ragged, her hair limp and lifeless and in sore need of a wash. She was a mess, and her life was a mess.

Faith tossed the stale toast into the trash and headed for the bathroom. Her wrinkled clothes hit the tile, and she slid into a hot bath. She spent the next half hour soaping herself with a nickel-size piece of Ivory. She'd run out of everything: food, toiletries, energy. . . .

No more.

She still wasn't her old self, she decided a while later as she stared at her reflection in the steamed-up bathroom mirror. But at least her hair was clean and shiny, her face freshly scrubbed. She might not look all that much better but she felt it. She changed into a button-down shirt and jeans, attached Grubby's leash, and headed for a nearby grocery store.

She didn't have enough arms to carry everything she'd run out of since she'd let her cupboards go bare. But at least she could get some food and essentials to see her through until she could find a means of transportation.

Of course, she could always commandeer the Suburban, but that would mean going to Faith's House and seeing the kids.

"What do you say, Grubby? You up for a new car?"

The dog barked and Faith smiled. Maybe tomorrow she'd go car shopping. Or the day after that. Eventually.

Sunlight beamed down on her. What was it they said about the weather in Houston? If you didn't like it, wait an hour. That summed it up, all right. It was brilliant and beautiful, with clear blue skies. It was the calm after last night's storm.

An hour later, she lugged five plastic bags, more than she'd intended, back home from the Food Mart. She was hot and panting by the time she reached her front porch to find Jesse Savage sitting on the steps.

A fact that did nothing to help the heat and the panting.

"Hey, little buddy. It's good to see you." Jesse scooped up Grubby.

Powerful hands cradled the small, furry body, and warmth stole through Faith.

Muscles rippled in his arms as Jesse stroked the puppy's head before setting him aside and reaching for Faith's groceries. "Here, let me."

"Where were you when I really needed you?" Faith handed him a couple of bags. "I think I pulled my shoulder completely out of socket a block back."

"You should have called me. I would have driven you."

Now, there was a thought. But as inviting as it was, after looking in the mirror that morning, really looking, Faith hadn't been so sure she wanted strangers to see her, much less a man who'd kissed her senseless the night before.

She didn't look much better now, but at least she was clean and had on some decent clothes. With that consoling thought, she led Jesse inside.

In the kitchen, Grubby licked excitedly at the dog food Faith opened for him as Jesse started unloading groceries.

"Shouldn't you be at Faith's House?" She spooned the last of the food into Grubby's bowl.

Jesse paused, a box of Wheaties in one hand, and grinned. "I am at Faith's house."

"I mean the other one."

"Once the kids were off to school and the breakfast rush over, Bradley said I could take a few hours off while he went to the hospital to check on Daniel."

"How is he?" The words were out before she could stop them.

"Not so good. The doctor says he's withdrawn. He won't talk to anyone. He just lies there. No reaction at all."

Compassion prickled through her, but Faith pushed the feeling aside. "He'll come around. He just needs a little time, a qualified counselor, somebody in his life who understands him."

"Like you?"

She shook her head. "I'm retired now. Bradley will do just fine. He's patient, caring, concerned, committed—everything a kid like Daniel needs. So"— she sighed, unloading one of the grocery bags— "what brings you over here during your break?"

"I couldn't help but notice that torn screen on your front porch."

"First garbage cans, now my screen." She started stacking cans of dog food in the pantry. "What are you, some kind of Mr. Fix-it guardian angel?"

"Well, I've always been pretty handy." Jesse's deep voice rumbled directly behind her, and a sizzle of awareness bolted up her spine. "But never much of an angel."

Her heart thudded a response and she took a deep, steadying breath. *Easy, girl. He's just a man, and you're just having an attack of hormones.* She'd neglected everything in her life for the past two weeks, including her sex life.

Of course, she'd also neglected it for the past five years, as well, which spoke volumes for her social life, or lack of one. With Faith's House to oversee, she'd never had time for a real relationship, and she'd never been into one-night stands.

She turned and stared up at him. Then again, a girl could always change her mind. Jesse Savage was certainly a convincing argument, especially standing so close to her.

So warm and real.

"You look like you're feeling better." His fingertips skimmed her cheek and she resisted the urge to turn into his palm. "No more dark circles." The pad of his finger traced the sensitive area beneath one eye and she trembled. "That's good, Faith. Really good."

"It feels good." She took another breath. Bad move. His scent—that undeniable musky maleness coupled with a hint of mystery—filled her head, pulsed through her senses. "I—about last night," she started, only to have the words stall in her throat. She swallowed. "I—I owe you an apology for running out of the hospital the way I did."

"Forget it. It's good to lose control once in a while. Sometimes we have to let off a little steam." He grabbed her hand, his fingertips caressing her bruised knuckles. A grin tugged at his lips. "Or a lot of steam."

"I was pretty fired up, wasn't I?"

She was referring to her outburst of anger. But when Jesse's gaze darkened, she knew her words had broached an altogether different subject.

Unconsciously, she licked her lips. He followed the motion with his eyes and her mouth went dry. It was going to happen again, and oddly enough, she wanted it to.

She wanted him. She wanted to feel the warmth he stirred inside her, to soak up the delicious heat, to chase away the cold grief that had taken up residence after Jane's death.

His breath touched her mouth, made it tingle, and her lips parted. Yes, she wanted to kiss him again—

"Cupcakes," he said, reaching behind her to pull the package off the pantry shelf. Wonder filled his voice. "You've got cupcakes."

So much for kissing. She forced her heartbeat back to normal. Not easy considering he was still standing so close. "Help yourself," she managed.

He leaned back, putting a few safe inches between them as he opened the package. He took a bite, and pleasure eased the lines of his face. "Damn, I forgot how good these were," he said in between bites.

"Forgot?"

"I haven't had them in a while."

"Why?"

He seemed at a loss. His jaws stopped working at the cake for a full second, his expression guarded, careful, as if he were hiding something. Finally, he swallowed. "A diet," he muttered. He took another bite of the cupcake. "No sweets. Have to keep the old bod in shape." He patted his flat stomach, finished off the cupcake, and busied himself pulling another out of the package. "You know what they say," he told her with a sheepish grin. "Abstinence makes the heart grow fonder."

"I thought it was absence."

"That, too." He bit into his second cupcake. Pleasure glittered hot and bright in his eyes. She'd never seen someone enjoy something quite so much.

"My kid sister used to bake a lot," he said, as if he read the question in her eyes. "She started off with an Easy Bake oven when she was about nine. By the time she hit thirteen, she'd graduated to the real thing." He turned to finish unloading the grocery sack on the table. "She didn't make cupcakes, but she made lots of real cakes—all chocolate. She loved anything chocolate, especially brownies. She could whip up the best fudge brownies in the entire world."

"You miss her a lot, don't you?" Faith scooted past Jesse to put a loaf of bread in the bread box. Anything to keep from watching his mouth work at the chocolate cupcake.

"Yeah." The word was gruff, a wealth of feeling behind the one syllable. She couldn't help but get the distinct impression that it was an admission Jesse Savage didn't make very often.

"You never did tell me what happened."

He averted his gaze and unwrapped another cupcake. "It doesn't matter. She's gone, and my brother, too." Silence settled around them as he leaned against the counter. "I never was much for baking, myself, but she always had something in the oven. The kitchen always smelled so sugary and warm. . . ." He shook his head, as if to shake away the sudden memory.

Faith closed her eyes to her own vision—a drawerful of Hershey's kisses and a young girl with dark hair and dark eyes, popping chocolate into her mouth while doing a particularly difficult math problem.

"What about you?" Jesse's voice pulled her back to the present. "Do you like sweets?" She nodded and he grinned. "That figures." He held out a bite to her. "Sweets for the sweet?"

She opened her mouth and let him feed her the small morsel. His fingertip trailed over her lip, and every nerve in her body went on full alert.

Their gazes locked for the space of several heartbeats before Faith managed to close her mouth. Then he reached out and wiped a smudge of cream from the corner of her upper lip. Electricity shimmered through her body.

"The inside's the best part." He slid his fingertip into his own mouth and sucked the dab of cream. The air stalled in Faith's lungs.

Her mind replayed last night's kiss and it was all she could do not to take his finger, slide it into her own mouth, taste the lingering cream and bittersweetness of delicious male skin. *Him*.

The forbidden thought sang through her head, and she actually felt herself lean forward, just a fraction of an inch. He was so close, the scent of chocolate and raw male like an aphrodisiac to her vulnerable senses.

"I'd better get to work on that screen."

He turned before she could form a reply and disappeared into the living room. Minutes later, she heard him outside working at the front screen, and she was left to wonder what had just happened between them.

Nothing, her brain cried out, but her hormones said otherwise. Something had indeed happened. Jesse had retreated. She'd seen the want in his eyes; then for whatever reason, he'd resisted his feelings, and her.

Grubby barked and Faith gathered her control. So he had no intention of kissing her again. So what? At least she'd felt that moment of contact last night, his body pressing against hers, desire rippling through her. She would savor the memory and chalk it up to experience.

If only she didn't feel so connected to him. When she looked into his eyes, those familiar brown eyes, it was almost as if she'd loved him in the past.

Whoa, wait a second. Love? She'd never met Jesse Savage, much less loved him. He was handsome and kind, and she was vulnerable. That explained everything. And nothing.

But Faith didn't care about explanations. She cared only about getting her life back together. She forced Jesse from her thoughts and concentrated on putting up the rest of the groceries. After that, she would tackle the mess in the living room, then scrub the bathroom. That should keep her busy.

Jesse Savage and his kiss were history.

If only she could manage to completely forget that he was only mere feet away. The awareness stayed with her, followed her through each chore, driving her to scrub and polish until her arms ached as badly as her reawakened hormones. Worse, even . . .

Nah.

Chapter Six

"The screen's fixed," Jesse announced an hour later as he opened the front door.

"Not soon enough," Faith muttered to herself. She sat on the sofa, sipping a diet soda, Grubby curled up in her lap.

"What did you say?"

She forced a smile. "I said it must have been rough."

"You're not kidding. The screen was torn, but the frame was nearly glued in place. I had to pry the thing off with a crowbar." Jesse set the toolbox he'd retrieved from Faith's garage just inside the front door and stepped into the room. His large form blocked her line of vision, the window at his back. Sunlight haloed him, a brilliant white surrounding a dark, mysterious shadow.

For the space of a heartbeat, the light grew in brilliance and Faith blinked against the onslaught.

Then the light faded just enough for her to make out his features—the serious set of his jaw, the intensity of his dark brown eyes with speckles of stardust in them. Stardust that gleamed and sparkled and burned so hot whenever he looked at her. Heat skimmed across her skin, stroking and soothing and—

"If you're not doing anything this afternoon"—Jesse's voice rumbled through her head, killing her thoughts—"why don't you come back to Faith's House with me?"

She shook her head and sipped her soda. "I don't think that would be such a good idea."

"It would be a great idea. The kids really miss you, and Bradley's this close to going over the edge."

"Bradley likes the edge. He comes from a long line of litigators. Stress and Danger are his middle names." Her attempt at humor fell short. Jesse simply stared at her, into her, and silence wrapped around them.

She concentrated on rubbing the back of Grubby's ears. Instead of licking his appreciation, he snuggled more deeply into her lap, his belly full after a can of dog food.

The ungrateful ball of fluff. Where was an appreciative wag when she needed one?

"I know about Jane." Jesse's words brought her gaze up to collide with his. She saw the pain, open and raw in his eyes. His pain. Her pain.

"I know what it's like," he added. "Remember, I lost my brother and sister not very long ago."

She didn't say anything. Instead, she forced her gaze away and shifted Grubby. He didn't so much as open his eyes.

"Sitting here by yourself isn't going to make the hurt go away," Jesse went on. "You need to get on with things, Faith."

She gave the puppy a little shake. His eyes opened, then drifted shut just as quickly.

"Faith." Jesse knelt beside her. His fingers touched her jaw, forced her gaze to meet his. "It doesn't mean you're forgetting her. She still lives inside you." He tapped his chest. "In here. You keep living and so does she. Inside."

He was right. She knew it. Deep down, beneath all the hurt and fear, she knew it. The realization was like opening a strange door, not knowing what lurked on the other side.

The door creaked open. But there was no living and breathing monster of grief waiting to rip her apart, devour her heart. He'd already attacked last night, and the only thing that waited for her now was peace, a cool, soothing peace to salve her wounds.

Faith closed her eyes against the sudden tears of relief.

"Remember that." His voice was soft, soothing. The pad of one finger caught a tear near the corner of her eye. "Okay?"

She nodded and his hand fell away. A strange sense of desolation swept through her.

"So what do you say?" he asked. "Come with me?"

She shook her head. "Sorry. I've got plans."

"Like what?"

"I'm watering my plants."

"That takes about twenty minutes."

"They're really dirty."

"Funny."

"You go on without me, Jesse." The teasing was gone, her voice quiet now, serious, her gaze pleading.

He shook his head. "I can't." The words were a low murmur, laced with desperation, and Faith got the inexplicable feeling again that she knew him from somewhere.

"There's just something about you. . . ." She stared at him, studying his features, her mind rifling through the past for some clue. "Who are you?"

His gaze met hers. "You know who I am."

"Yes, but I don't know why you seem so familiar to me. It's almost like I've met you before."

"You haven't." He averted his gaze, fixing his attention on Grubby. Long, lean fingers massaged the back of the puppy's ears, so soft, soothing, and Faith's mind traveled back, to a dark room at Faith's house in the dead of night, and a teenage girl curled against her. . . .

"I try to remember," the girl's small voice whispered. "But when I try, the nightmares come. I hear the screams, feel the pain, but I can't see anything. I can't see anyone!"

The girl's tears flowed unchecked, splashing onto Faith's arm, which was anchored about her, and something seeped into the crevices of Faith's heart. As she did every night when the nightmares came and the screams started, she settled herself firmly on Jane's bed and held her. Tight. Then she watched the play of shadows as moonlight winked outside the window, and she stroked the girl's soft, shiny hair.

"I used to be afraid," Faith said, reliving her own past, her own battle with the darkness. "Just like you. When my parents died, I thought I'd died, too. I couldn't imagine never seeing them again. Each day, it hurt to wake up knowing they wouldn't be there. And it hurt to go to sleep, knowing they would be. Knowing I would see them but never really touch them again. God, it hurt so much."

"That's what I'm feeling," came the small voice.

"My chest hurts almost as bad as my head. There's somebody I miss. I know it, I just can't seem to picture them."

"You will," Faith whispered, hugging the girl closer when her thin body shuddered. *"Just give yourself time."*

"What if I don't?"

"Then we'll make new memories for you to have, to fill up the empty spaces inside. Don't concentrate on trying to see a face; just focus on what you feel. The loss means love, Jane. You had a family, someone you loved dearly, and they loved you. Even though they're gone from your life, what you felt for them, and what they felt for you, lives on inside of you, in spite of your failed memory."

"You think so?"

"I know so. They might be gone, but their love lives on inside you. You keep living, waking up, and so do they. That's why you have to keep going. For yourself, and for them."

Grubby's faint whimper jerked Faith back to the present. She stared down to see Jesse's tense fingers, the knuckles rigid, nearly white, paused atop the dog's head.

Her gaze lifted to meet his and they simply sat there for a long moment, Faith trying to read the expression in the depths of his eyes and Jesse . . . She didn't know why he stared at her. It was as if he already saw deep inside, into her thoughts, his gaze probing and delving until nothing remained a secret.

Grubby gave another whimper, obviously none too pleased that Jesse had stopped his stroking. The sound shattered the breathy silence surrounding them.

"He's spoiled," she remarked, tearing her attention from Jesse to focus on Grubby's wriggling form.

Jesse gave a comforting pat to the puppy's head, then withdrew his hand. "You're a born nurturer."

She smiled, a sad curve to her lips. "I used to be." Sad? That fact shouldn't make her sad. It was her nurturing that had gotten her into this mess. This hurt.

"You still are, Faith. You're just doing a damned fine job of pretending otherwise."

"I didn't know psychoanalysis was your area of expertise. Or is that just a part-time hobby like the home repair?"

He smiled, a slow tilt to his sensuous lips that sent her heartbeat into overdrive. "You'll go back to the kids eventually," he said with dead certainty. "You know that, so why put it off? You can't hide forever."

She could try, she thought. She wouldn't hurt the way she'd hurt for Jane ever again, and that meant keeping her distance from the kids. She couldn't care again. Not like that.

Never again.

It was as if he read the thought as it rooted in her mind. His expression hardened. Anger turned his eyes a deep, bottomless obsidian that would have been frightening if he hadn't been so close. So warm.

This time she reached out. Her fingertips touched his jaw, traced the strong curve, and his features softened. "I'm not going back. I can't."

They stared at each other then, and again Faith had the feeling that he wanted to kiss her.

If only he would. It had been so sweet last night. So consuming. So electrifying. So . . .

"I'd better get going." He stood up and stared

109

down at her. "I told Bradley I would help with Ricky's schoolwork this afternoon."

She came so close to reaching for him. Instead she balled her fists, took a deep breath, and tried to steady her pounding heart. She was stupid.

And desperate.

And lonely.

The three didn't make for a very good combination.

"If you're doing math, make sure you keep his hands on the table," she said when he reached the front door.

He halted, hand on the doorknob. "Why?"

"He counts on his fingers if you give him half a chance. He can do it up here"—she tapped her forehead—"when he wants to, especially if you have Emily ride shotgun with you. He likes to impress her."

"But they're constantly fighting."

She smiled. "That should have clued you in right away."

"You're really good with them, Faith."

She closed her eyes for a long moment, visions of Ricky and Emily and the other kids running through her head.

Finally, she slanted him a glance and a smile. "You're pretty good with kids yourself. Otherwise Bradley wouldn't have kept you."

"He was desperate."

"He's got good instincts." She smiled. "I'd say he got a real bargain—a guy who's good with kids, great at home repair, and does part-time psychoanalysis. Definitely a prize find."

He smiled again, lips parting to reveal a row of straight white teeth, a stark contrast against his tanned features. "I'll stop back by tomorrow," he said, twisting the knob. The door creaked open. "Your rain gutter's torn near the back porch."

"It won't work, Jesse. I'm not going back to Faith's House no matter how often you show up here and analyze me."

"I'm not talking analysis. I'm talking rain gutters."

"Right." She smiled. "I appreciate the screen, though. Thanks for thinking of me."

His smile died as he regarded her. "You're all I think about," he murmured a moment before he shut the door behind him.

At least she thought that was what he'd said.

She had to be hearing things. Her imagination. Wishful thinking. A very enticing fantasy.

Common sense told her that, but it didn't stop the words from echoing in her head and following her into her dreams an hour later.

You're all I think about.

He covered her, his hard length burning into her as Faith opened herself and welcomed him deep, deep inside. It had been a long time since she'd been with a man, and even longer since she'd wanted to be with one. A lifetime, it seemed.

He was hot, huge, and she was wet and eager and . . .

She awoke near nightfall to find herself sprawled on the sofa, drenched in sweat. Her T-shirt stuck to her despite the freezing air that swirled from the air conditioner.

Sitting up, she stared into the growing shadows of dusk and felt for Grubby's soft body. He was gone, probably sleeping on his pallet in the kitchen.

Faith hugged her arms and trailed her hands over her skin, wishing with all her heart it was Jesse's touch she felt rather than her own.

* * *

"Leave me alone!" Emily wailed. She gathered up her math book. "I have better things to do with my time than stay up past curfew to try to help an ignorant pighead who keeps calling me Einstein Emmie. I need my beauty sleep, you know. I've got school tomorrow, and two tests, and it's already a quarter after ten. And I am not an Einstein!"

"What'd I do?" Ricky turned to Jesse once Emily had stomped up the stairs.

"You called her an Einstein."

"She *is* an Einstein."

"Maybe, but I think she'd like you to notice more than her brain."

"Like what?"

"Like how shiny her hair is or whether or not she's wearing a pretty blouse."

"But she doesn't draw attention to any of that stuff. Instead she's in my face, telling me how smart she is and how dumb I am." He eyed Jesse. "How come you know so much about girls?"

"I had a younger sister. We were pretty tight."

"I had a sister, too." A bleak look covered Ricky's face. "I haven't seen her in a while. When my mom left, my kid sister was just a baby. Then Welfare came and took us both, then split us up. I haven't seen her in about ten years."

"That's tough, man."

Ricky stiffened. "It ain't no sweat off my back." He turned his attention to the textbook. "I can't believe they expect us to know all this crap." He cradled his head in his hands. "Em's right. I'm no good at this. It's too late. My brain's too small. Hell—er, I mean, heck, I probably don't even have a brain."

"It's there, Ricky. Just try."

The boy eyed him. "Do I have a choice?"

Jesse shrugged. "You can let Emily ace the test while you get burned. It's up to you."

After five minutes of calculation, Ricky produced the right answer, beamed a smile, and headed up to bed.

Jesse and Bradley and Mike spent the next fifteen minutes doing a last-minute check on bedrooms, making sure all the lights were out and everyone was accounted for.

Mike, who was studying nutrition at a local junior college, disappeared into the dining room to read, while Jesse and Bradley collapsed in the den.

"Every day I tell myself no more, and every day here I am." Bradley sank down on the sofa and motioned to a nearby chair. "Take a load off."

"Why do you do it?" Jesse settled into the chair.

"Paying my dues, I suppose. I was one of those rich kids who had everything. Big home out in River Oaks. Great parents. Plenty of food in my stomach and new clothes on my back. I went to a private school, St. John's here in Houston, then headed to Rice to major in prelaw."

"Faith mentioned something about you coming from a law family."

"It's in my genes. There was never any question that I would carry on the family tradition and head straight to the famed halls of Winters, Winters, and Winters, the best defense firm in the country."

"So why didn't you?" There was no worry in Jesse's voice, just mild curiosity. He'd learned how to mask his emotions, be cool and distant a long, long time ago—no matter how hot the situation. Just because this guy might have some knowledge of the law didn't mean he would remember one of Houston's finest being brutally slaughtered. Murders were a dime a dozen in Houston. Even murdered cops, and Jesse had only been on the force in Houston for a few months.

"Well, it seems the dog-eat-dog world of litigation isn't genetic after all. In fact, I stay far away from the Triple W."

"So you don't like law?" Jesse's fingers eased on the arms of the recliner.

"My dad doesn't like me," Bradley corrected. "I'm the black sheep, the crazy uncle my brothers tell their kids about."

"You don't seem crazy to me."

"I gave up a few hundred grand a year, Armani suits and a high-rise apartment in downtown for this life of domestic bliss. My father is a lawyer, and my mother, and my two brothers. And before them, it was both grandfathers, a few uncles."

"Your mother, too? Then how come it's only the triple W and not a quadruple?"

Bradley smiled. "My mother's a feminist from way back. Kaye Morgan-Winters."

"From the DA's office?" Jesse's heart picked up speed but he merely raised an eyebrow at Bradley.

"The one and only. She'd sell her BMW before she'd give up the hyphen in her last name and become a plain old Winters. You know her?"

"I've heard of her."

"She was the only member of my family who tried to understand my decision. But she was too addicted to Gucci shoes and Donna Karan suits to be all that supportive. I love her and she loves me, but we don't communicate very well. She likes to talk shop and I can't seem to get past what I'm making for dinner, or who has homework and who doesn't, to take much of an interest."

Relief eased through Jesse and his muscles relaxed. "So when did you stray from the path?"

"When I hit my senior year at Rice. I decided to substitute at a local high school to make some extra money. Subbing's easy once you let the kids know who's boss. They worked quietly while I used the time to study for this hellacious criminal justice class."

"And?"

"Well, my first subbing job was at this dirt-poor high school in the fifth ward. For the first time I got to see how the other half lived, and I didn't like it. It wasn't fair that some kids were born with a silver spoon, while others got a rusty one. I went home that first night and said that exact phrase to my dad."

Jesse grinned. "I bet he loved that."

"He nearly had a heart attack. Anyhow, there went my law career. I got my teaching degree, a master's in sociology, and now I'm a counselor. The pay isn't great, the hours suck, but the benefits can't be beat." He yawned. "I can actually sleep at night, guilt-free, which is more than I can say for half the lawyers I know."

Bradley's eyes drooped closed then. His head bobbed. Deep, even snores flared his nostrils in a matter of seconds.

Jesse headed outside and up the stairs to the garage apartment. It wasn't much, just a small room with a single twin bed, a bureau, and a connecting bathroom, with a small sink and stove in the far corner, but it was clean and well cared for and Jesse liked it. Plaid curtains covered the one window and a matching plaid bedspread sat folded at the end of the bed.

Exhaustion pulled at his body and he stretched out on the bed, too tired to undress or even slip beneath the covers.

He needed to sleep, to come up with a surefire

plan to lure Faith back to the kids. So far his urging and prodding weren't doing a bit of good, and time was running out. He had all of a week and a half left. Then he'd either be here for a lifetime more, or finding forgiveness and gaining peace. He had every intention of doing the latter. If only Faith wasn't so damned stubborn.

He closed his eyes and saw her sitting in the darkness, holding Jane, and his heart twisted in his chest. His hands trembled, the feel of smooth silk tickling his palms. He'd felt Jane's smooth hair, absorbed every shudder, as if he'd been Faith herself.

He had been. For those few moments, they'd been one. He'd been inside her, his arms tightening reflexively around the girl's small body, her tears splashing against his hand. Jane had fit against him so well, as if he'd held her before, her voice oddly familiar, tugging at feelings he'd always kept so deeply buried.

But of course the little girl was familiar—to Faith. Jesse had been inside Faith's head, feeling her feelings, hearing what she heard. It was all familiar because she'd held the girl night after night, soothed her, wiped away her tears.

Linked. Connected.

He shook away the thoughts, concentrating on the future. Tomorrow. Faith had to overcome her fears, and Jesse had to help her.

How?

The dilemma beat at his brain, making him toss and turn until he could no more sleep than he could force her image from his mind. He threw his legs over the side of the bed and strode to the window, staring out over the darkened front yard of Faith's House and beyond.

Faith. The word whispered through his head, and

116

Jesse closed his eyes, feeling the weight on his shoulders, the burden so heavy, driving him to his knees.

The grooves in the hardwood floor bit through his jeans, but he didn't feel the discomfort. He felt only urgency, desperation. He threw his head back and stared at the ceiling, but his gaze went beyond, to the black velvet sky overhead, and farther yet.

A pinpoint of light twinkled, expanded, growing in diameter like a door opening in the blackness. A bright white beam plunged through the velvety blackness, searching for him. The light appeared to him like the first ray of the sun breaking through a stormy sky. Heat sizzled over his skin, soothing and warm, chasing away his fears and insecurities, leaving nothing but serenity. Peace. A small taste of the peace to come.

Eternity waits for you, the voice whispered around him, inside him. *No more pain, no more guilt.*

The light swirled around him like the strong arms of a comforting embrace; then it narrowed, disappearing into a dot that soon vanished, leaving Jesse cold and alone.

And determined. He wanted more than a taste. He wanted freedom from his own pain, and he meant to have it.

Faith Jansen was coming back to the land of the living, whether she liked it or not. As much as Jesse sympathized with her, he wasn't about to let her screw up his chance at eternity.

For all Jesse's determination, sleep still didn't come. Wide eyed, he found himself staring at the ceiling. Oddly enough, it wasn't Faith's image that haunted the dark corners of his mind.

Instead, it was the vision of a young girl with dirt-smudged cheeks who strummed a battered guitar. Trudy's haunting melody filled his head, and a shiver rippled through him. He could see her as clearly as Faith's crystalline tears, her tiny form huddled in the corner of the abandoned apartment.

Goose bumps danced along his arms. The smell of rotten garbage and tepid water filled his nostrils, as if he were actually the one in the corner. Scared. Alone. Hungry.

No, he was none of the three, but he had been, once. Many times. In his childhood he'd been the poor neglected kid with two alcoholic parents; then as an adult he'd met other kids, seen their hard luck, cursed it, and tried to help.

But things were different now. He couldn't afford to go back there. The place stirred too many demons, too many distractions to keep him from his mission.

"No," he muttered, all the while swinging his legs over the side of the bed. He fought the guilt, the pull, but it was useless.

Finally he gathered up the blanket stretched across the mattress, rummaged around downstairs in the kitchen for the leftovers from that night's dinner, then headed out the door.

The walk took less than twenty minutes, but it seemed like forever. Like a convicted criminal walking the last few feet to the electric chair. Death waited at the end of the journey.

Or in Jesse's case, the memory of death.

He walked into the gaping hole that had been the building's front door. His boots thudded, wood creaked, rats scurried. A chill crept through Jesse as he reached the third-floor landing. This was a mistake. He shouldn't be here. He didn't want to be here—

The thought ground to a halt when he saw the young girl. Trudy lay nestled beneath his tattered letterman's jacket, her knees pulled up under her chin. She looked so small, so lonely, so lost.

Thanks, Jesse. You're the best big brother in the world.

The soft voice filtered through his head, and his chest tightened. He fought back the memories, but they came anyway, surrounding him, swamping him.

"Do you have to go to work tonight?" Rachel asked.

"There's a major stakeout tonight. They need every available man." He walked around the kitchen, gathering up his gun and badge, while his younger sister stood in the doorway, her nightgown trailing past her bare feet, a worried frown on her freshly scrubbed face. "I'll be back before you wake up in the morning."

"What about me and Jason?"

"You two will be fine. Jason's sound asleep, and you've got my beeper number if there's a problem, or you can call the station. You know the routine, honey."

"I know." She shook her head and cast troubled eyes on him. "I don't like it here. I wish we could go back home."

"This is home now, Rachel."

"Things are different here. People are different. Jason's new friends . . ." She gave him a pointed, wide-eyed stare. "I really think you should stay here tonight. It's just one night."

"One night I can't possibly miss." He paused in buckling on his holster. "What is it about Jason's new friends that's got you so wound up?"

She looked undecided for a long moment, then

119

shook her head. "Never mind. You go on. I'll see you in the morning."

The urge to go to her, pull her into his arms and reassure her nearly overwhelmed him. But a lifetime of hiding his emotions, holding himself in check, always being the silent pillar of strength—a position forced on him by circumstance and a mother who neither loved nor wanted him—won out over the softness his little sister stirred. "I'll be back soon. I know this graveyard shift is hard on everybody, but it's just for a little while, until I make detective. That's why we came here. So I could move up the ranks. A few more months walking the night beat and then we'll have enough money set aside to get a better place. A nicer neighborhood. It'll be better than Restoration. You'll see."

She gave him a smile, but the worry never left her eyes.

"Be careful."

"Sleep tight, sis. . . ."

Her troubled eyes had followed Jesse all the way to the station and on his shift that night. He'd been right in the middle of a raid on a crackhouse when he'd felt the twist in his gut, the dead certainty that something was wrong—

Paper rustled, breaking his train of thought, and his gaze shifted to Trudy. She sighed and snuggled deeper into his jacket.

He spread a blanket around her, tucking in the edges. Then he placed the bundle of food near her guitar and pulled a note from his pocket.

If you need help, he scrawled in big black letters, along with the address for Faith's House.

"Hey—" Trudy's startled voice came up short as she scrambled backward. "Oh, geez, you scared the crap out of me!" She clutched the blanket around her. Her eyes narrowed suspiciously. "What are you doing here?"

"I thought you might be hungry." He picked up the bundle of food and handed it to her.

She gave him a wary look that quickly disintegrated as she stared into his eyes. Then she peeled back the plastic wrap and sank her teeth into a cold piece of fried chicken.

"So what's the catch?" she said in between mouthfuls. "I mean . . ." She chewed some more and swallowed. "There's always a catch. You didn't just bring me this stuff free of charge." She waved the chicken leg at him. "So what do you want?"

"For you to consider leaving this place. I can hook you up with someone who could help you."

"Shit!" She threw the chicken bone at him and he ducked. "I knew it! I knew you were too nice to be real. You're a pimp. A damned, dirty pimp. Look here, I ain't into that, you hear?" She started to scramble free of the blanket. "You can take your stuff back and stick it where the sun don't shine—"

"I'm talking about a shelter." Her movements instantly stilled. "I'm not a pimp. I work at a place called Faith's House. It's a shelter for kids like you."

"You might as well be a pimp, 'cause I hold shelters in about the same regard, and I ain't going to one. I like it fine right here." At his pointed look, she added, "Okay, it's not all that great, but it's not bad either."

"It's a filthy hole in the wall. You said as much yourself the last time I saw you."

"Things have changed. This is my place now. I even cleaned up." She pointed to a broom leaning against the far wall. The bristles were grizzled, half of them missing, but he could see where she'd swept the floor.

"People were murdered up here," he reminded her. "One of them right there." He pointed to the familiar stain and then the spot just to the right where Jason had taken his last breath.

"Maybe . . . I mean, I know what went down, but it don't seem creepy to me." To emphasize her point, she pulled out a small switchblade. "I can take care of myself. I ain't afraid of nothing."

"I'm not talking about a physical threat. This place"—he looked around him—"it's a bad memory. It *feels* bad."

"Not to me." She grew quiet for a long moment. "I know it ought to scare me, but it don't. I feel sort of, I don't know, protected, I guess. I been alone most of my life, but here, it feels different. Like I got company." She stared at him. "You believe in ghosts, like friendly ones?"

"Like a guardian ghost?"

She nodded. "I never bought into any of that crap, but since I been staying up here . . . It's like I feel a presence, you know?" She pointed to the blood-stained floor, all that was left of Jesse's old life. "When I'm in that spot right there, it's like I can feel that guy. Like his ghost is here watching over me or something."

He laughed, a bitter sound that made him grimace. "There's no ghost up here. And if there were such a thing, the guy that died right there wouldn't be anybody's guardian; I can guarantee that."

She leaned forward. "Did you know him? Is that why you came here the other night?"

He stared into the darkness, his gaze fixed on the broken window, where cool air whistled in, flapping the plastic covering that someone had tried to tape in place.

"Yeah," he said after a long moment. "I knew him, and trust me, he wouldn't be anybody's guardian."

She settled into her corner, tucked the knife against her chest, and pulled the blanket up around her. "Tell me about him."

"Why?"

" 'Cause I want to know. I feel like I already know him in a way. Sometimes when I'm sitting here, I look across the room and I swear I can see someone. Just the faint outline, but it's there. Like somebody's watching me."

"Nobody's watching you, honey. But they should be. You're too young to be out on your own." He settled down on the floor, his back against the wall, his legs stretched out in front of him. He sat there for several minutes before he finally found his voice, and his courage.

"He was a cop from a little town called Restoration, no more than a couple of thousand people—just on the other side of Fort Worth. The town was small, all of two cops on the entire force, with very little room for advancement, so the guy packed up his brother and sister and moved them here. More money, better opportunities. They'd moved into this neighborhood temporarily until the cop could save up enough money for something better. He was this close to making detective." He leaned his head back and closed his eyes. "He really wanted that promotion. He'd been looking to buy a little house on the south side, near Channelview. A little place, three bedrooms, a yard." He stared at her then, their gazes colliding. "Really clean, you know?"

She nodded, as if she could see his dream, or rather, her own. "Yeah. Clean."

"He was so busy hustling after this promotion, he didn't spend too much time at home. He never had to worry about his kid sister; she was really smart, an A student, always followed the rules, an all-around good kid. His brother was another story. He was smart, but impulsive, and if there was trouble nearby, he was always neck-deep in it. That's what happened that night."

"The night of the murder?"

He nodded. "Restoration was a small, hole-in-the-wall town. No drugs. Very little crime. They moved here, and all of a sudden they were surrounded by scum. The kid brother fell into a bad group of kids who ran drugs for a local dealer. He wanted to fit in, to be liked, to make some of the money he saw his friends flashing around. Anyhow, he started running small amounts of crack for this dealer, and skimming off some of the cash on the side. The dealer came after him. Here." He glanced around the room, his gaze cutting through the darkness. "The sister was asleep in the other room. The kid brother was right here, having a showdown with the dealer. The cop came home in the middle of the meeting and all hell broke loose."

This ain't none of your business, Savage. It's your brother we want. We got a little lesson to teach him—

"Holy crap." Trudy's words shattered the voice that haunted Jesse's thoughts.

He closed his eyes. "It was all over so fast. The dealer pulled a knife. The cop drew his gun, but he didn't have a chance to use it. He went down with the first plunge of the blade."

Jesse winced. His hands started to tremble and a wave of pain washed across him. The voice blared in his head with renewed determination.

You're home early, cop. Way too early . . .

". . . know so much?"

Jesse shook away the past. "What?"

"How do you know so much?"

"The cop was . . . my friend." He ran tense hands through his hair. "We were tight."

"Hey, that's tough, man."

"Yeah." He climbed to his feet. "There's the address for the shelter. Think about leaving this place."

"I ain't going to no shelter."

"Think about it."

"Mind your own business."

He was halfway to the door when he heard her voice.

"You ain't gonna call CPS on me, are you? I'll just take off. I been that route before."

He shook his head. "I told you before that I wouldn't."

"Thanks for the food and the blanket." Her words followed him out the door.

His legs made quick work of the hallway, then the stairs. With each step, the walls seemed closer, caging him, strangling him, and he struggled for each breath.

You're home early, cop.

It's your brother we want.

Your brother . . .

The words pounded through his head, making him sorry he'd come back here. He didn't want to remember. To feel the pain again, to hear that damned voice.

To feel the hatred stir to life.

Peace, his soul cried. *Peace and forgiveness and Faith.*

He didn't bother walking to the front of the building. Instead he headed for the nearest exit once he reached the ground floor. Wood groaned and cracked as he thrust his weight at the back door. He burst out into the night and leaned over, gasping for air.

Calm, he told himself, but his heart pounded furiously. It was so damned loud. Why hadn't he listened to Rachel? Why hadn't he stayed home that night? Why had he moved them from peaceful, crime-free Restoration to this drug-infested city? Why, why, *why*?

Breathe, he told himself, and he did. Over and over until his lungs relaxed and he managed to straighten up.

His gaze went to the small row of sheds out behind the apartment building. One had a door hanging half-off its hinges; the other had a broken window. The paint was peeling, the wood rotting in most places. His gaze went to the third one. It was shabby like all the rest, but the door was still in place. The windows had been broken out, but they were too high and small to attract vandals, the shed in much too sorry shape to entice anyone.

Walking over, Jesse fingered the padlock on the door. It didn't budge. Still as sturdy as the day he'd snapped it on. He hunkered down and moved a small rock near the corner of the shed. A hole about two inches wide sat beneath the rock. Jesse shoved his hand just inside the hole. Metal brushed his skin. Bingo.

He slid the key into the padlock. The shed door creaked open. Silence yawned at him and he walked inside.

The motorcycle was still there underneath the tarp, and Jesse couldn't help but smile. No one in this broken-down neighborhood had ever fathomed what lay hidden inside the rotting shed. Then again, it had been just under a year. Sooner or later someone would have broken in and taken the bike.

He didn't worry over sooner or laters. He concentrated on the now and his incredible good fortune. His hands trailed over the frame, pushing away the layer of dust that coated the shiny chrome and paint.

"I don't know anything about motorcycles." With a critical eye, Jason surveyed the piece of junk Jesse had found at a local salvage yard.

"That's the point. We're going to learn. We'll put it back together ourselves."

He and Jason had managed to get the entire thing rebuilt, complete with a new motor, tires, and a paint job, in the first two months they'd been here. Jesse had thought to keep his brother occupied, take up his time so he didn't miss Restoration all that much.

Bitterness caught in his throat. Apparently restoring the machine hadn't taken nearly as much time as it should have. Jason had still had the chance to fall in with the wrong crowd and find himself a mess of trouble.

Jesse tamped down the regret and concentrated on the motorcycle. Wheeling it out into the lot, he did a quick check of the motor. Other than a thick layer of dust, everything seemed intact. He straddled the seat, flipped the key, and kicked the starter. The motorcycle coughed, sputtered, then died. He tried again, and again. Finally it caught.

Jesse gunned the engine with one hand and trailed his hands over the initials carved into the handlebars. He and Jason had done that first thing before they'd ever started to piece the '79 Harley back together. They'd marked the bike as theirs, without any words having been spoken between them.

That was the problem. Jesse had always held his feelings in, never one to open himself up to heartache twice. He'd gone that route before, poured out his love to a mother who'd never loved him back. A woman who'd treasured a bottle of cheap bourbon more than her own son. And so he'd held back from his siblings.

But he had loved them. That was why he'd headed to work every day, pulled double shifts, provided for them as best he could. Why he'd uprooted them and brought them to Houston. For a better life.

And the entire time—ten years of being their provider, their protector, their mother and father—he'd never once said the words. He'd done to them what his mother had done to him. And though he knew instinctively that Martha Savage had loved him in her own way, he'd always wanted to hear her say it.

The boy he'd been had needed it so desperately. She should have told him, and because she hadn't, he'd never completely forgiven her.

He should have told Rachel and Jason.

A knifing pain stabbed at his chest, and he took a deep breath. It wasn't too late. Fulfilling his mission with Faith would give him another chance.

To speak the words.

To ask their forgiveness, tell them he loved them, and rid himself of the guilt eating at his soul.

His fingers traced the carved initials again. He hadn't even had the chance to teach Jason to ride.

With a kick of the clutch, he sent the bike flying out of the lot. He hit the street and roared into the night, as if he could outrun the memories that lived and breathed in the old apartment building.

But Jesse couldn't outrun his past, any more than he could break the invisible ties that connected him to Faith Jansen.

Chapter Seven

True to his word, Jesse returned the next day to fix Faith's rain gutter.

"You don't have to do that," she told him as she stood outside on her back porch and shielded her eyes against the midmorning sun.

He was little more than a silhouette standing in the mouth of her garage. His toolbox lay open on a small workbench. Metal chinked, tools clanged as he retrieved the needed equipment to repair her failing rain gutter.

"You'll be singing a different tune when the next storm hits and that gutter comes crashing into your roses."

Her gaze went to the neglected bushes lining her porch. A few pink buds pushed past the overgrowth of thorns and weeds. She swallowed against the sudden tightness in her throat.

"I would still feel better if you let me compensate you."

He filled up the opening, a darker shadow against softer gray ones. She couldn't make out his features, just the bright glitter of his eyes. His gaze crossed the several feet of overgrown grass to rake over her, and she suddenly wished she'd thought to put on something more than a tank top and shorts. "I mean, it's an awful lot of work. I'd really be happy to pay you."

"All right." Another sweep of those twinkling eyes and her skin tingled.

"Why is it I get the feeling that you're not interested in money?"

He gave no answer other than a smile, a devilish flash of white that sliced through the shadows and pebbled her nipples.

She took a deep breath, the effort pushing her breasts against the soft cotton of her tank top.

He stepped from the shadows. The smile vanished as his strong legs ate up the distance to her. He stopped just shy, dropped a few tools on the grass, and wiped at a thin trickle of moisture winding a path from his temple to his stubbled jaw. "Actually, I did have something different in mind."

"And"— she cleared her throat—"um, what might that be?" As if she had to ask. She could see his answer plain as day in his eyes. Those beautiful, mysterious brown eyes that held just a hint of gold around the iris.

Dark and haunting, he stood on the ground two steps below her, their eyes level, gazes holding. It was as if a brilliant heat burned inside him, and when he looked at her, really looked at her, she glimpsed the fire within. The light. The desire—

"Iced tea," he said, his gaze shuttering, as if he'd

just remembered something important. "A glass of iced tea," he repeated. "For the repairs." He turned away from her then. Strong arms reached for the half-hanging piece of gutter, and it was as if she didn't exist. He went about his work, his attention fixed on his task. Muscles rippled beneath the damp cotton of his T-shirt. Sweat beaded on his face, dripped down his corded neck. She had the incredible urge to reach out, catch a drop of perspiration, and taste the saltiness of moisture and skin against her tongue. . . .

He shot her a sideways glance, his gaze colliding with hers for a heart-stopping moment. His eyes glittered hotly, the look having nothing to do with the sun and everything to do with the lustful thoughts racing through her mind. He knew. *He knew.*

Impossible.

She forced herself back into the kitchen, her heart hammering, her nipples still erect and throbbing. What was the matter with her? She was acting like she'd never been looked at by a man before.

Not this man.

So what?

She didn't want his looks, his hungry gazes. She didn't want to see the gold shimmering in his eyes, and she didn't want to be having such erotic thoughts about him.

She wanted solitude. Time to herself. Time to heal.

She put the tea on to brew and busied herself feeding Grubby his breakfast, determined to ignore the hot and sweaty man moving around so close to her back door. But how could she when she heard every chink, every clang, every deep, even breath that he drew . . . ? Impossible.

Still, the sound filled her head, and she couldn't help but wonder if she was really hearing him, or her imagination. There was a quick way to find out. She could take a little peek, test the rise and fall of his chest, and assure herself she was crazy.

Faith peered past the kitchen curtains and found herself staring into those disconcerting eyes. She jerked back and heard his deep rumble of laughter.

Stiffening, she swept aside the curtains again and glared at him.

"You scared me."

"You shouldn't be spying on me."

"I wasn't spying. I was seeing if you were finished."

"You shouldn't be lying either, but I'm willing to forgive you if you get me something to drink." He wiped his sweaty brow. "This sun is killing me."

"The tea's almost ready," she promised and as if on cue, the kettle whistled. A few glasses, a lot of ice cubes, and a cup of sugar later, she walked out onto the back porch and handed him a cold glass dripping with condensation.

He drank the contents in one long swallow, his Adam's apple bobbing, streams of ice-cold tea chasing down his chin.

Faith swallowed.

"Another?" he finally asked, holding his glass out.

When she returned a few minutes later, she had a glass for him and one for herself. He settled down on the steps and patted the seat next to him.

"I won't bite," he promised.

That's too bad, she thought to herself, the sight of him voraciously downing the glass of tea still vivid in her mind.

He grinned and her heart skipped a beat. "Unless you're real nice to me," he added, and a wave of heat swept up from her toes, clear to the roots of each hair on her head, pausing in between to concentrate on a few strategic spots that made her shift uncomfortably and gulp at her own iced tea.

Geez, it was hot. Even for Texas.

They spent the next hour drinking iced tea, the lush scent of roses surrounding them.

"So, you like to garden?" His gaze went to the weed-infested rosebushes.

"I dabble when I'm in the mood. Every Saturday afternoon I used to come out here with—" The name stuck in her throat and she took a sip of tea. "Saturday was my trimming and weeding day," she finished.

"I don't know much about gardening, but if you show me what to do, I could help you whip these babies back into shape. From the looks of things, you could use an extra pair of hands."

She'd once had an extra pair. Jane had been so eager, so careful with the trimming shears.

Faith's gaze dropped to his large, tanned hands, the nails short, fingers long and tapered, but not elegant. Nothing about Jesse Savage was elegant. His hands were powerful, strong, confident, comforting . . . as if they could hold the weight of the world one minute, and cradle the fragile body of a helpless, spoiled puppy the next.

"So, what do you say?" He took a swallow of tea. "You want some help clipping these bushes back into shape?"

"If I say no?"

He grinned. "Your lips might say no but your eyes say yes, honey."

The cheesy line made her smile. "Which means you won't take no for an answer?"

He shrugged again. "I've never been really good with rejection."

Her gaze went back to his hands, to the puckered ridge of flesh that ran across the back of one. Again, she felt the urge to reach out, to comfort. "If I say no, you'll show up anyway, won't you?"

"Probably." He clasped his hands, rubbing them together.

"Then be here tomorrow morning after the kids leave for school." She stood and dusted off the back of her shorts. "We'll get started then. And when we're finished," she added before going back into the house, "the hose on my clothes dryer is loose, there's a stubborn ceiling fan that won't turn in my kitchen, and I've got fire ants near the back fence. If I can't get rid of you, I might as well keep you busy."

"I've created a monster," she heard him murmur as she closed the door.

His deep rumble of laughter followed her, sending tickling fingers of warmth dancing up and down her spine. And when Faith placed the empty tea glasses in the sink and spotted the Houston Rockets mug sitting on the drainboard, she didn't feel the cold bite of regret.

A smile crooked her lips, and Jesse's voice echoed in her head, ringing with an undeniable, comforting truth.

She lives on inside you. Inside . . .

The next morning, Faith met him on the back porch with her gardening tools. They worked through the morning until every weed had been pulled, the bushes had been neatly trimmed, and the frail buds tended. They drank iced tea and talked about Bradley and the kids, and afterward, Jesse headed back to Faith's House.

They repeated the same routine the next day, only Faith tended the rosebushes alone while Jesse worked on the dryer; then she fed him lunch. Food in exchange for work. That way she didn't feel quite so indebted to him.

That was the only reason, she told herself. It certainly wasn't that she liked his company or wanted to keep him around a few extra minutes each day. The last thing she wanted was company. Anyone's company. She was an island unto herself. If only Jesse Savage didn't seem so intent on an invasion.

Not that an invasion would be bad, she amended. A physical one, at least. It had been so long, and she was so lonely. She didn't realize just how much until Jesse climbed onto his motorcycle every day and roared away.

Hormones, she told herself. She was a young, healthy woman who'd been without a man for a long time. And though she'd never been promiscuous, maybe the three times she'd actually had sex had awakened her physically, though they'd done little emotionally. She knew what it felt like to be touched by a man, and her body was craving it. Craving *him*.

She ached for his voice rumbling in her ear. His smile warming her insides. The brush of his skin against hers whenever he happened to move past her. The sparkle in his dark eyes when he laughed.

Just biology, she assured herself. Because she couldn't, *wouldn't* feel anything more for Jesse Savage.

Or anyone else, even though he tried to persuade her otherwise. He was subtle, but no matter what they talked about, he always brought the conversation back to Faith's House. To the kids.

She heard all about Ricky and Emily, and the nine others. And she received a daily report on Daniel's progress, or lack of, at the hospital.

"Maybe you could talk to him," he told her a few days later after he'd finished annihilating the ant beds in the backyard. They sat on the porch steps, side by side, drinking iced tea as the sunny sky grumbled above them.

She shook her head. "I'm no psychiatrist." She shielded her eyes and stared up at the sun. No clouds, yet the unmistakable growl of thunder gave the sweet promise of rain.

"You probably know a hell of a lot more than most psychiatrists. And you're his foster mother," Jesse pointed out.

He was right on both counts. She wasn't a doctor, but she was a trained counselor with a degree in sociology, not to mention she'd been working with kids for years. She knew how they reasoned, reacted—what made them tick. And she'd yet to sign over Faith's House to Bradley. She'd been too busy tending her rosebushes and making tea. But she would find the time, she promised herself.

Soon.

Eventually.

"Technically I'm Daniel's foster parent, but Bradley is acting in my absence, with CPS approval, and he's just as good as I ever was. Daniel's his job." The sky grumbled again and Faith added, "I hope it rains soon. I'm watering the rosebushes, but they need a good shower to really bloom."

"But Brad isn't getting anywhere," he added, ignoring her attempt to change the subject. "Daniel won't even talk to him."

"Then he certainly won't talk to me. He hates me."

Faith could still remember the coldness in the boy's blue eyes, his hatred stirring her own feelings until they'd boiled over and she'd run out of the hospital.

"He senses something inside you and it makes him uncomfortable. Probably because he knows you care. Boys like Daniel don't want anyone to care about them."

"Why is that, Dr. Spock?" She turned her attention from the sunny sky to the shadowy man sitting next to her.

"Because then he'd have to care in return."

"He has the right idea." She took a long sip of tea. "No caring, no hurt."

"Amen," Jesse murmured, or at least she thought he did, but when she asked him, he just shook his head and muttered, "I said he's almost a man. A few more years and it'll be too late for him."

"It's never too late." She said the words before she could stop them. "Can we please stop talking about this?"

"You know I'm right."

"I know if you don't stop needling me about all this—" Her words stalled as a fat raindrop splashed onto her bare leg. "It's raining," she said, turning a smile on Jesse.

As if her words had opened up the heavens, a steady sprinkle began to fall, cool specks of relief against the onslaught of the sun's bright rays. "Thank God," she murmured, jumping to her feet to inspect her roses. Rain beaded on the velvety smooth petals, and Faith breathed a sigh of relief. "There you go, babies," she crooned. "Drink up."

"Look at them," she said with all the pride of a new mother. "They look healthier already."

"Very healthy," he agreed. Something about the husky tone of his voice drew her gaze, and she found

137

him staring at her. Her tank top was already soaked, molding to her breasts to leave little to the imagination. Her nipples hardened at the realization, making distinct impressions. Jesse swallowed. Hard.

"I—I was talking about the roses."

"So was I," he said, but his gaze didn't move.

Faith drew a much-needed breath, the action making her breasts heave, swell.

He swallowed again, his gaze fixed, his body as still as a statue.

They simply stood there like that for endless moments, him staring, her breathing, the rain falling softly around them.

Water drip-dropped down Jesse's dark skin, soaking his own T-shirt until she saw every ripple of muscle, every ragged breath he took. And suddenly the urge to touch him superseded the urge to draw breath.

She reached out, her fingertip circling one dark male nipple outlined beneath the wet fabric of his white T-shirt. He sucked in a breath, not moving for the space of a heartbeat as she touched and stroked.

"They were thirsty," she said, her mind on the roses, yet her body completely tuned to his.

"I know the feeling." His words were hoarse as her fingertip trailed down over the cotton-covered ribs of his abdomen. "I'm hungry myself."

"You mean thirsty."

"No," he said, catching her wrist to halt her exploration. "I mean hungry. Starving." Then he pulled her up against him.

The motion was desperate, like a man gone too long without sustenance. His arms encircled her. His hands spanned her waist, then cupped her buttocks to pull her flush against him. He lifted her, urging her legs up on either side of him.

He slid her up the hard ridge of his groin until he was eye-level with her chest. Hot breath puffed against one throbbing nipple; then his tongue flicked out. Heat licked the tip of the sensitive peak and a burst of electricity sizzled to her brain. She moaned, bowing into him, needing his mouth on her.

As hungry as he was, he seemed to delight in watching her. He touched her with his tongue again and licked her longer, more leisurely, savoring the ripeness of her. She gasped and clung and quivered.

"Please," she said, arching her back. "I need—"

Before she could finish the desperate plea, his lips closed over her nipple and he sucked long and hard on the throbbing tip, the wet material of her shirt little protection against the searing heat of his mouth.

She threaded her fingers through his hair, tilted her head back, and gave herself up to sensation. Cool rain sprinkled her face, but it wasn't enough to quench the fire at her breast. The flames spread, burning over her skin until she felt ready to disintegrate.

The pressure of his mouth increased, his tongue stroking her, his lips suckling. Each pull on her nipple sent an echoing thrum between her legs. She clutched at his shoulders, desperate for . . . more, less, *anything* to relieve the pressure building inside her.

His hands held her steady, scorching her through the denim of her shorts, nestling her crotch against his belly.

Then he moved her, a lazy brush of her sex up and down the muscled ridges of his abdomen, and the pressure reached maximum intensity. A gasp tumbled from her lips and she came apart in his arms, reeling with the force of her climax. She collapsed against him, her arms wrapped around his shoulders. He was so warm, so strong, so . . .

The realization of what had just happened hit her like a two-by-four. She blinked. Had she really . . . ? And they hadn't even . . . Yet she'd . . . And he hadn't even touched her *there*. . . . Not directly, anyway, and . . .

She closed her eyes, buried her face in his neck, and then she started to cry.

"Shhh," he said, stroking her rain-slick skin, his palm warm and comforting. "Don't be embarrassed, sweetheart. Not with me. Not ever."

"But you didn't," she mumbled into his neck. "And I shouldn't have."

"It's all right," he murmured.

"I—I'm sorry," she went on. "It's just been a long time since anyone has"—she swallowed—"touched me like that." *Try never*, she added silently.

I'm glad. . . . His deep voice rumbled through her mind, which was odd considering his mouth was pressed to her hair, his lips unmoving.

Obviously not. She'd heard the words. Clear, distinct, unmistakable—

"The rain's stopped," he said, killing her thoughts. He eased her down his body and they stared up into the still-sunny sky.

"You're all wet." She pushed a strand of hair back from his jaw. Despite their moment of shared intimacy, she felt awkward. Unsure. If only he would say something.

"I really should get back." His words were short, clipped, a direct contrast to the raw need making his dark eyes shimmer like liquid onyx, and the bulge straining beneath the front of his jeans.

Guilt ebbed through her. He'd given her so much and she'd left him huge and hurting.

"Why don't you come inside for a little while? I could toss your shirt into the dryer."

He was silent for a long moment and she saw the inner battle in his eyes. For some reason, he fought the need bunching his muscles tight, raged against the idea of going inside with her, *inside* her.

"I have to go." His gaze shuttered and there was no more conflict in him. Just steely resolve. "Bradley's probably waiting for me."

"I'll see you tomorrow then." *Please,* she added silently. Her cheeks burned. The sun, she tried to tell herself, but she knew better.

"Tomorrow," he promised, his eyes softening just a hint, and an odd sense of relief swept through her.

Then he turned and walked away, and the relief gave way to the hard press of loneliness that had become her permanent companion the past week, since Jesse Savage had walked into her life, and out. Day after day.

Only today was worse.

At least she'd had the rain, she told herself. The roar of his motorcycle faded into a distant drone until she heard nothing except the buzz of insects and the whispering quiet of freshly watered grass baking in the sun.

And so she didn't have to worry over the cause for all the wetness on her cheeks. It was rainwater, because Faith Jansen wouldn't cry over anyone. She wouldn't let herself care that much.

Never again.

It was happening Jesse thought.

His lust was overriding his common sense. But hell, she'd climaxed right there in his arms, with no

141

more than the touch of him. And she'd been fully clothed.

He tightened his grip on the motorcycle and took a sharp right at the next intersection. The bike rumbled beneath him, vibrating the muscles of his thighs as he sped forward.

The air lashed at him, but the smell of roses and rainwater and hungry female—*her*—stayed with him, filling his senses. Just as the sound of her—soft pants and delicious moans—haunted him, drowning out everything, the honk of a car horn, the whir of traffic, the skid of brakes as he roared through the city, desperate for some air. Some distance.

He had a mission to fulfill, and sliding fast and deep between Faith's thighs wasn't part of the deal. If only he could remember that whenever he was near her. He tried. Heaven knew, he tried. But in the face of her desire, he seemed powerless to resist. She wanted him. Badly. That fact coupled with the bald truth that Jesse—the flesh-and-blood man— needed a woman. He was, after all, only human right now, with weaknesses. Needs.

Human, he reminded himself.

But while he might be flesh and blood, there was a spirit inside the man. A light. A miracle waiting to happen.

The trouble was, whenever he was with Faith, he forgot his situation. She made him think like a man. Want like a man. Feel like a man.

Dammit!

He rode long and hard, until he wound up outside the city limits, on a nearly deserted highway surrounded by rolling fields. Only the occasional passing of a car penetrated the serenity of the place. It was nature at its simplest. A place where nothing grew but wildflowers and silence.

Jesse turned off onto a dirt road and followed a winding path farther away from the road and civilization, until flat, motionless fields surrounded him in every direction. Then he parked his motorcycle and started walking.

He walked until the high afternoon sun beat down on him and the humid air robbed the breath from his lungs. He finally sank to his knees and bowed his head. He was hot. Tired. Desperate.

If only he didn't want her so badly.

"I can't do this. I—we're too closely linked. It's killing me," he cried, staring up at the sky, into the blinding sun and beyond. Into a more brilliant, soothing light.

Focus, Jesse, came the clear voice. Not a single voice really, but a symphony of melodic sounds joined together as one. The light. *Keep your mind on the future*.

But even as the reassuring words rang in his head, he felt little comfort. Only an angry tightening inside him, pushing and pulling at his control.

Think about the mission. About eternity.

Easier said than done, he thought as he walked to his motorcycle and headed back to Houston. He was already hours late for his afternoon shift at Faith's House. He needed to think about the kids, about what excuse he was going to give Bradley for being late.

The trouble was, he couldn't think right now. He just felt the excruciating heat in his groin, the rush of blood through his veins, the rapid beating of his heart, and the overwhelming need to be inside her.

He entered the city limits just as the sun dipped below the horizon. Exhaust fumes burned his nostrils, and the chaos of the city beat at his ears, yet Jesse wasn't aware of any of it.

He knew only the fresh smell of roses and rainwater teasing his nostrils, the soft sigh of a woman whispering through his senses, testing his determination and worrying his resolve.

Bedding her could only end in disaster. He was leaving when everything was said and done. He had an eternity waiting for him, and Faith didn't figure in.

His head knew that. Now if he could only get the message through to his body, and his heart.

True to his word, Jesse returned the next day, but things were different. Gone was the easy rapport they'd shared for the past few days. When she handed him a glass of iced tea, he didn't motion her down beside him on the porch steps. Instead he gulped the drink and returned to trimming her overgrown hedges near the back fence, while Faith once again tended her rosebushes.

She threw herself into her work, yet she was always acutely aware of his presence. Her nerves were on edge, her mind regretting those few shared moments in the rain, while her body longed for a deeper contact.

She was crazy to want a man who obviously didn't want her.

Then again, she didn't really believe his indifference. Maybe if she did, it would be much easier to ignore him and dismiss her own feelings. But while he worked savagely at the bushes, he was as aware of her as she was of him. She'd glimpsed his gaze a time or two, the heat sparking his dark eyes before he turned away.

The silent treatment lasted for several hours, until he'd finished trimming and was about to leave.

"Ricky asked Emily to the community dance day after tomorrow."

"You're kidding." She smiled, feeling her tension ease for the first time that afternoon. "When did he do it? How did he do it? What did she say?"

He grinned. "He did it last night while she was tutoring him in math, and he just came out and asked her, very polite and direct. He complimented her shirt and her hair, then popped the question."

"Ricky? My Ricky?" She shook her head. "The last nice thing he said to her was that she had a big brain, and she didn't consider that quite the compliment he'd intended."

"He's been practicing."

"And I bet I know who's been teaching him." She eyed Jesse for a long moment. "He's really taken to you, hasn't he?"

Jesse shrugged. "He's a good kid. They all are."

"Yes." She sighed, staring down at the tips of her worn tennis shoes.

"You should have seen him. He was so nervous, he actually put his shirt on inside out before he came downstairs."

"I wish I'd been there."

"Do you?" With a tender hand beneath her chin, he drew her gaze up to meet his. "It's not too late. You told me so yourself. The kids miss you, Faith. They ask about you every day."

"I . . ." She pulled free and looked away. "I'm really glad for Em." A moment of silence passed before she met his eyes again. "Tell her that for me, okay?"

"Wouldn't you rather tell her yourself?"

She shook her head, a smile playing at her lips. "You don't give up, do you?"

"A guy has to try." Then he walked away from her.

Faith stifled the familiar ache that shot through her and picked up her gardening tools. It was going to be another long night, especially since Faith had more than just Jesse to think about.

Ricky and Emily going on an official date . . .

And she was going to miss it.

By choice, she reminded herself.

But at that moment, missing the shine in Emily's eyes as she put on her best outfit, and the way Ricky puffed out his chest to make himself stand taller, made her regret her decision.

Maybe she could just drop by the house tomorrow night, just to say hello and catch a quick peek at the kids—

No. That would only make walking away harder, on herself and the kids. It was better for everyone if she just stayed away. No risk. No attachment. Distance was easier.

If only it weren't so lonely.

Chapter Eight

That evening, Faith sat outside on the back porch and watched the sun fade over the top of the garage. Laughter floated on the wind, along with the excited sounds of kids playing. The voices made her feel a little less lonely, and so she sat there until all light faded and darkness forced her to go inside.

Otherwise, her nightly ritual was the same. She ate dinner with the TV blaring, then busied herself doing some chore or another until she collapsed from exhaustion. Nearly a week had passed since she'd started to come back to the land of the living, and she'd scrubbed every room in the house.

All except for one.

Each day she went a little closer to Jane's room. The girl hadn't actually lived with Faith, but her things had been transferred to Faith's spare bedroom to make room for another child at the foster home. The door had been closed for the past three weeks since the funeral, until last night.

A handspan of space filled her peripheral vision as she sat cross-legged on the living room floor and alphabetized what was left of her CD collection. When that was done, she played ball with Grubby, tossing the red nylon ball toward the hallway, toward the door.

The little dog wagged his tail and wiggled after the ball. His excited body thumped against the wood, and the door creaked open an inch more.

Not yet, she told herself, forcing her attention elsewhere. She retrieved a can of disinfectant and attacked the baseboards in her living room, a time-consuming chore that taxed her muscles and drained her mind.

Three hours later, well past midnight, she crawled into bed, too tired to think or dream, or so she thought.

Faith . . . The voice called to her from somewhere deep inside herself. But it wasn't her own voice. It was Jesse's. The deep timbre rumbled through her body, sending a wave of tremors washing over her senses.

I need you, Faith. You're my only way out. You have to help me. You have to believe again.

She railed against the thought even through the haziness of sleep. She couldn't. She wouldn't. . . .

I know you're afraid, but you don't have to be. Not anymore. You're not alone. You'll never be alone. I'm here, Faith. I'm here—

Her eyes snapped open to the darkness of the bedroom. She jerked upright, her heart pounding furiously, tears streaming down her cheeks.

Tears, when she'd been certain they'd all dried up by now.

The wetness trickled down her face, her neck, and Jesse's voice echoed in her head.

You're not alone. I'm here. I'm here. . . .

She threw back the covers and padded down the hallway to Jane's room. The door creaked open and she flipped on the light. Stacks of boxes filled the corners. Stuffed animals littered the bed, along with piles of clothes still on the hangers. So much stuff, even though the girl had only been at Faith's House a little under a year.

Faith scooted some of the things aside and settled herself on the mattress. She touched the soft fur of a hot pink teddy bear—a Valentine's present to Jane from Ricky—and a smile pulled at her lips. She stroked the furry head for a few seconds before reaching for the nearest box. Her fingers trembled and paused. Maybe this wasn't such a good idea. Maybe—

I'm here, came the deep, soothing voice. *I'm here.*

She pulled back the cardboard flaps. With a rush of tears and a silent prayer for strength, she went to work.

Bam, bam, bam. The pounding on the front door drew Faith's attention. She glanced up from the last box she'd been sifting through and stared past the bedroom doorway into the living room. She blinked.

Morning sunlight pushed through the slats in the blinds, showering the living room with brilliant white bars of light. Geez, she'd been at it for hours, she realized with a quick look at the nightstand clock.

"What's wrong?" Jesse's all-seeing eyes swept her from head to toe the moment she hauled open the front door.

"Nothing," she murmured, and realized the statement rang true. There was nothing wrong. She'd made it through each box, faced the contents and the memories, and here she was, alive and breathing. She smiled. "Absolutely nothing."

His gaze swept her again, lingering on her face. Finally he grinned. "You look awfully pleased with yourself. What have you been up to?"

"My ears in boxes." She motioned behind her to the stack of cardboard spilling out of the bedroom into the hallway. "A few are filled with clothes. I thought I'd send those to the girls at Faith's House. The rest are going to Mrs. Moses at the mission. She's sending somebody to pick them up."

"If it's only a box or two, I can take the stuff for Faith's House after I finish with that ceiling fan you mentioned. The kitchen, you said?"

She nodded. "Thanks, Jesse."

"Thanks for fixing the fan, or taking the boxes?"

"Both." *And last night,* she added silently.

He smiled then, a slow sweep of his sensuous lips that lit up the room brighter than the sunlight. "My pleasure," he said as he followed her into the kitchen.

Jesse tested the ceiling fan switch while Faith put a pot of coffee on to brew. Then she sank down into a kitchen chair, heedless that she was wearing nothing but an oversize T-shirt and white socks, and rested her head on her arms. Tired. Relieved.

"Did you sleep at all last night?"

"Not much," she murmured. Her eyes drifted shut, her ears tuned to the steady sound of Jesse's breathing, the *thump-thump* of his heart. No, that had to be her own heart, because he was standing clear across the room.

"Try not at all," he said somewhere in the vicinity of her left ear, and she realized he was very close.

Strong arms closed around her and she felt herself being lifted, carried. She wanted to snake her arms around his neck, pull him closer, lose herself in the heat of his eyes, his mouth. But she was too tired; the security was too lulling. She did little more than sigh as he tucked her into bed. The blankets closed around her and sleep claimed her completely.

Faith had never slept better in her entire life.

She opened her eyes just as afternoon shadows started to creep across the bedroom. Her gaze lingered on the jewelry box sitting in the middle of her dresser. One down, one to go, she thought. But not now. She felt too good, too purged.

She yawned, stretched, and padded to Jane's room. The boxes were gone, the room clean. Obviously Jesse had seen to everything while she'd been asleep.

She flipped off the light and left the door wide open. There were no memories lurking inside anymore, no monsters. Her stomach gave a traitorous grumble and she smiled. Minutes later, she was digging in the pantry for something to eat. Not just anything. She had a craving tonight that only one thing could satisfy. . . .

"There," she said, pulling the box off the back shelf of her kitchen pantry. She reached for a bowl, eggs, and a spatula and went to work. A half hour later the delicious aroma of chocolate filled the house as Faith gathered up trash and yanked open the back door.

"Yikes!" She came up short as a solid mass of man blocked her path and she realized that she'd forgotten to lock the burglar bars. A mistake she'd made numerous times in the past, before Jane's death.

Fear bolted through her until her gaze jerked up and she found herself staring into Jesse's dark brown eyes. Gold flecks twinkled with amusement.

Faith held a hand to her rapidly beating heart. "Thanks a lot. You scared the pants off me."

His gaze swept down and she saw a flicker of disappointment.

"I meant that figuratively."

"A shame."

"What are you doing here?"

He sniffed, a smile creasing his face as he stared past her into the kitchen. "Is that what I think it is?"

She frowned. "Yes, and you're not getting any after scaring me like that."

He gave her a wicked smile. "Have a heart, Faith. You're dealing with a desperate man. I haven't had any for months."

She was sure his *any* referred to something entirely different than a plate of brownies, especially when he passed so close to her. He was so warm, scorching, and she barely resisted the urge to lean forward and touch her lips to his shoulder.

Distance quickly yawned between them as he left her to pounce on the platter sitting near the stove.

"A beautiful woman who can cook," he said after biting into a warm brownie. "I'm impressed."

"Don't be. I used a mix. You can thank Betty Crocker."

He looked so at home standing there, filling up her kitchen. It was as if it were the most normal thing in the world for him to be leaning against her counter, scarfing down brownies and making her feel warm in all the wrong places. Or the right places, depending on which way she looked at it.

Considering he hadn't so much as touched her

since that day in the rain, the warmth was definitely in all the wrong places.

"You handed the boxes over to the mission for me. Thanks."

He ate another brownie before carrying the platter over to the table, where she joined him. "No trouble. Mrs. Moses came by while I was fixing the ceiling fan."

"And you straightened up the room."

He shrugged. "Once the boxes were gone, it was pretty clean. So what are you doing tonight?" He stared down at the platter. "Eating brownies all by yourself?"

"Maybe," she said, retrieving a dog biscuit for Grubby, who licked at her ankles. "Grubby and I thought we'd play a little solitaire"—she indicated a stack of cards sitting on the counter—"and I'd have a chocolate fest."

"Sounds like a plan." Jesse ate another brownie, and Faith drank in his appearance, noticing for the first time that he was wearing a button-up denim shirt tucked into denim jeans with a woven brown belt.

"Big date tonight?" she asked, wondering why the idea should bother her so much.

"Maybe later," he said, eyeing her as he took another bite of brownie. "I thought I'd play a few hands of solitaire first."

"Two people don't play solitaire."

"Then name your game." He retrieved the deck of cards, flipped the chair around to straddle it, and started shuffling.

"You don't have to sit here and baby-sit me, Jesse. If you have someplace to go . . ." *Someone to see*, she added silently. The notion sent a pang of hurt rippling through her. "Don't feel obligated. Just go wherever it is you were going."

"Later," he said. "Now I'm up for a little poker." He started dealing. At her hesitation, he added, "You can play poker, can't you?" Challenge glittered hot and bright in his eyes, and Faith found herself reaching for the cards.

"I can play anything you can deal, mister."

"Good." He glanced at his hand, then grabbed two brownies and placed them in the center of the table. "I raise you two."

Faith smiled and met his challenge. A half hour later, she'd won a half dozen brownies, and eaten at least three.

"We have to stop." She groaned, patting her stomach. "Or else I'll have to unbutton my pants."

At that comment, Jesse shoved a stack of winnings to the center of the table. "Show me what you've got."

"Very funny," Faith grumbled. "But I'm serious."

"So am I."

Faith stared at him for a long moment and debated the truth of that. On the one hand, he looked dead serious. She could see the gold glinting in his eyes, feel the heat coming off him. On the other hand, he didn't so much as make a move toward her. He was careful not to brush her hands when he dealt, equally careful to keep from staring at her any more than necessary.

"I quit," she said, tired of games. Of wanting something she obviously couldn't have.

"Wait." One large hand reached out and covered hers. His skin burned into hers, oddly soothing and disconcerting at the same time. "What do you say we change the stakes?" He unbuttoned the top button of his shirt and tugged at the collar.

Faith shook her head. "If you're thinking about strip poker, think again. Especially after I just gained five pounds from that last hand."

He grinned. "As tempting as that sounds, I had something a little different in mind."

Heat flooded her face for an embarrassing moment. Okay, so she'd read him wrong. That seemed to be a habit she couldn't shake when it came to Jesse Savage.

"What then?"

"I'm chaperoning the dance at the community center tonight."

"Em and Ricky's first date?"

He nodded.

She tilted her head and slanted him a glance. "So what's the deal?"

"If I win this next hand, you come along and help."

She was shaking her head even before he finished. "No, thanks. I think it's time to call it quits." She moved to get up, but his hand closed over hers again, and this time he didn't let go.

"What's the hurry? Have *you* got a hot date or something?" His gaze raked her from tank top to jeans, to her bare feet peeking from beneath the table.

"Only with my TV set."

"Then you can cancel."

"I don't want to cancel."

"You should have seen them," he said matter-of-factly, leaning back to shuffle the cards. He watched her from beneath partially lowered lashes. "Ricky bought her a corsage."

"What kind?" The words were out so quickly, she didn't even consider holding them back. "Carnations?" She sighed. "Em loves carnations."

He raised an eyebrow at her. "You really want to

155

know, then come with me and find out."

Yes. It was there on the tip of her tongue; all she had to do was let it go, but something held her back. A tightening in her chest, a closing of her throat.

She shook her head.

"Carnations," he went on. "Red ones to match her sweater."

The excitement snagged her attention again. "A red sweater? With jeans or a skirt? Don't tell me she actually put on a skirt?"

"If I win, you can see for yourself." He started dealing her a hand. "That's the bet. I win and you come to the dance with me."

"And if I win?"

He stopped shuffling, his dark eyes boring into hers for a long moment. "Then I'll leave you alone about the kids."

She willed her hands to close around the cards he'd dealt her, but for some reason Jesse's wager held little appeal. Maybe because she wanted to see the kids again. As much as she fought against herself, against the hurt she'd felt, she wanted to see them, to hug them, to hear them laugh again.

"What's the matter?" he asked when she hesitated. "Afraid I might beat you?"

She had to smile at that. "You've lost every hand." And that was the trouble, she quickly realized. She was afraid she would win and he really would stop badgering her about the kids.

"I'll win," he said, his voice so calm, so self-assured, she knew in an instant that she'd been suckered. He'd been losing on purpose.

"I know what you're up to," she told him. "I did the same thing with Ricky."

"How's that?"

"He was ditching school so I challenged him to a

game of pool. We played forever, and I lost every game. Then we played the final round."

"And you beat him."

"Exactly. Of course, he thought no girl could beat him, so he gladly played a winner-take-all last game."

"I assume he stopped ditching school."

"He's rough, but he keeps his word. He had perfect attendance last year because I suckered him, just like you're suckering me."

"Are you playing or not?" He motioned to her cards.

With a smile, she picked them up. "You're on."

Why?

The question pounded through her head but she refused to think about it. Maybe she was just tired of being cooped up in the house. Maybe she didn't want to watch Jesse walk out the door in ten or fifteen minutes. Maybe she wanted to see the kids and this was her only way of doing it without violating her self-made promise to stay away. Maybe all three.

Not that it mattered.

The only thing that mattered was the terrible hand Jesse dealt her and the look of victory as he laid down a full house.

"I win." He pulled her to her feet and stared down at her. "Now go put on your dancing shoes. We've got a date."

This was *not* a date, Jesse reminded himself as he stood in front of Faith's house and stared at the woman who appeared in the doorway.

She wore a loose-fitting pink and green sundress that fell to midcalf and covered a hell of a lot more than it showed. The material was soft, flowing over curves and dips to merely hint at what lay beneath.

His gaze swept her once, twice. No, it wasn't a date dress. No plunging neckline or tight bodice or short hem. The only thing that even whispered *date* was the lack of sleeves. He had a tantalizing view of tanned shoulders and arms that sent an ache straight to his—

Wait a second. Arms? He was getting turned on by the sight of her *arms*? He was definitely hard up, and this was not, repeat, *not* a date. With that thought firmly in mind, he busied himself straddling the motorcycle and starting the engine.

"This is great," Faith said, bunching her skirt between her legs and climbing behind him. "I've always wanted to ride one of these things." Her knees nudged the backs of his and she wrapped her arms around him.

He gunned the engine and sent them bolting out of the driveway. The air rushed at him, but it did little to cool the heat inside him. Not with Faith pressed so tightly against his back, her thighs flanking his.

The three blocks to the community center passed painfully slowly, yet too damned fast at the same time. He wanted to feel her, yet he didn't, his emotions a constant seesaw where Faith was concerned.

But distance had to win out, because Faith was just a means to an end. Business, he told himself as he swerved into the community center's parking lot and killed the engine.

The Heart of Houston Community Center was a converted warehouse about the size of a school gymnasium not far from the local junior high and high school where most of Faith's kids, except for the youngest, attended school. The center served as an after-school hangout for the neighborhood kids, as well as a haven for them when things got too rough at home. There was a center director on duty at all times, and every other month the center and a few of the local teen shelters and group foster homes, such as Faith's House, got together to organize a dance for the kids.

Lights blazed in the windows, and the walls vibrated with the rhythm of a rap song blaring from the speakers as Faith and Jesse crossed the parking lot.

"The place looks really crowded tonight."

Faith's soft voice drew Jesse's attention, and he noted the trembling of her lips. A shiver rolled through him, part fear, part anxiety, and part restless anticipation. He realized as he followed Faith to the double doors that they were her feelings coursing through him, and he couldn't help but reach out and place a comforting hand on her shoulder.

Inside, streamers were draped from the basketball hoops and the darkened light fixtures. Swirls of colored lights flashed with the beat of the DJ's music, illuminating a swarm of teenagers. Some were dancing in the middle of the floor; others stood on the sidelines talking or drinking punch.

No one paid too much attention as Faith slid into a darkened corner of the bleachers.

"Don't you want to say hello?" Jesse motioned past a cluster of kids to Bradley, who manned a refreshment table with a handful of other adults.

"Maybe later," she said. "I think I'd like to just sit here for a while." They both watched as Bradley ladled punch and sniffed every cup. "Someone always tries to spike the punch," Faith explained at Jesse's puzzled glance. A smile tugged at her lips. "Bradley's a stickler when it comes to seeing that the kids stay sober. I think they try to spike the drinks, not to get drunk, but just to see him go through the ritual."

Jesse smiled, but the expression died as Faith's nervousness washed over him. She worried her bottom lip, held her arms about herself, and stared at the sea of kids.

"I hate to leave you sitting here, but I need to report for duty." At that moment, a fast song blared from the speakers and someone upped the volume. "Will you be all right?" Jesse tried to shout over the increased noise level.

"What?"

"I asked"—he leaned down, his lips grazing her ear—"if you'll be all right." The fragrance of roses filled his nostrils and he inhaled deeply.

"I'll be fine," she whispered.

He didn't actually hear her voice, though he saw her lips move. Still, the words were there in his head, as vivid and intoxicating as her scent.

Focus, his mind screamed, and he jerked away.

"What's wrong?" she mouthed.

He motioned to Bradley. "I'll check on you later," he shouted, and she nodded.

Still, he couldn't bring himself to move. She looked too uneasy, too skittish.

He leaned back down to the warm shell of her ear and the delicious scent. "You're not planning to slip out the back door, are you?"

She turned toward him, her lips grazing his jaw. They were so close, the shadows of the bleachers swirling around them, wrapping them in a private cocoon. Just a quarter of an inch and he could kiss her, taste her.

"You won the bet," she said, her eyes fixed on his. "I'm not going anywhere until you finish."

"Promise?"

"Promise."

He must have looked doubtful because she nudged his arm, the motion shattering the strange spell that had wrapped around them.

"You're here to keep an eye on the kids, not me," she said, motioning him away. Bradley sniffed a cup of punch and made a face. Then he hefted the punch bowl into his arms and headed for the kitchen. "He needs you more than me," Faith said, laughter in her voice.

Liar. The moment the thought flitted through his head, her gaze jerked up to collide with his. Questions swirled in her eyes, and Jesse damned himself for the slip. He could feel her, so the reverse was also true. But Jesse knew about the connection and he'd spent years guarding his emotions, holding back; Faith had felt little from his end so far. If she had felt anything, undoubtedly she'd have thought it was her imagination. What they shared was unbelievable. Impossible. At least, it must be from her point of view.

"Stay put," he said and turned away, before he could slip again.

He spent the next two hours inspecting punch, flashing a high-powered flashlight into makeout corners to send the kids scattering, and keeping an eye on Faith.

As deep in the shadows as she was, no one even knew she was there. She watched from the most remote corner, smiling every now and then, especially when Ricky finally worked up the nerve to ask Emily to slow dance.

The sight of Faith, sad yet happy at the same time, tugged at something inside of Jesse. She'd *wanted* to come tonight. He knew it, yet her fear still kept her from really enjoying herself. From joining in and abandoning her spot on those damned bleachers.

But he meant to change all that.

"Let's dance," he told her when a slow song started up and he managed to find someone to man the flashlight.

She shook her head.

"Don't you know how?"

She shrugged. "Mr. Wells—he was my guardian after my parents died—didn't let me date until I turned eighteen, and by then I had my hands full with college classes and volunteer work."

"You've never been out dancing with a man before?"

"Sure I have. I can do a mean limbo—Ricky taught me how at the neighborhood luau last year— and there were plenty of men in line in front of me, and behind."

"That's not what I meant." He grasped her hand, her fingers so small and warm in his. "I'm talking man to woman, body to body, couple dancing. Come on." Before she could shake her head, he hauled her upright and led her from the shadows, down the bleacher steps, toward the floor.

"I don't think this is such a good idea. What if I step on your feet?"

"It's a great idea, and I doubt you could do much damage."

"This isn't the kind of music I'm used to—"

"Ms. Jansen!" a girl shrieked from a few feet away. In seconds, a cluster of heads swiveled in their direction. Excited murmurs floated through the group, and then at least a half-dozen kids started toward them.

Jesse read the terror in Faith's eyes, but it wasn't because she was facing the kids from Faith's House.

No, her gaze was riveted on one in particular.

"It can't be." The words were a bare whisper as she stared at Emily as if she were seeing a ghost.

She was, Jesse realized as Faith's gaze centered on the bright red sweater the girl was wearing. It had been in one of the boxes Jesse had brought from Faith's that afternoon.

"It's Emily," Jesse said, urging her gaze to his. "Emily," he repeated.

"Emily?" She shook her head. "But it's her." Faith's gaze shifted back to the girl, and she blanched. "Oh, my God." She jerked free of his hand, turned, and bolted for the nearest exit.

"Where'd she go?" Emily asked as she came up to Jesse, a group of kids on her heels. "We wanted to say hi."

"I think she's feeling a little under the weather. Let's give her a little time to get herself together." Jesse motioned the disappointed group back toward the dance floor before going out the rear exit in search of Faith.

It was a good fifteen minutes before he found her leaning against the back of a neighboring building, her breathing heavy, as if she'd just escaped death by a fraction of a second.

"It was Emily," he said, placing his hands on her trembling shoulders. *"Emily."*

"I . . ." She swallowed. "I know that. I saw her earlier dancing with Ricky. But when she started walking toward me and I got a really good look at the sweater, it was like seeing—" The name seemed to stick in her throat. She stared up at him, her eyes wide and frightened. So damned frightened. "I shouldn't have come tonight. I wanted to. I was hoping . . ." Her words faded as she took a deep breath. "I don't know what I was hoping. I just know I can't do it again. I can't be their friend, their foster mother. I just can't." Her eyes glittered brightly, reflecting the moonlight that cut through the darkness of the alley. "Can't you understand?"

No. He couldn't. She had to come back, to be everything she was before. She had to stop screwing up his chance at eternity.

"Yes," he murmured, the word wrenched from someplace deep inside that only she could touch. "I can." He pulled her into his arms and held her. "I can," he whispered again into the softness of her hair.

"I'm so sorry," she cried. "I wanted to see Emily and Ricky, and the others. I wanted to be a part of them, but I can't. I just can't . . ." Her words faded into a sob that she buried in the curve of his neck.

It hurts too much. Her soft voice cried through his conscience, and he knew the sudden urge to comfort, to reach out. Not simply because feeling Faith so close to him was stirring his passions, but because her nearness stirred something else—a fierce protectiveness that made him want more than just her body. He wanted her heart. Her soul.

He wanted to make her stop crying.

"Hey," he murmured, stroking her hair. "I think we're almost dancing." A faint breeze carried the slow song playing at the community center. The melody reached out, filtered through the air, and surrounded them.

"We're just standing here." He felt her lips move against his shoulder.

He rocked her slowly from side to side. "How about now?"

She tilted her head up and smiled at him. "Close enough. I don't know what it is about you, Jesse, but you always chase away the cold and make me feel

164

so warm. So alive." She fit her head back in the curve of his neck and hugged him tighter. "I really need that right now."

Her desperation seeped through him, swamping all reason that screamed for him to turn, to walk away from her now before it was too late. Before he did more than simply hold her.

"I need you," she murmured, pressing herself against him, her curves molding to his, awakening his body the way her words awakened his spirit.

Then there was no reason. No logic.

Just her.

And him.

The two of them.

The connection. That was what drew him to her. He knew that, somewhere in the back of his mind where he'd pushed all *right* and *wrong*. It wouldn't have mattered if an entire football stadium had separated them; he would have felt her heart beating. But what he was feeling now—this urge to protect, to pull her inside himself and shelter her—was different somehow. Stronger. More potent.

"I'm sorry I freaked out inside. I just miss her so much, I guess my mind was playing tricks on me." She sniffled and Jesse felt a drop of wetness trickle down his skin. Tears.

He wasn't sure whether it was her tears, her voice, or his own lust that did him in. Maybe all three, or maybe something more, something so big even he couldn't comprehend it.

He only knew that he needed to touch her, really touch her, to chase away the tears and drive the sadness from her words.

It wasn't the right time or place. His brain told him that, but his pounding heart—*her* heart—told him something altogether different, and as much as Jesse wanted to resist, he couldn't.

Not her. Not himself. Not this thing between them.

With a curse of surrender, he tilted his head, touched his lips to hers, and kissed her deeply.

Chapter Nine

The moment he dipped his tongue past her parted lips, what had started out as a slow exploration, a tentative sip of her sweetness, turned into a starving man devouring his last piece of bread. He deepened the pressure on her mouth, stroking her lips, her tongue, learning every secret. And still he wasn't satisfied. He wanted more.

He wanted her to come apart in his arms, wanted her soft moans echoing in his ears. He wanted . . . her. Now.

He backed her against the side of the building, leaned into her, and lifted the edge of her dress. His hands slid up, caressing the silky smoothness of her thighs while she grasped at his shoulders, clutched the muscles of his back, wanting what he wanted. More, perhaps.

No! a part of him raged. There couldn't be more. No tomorrows. No future. *No!*

But the command was drowned out by the fierce pounding of blood through his veins. Desire fired his senses, giving rise to a painful excitement that sent an echoing throb clear to his temples.

She moaned into his mouth as his fingers found the wispy lace of her panties. He slid his hands inside to grasp her bare bottom.

"Open for me, Faith. Open . . ."

Her legs came around him and he lifted her, pulling her silk-covered heat against the straining denim of his crotch. He rubbed her the way he had that day in the rain, only harder this time. Up and down, until a breathless moan tore from her throat.

". . . are they? I know they came out here." Bradley's voice barely penetrated the pounding in Jesse's ears.

". . . take that side, and I'll check back there. The motorcycle's still here, so they're around somewhere."

He heard the footsteps though he knew they were a good distance away. His senses were magnified with Faith in his arms, her heat so close and sparsely covered he could lose himself with nothing more than the opening of his zipper. . . .

Jesse eased her down onto wobbly legs and let her skirt fall back around her knees just as Bradley rounded the corner.

"There you two are." He squinted into the darkness. "Is everything all right?"

"I . . ." Faith touched a hand to her swollen lips, surprised and dazed and oddly disappointed all at the same time.

Jesse felt her confusion, the way her blood was racing, and the double thud of her heartbeat, so fast and furious.

"Faith needed a little air," Jesse told Bradley. "And

168

I didn't want her wandering around out here by herself."

"Yes." She managed to find her voice. "It—it was so hot inside." She wiped a hand across her sweaty brow. "It's not much better out here."

"Then come on back inside."

She shook her head. "I'm really tired. I think I'll call it a night." She turned to Jesse. "Do you mind?"

He shook his head and she smiled—a soft, secretive smile reserved for lovers—and it was all he could do to keep from busting out of his jeans.

Damn, it was only a smile.

Then again, his response was fueled by her emotions. It wasn't his own desire and lust that sparked his reaction; it was hers. He felt it as his own, more intensely, in fact, and he was a slave to it.

"Take care then," Bradley said to Faith. "And I'm glad you showed up."

"So am I." The words rang with a truth that seemed to startle her. "Tell Emily I'm glad that Ricky finally came around. And"—she swallowed—"tell her I'm sorry I ran out on her. For a second there, she just reminded me so much of . . ." Her words fell away and she shook her head. "Just tell her I'm sorry."

"There's nothing to be sorry for." Bradley stood, hands on hips, and shook his head. "She understands, Faith. We all do. You're not the only one who lost Jane." Then he turned and disappeared around the corner.

"Jane touched a lot of people," Jesse said after a few silent moments. "She must have been pretty special."

"Yes," Faith murmured. "It's getting late." She smoothed her skirt. "I really am tired."

"You can talk about her, Faith."

"This really isn't the place."

"There's never a right place. Just say her name. Tell me something about her."

She shook her head and moved past him. Her footsteps, like the angry pounding of a fist, shattered the dark silence that separated them. She rounded the building and headed for the parking lot.

He caught up with her a few steps later and jerked her around to face him. "You think if you push her out of your mind, try to bury your hurt, it'll just disappear?" His grip on her arm tightened as he glared down at her, suddenly angry with her for being so damned stubborn. And even angrier with himself for caring one way or another. "It won't. It'll eat you up inside until you let it out, just like the anger. Remember that night outside the hospital? You let the anger go then, and it helped. Now let the hurt have its turn. Let it go."

Eyes like hard chips of jade stared up at him. "Why don't you stick to home repair and baby-sitting? You're not much good as a shrink." She yanked her arm from his grasp and whirled to keep walking.

"Dammit, Faith, I'm serious. You can't keep your feelings bottled up inside. Let them out. Let Jane out. Stop trying to pretend she never existed."

She came to a dead stop and jerked around and he knew he'd hit upon the truth. He saw it in her fighting stance, felt it in the fast, furious beat of her heart.

"She did," he said, his voice tempered by the trembling of her bottom lip, such a slight motion—yet he saw it, felt it, responded to it. "She lived and breathed, and you loved her. You can't forget that."

Pain wracked her features, twisting her brow, tightening her mouth until she looked ready to scream. Her eyes filled with tears and Jesse knew she was near the breaking point.

"Let it out, Faith. Say her name. Tell me about her."

"I . . ." She shook her head, her expression hardened, and she blinked. "Take me home." She turned and rushed through the parking lot. Gathering her skirt around her legs, she climbed onto the back of the motorcycle, a stony look on her face.

The urge to reach out, grab her shoulders, and shake some sense into her nearly overwhelmed him. He balled his fingers and straddled the bike, acutely aware of the rigid statue of a woman sitting behind him.

The ride home was short and silent. Jesse could feel the turmoil raging inside her, and he wanted with everything he had to help her, to reach out. The irony of it brought a bitter smile to his lips. He was a man who'd spent a lifetime bottling his own feelings, masking his emotions, so damned afraid that someone might see that he actually felt something, and use it against him, to enslave him the way his mother had before she'd died. Yet here he was, trying to help a woman overcome the very same problem—she was afraid to feel. To care. To love. To admit any of the above.

The entire situation was crazy. And doomed.

He pulled into her driveway, killed the engine, and sat there while she walked to the door, a few feet that might well have been a thousand miles.

Faith was too far gone, and no matter how he tried to bridge the gap between them, she simply moved farther away, erecting more obstacles until he didn't stand a chance in hell of saving her. She was so distant, so emotionally guarded. And so damned stubborn.

Jesse admitted to himself for the first time that he might not be able to fulfill his mission. How could he deliver a hope-renewing miracle in a little less than a week when he couldn't get close enough to her, emotionally close enough, to find out what she cherished the most?

He watched as she unlocked the door and disappeared into the shadows inside. He was about to start the engine when he heard her soft voice and realized she hadn't closed the door.

"She liked teddy bears."

His gaze pierced the darkness and met hers for a long second; then she was gone, disappearing inside.

She liked teddy bears

The phrase lulled him to sleep that night. And for the first time, there were no nightmares about death and past regrets, no urgent dreams of Faith and an uncertain future.

When Jesse Savage closed his eyes, he knew only peace.

"Get dressed," Jesse told her the next afternoon when Faith opened the front door wearing sweats and a faded pink T-shirt. "We're going out."

She shook her head, walked back into the house, and settled Indian-style on the couch. "Not on your life. There's a Mel Gibson marathon on cable tonight and I'm baking lasagna." Jesse made a face and Faith smiled. "Megan still hasn't made it back from the honeymoon, huh?"

He nodded. "How did you know?"

"Because the only thing that Bradley can cook is lasagna. Are the kids as sick of it as you are?"

"They've been pooling their allowances and smuggling in hamburgers, and the neighbor's dog is this close to bleeding tomato sauce."

She laughed. "Then I won't offer you any dinner."

"Actually, I was going to offer you dinner. I know this place that has really great Tex-Mex."

"What about my lasagna?"

"It'll keep in the fridge."

"And Mel?"

"He'll keep on video."

She eyed him suspiciously. "This Tex-Mex doesn't happen to be served in the dining room at Faith's House?"

He touched his hand to his heart in a dramatic gesture and widened his eyes innocently. "Would I resort to such a low trick?"

"Maybe."

"Actually," he said with a grin, "that's not a bad idea. But tonight's strictly on the up-and-up. Just you and me, some great food, and a little conversation."

"About Jane?" she asked, surprised that the name didn't stick in her throat as it had so many times in the past.

"If you want." He stared deep into her eyes, the gold flecks in his gaze sparkling with compassion and something else.

The slow-burning hunger she'd glimpsed the night before when he'd kissed her and . . .

She didn't want to think about the *and*. The kiss was enough food for thought. Enough to consume her thoughts.

"And if I don't want to talk about her?"

"Then don't. It doesn't matter. I just thought it would do us both good to get away from everything for a while."

More than his words, his gaze—that unspoken reminder of last night, of things to come—drew her off the sofa.

She changed into a blouse and a gauzy skirt she'd bought last summer but hadn't had the opportunity to wear. It was the sort of outfit that begged to be taken home, only to sit in the closet awaiting the perfect time and place that never presented itself. Too casual for a summer evening at the opera. Too dressy for a softball game.

It was perfect for eating Tex-Mex with a sinfully handsome man.

The material, a shimmering jade, caressed her skin with every movement as she moved about the bedroom brushing her hair and spritzing perfume. Back and forth, side to side in a sensual glide of fabric that coaxed her nerves to life and made her acutely aware of her femininity. Sexy.

Yes, perfect for an evening with Jesse.

He was waiting for her when she walked out of the bedroom a good twenty minutes later. He raked her with an approving gaze and she smiled. Then she hurried to check on Grubby before accompanying Jesse out to his motorcycle.

"Where are we going?" she asked as she gathered her skirt and climbed behind him.

"Flaco's. It's a little hole-in-the-wall place a good half-hour outside the city limits. Not much to look at, but they serve the best mesquite-grilled fajitas in Texas." He gunned the engine and the roar ended any further talk.

Seconds later they were speeding north on Highway 59. They left the city, the Houston skyline quickly fading behind them. The traffic thinned, dusk fell, and the occasional fast-food joint and gas station soon gave way to farmhouses and green stretches of pasture. They drove on until a blanket of velvet darkness spread above them, and it seemed the endless highway stretched clear to heaven.

"This place is way out of the way," she shouted against the streaming wind.

"What?"

"I said, this place is pretty far out. How much farther?" As she said the words, the bike started to slow. Faith saw a narrow dirt road a second before Jesse turned. Gravel spewed as they headed down the narrow stretch, to what looked like an old farmhouse. But it was more than a farmhouse, Faith quickly discovered as they drew closer. Multicolored Christmas lights draped the outside, illuminating a parking lot full of cars.

Jesse swerved into an available parking spot and killed the engine. Lively mariachi music carried through the open windows, along with laughter and a steady stream of voices.

"Welcome." A Hispanic woman beamed at them when they walked through the doorway. At Jesse's request, she led them through a crowded dining room, out onto a secluded patio that housed a table for two. A fat red candle occupied the center of the fuchsia-draped table, the flame flickering with each whisper of wind.

"So tell me about yourself," Faith said once the waitress had disappeared with their orders. She stared across the table at Jesse, into his dark eyes. "You wanted to talk tonight, so talk."

"I wasn't thinking about myself."

"You've picked my brain enough. Now it's my turn." She glanced around, her gaze touching on the garish papier-mâché parrots hanging from the wooden beams that crisscrossed overhead. Plants sat atop the frame. Vines draped down, forming a green umbrella above them. Baskets of fuchsia flowers and empty tequila bottles sat here and there atop the waist-high ivy-covered wall that bordered the patio. "How did you find this place?"

"When my brother and sister and I were on our way from Restoration, we stopped here."

"How long ago was that?"

"A little over a year."

"Have you eaten here since?"

He shook his head. "I never really had the time."

"Busy working?"

He nodded and sipped at the bottle of Corona the waitress had placed in front of him. "I told myself I would get back out here soon, but you know how that goes. Always a day late and a dollar short."

"And what brought you to Faith's House?"

You, his gaze seemed to say, but Faith knew it was just her imagination. How could she be the reason when she'd never even met him before he'd come knocking on her door for a job?

"I like kids and I needed a job."

"And you missed your brother and sister?"

He took a long drink of beer before nodding. "That, too." The sudden flicker of pain over his features sent an ice pick straight into her heart. Instinctively, she reached across the table and covered his hand with her own.

He stiffened and his gaze dropped to stare at the point of contact between them. When he caught her stare again, the flecks in his eyes seemed brighter, more mesmerizing. "I've been sort of out of it since they died, just drifting here and there. Then I saw the ad in the paper." He took another drink and grinned, the pain gone as quickly as it had come. "Being at Faith's House brings back a lot of memories for me. Ricky reminds me a lot of my kid brother. He's about the same age, always into trouble. But Bradley really knows how to handle him. He's like a cross between Ward Cleaver and the Terminator."

The way he shifted the conversation from himself to her kids was so smooth, Faith didn't notice until it was too late. Until he'd made her smile with stories about all the kids, and remember her own times with them. Then she could no more shut out the past than she could have pulled her hand away from Jesse Savage.

The memories rolled through her mind, making her happy and sad all at the same time. She alternated between laughter and a nearly overwhelming sense of loss. On more than one occasion, her eyes filled with tears, but before a single drop could squeeze free, Jesse would stroke her palm or simply stare into her eyes, and her sadness dissolved.

"Thank you," she finally told him a half hour later.

He grinned. "Don't thank me until you've tried the main course. The shrimp fajitas are basted with a red pepper sauce that'll set your mouth on fire. That's what that stuff is for." He gestured to the small bowl of pale golden liquid the waitress had placed between them. "It's for dipping. Tastes like lemon and honey and cuts the effect of the pepper."

"I wasn't talking about the food. What you said last night, about me trying to pretend she"—she swallowed—"Jane never existed." Her gaze locked with his. "You were right. I didn't even want to say her name because I knew it would hurt."

"Does it?"

"Yes and no. It hurts, but now it's a good kind of hurt." She closed her eyes for a long moment, expecting the tears. Oddly enough, they didn't come. Instead, a strange sense of relief washed through her, soothing the grief. "She was only at Faith's

177

House a short time, a little less than a year, but we became so close."

"But you're close to all the kids, according to Bradley."

"*Was* close." She shook her head. "Not anymore, and it was different with Jane."

"How?"

"She had this look about her that was so different from the others. She had the same haunted expression they all have, the look of a victim, yet it wasn't the same. She didn't come from an abusive home. I knew it in my heart the moment I met her. She was lying in a hospital bed after emergency surgery to repair damage to her lungs—she'd been brought to the hospital with severe chest wounds. Anyhow, she stared up at me and I knew whatever had happened to her hadn't been the result of an abusive home. She'd come from a loving household. The proof was there in front of me—a young girl with no bruises other than her wounds, no shadows lurking in her eyes. Nothing but the pain of losing all memory of her past." Faith's gaze locked with his. "I recognized that pain because it was what I'd felt when I'd lost both my parents in a car accident."

"How old were you?"

"Sixteen, just a few years older than Jane. But I was luckier. I had my memories, at least, and my parents were well-off, so I didn't have to worry about where my next meal was coming from. One of my father's business friends, Mr. Wells, took over guardianship until I turned eighteen and collected my trust fund and inheritance. After college, I used part of the money to fund Faith's House, my graduation present to myself."

He grinned. "Most kids would have bought a new car."

"I wasn't most kids." She shook her head, her gaze fixing on the small bowl of sauce. "After my parents died I never really related to everyone else. I always felt separate from my friends, like I was on the outside of a bubble looking in. They had their families and I didn't have anyone. I had Mr. Wells, of course, but he was little more than a stranger. When my parents died, this man showed up out of the blue, claiming he owed my dad and I was his responsibility, according to my parents' wills. I'd met him only a few times while growing up. I didn't even know he and my dad were close."

"Was he good to you?"

"He kept a roof over my head and designer clothes on my back, if that's what you mean."

"Was he nice?"

"I don't really know. I guess he was. He was polite, the few times he actually spoke to me. But otherwise, he was a portrait hanging over the fireplace, a picture on the front of *Fortune* or *Houston Businessman*. He spent three-fourths of the year away on business, and the rest of the time at his office or the country club, anywhere but home. The only person I saw regularly was the housekeeper. I was basically alone, scared. Just like Jane."

Faith's gaze shifted to the stubby candle. She stared into the flame and saw Jane, the little girl's brown eyes wide and frightened, her brow drenched in perspiration, her face twisted in fear. "She came to live at the foster home as soon as the hospital released her. I used to spend most of my nights at Faith's House with the kids. I covered weeknights and Bradley did weekends. When Jane first arrived, I stayed every night so I could be near her. She would wake up crying and I would go in and hold her. We didn't talk at first. Just held each other." She

179

tore her gaze away from the image to look at Jesse "I knew what she was feeling. The loneliness, mean, and the fear. The nightmares lasted about a month or so; then they gradually stopped. She stopped being frightened and started living again."

"Thanks to you."

"Thanks to herself. She had strength about her, a will to live. I guess that's what tore me up the most. Here was this girl who wanted to live, who fought for her life—only to have it snatched away again. I all seemed so unfair. I mean, I've lost kids before Not to death, mind you, but to the streets. Those losses weighed on me almost as badly, but not quite because those kids turned away by choice. Jane had no choice. She was taken." Faith dashed away a tear and sniffled.

"So she liked teddy bears, huh?" Jesse's voice broke the sudden quiet that had twined around them.

Faith smiled and dashed another tear away. "She collected them. All shapes and sizes. I gave her a purple one with pink polka dots for her birthday."

"Sounds . . . colorful."

"It was. She loved it. She always loved everything anyone gave her. She would get this great big smile on her face. Seeing her smile always gave me the best feeling—like standing outside in the sunshine after you've been sitting in the freezing air conditioning all day."

"The heat washes over you and seeps clear to your bones," he said, and she smiled.

"Exactly. You know the feeling?"

He leaned over, the pad of his thumb smoothing away another tear. "It's the same feeling I get when I look at you."

Chapter Ten

The meaning of Jesse's words stalled the air in Faith's lungs, as much as his tender touch sent a ripple of awareness through her.

"Here we go," the waitress declared, arriving with their food, and Faith couldn't have timed it better.

No quiet, empty seconds to analyze her reaction to Jesse. No chance to chastise herself for responding physically, or warn her heart against anything emotional. Tonight she was determined to enjoy his company and the strange freedom surging through her.

Freedom from the anger and grief.

She'd exorcised them both now, and she was still in one piece. Still alive, and feeling more alive by the second with Jesse staring so intently at her.

"This looks really great," she said, reaching for a shrimp. She dipped it into the succulent honey sauce and took a bite. A range of tastes, spicy to sweet, exploded on her tongue, and she chewed slowly, relishing the flavor.

"I never would have guessed the food would be this good," she said after she'd swallowed. "Not with the way this place looks on the outside."

"Looks can be deceiving."

"You're telling me." She dipped another shrimp into the sauce and stared pointedly at him. "You know, every time I look at you I get this strange feeling I know you from somewhere." She licked at a dribble of honey that had oozed down the shrimp onto her thumb. "It's not really your face. It's your eyes, I think. They're so . . . distinctive. I feel like I've looked into your eyes before." She shook her head. "But then if I had, I can't imagine not remembering."

He gave her a slow, lazy grin and reached for a shrimp. "So I'm unforgettable, am I?"

"Unfortunately."

"And why is that?"

"Well"—she licked a drop of sauce from her knuckle—"because guys like you aren't the permanent kind—too many deep, dark secrets hiding in your closet. You're more the love-'em-and-leave-'em kind, I think. One of those wild boys who thinks commitment is a four-letter word."

"That's exactly the kind of man I am," he said, grabbing the shrimp from her hand before she could take another bite. "And you'd be smart to remember it." He plopped the shrimp into his own mouth.

"And why is that?" She reached for another shrimp, dunked it, and licked at the sauce, her tongue swirling around the edges, catching drops of the bittersweet liquid.

His gaze fixed on her mouth, and the flecks in his eyes seemed to glitter brighter, hotter. "Because we're different," he said in a growl. Gone was the comforting companionship they'd shared earlier. An edge sharpened his words. "You want the morning after, and I only want the night before."

"You don't know what I want."

"I'm getting a pretty damned good idea," he muttered, downing three-fourths of his beer before he pierced her with a frustrated glare. "Would you just eat the damn thing and be done with it?"

She paused, the shrimp at her lips. Sauce lingered on her tongue, and she quickly realized the cause of his sudden discomfort. Her cheeks burned. "Sorry." She put the shrimp on her plate and reached for a napkin. "I didn't realize . . ."

"That's what makes it so damned hard to take," he muttered. "So damned hard, period."

At his words, awareness prickled her nerve endings, and she couldn't help herself. She smiled.

"It's not funny," he bit out, shifting in his seat to ease his discomfort.

"Of course not."

"A guy can only take so much."

"Sure he can."

"And with you . . . and those lips, and . . . well, it's frustrating. Damned frustrating."

"Certainly."

He shot her an annoyed look. "Would you stop that?"

"What?" She batted her lashes innocently.

He glared at her long and hard for several seconds. "Nothing," he finally said in a hiss. "Just have a little mercy, all right?"

"I didn't mean to get carried away." *Liar*. Okay, so she hadn't been consciously licking the shrimp, but subconsciously?

She couldn't deny that she liked the way his eyes

flashed midnight fire, the way the gold flecks sparked, flared when he watched her mouth.

"These were just so good, I couldn't help myself," she went on. Without breaking eye contact, she picked up the shrimp, went for the sauce, and raised the scrumptious morsel to her lips.

"Stop it."

"What?" She gave him a wide-eyed stare and licked the edge of the shrimp.

"You don't know what you're doing, Faith."

"I'm just eating."

"You shouldn't test a man like me."

His voice carried an undisguised threat that sent a tingling of fear through her. Rather than deterring her, however, it prodded her on, feeding the excitement pumping through her veins.

"You mean a love-'em-and-leave-'em, commitment-fearing man like you?"

"Exactly." He gripped her hand and plucked the shrimp from her fingers. "You won't find a wedding band and a two-story house with a white picket fence waiting for you. There won't be any tomorrows with me."

"What about tonight?" Their gazes locked and she saw her own hunger mirrored in the depths of his eyes.

"It wouldn't be enough."

"Maybe it would be. Maybe tonight's all I want."

He laughed, a bitter sound that echoed a lifetime of lost dreams and sacrificed hope. "That wouldn't be enough. Not for you."

"That just goes to show how much you know. I've turned over a new leaf. I've decided to live for the moment. For now."

He stared long and hard at her, through her, it seemed, and for a brief moment she felt another tingle of fear, followed by a niggling doubt.

She forced the feeling aside. She wasn't going to fear the future. Now, she told herself. And with that in mind, she picked up another shrimp and swirled it in the sauce. Then she suckled the tip in silent challenge.

"Damn, you're stubborn."

"No, just hungry." She popped the entire shrimp into her mouth and chewed slowly while he watched.

"Tonight then," he finally murmured, his voice hoarse and raw, and Faith had the feeling she might have bitten off more than she could swallow.

Especially when Jesse stood up and positioned his chair next to hers, so he sat at her left rather than across. He was so close.

Then his hand slipped under the table. He pulled at the hem of her skirt, pushing the fabric up to bare her knee, her thigh, until his fingers trailed over the silk of her panties. Her breath caught and he smiled.

"Last chance," he whispered, his lips grazing her ear. "You might want this now, but you'll regret it tomorrow."

"There is no tomorrow," she managed, her lips trembling, her body keenly aware of his. "Just now."

His smile died and the hunger in his eyes blazed. His fingertips traced the lace strap of her panties before hooking the edge. She shifted just so and he shimmied the fabric down her legs, pulled the undies free and stuffed them into his pocket.

A twinge of embarrassment went through her as cool air ruffled under her skirt to tease her bare flesh; then Jesse's fingers followed and she felt only a slow-burning heat that started at the tips of her toes and swept up.

The next thirty minutes passed in a heated blur

for Faith. She wasn't sure how many more shrimp she ate, how many Jesse fed her, or how many he devoured himself. Enough to make her swallow several times as she watched his perfect lips weave their magic, all the while his fingers danced along her inner thigh. He never went higher than a few inches above her knee, yet he might well have been touching her *there*. Her insides quivered, and a slow ache burned from her nipples to the moist heat between her legs.

Tonight. His voice echoed the promise in her mind, and Faith was more than eager when Jesse finally clasped her hand and led her from the restaurant.

"Can I drive?" she asked when they reached the motorcycle. "I always did want to learn how to work one of these things."

"This is not a thing." One large hand trailed over the handlebars in a loving, reverent caress that actually made Faith jealous. "It's a seventy-nine Harley. A classic." His narrowed gaze swept her flushed face. "You really want me to teach you how to drive her?"

Faith nodded with an eagerness she hadn't felt in a long time.

"Be my guest then." He motioned for her to get on and climbed behind her.

She was a quick study. In ten minutes they were rolling down the gravel drive. In twenty, they were zooming up the dark stretch of Highway 59, headed farther away from the city limits.

The wind whipped at her face, sneaking beneath the edge of her skirt to whip the material back and forth in a sharp motion against her thighs. A shiver crept through her, but it had nothing to do with the cool wind and everything to do with Jesse. He wasn't touching her anymore, and she felt the loss as keenly as the quiver in her middle, the moisture between her legs.

Powerful thighs framed hers, his chest a solid wall of promising warmth behind her. If she leaned back just so . . .

She leaned into him and felt his entire body go stiff.

It was all so confusing. One minute he wanted her. She knew he did. And the next . . . He was cool, aloof, detached, as if he never meant to touch her again. Like now . . .

But Faith needed him to touch her. She was so cold by herself. Yet when she looked into his eyes, he warmed her from the inside out. His eyes started the fire burning deep inside her belly, until she wasn't cold anymore. Or empty. Or lonely.

The motorcycle swerved and panic bolted through her.

"Pay attention." The deep voice slid into her ears. She wouldn't have heard him over the rush of wind, but he was so close, his lips grazing her ear. His hands came around her to grab the handlebars. "You have to hold her steady. Like this." His hands, so strong and purposeful, closed over hers. "Keep your mind on the road."

But her mind wasn't on the road. It was on him and the way he seemed to surround her.

"Concentrate."

"You try concentrating without your underpants." She wouldn't have said it under normal circumstances. But with the wind rushing at them, the bike vibrating beneath, she felt a little wild, and reckless.

Laughter rumbled in her ears, thrummed through her senses. "I guess that would make it a little difficult."

She took a deep breath. "Try next to impossible."

"Not impossible. Not yet."

"What's that supposed to mean—" The words stalled in her throat when one of his hands dropped to her bare leg. His fingers splayed against her flesh and slid toward the inside of her knee, working the hem of her skirt up as he went.

Her grip on the gas faltered and the motorcycle jerked before Jesse recovered their moderate speed with his other hand.

"Careful. Remember, it's all in the hands." His hand left her knee to force her fingers back to the handlebars; then he dropped his attention back to the spot he'd already set on fire.

"Motorcycles aren't that much different from people," he went on, one hand over hers guiding her grip on the gas, his other on her leg. "They'll do just what you want, as long as you know how to stroke them. If you want a nice, slow, leisurely ride, you keep your touch loose, not too much pressure." His fingers made lazy circles on the inside of her thigh, and a slow heat seeped through Faith.

"You want a fast, hard ride, you tighten your grip and exert more pressure." His fingers swept higher, his touch more intense as he moved beneath the edge of her skirt and higher until he was a scant inch shy of the moist heat between her legs. "See the difference?" he murmured against her ear, his deep voice gliding along her nerve endings.

Forget a reply. Her heart pumped much too furiously for her to form any words.

"Faith, are you with me?"

She was ahead of him. Way ahead, she realized when his thumb brushed the center of her desire and sensation speared, hot and jagged, through her body.

They would have run off the road if one of Jesse's hands hadn't been resting atop hers, guiding the bike when Faith's thought processes short-circuited.

"You're so wet." The words were more of a groan. "So warm and wet and . . ." His voice faded into the buzz of wind and excitement that filled her ears.

She tilted her head back, resting it in the curve of his shoulder as she gave over to the ecstasy beating at her sanity and let him take control, of the motorcycle and her aching body.

He slid a finger deep inside her and the air bolted from her lungs. He moved and she did, too, shifting just so, riding his fingers the way the two of them rode the bike, her legs tightening around the powerful machine, her insides tightening around him.

The ride was wonderful, exciting, leaving her breathless and dizzy by the time Jesse steered them over to the side of the road.

The highway was deserted, the night sky an endless stretch of stars above. He was off the bike, pulling her after him before she could blink away the stars spinning in her head. His mouth covered hers, his lips plundering hers in a kiss that sent a flood straight between her already damp thighs.

He backed her up against a nearby tree, his arms braced on either side of her, his lips blazing a trail from her collarbone, down to the vee of her blouse. His fingers made quick work of its buttons until he parted the material, unsnapped her bra, and shoved aside the lacy cups. Then his hot mouth closed over her nipple and a moan parted her lips.

He teased the ripe peak with his tongue before he sucked so long and hard and deep that she thought she would come apart right there in his arms. Again. The shameless way she'd done that day outside in the rain.

It was all so overwhelming. She'd never achieved release before that day. She'd had sex, yes, a few times with her steady boyfriend back in college. But he'd never done this to her, never made her feel a fourth of what Jesse did.

Jesse was different. Jesse gave her . . . *heaven*.

The word echoed through her head a heartbeat before he pulled away. The wind skittered across her bare flesh, and a heated curse echoed in her ears.

She opened heavy eyes to see him stalk to the edge of the road and rake tense fingers back and forth through his hair.

"Jesse?"

"It's late," he finally said, his voice gruff.

"What?" She fought to gather her wits and understand what had just happened.

"We'd better get back." Without sparing her a glance, he climbed onto the bike, flipped the key, and gunned the engine.

Somehow she knew he meant his coldness to anger her, but Faith was far too wound up, too hot and desperate to feel anything other than a numb shock. Then as the motorcycle engine roared in her ears, reality started to set in, and along with it, a slow-burning rage.

"You lied to me. You're not even a love-'em-and-leave-'em man. You're worse. You're a tease."

He didn't respond. He simply sat there. Moonlight sculpted his features, accenting the taut lines of his face, the banked tension gripping his shoulders, his very evident excitement making his jeans bulge.

He wanted her, and she wanted him like she'd never wanted any other man before. Not out of curiosity or a sense of obligation. She just wanted him; it was plain and simple.

190

Or it would have been if he hadn't been so set on resisting this thing that flowed between them, this connection, which was so powerful and consuming. So out of this world.

Faith yanked the edges of her blouse together, worked the buttons, and smoothed her skirt down before walking to the motorcycle, her legs rubbery, her body tingling.

Before she could completely seat herself behind him, he pulled onto the highway and headed for town.

The seduction was over. Unfinished. And Faith was still empty and cold and so damned lonely, even though Jesse Savage sat a scant inch in front of her.

So close all she had to do was reach out.

But she wouldn't. Not again. The next move would be his. That realization brought fresh tears to her eyes because Faith knew in her gut it would be a cold day in hell before Jesse Savage made any move toward her again.

Stupid!

Jesse had lost his sanity. Floating around in that great big void between heaven and hell, light and darkness, he'd gone crazy. That was the only explanation for the way his body ached, throbbed, even though he'd dropped Faith off three hours ago. He had spent the time since riding around, and now walking, doing his damnedest to cool off, to forget.

With distance between them, it shouldn't be hard. He shouldn't be so hard. He shouldn't feel her emotions, her desperation, her desire. It was all her. He knew that.

He glanced down at the prominent bulge in his jeans. Okay, so his own lust had figured in, but it was nothing personal. He'd been floating in the nothingness, alone and sexually deprived. Of course, when confronted with a female, one who definitely wanted him, he was bound to react. It was a physical reaction. Nothing deeper. He didn't want Faith Jansen. He just *wanted*, period.

Focus.

The word whispered through his head like a cool wind blowing over a blistering landscape. Yes, he had to focus.

Then he heard her—a soft sigh here, a giggle there, a deep, relaxed breath. . . . And he smelled her—a sweet, feminine heat with a touch of wildness. Roses and rain.

The panties he'd slid from her silky smooth legs burned through his pocket, scorched his bare skin.

Yanking the scrap of silk from his jeans, he went to toss the panties into the nearest trash can but his fingers wouldn't obey. With a violent curse, he shoved the soft material back into his pocket.

Focus.

He concentrated on taking deep breaths, one after the other as he walked. No thinking, just step after step. By the time he returned to Faith's House, it was well past midnight. He staggered up to the garage apartment, collapsed into bed, and gave in to the sleep clawing at his brain.

Chapter Eleven

"Headlining today's newscast is the horrific fire that swept through a downtown apartment complex—"

Faith sat on the living room sofa, the sun beaming through the window, and punched the button on the remote control, flipping past several talk shows.

". . . today we're talking to the sons and daughters of parents who've joined deadly religious cults."

". . . did you know your husband was having an affair with your daughter's boyfriend's mother?"

". . . we're featuring cross-dressing fathers and sons and the women who love them."

Okay, so it looked like cooking or music television. What a choice. She settled for the local video channel and turned her attention to the plate of leftover brownies sitting next to her.

A shadow appeared outside her living room window and her hand paused inches shy of the plate.

Her heart lurched forward like a prime race car at the Indy 500. Her gaze darted to the front door, which she'd left unlocked, along with the burglar bars, when she'd gone out to retrieve the newspaper earlier. A disastrous news report blared through her head.

WOMAN FOUND MURDERED IN LIVING ROOM.

No, make that STUPID WOMAN WHO FORGOT TO LOCK HER DOOR FOUND MURDERED IN LIVING ROOM.

She was about to lunge for the dead bolt when the shadow bent down and she heard her lawn mower sputter to life. She crossed the room and stared through the open drapes at Jesse Savage.

Okay, SO STUPID WOMAN FOUND DEAD OF OVER-ACTIVE IMAGINATION. He strode back and forth across her lawn, pushing the mower she kept out back in her garage. She drank in every detail, from his dusty black boots and faded jeans to the black T-shirt stretched over his torso. Strong hands gripped the handles and guided the machine. His forearms flexed. Biceps rippled.

Faith swallowed and her attention shifted.

His steps were sure and steady despite the over-grown grass. Thigh muscles bunched. Released. His tush swayed just so. . . .

She swallowed again before forcing her gaze away.

"Relax," she muttered to herself and forced a calming breath. It wasn't as if she were some love-starved teenager lusting after the lawn boy. She was a grown woman, and he was just a man.

Okay, so he was more like *man*—six feet plus of carved muscle and enough sex appeal to send Aphrodite herself into a tailspin.

Faith couldn't help but smile.

Her lips still tingled from his kisses. Her nipples

puckered at the memory of his mouth and tongue, and a flood of heat washed through her at the memory of his hands. . . . Geez, he had really great hands, and . . . he liked brownies.

Her gaze lit on the platter sitting on the sofa.

Minutes later, she slipped outside and sat down on the front porch steps to watch him. She had a really great view for all of one minute before he noticed her.

He cut the mower engine, planted one hand on his hip, and faced her.

"Hungry?" She held up the plate of brownies.

He shook his head and wiped at the sweat dripping down his temples.

"How about thirsty?" She held up a glass of lemonade, then patted the spot next to her. "Take a break."

"I've got a lot of work to do."

"You work too much. Besides, it's my yard, so that makes me the boss. I'm ordering you to take a break."

He strode toward her but he didn't take a seat. 0Instead, he simply stood there and took the glass of lemonade she held up.

Tilting his head back, he gulped the contents of the glass. Liquid dribbled down the corners of his mouth, and Faith took a sip of her own lemonade to soothe her suddenly dry throat.

"Thanks." He handed her back the empty glass.

"You sure you don't want a brownie?"

"No, thanks."

"How about a sandwich? I could rustle up some bologna and cheese. Or maybe some roast beef. My fridge is full now."

Another shake of his head.

"Then what do you want? I mean, I know you live

for lawn maintenance, but that's not what keeps you coming back. At least I don't think so. So what is it, Jesse? What do you *really* want?"

He gave her a pointed stare. "I really want you to come to Faith's House with me today."

"No."

"Yes."

"We've had this discussion before."

"This isn't a discussion. I'm not asking you, Faith. I'm telling you." His jaw tightened with determination. "Those kids need you. Are you blind? Couldn't you see how much they missed you night before last?"

"That's because I haven't been gone for very long. They'll forget about me." They will, she added silently, desperately trying to sway that traitorous part of her that insisted otherwise.

He looked ready to throttle her. "You can't just walk away."

"I'm not. I'm turning things over to a very capable person—Bradley—then I'm retiring, and it's none of your business."

"It is my business," he muttered, then swore. "It is."

"Why? Why does it matter to you, Jesse?"

"Because." He stared down at her, his gaze reflecting the sun that streamed down around them. His eyes burned hotter, whiter, a pulsing iridescent heat that drew her, called to her.

Impossible. It was obviously a trick of the light. She raised a hand to shield her eyes and blinked.

On the fourth blink, his gaze cooled and she found herself staring into dark, mysterious pools that revealed not a hint of the thoughts racing through his mind.

"If you're going to tell me that the kids need me,

don't. They need somebody who doesn't hold back, and I'm afraid that's all I can do now. I can't give one hundred percent." Her voice threatened to crack and she swallowed, as if that could make saying the words easier. "I don't want to hurt anymore. And that's what caring does. It hurts."

He wanted so much to argue with her. She could see it in his eyes, in the tension that filled his powerful body, but he didn't say anything. He just glared at her, as if he could exert his will on her with those unnerving eyes of his.

"So you'd just rather look out for number one," he finally muttered.

"Exactly."

"And if a few people get lost by the wayside, it's okay."

"No, it's not okay. But somebody else can play hero and pick them up."

"And what if no one does?"

"Someone will," she insisted. "Someone like Bradley. Like you."

He laughed then, the sound bitter and pained, and she had the urge to draw him into her arms.

"I've never been much of a hero."

"You saved me from Daniel."

"It's my job."

"It wasn't. Not then. You risked your neck before you had the job."

"I didn't have a choice."

"Because you're like Bradley. You can't resist a cry for help."

"*Your* cry," he said, his words ringing with an honesty that reached out and tugged at her heart. "I can't resist your cry for help."

"Well, I'm through crying and I'm through with the kids." Her voice softened and she rubbed at her suddenly tired eyes. "You don't know me around kids. I get close and *bam*, I'm sucked into their lives. I have this constant need to nurture, to help." She shook her head. "I don't want to be wrapped up in someone else's life. I don't ever want to feel the way I did when they put Jane into the ground. I felt my soul ripped away. I—I don't ever want to feel that way again, and that means keeping my distance."

"You're running away," he said.

Her gaze collided with his. "I'm not running away, Jesse. I'm *turning* away. I'm not capable of opening myself up and putting other people first anymore. That part of me is gone. I'm just plain old selfish Faith."

"This wasn't selfish." He held up the glass of lemonade and indicated the plate of brownies.

"Oh, no?" She raised an eyebrow at him, a grin tugging at her lips. "And you think I'm the one who's blind?" When he looked bewildered, she went on, "I wanted an excuse to come out here. To get close to you. I . . ." She swallowed. "I keep thinking about last night."

Something ignited in his eyes the moment the words were out of her mouth. She glimpsed desire, desperation, hunger, and . . .

"I've got grass to cut," he muttered, turning away before she could see any more.

Anger rolled through her. "And you think *I'm* the one who's running away? You could teach me a thing or two."

"I'm not running from my responsibilities."

"No, you're running from your feelings."

He whirled. "If you think pissing me off is going to get me off your back about the shelter, then think again."

"Faith's House was the farthest thing from my mind. I'm talking about you and me."

"There is no you and me."

"I don't think I ate by myself last night."

"Last night was last night. This is today. *Tomorrow*," he said, the word hanging between them, a reminder of what had happened. What hadn't happened.

He finally shrugged and turned back to the the lawn mower.

"You won't forget what happened last night," she told him, her gaze riveted on his back.

"I already have."

"I couldn't sleep at all."

"I slept like a baby."

She folded her arms across her chest. "Liar."

He straightened and wiped at the perspiration beading his forehead. "Look, Faith. Last night was . . ." He shook his head. "It shouldn't have happened. I'm sorry it did. It was a mistake."

"One you don't intend to repeat?"

"I can't."

Faith resisted the urge to break the platter of brownies over his head. "And why is that?"

"Because I don't want to," he ground out.

And he thought she was being stubborn? "You're a liar, Jesse Savage. You want it more than you've ever wanted anything." *Just like I do*, she added silently.

He stiffened, the muscles in his arms bunched tight as he simply stared at her for a long moment.

"What I want more than anything," he finally said, his voice fueled with a sudden desperation that melted Faith's anger like an ice-cream cone beneath the blazing Texas sun, "is for you to go back to the kids, to Faith's House where you belong. You're their foster mother. Their role model. Their *savior*."

She closed her eyes for a long moment, fear battling with the sudden desire to do as Jesse asked, to go back to the kids, to be there when they needed a shoulder to cry on, to listen to their problems and their pasts, to help them—

She shook her head. "You've got the wrong person," she managed, though saying the words hurt with the effort. "I'm nobody's savior." Then she stood and walked inside.

"Wait—" Jesse hit the steps behind her, but Faith closed the door.

Tears flooded her eyes as she slumped back against the door and slid to the floor, her knees bunched against her chest.

A collage of images played through her mind, faces from the past, kids whose lives she'd touched so briefly, and it hadn't been enough. They'd found their way back to the streets. They hadn't wanted a savior, but Faith had kept going, kept trying.

But Jane had been different. . . .

Faith buried her face in her hands and let the memory return, almost eager to be reminded of her powerlessness, almost pleased to see the bald proof that Faith Jansen couldn't save anyone.

"Good morning, Faith." The nurse came up beside Faith, who stood in the hospital lobby waiting for the elevator, a stack of magazines clutched in her arms.

"Morning, Betty. Did you hear about yesterday?" The doors opened and Faith stepped into the elevator. The nurse followed.

"Can't say that I did." The doors closed and the nurse turned a questioning gaze to Faith. "It was my weekend off. I just came on duty. What happened?"

Faith couldn't hold back her smile. "She squeezed my hand."

"Oh, my! That's wonderful!" The nurse's smile eased some of the chill that had settled into Faith's bones over the past several days since Jane had been hit by the car. "You just keep on reading to her like I told you. That girl will come out of it yet. Four days isn't very long. I've seen 'em wake up after a month or more. You just keep the faith, honey."

Faith nodded. "I've got the latest issues of all her favorites right here. An afternoon with Teen Beat's hottest hunks and she'll be opening her eyes next."

A bell sounded and the doors opened to the third floor. The nurse stepped off the elevator and turned to Faith. "I bet the whole floor is buzzing about the breakthrough. I'll try to get up later on my break to see you. Congratulations!"

The doors swooshed closed. Faith leaned back against the wall and closed her eyes. Her smile broadened. She could still feel the slight pressure of Jane's fingers against her own. Just a faint movement, but enough to let Faith know the girl was still with her. Still alive. Still fighting.

Jane was a fighter, all right, and so was Faith. She wouldn't let the girl give up. It didn't matter that the doctors said Jane might never wake up, that her injuries were too severe, that she was just lingering until her poor body gave out completely.

There was always a chance. Hope. The hand squeeze proved it. Jane would beat the odds as she had when Faith had first met her. The girl had overcome a deep stab wound to the chest, healed after a lengthy surgery, and survived the nightmares that had followed. Jane had made it through then, and she would now. Faith would see to it. She would keep the faith.

The elevator doors opened again and Faith got off,

heading down the hallway of Ben Taub's trauma unit.

Yesterday a hand squeeze. Today . . . Maybe Jane would actually open her eyes. Maybe she would move her lips. Maybe she'd even say something—

The thoughts screeched to a halt when Faith reached the open doorway of Jane's room. Shock bolted through her as she stared at the empty hospital bed. She closed her eyes, praying she was seeing things. But the truth pounded at her, burrowing inside and killing all hope.

There were no familiar sounds: no hum of the respirator, no steady beat of the heart monitor, no morning talk show blaring from the television set. There was nothing but a chilling silence that sent goose bumps racing along her nerve endings.

"Ms. Jansen," came the deep, emotionless voice of Jane's doctor. "I've been trying to reach you all morning."

"Where is she?" Faith asked, the question no more than a rush of breath.

"Early this morning, I'm afraid . . ." He paused, the brief hesitation like the final seconds before an execution. "I'm afraid she just couldn't hold on any longer."

No! The cry exploded inside her head and shattered her control. Then came pain, gripping every inch of her body, squeezing her heart, strangling her soul. Not Jane!

But even as denial snaked through, the truth surrounded her in the stark white sheets of a newly made hospital bed, the soft, undisturbed purr of the air-conditioning, the stinging scent of the freshly sterilized tile floor, the small sack of stuffed animals and clothes that the doctor placed near her feet.

"Here are her things. I had hoped to talk with you before you found out this way. . . ." The doctor's

words faded into a blur as the magazines slipped from Faith's numb fingers. The floor started to tilt.

Her lungs burned with each breath. Her head throbbed. She clutched at the door frame to keep from falling, as if she could hold on to herself, to Jane.

But it was too late.

The knowledge beat at her brain until she wanted to cry, but the tears wouldn't come.

"She was wearing this," the doctor said. "I wanted to hand it to you myself. I was afraid it might get lost among all her other stuff."

"Aw, hell."

Jesse's soft words jarred Faith back to reality, to the floor where she sat, the door at her back, and the man on the other side. So close. She felt the pressure of the door against her shoulder blades and knew he sought to touch her, compelled her to open the door, throw herself into his arms, and cry out her troubles.

And everything would be all right.

Then she could go back to Faith's House. To her life—

But then the pain would come all over again. With some other child. Some other lost soul. The pressure against her back ceased and she knew Jesse had gone.

She forced her eyes open and climbed to her feet. Rushing into the bedroom, she hurried over to the jewelry box and threw back the lid. Nestled inside was a gold half circle attached to a matching chain.

She was wearing this. . . .

With trembling fingers, Faith picked up the piece of jewelry. It was a friendship circle, or rather half of one. The circle came cut in half to be shared between two friends. Jane had worn one half and given

the other to Faith as a present. As long as they each
wore their half, their friendship could never be broken, the bond between them could never be severed.

But half of the circle was buried now, and Jane
was dead. Faith hadn't been able to save her. Hope
and optimism and dogged determination had meant
nothing in the face of tragedy.

On that bitter note, Faith attached the chain
around her neck and dropped the half medallion beneath the neck of her shirt. A reminder, she told
herself, that she was no one's savior.

Yet as the metal nestled between her breasts, its
chill resting where her heart thumped furiously in
her chest, a sense of peace stole through her. Peace,
not bitterness or loneliness or grief.

Instead of being reminded of Jane's death, Faith
found herself remembering the girl's life—the way
she'd smiled and laughed and drunk soda out of her
Houston Rockets mug. And despite the tears
streaming down Faith's cheeks, a smile touched her
lips.

Chapter Twelve

An hour later, Jesse finished Faith's yard, put away the mower, and barely resisted the urge to break down her door, throw her over his shoulder, and physically drag her back to the shelter. He could have, except for his conscience, making him feel like the biggest jerk in the world. Who the hell was he to ask her to open herself up to the hurt again?

Even as the question raced through his mind, he damned himself. It didn't matter if she did wind up hurt, as long as he got his chance at heaven. At forgiveness. That was all that really mattered. He had himself to worry about. His own salvation.

He climbed onto his Harley, revved the engine, and took off. Damn the link between them. That was the problem. Every time he turned around, he was seeing into her thoughts, reliving her past, and it did something to him. The memories touched feelings he'd buried a long time ago, chipped at the wall he'd built around his heart. A wall so thick that no one could touch him or hurt him.

Except her.

A wave of anger swelled inside him and he nearly sent the bike into a tailspin as he swerved into the driveway at the foster home.

When Jesse strode into the kitchen, he found Bradley layering noodles, tomato sauce, and ricotta cheese into a casserole dish. The smell of oregano and garlic bread burned his nostrils, and he felt a momentary twinge of guilt for the poor dog next door. It was lasagna night. Again. Now *that* really topped off his day.

He collapsed into a kitchen chair, spread his legs out in front of him, and ran a tired hand over his face.

"How's Faith?" Bradley asked, pouring a can of tomato sauce into the dish.

"Out to set a record for most difficult female."

The counselor chuckled, added a layer of noodles and more sauce. "I see you two are getting to know each other pretty well. I've always been more the flowers-and-candy type myself. I never thought about home repair as a way to a woman's heart."

Jesse shrugged. "I'm not looking for a way to her heart."

"Then what, pray tell, are you doing over there every morning while I'm toughing it out at Daniel's therapy sessions?"

"Looking for a way to her conscience." A way to touch her, he added silently. All he needed was to find something in the world she wanted, something his miracle could give her.

But Faith didn't seem to want anything other than Jane, and though the miracle he had to give could breathe life into a dying man, resurrecting someone already dead was strictly off-limits.

"If her conscience is what you're after, I'd say you're on the right track. I nearly spilled a cup of punch when I saw her at the dance. I don't know how you coerced her into going, but I'm in awe."

"Don't go paying homage yet. She went to the dance, but it didn't do any good. She's still determined to stay away from the kids."

Bradley layered in cheese, then more noodles and sauce. "That's what she says, but I know Faith. If she was really set on staying away, you and a freight train couldn't have towed her to that dance. You said it yourself. She's stubborn. But she obviously misses the kids."

"Not enough."

"Not yet," Bradley said, glancing over his shoulder. "But she's coming around. Thanks to you. My only question"—Bradley paused to wipe his hands on a nearby dishtowel—"is why you? I'm the one who ought to be over there begging and pleading. If I thought it would work, I would be. I'm barely thirty-two and I'm going to be legally responsible for twelve kids if I sign Faith's papers."

"So don't sign them."

"I have to." Bradley sighed. "I couldn't turn my back on the kids and hand them over to a stranger. I'll sign, but I'd rather not. I want Faith back. I *need* her." He gave Jesse a pointed stare. "But you don't. You're not the one holding it all together, tossing and turning, worrying about dental appointments, grocery shopping, lunches, summer camp. So why are you so set on bringing her back?"

Jessie shrugged. "The kids miss her. They talk about her all the time. And she misses them. She nearly had a heart attack when I told her about

Ricky and Em's date. That was her motivation to go to the dance. She wanted to see what Emily was wearing for her date with Ricky."

Bradley laughed. "Sounds like Faith, all right."

"She's more unhappy away from them," Jesse went on. "But she refuses to admit it." He raked tense fingers through his hair and stared at the floor. He was at a complete dead end.

"Faith's stubborn," Bradley said as if reading his thoughts. "But she's worth the effort."

Worth a miracle, if Jesse could find something, anything he could give her, do for her, that would renew her faith and bring her back to the kids, and soon. In less than a week. Otherwise . . .

He shook his head. He didn't want to think about otherwise

"The dance," Bradley was saying, "was the first time she hasn't attacked me with those damned papers. In fact, I haven't even heard her mention them for nearly a week now, which has to mean she's coming around."

"Not fast enough."

"Give her time. Jane's death was hard on her. She misses the girl and she's nursing a lot of guilt over what happened, especially since she was standing right there."

Jesse stiffened, his gaze colliding with Bradley's. "She saw the accident?"

The man nodded. "Jane crossed the intersection maybe a yard or two in front of Faith. Five seconds more, and Faith would have been the one who got hit."

"Aw, *hell*." Jesse rubbed his throbbing temples.

"She's been a zombie since the death, but you're changing all that. I have to tell you, you're good with people. The kids and, of course, Faith. Just be patient with her."

If only things were that simple, but Jesse didn't have patience, much less time. Time was precious. His power was active for all of two weeks, half of which he'd already spent. Then he had to deliver the final product and move on to an eternity in heaven, or renege and spend the rest of his life in hell. This flesh-and-blood, living, breathing, frustrating hell.

"I didn't know she'd seen the accident," Jesse said, the words leaving a bad taste in his mouth. He closed his eyes, feeling her pain, her determination to stay indifferent, isolated. "No wonder."

"It doesn't seem fair, does it?" Bradley popped the casserole dish into the oven and set the timer. "The way life can turn on a dime, I mean. You go through the motions, play by the rules—do unto others and all that—then zap, something happens and you lose."

"Everybody loses," Jesse muttered. "There's no winning this game. The ones who make up the rules see to that." With insurmountable surprises.

"No argument here, but I'll tell you like I tell the kids; it isn't whether you win or lose; it's how you play."

"I'm tired of playing."

Bradley retrieved a soda from the refrigerator before sitting down at the table opposite Jesse. "Well, buddy, you haven't got a choice. None of us do. We're here, so we play." A slam of the front door punctuated his words, followed by a stream of voices. "Looks like we're on duty," he added as the first of a dozen kids barreled into the kitchen.

Dinner was chaos. Homework was a string of arguments. Bedtime was nearly a knock-down, dragout, and Jesse relished every minute of it. He never

209

completely forgot about Faith, but at least he had a distraction from her image dancing in his head, her voice whispering through his senses, her scent unraveling his concentration, her memories wreaking havoc on his determination.

When darkness fell, however, Jesse had to seek a different distraction. Or rather, the distraction sought him.

He was simply concerned about Trudy, he convinced himself as he parked his bike in a well-lit parking lot and walked the few blocks to his old apartment building. She was young and alone, hungry and cold, and he needed to check on her.

But deep down, Jesse knew the real reason he went inside. The past called to him, louder than his conscience, and he had to go back. To relive his memories and face who and what he'd been. To feed his hatred—the only thing that could completely distract him from what seemed an impossible mission with Faith.

"Trudy?" The apartment was entirely dark. Empty. Worry crept through him, until he saw the dark stain on the floor.

The bloody reminder of the life he'd once had. The memories rushed at him and he closed his eyes.

"Rachel," his voice was little more than a desperate croak. He blinked, trying to see his sister's face one last time. . . . No! It wouldn't be the last time. Jesse couldn't lose them both. Jason was already so still.

Jesse summoned his dying strength and focused. There. He could see her. Blood seeped from her chest. Her lips were slightly parted, her eyes open, her face expressionless. . . . No!

He blinked frantically, as if with each lift of his eye-

lids he would be more likely to see her smile, move, breathe, flinch—something, anything to let him know she was still alive. That her end hadn't come. Not hers. Not his little sister's—

A boot landed in Jesse's middle. Pain shot through him, a searing agony in his skull. His vision clouded and he sucked in a breath as two shadows hovered around him.

"That's for walking in on our deal and screwing things up, cop." Another kick, and blackness swamped the pain. "And that's for your no-good brother. He wanted out, so now he's out. Permanently." Laughter followed Jesse into oblivion, along with another vicious kick to his ribs. Bones cracked, but the pain was fleeting now. Unconsciousness was coming quickly.

"Leave him alone, man. He's dead. Man, this is bad news. You took out the girl, too. There was no need for that!"

No!

". . . take it easy, baby. We're almost there."

Jesse opened his eyes to the darkness and the sound of voices drifting from the hallway outside apartment 3B. His heart slammed against his ribs, his breathing quick and shallow and painful.

"Down here, baby."

"Forget it," came a stubborn female voice. "That place gives me the creeps. I ain't going in there."

"Come on . . ."

"I *ain't* going in there."

"All right, all right. Just chill, baby. I know this quiet spot on the second floor. I'll send you to the moon and you can get me off."

"Anywhere as long as it's not there. There's a ghost in that place."

"That's a load of crap. There ain't no ghosts in there."

Jesse walked out into the hallway and two pairs of eyes widened. He stared at the young teenage couple as they jerked to a stop several feet away. Anger raged through his veins, firing his body as hot as his blood.

"Holy Toledo . . . his eyes . . ." The boy stumbled backward.

"I told you," the girl shrieked, whirling to follow him. "I *told* you."

The couple scrambled for the stairs, and Jesse took a deep breath. He turned a fraction and caught his reflection in a fragment of broken window glass. Two pinpoints of white-hot light gleamed from his eyes, and he clamped them shut.

Control, he told himself, willing his body to cool, his mind to forget, his vision to return to normal. He had to stay in control. But even as he fought to keep his emotions in check, the anger raged inside him, demanding release. His need for vengeance warred with the light that lived and breathed inside the man now.

You took out the girl, too.

He stormed down the stairs, shoved open the door, and stumbled out onto the sidewalk.

In his mind, he saw the knife plunge down and pierce Rachel's arm. *One strike* . . . Another stab near her shoulder. *Two* . . . Then the blade sank into her chest. . . . *Three* . . .

You're out!

"Hey, buddy. Watch where the heck you're going—" The words died the moment Jesse's gaze fixed on the man he'd slammed into.

Well, if it ain't the nosy big-brother cop. Hey, cop? You want a piece of little brother's action? The words echoed in Jesse's memory as he stared at the familiar man. The air bolted from his lungs, a wave of rage burning through his body, like fire sweeping through dry brush, sucking up the oxygen.

He blinked. It couldn't be. . . . His mind rifled back through the past and he saw the man hovering over his own near-dead body, staring down at him with anxious, nervous eyes while his partner, the murderer, finished off his sister.

The past year had changed him little. The guy was still dirty-looking with long, greasy hair and red-rimmed eyes. Still nervous and anxious-looking. Still alive.

The last thought grated on Jesse's nerves as much as the man's hoarse voice.

"Holy mother—" the guy muttered, stumbling backward. "You—you're dead." Fear and shock held his eyes wide.

"No." Jesse gripped the man by the collar and hauled him close, until he smelled his sour whiskey breath. "You're the one who's dead." He slammed him up against the apartment building.

"But—but I saw it." The guy shook his head, his stubble-covered jaw chafing the back of Jesse's hand, a grating reminder against the tender scar. "I saw Bryan cut you, man. I *saw*."

Bryan . . . The name echoed in Jesse's head. Now his murderer had a name. Bryan. And Jesse had a way to find him. A way to quench the rage so close to boiling over inside him. Then he could focus on Faith, on his true mission. This was the reason for his failure so far. It wasn't Faith's stubbornness. It was Jesse's preoccupation; he'd been too angry and bitter over his own past to help anyone over theirs. Vengeance could soothe the anger, help him focus. *Bryan.*

"Where is he?"

The man shook his head, an incredulous look on his face. "I—this is crazy. You ain't really you." He started to laugh—a nervous, high-pitched laugh that rang with fear and the coke he'd probably been snorting. "You're dead, man." Another burst of laughter. "Dead!"

"Where?" Jesse demanded, tightening his grip on the man's collar. "Either you tell me where he is or I'll kill you right here, right now. Your choice. A choice I never had." Jesse's fingers closed around the man's throat and squeezed.

"The Dungeon," the man rasped, and Jesse loosened his grip enough to let him gasp for a breath.

"The Dungeon?"

"On the corner of Fifth and Travis. Late," the guy said, gulping. "You can find him there late"—he swallowed—"after ten or eleven when he finishes his rounds. He likes to kick back, down a few brews."

Jesse's fingers flexed, tightened, and the man's eyes bugged out.

"Don't," the guy pleaded. "I—I told you where Bryan is. Lemme go."

"You let him kill my brother and sister."

The guy shook his head frantically. "I—I didn't want no part of that. I tried to help her."

"You let him stab her after he did the same to my little brother! He killed them both and you watched. Dammit, you *watched*," he said in a hiss, fingers convulsing, tightening.

"But I didn't kill 'em, man, and I tried to set things right with the girl." He struggled, saliva trailing from the corner of his mouth. "I tried to help her. Bryan's the one who stabbed 'em both. You, too."

Bryan.

Jesse flung the man back against the brick building and whirled. The murderer's name pounded in his head like a war chant.

It was war. A war for Jesse's soul. For his peace of mind. For justice, and forgiveness.

"You're dead," the man's voice followed Jesse as he walked through the alley. "You ain't real. I saw you bleed. I saw you, man. You're dead."

He was, and so was Jason. Thanks to Bryan.

Jesse stormed down the street toward his motorcycle. The Dungeon was about ten minutes away. If he hurried, he could be there in time to pay good old Bryan a little visit.

He cut through another alley and picked up his pace, the scar on the back of his hand tingling. His body came alive then in remembrance. Six stab wounds, and each of the scars fired to life, sending shock waves of pain skidding across his nerve endings.

A life for a life.

In the far corner of his mind, he glimpsed Faith. She waited for him, calling to him, promising salvation.

But she was no one's savior. He'd seen that for himself. He'd felt her hopelessness. And he didn't blame her for retreating, for giving up her work. He tasted the same bitterness, like a mouthful of sea-water burning his tongue, choking him. It wasn't fair. Dammit, it wasn't fair—

A small cry pushed past the roar in Jesse's ears, and he came to a dead stop. A bare bulb flickered nearby, sending skittering shadows across the muddy, garbage-lined alley just to his left. The heartbreaking sound continued, carrying from the far end, niggling at his conscience despite the turmoil inside him, and he couldn't resist.

He moved deeper into the alley, his gaze searching the narrow dimness. With every step the noise grew louder. A whimper here, a sniffle there. Then he saw her.

Trudy was slumped against a brick wall, her nose bloodied, her eyes puffy. Her guitar lay broken beside her.

His rage dissolved the instant he saw the tear trickle down her bruised face. The past faded into a blur and there was only now. The present. The poor girl broken and bleeding and calling out to him.

"What happened?" He reached her in three long strides, boots stomping trash and muck, and hunkered down in front of her.

"Jesse? Is that you?" She stared at him through eyes no wider than slits.

"Yeah, honey. It's me. What happened?"

"They"—she swallowed, struggling for a breath—"beat . . . me up for my . . . my shoes."

His gaze went to her bare feet and something twisted inside him.

"They took your letterman's jacket, too, and the money I had left."

"It doesn't matter, honey. All that matters is you're still alive." With gentle hands, he examined her face. She winced and grunted several times, and he frowned. "I've got to get you to a hospital."

"No!" She struggled against his hands, pushing him away all the while fighting to sit up.

"But you're hurt."

"They'll—the hospital—they'll turn me in," she managed after a deep gulp of air. She shook her head, her face contorting with the effort. "Nothin's broken. They just punched my, ugh"—she grimaced, touching a tender hand to her puffy cheek—"my face a few times. I'll be all right. Honest."

Jesse checked her arms, legs, ribs, moving her this

way and that to make sure she was telling the truth before he took a thorough look at her face. "Your eyes are pretty bad. Can you see?"

"Yeah . . ." She felt for his face. "Well, maybe not so good."

He muttered a curse. "We're getting out of here."

"If you could help me back to my place . . . the apartment . . ."

"Forget it. You need rest, some ice for your eyes, and somebody to clean those cuts." He gathered her in his arms.

"No!" She fought him, but Jesse wasn't about to leave her alone again, fresh pickings for the scum who roamed the alleys and the abandoned buildings. "Just leave me alone. I don't need any help. I'm fine. . . ."

He hoisted her up over his shoulder, his arms firm but gentle, and navigated back to where his motorcycle was parked.

"I told you to leave me be, dammit!" She pounded his back, ranted at him, and sucked air in painful gasps. "You ain't my boss."

"No," Jesse said, depositing her on the seat. He climbed behind her before she could scramble off, and kicked the bike to life. "I'm your friend, and I'm a helluva lot bigger and meaner than you. So settle down."

"Fat chance. I ain't going to no hospital." Trudy struggled, her efforts useless with Jesse's arm locked around her waist. But she tried anyway. She was so desperate, so spirited. So much like Rachel.

"We're not going to the hospital."

Her movements paused. "Then where?"

"To salvation," he replied, sending the motorcycle speeding forward. "Yours, and mine."

*   *   *

"I'm coming." Faith peeked past the curtains before throwing open her front door. "My God, what happened?"

Jesse stepped inside, a bruised and battered teenage girl cradled in his arms. "Somebody beat her up. She's got lacerations to the face, bruising—do you have a first-aid kit?"

Faith nodded. "Bring her in here." She led him to the spare bedroom that had only recently housed all of Jane's belongings. "Lay her down." Faith motioned to the double bed adorned with a red and gold patchwork quilt.

While Jesse settled the girl upon the bed, Faith retrieved a large tackle box marked with a bright red cross on the handle, a bowl of warm water, and some washcloths.

"Let me get a good look." She pushed Jesse aside and went to work, gently bathing Trudy's face with a cloth before applying ointment and a bandage here, another there.

"How bad is she?" He hovered over her shoulder, a worried look on his face, and Faith had the overwhelming urge to pull him into her arms.

"She's bad, but not too bad. Nothing life-threatening." She reached for a fresh washcloth.

After several more minutes of bathing and doctoring, she closed her medical kit and reached for an oversize T-shirt and thick socks she'd retrieved from her bedroom. "Go on into the living room," she told Jesse, ushering him from the bedroom, "while I help her get changed."

The door closed and Faith turned to the battered girl.

"I'll be fine in my own clothes," the girl mumbled, her slitted, puffy gaze fixed somewhere to Faith's right.

"If your vision isn't better by morning"—Faith walked toward the bed, a watchful eye on the girl— "I'm taking you to the doctor."

"Like hell," the girl muttered, her gaze still riveted in the direction Faith had come from. "I see all right."

"Oh, yeah?" Faith asked.

The girl jumped, her gaze swerving to the side of the bed where Faith now stood. "So it's not great now, but it'll get better."

"I hope so, but if not, we're hitting the clinic."

"I don't like clinics. Or doctors."

"The worst that'll happen is he'll give you a shot, some antibiotics."

The girl laughed, her face twisting into a distorted puzzle of bruises. "And I could find myself hand-cuffed to some social worker, on my way to a place worse than the one I came from. No, thanks. I'll do fine on my own."

"You could always go blind," Faith said, sinking down onto the edge of the mattress. "Think you could survive on your own then?"

The girl's frown twinged with worry and she gave Faith a wary glance. "But I ain't got no money."

"I'm paying."

"Why?"

"Because you're a friend of a friend, and friends help each other out. Now try to sit up so we can get you out of these clothes." She reached for the girl with gentle, practiced hands.

"How is she?" Jesse asked a half hour later when Faith sank down on the couch next to him, the girl's tattered clothes bundled in her lap.

"Sound asleep. She all but passed out before I even finished helping her off with her socks. She was tired." She slanted a glance at him. The living room was lost in shadow, the only light the play of the street lamp sifting through the blinds. Slats of yellow played across his dark profile, giving his features a harsh edge.

"So who is she?" Faith asked.

"Just a kid I met last week. Her name's Trudy. I don't know about a last name. She's on her own. Lives in an abandoned apartment building over off Elgin."

"How do you know her?"

"It's my old building." He slumped back against the couch and closed his eyes. "Where I used to live when I first moved to Houston. I haven't been there for the past year, and I went back to see what had happened to it. And there she was."

"You should have called CPS."

"I promised her I wouldn't. Besides, it wouldn't have done any good. She would have taken off and ended up in another building, in another part of town. At least this way I could keep an eye on her. I took her some food and a blanket the night before last, and the phone number for Faith's House."

"Let me guess." She leaned back and surveyed him. "She told you to go to hell, right?"

"Not in so many words, but yes." He passed a hand over his eyes, looking tired and drained. "She's been through a lot. She hasn't said much, but from what I can figure, her mother is a junkie and a prostitute. No father. I don't know about brothers and sisters. She doesn't seem to have anybody."

"So you're playing the hero?"

"I'm nobody's hero, Faith." He leaned down, forearms resting on his thighs as he clasped his hands together. He looked extremely weary all of a sudden. So . . . vulnerable. The strength that normally cloaked him seemed to slip away and she saw the man beneath. A weary, frightened man.

"I'm about as far away from a hero as you can get," he muttered. "Trouble. That's what my mother used to call me. 'Here comes trouble,' she'd say. 'Just like your father.'"

"And what did your father say?"

"Not much. He was drunk most of the time. They both were. Then when my mother got pregnant with my little sister, my dad split. He couldn't take care of two kids—me and my kid brother—much less three." He laughed, a bitter sound that brought tears to Faith's eyes. "My mother was so drunk, she didn't even notice he'd left for near a week."

"Drunk and pregnant?"

"Good old Mom." For all the sharpness to his words, his voice trembled.

"Thankfully Restoration is a real small town," he went on after a moment of silence. "The sort of place where everybody knows everybody else's business. Anyhow, when my dad left, a few of the church ladies stepped in to help. They got my mother to sober up, at least for the duration of her pregnancy. It was a miracle, but my sister was born without any complications or problems. Then my mother went back to drinking while I took care of my brother and sister."

"How old were you?"

"Just turned fourteen."

"You were taking care of a newborn at fourteen?"

He nodded. "And a toddler. My brother was two."

"What about the ladies from church? Did they help?"

"Mom crawled back into a bottle, drunk and unappreciative. They washed their hands of her. And us."

"I can't believe they didn't call CPS."

"They did. A county case worker came out to our place a couple of times. But the visits always seemed to be on my mom's good days. She seemed halfway normal; the kids were fed and clothed. The house was small, but clean."

"So they stopped coming?"

He nodded. "I kept everything together, everybody, for the next few years. I kept thinking if I held on a little longer, my mom would come around. She couldn't ignore her kids, right?" He shook his head. "But after that she drank harder, heavier, until one day she passed out and never woke up." He covered his face with his hands for a long moment. "That was close to five years after my dad left. I was eighteen. Jason was six and Rachel was four."

"That's terrible." Her hand covered his shoulder, feeling the tightness of his muscles, the tension that thrummed through him.

"It was the worst day of my life," he went on. "I remember standing there, staring at her grave, begging her to come back." A harsh laugh passed his lips. "I don't know why. She was never really there anyway, but at least while she was alive, I never felt quite so alone. As long as she lived, there was hope." He laughed again. "Stupid, huh? But I was just a kid, and there I was looking at her casket, and it was so . . . final." He raked tense fingers through his hair, his muscles rippling from the movement, drawing tighter, stiffer beneath Faith's hand.

"I'm sorry, Jesse."

"Don't be," he muttered after a drawn-out moment of silence. "Things were actually easier after that. No more watching my mother kill herself. She was gone and so the three of us got on with living. I quit school, took a job as a mechanic, and supported my brother and sister. In the meantime I finished my senior year in night school, then went on to night classes at a local college."

"That sounds pretty heroic to me."

"I'm no hero, Faith. Far from it." He grew quiet, his gaze fixed on the play of shadows across the carpet. "I let them down when they needed me most," he finally said, his voice quiet, raw. "They didn't want to leave Restoration, but I made them. We had to. There were no jobs there, certainly no room for advancement. No future. So I brought them here." He turned to her then, and the pain glazing his eyes touched her like a vise squeezing her heart. "But there was still no future because they were killed a few months after we arrived."

"Oh, Jesse . . ." She slid her arms around him, pulling him tight, desperate to take away his pain as surely as he'd taken hers, shared it, that first time he'd kissed her.

"It was my fault." His arms snaked around her and he hugged her so fiercely she had trouble drawing her next breath. "I brought them here, and now they're dead."

"But how? What happened to them?" She stroked his hair, her fingertips skimming the silken strands, stroking his neck, his jaw, his cheeks—

The drop of wetness hit her knuckle, slid down over her palm, and her heart crumbled.

"It's okay," she whispered. "It wasn't your fault. I'm sure—" Her reassurance fell short as he abruptly released her and pulled away. She glimpsed a streak of wetness on his face; then he bolted to his feet, his back to her as he moved toward the door.

"Don't go, Jesse. Talk to me. Finish what you started."

He shook his head. "I need to get out of here."

"Why did you bring Trudy here?" Her question stopped him in the doorway, his hand on the knob. "Why didn't you take her to Bradley?"

"He would have called CPS," he said without turning around. "I promised her I would help, no strings attached."

"What makes you so sure I won't call CPS?"

"Because you know she'll run and you don't want that." She saw his fingers tighten on the doorknob. "You want to help her."

"You're wrong there. I don't want to help her. I don't want to help anybody."

He turned on her then, his dark, turbulent gaze colliding with hers. "So why didn't you slam the door on us?"

"I should have."

"But you didn't. You care a hell of a lot more than you let on. Admit it, Faith." His voice was low and angry, his expression fierce as he stalked toward her, stopping inches away. His fingers flexed, as if he wanted nothing more than to wrap them around her shoulders and shake some sense into her. "You *do* care. It's who you are. You couldn't turn your back on Trudy. It goes against everything you believe in. Admit it, Faith. Just *admit* it!"

She met his glare, her words soft, quiet. "Okay, I admit it. I do care, but it's not what you think. I didn't open the door for Trudy. I opened it for you. I care about you, Jesse. *You.*"

And then she turned and walked into the bedroom, shutting the door behind her. Sweat slid down her temples, between her breasts, the air stifling despite the hum of the air conditioner. Rushing to the window, she slid the glass up and welcomed the slight breeze that curled into the room.

Resting her forehead against the glass, Faith

closed her eyes and did her damnedest not to react to the sound of the front door slamming shut.

She flinched, though, and as always when Jesse Savage walked away from her, a sadness swept through her. A police car roared by, its siren wailing, echoing the lonely cry of her heart.

Regret welled inside her. Had she actually confessed that she cared for him? When she'd sworn never to care for anyone again?

This was different. She'd refused to get involved with kids again, but this was Jesse. Kind, considerate, sexy as sin Jesse who made her feel things no man ever had.

She wiped at a drop of sweat sliding down her collarbone, and her arm brushed the sensitive tip of one nipple. Electricity shot through her. Her body thrummed, her senses still alive from being so close to him.

But it wasn't simply her body that missed him. It was her heart, as well. He'd opened up to her, shared a piece of himself, and she couldn't help but want more.

Foolish, she knew, because Jesse Savage had made it painfully clear that he wasn't the man for her, not physically or emotionally.

"You should have locked the door in my face." His deep voice rumbled in her ear, shattering her thoughts. His warm breath teased the curve of her neck, and Faith turned to find Jesse Savage standing directly behind her.

Very close, and very naked.

Chapter Thirteen

Faith went rigid, instantly alert to the powerful presence directly behind her, seemingly surrounding her.

He'd walked up behind her and she hadn't heard a thing. No footsteps. No sound of the door opening and closing. Nothing, as if he'd floated through the wall and into the room—

The siren had covered it. Of course! A giddy sense of relief tingled through her.

"You should have turned me away, for both our sakes." He touched her then, just the light caress of his fingertips up her bare arms before his warm hands closed over her shoulders. "You and me, it's no good."

Faith held her breath, afraid he would turn and walk away. As always.

"I know that," he went on, as if trying to convince himself—even now, even naked and touching her, and so close to doing more. "I tell myself over and over that there can't be anything between us, there shouldn't be, but here I am anyway. And I'm so tired of fighting. So damned tired." His grip tightened. His fingers burned into her, branded her. "I shouldn't feel this way about you, about anyone."

"It's because I'm incredibly beautiful," she offered, her tone light, teasing, her words meant to ease the sudden anguish in his voice.

"It's more than that," he told her seriously.

"Sexy?"

"More."

"I'm both, a double whammy, so you can't keep your hands off me."

"I can't keep my *mind* off you. You're all I think about. All I breathe. All I hear." He nuzzled her ear then, his deep voice sending ripples of goose bumps up and down her skin. "All I can think about is being inside you, feeling you around me, sucking at me, making me so crazy I can't think straight."

Then Jesse slid his hands down her arms in a seductive caress that sent the blood thrumming through her veins. He encircled her rib cage, cupped the full weight of her breasts, and Faith's teasing faded into a low moan.

He caught her nipples and worried the sensitive nubs. His fingers scorched through the thin fabric of her nightgown to send sizzles of heat pulsing through her body.

"You feel so good." He rolled the tender peaks until they were erect and throbbing and it was all Faith could do to keep from crying out.

Then his hands fell to her thighs. His fingers bunched the fabric until she felt his touch against her bare skin. The next few seconds passed in an impatient blur as he pushed her panties down. His foot caught the scrap of underwear at her calves and shoved the lace to her ankles. She stepped free just as his arms came around her waist. He cupped her sex, his fingers parting the silky folds to explore every steamy secret.

Her breath caught as he slid one finger deep inside her. Instinctively, she tightened around him and he groaned.

"I've felt you like this, seen you so many times in my head." His lips moved against her ear, his tongue tracing the outline to dip inside. "I thought about what it would be like between us. How warm and wet you would be." He slid another finger into her and a low moan burst from her lips. "How tight."

He worked her then, moving inside her, stroking, plunging. He knew just how to touch her—how to push himself deep until the air lodged in her throat and her senses flooded with sensation. When she knew she couldn't take any more, he withdrew, just enough to let her catch her breath; then the exquisite agony started all over again.

"Please . . ." The word was a ragged gasp of air as her hands clawed at his forearms.

"Once," she heard him murmur, the words barely audible over the thunder of her heart, the rush of blood through her veins. "I need to feel you like this, under me, around me, just this once and then I can get you out of my system. I *can*."

Another deft move of his fingers and she came apart in his arms. It was quick and mind-shattering. Shudders vibrated through her body, skimming along her ragged senses in wave after wave of sweet sensation. She slumped back against him, weak and damp, her breath raspy, her heartbeat a frenzied rhythm in her ears.

He caught a drop of perspiration at her temple

with the seductive glide of his tongue. But it wasn't the contact that stalled the air in her lungs. It was his voice.

"No one's ever really cared about me before."

She opened her eyes then and caught a glimpse of his face in the window. She saw the streak of moisture on his cheek, just as surely as she heard the catch in his voice.

"My brother and sister, yes. But no one else. *No one.*"

Jesse watched her reflection in the window, his gaze fixed on the flash of emotion in her eyes at his raw admission. She cared about him, *really* cared. It was there, evident in her gaze, and he felt a hand reach inside him and tear at his heart.

Pleasure washed through him, and at the same time he wanted to drop to his knees and rage at fate for letting this happen. It was so unfair. Faith needed to care again, but not about him. About anyone but him! This relationship could only bring her pain and heartache in the future. Loneliness.

He couldn't do this, he realized with a tortured heart. He wouldn't. He moved to pull away from her, but she grabbed his hand and placed a kiss on his palm. It was a featherlight gesture, but it struck him more fiercely than a gulf hurricane ripping apart a sailboat.

He knew then that she wasn't worried about the future. Faith was anchored in the here and now, and she wanted him.

Here. Now.

Though he knew he could bring her only sadness later on, he could give her heaven at this moment. Pure, blissful heaven. And maybe, just maybe, it would be enough to sate him, to get her out of his system. His body would be satisfied, his mind free and clear to pursue his mission. Maybe . . .

She trailed her lips over his palm before drawing his finger into the warmth of her mouth. She suckled him and Jesse closed his eyes as need hit him like a solid punch to the stomach, and *maybe* faded into dead certainty.

He groaned, his arousal throbbing, pressing between her buttocks, hot and desperate for entry.

"Wait—" she started. "I—I'm on the pill, but we should really use something . . . " Her words trailed off and he felt her embarrassment, almost as fiercely as she felt her desperation, her need.

"I haven't been with anyone in a long, long time. I won't hurt you Faith. I can't."

His eyes opened and he caught his reflection in the window. Two pinpoints of white light gleamed back at him.

"Jesse." Faith sighed, a heartbeat before she tried to turn her body into his.

"No!" His hands locked around her waist, anchoring her in front of him. He blinked, frantically trying to force the light away, but he couldn't.

The knowledge of what he was stared back at him, a glaring reminder of why he shouldn't do this, now, with this woman.

"Just once," he murmured the plea. *Just once*.

"What is it?" She tried to face him. "What's wrong—"

"Ssshhh," he murmured. He kept her from turning as he urged her away from the window, toward the wall. "I want you to feel me. Just close your eyes and feel me." He positioned her arms slightly above her head, flattening her forearms against the wall from elbows to fingertips. The position bent her at the waist, her bottom raised in undeniable invitation.

"But I need to see you, too." She wiggled against

him, and a groan echoed deep in his throat. "Please."

"You see me perfectly." He leaned over her and kissed her temple. "In your mind"—his breath ruffled the silken strands of her hair—"where it counts." He swept his hand across her belly, up over her breast, his palm gliding over her nipple to rest atop the furious thud of her heart. "In here," he added. "And"—one hand gripped her waist as he entered her—"*here*." His other arm locked around her, anchoring her for a full upward thrust until he was buried to the hilt.

The blood drummed so loudly in his ears, he barely heard her gasp of pleasure, her sob for more. Her body was warm and ripe, milking him even though they were both standing so perfectly still. For several deep, shallow breaths, he just stood there, relishing the sensation.

Then she shifted, swaying her hips this way, then that, and where the husky sound of her voice hadn't been enough to jar him from the pleasure of being buried inside Faith Jansen, the movement drew him back to reality. To the woman whose bottom strained against him, and to the fierce throbbing in his loins. And suddenly standing still wasn't nearly good enough.

He began to move, working in and out. Pleasure splintered his brain with each furious thrust, then a slow, breath-stopping withdrawal. In and out, fast and slow, until Jesse hovered at the brink of explosion.

She came quickly, crying his name as violent tremors racked her body. He followed her, spending himself into the moist heat that gripped him so tightly.

So perfectly . . .

She slumped against him, limp and immobile, her

eyes closed, her lips parted, her breathing quick and frantic. He scooped her up and placed her on the bed.

The nightgown rode up on her hips, revealing a triangle of rich brown curls damp with the evidence of their coupling. His gaze fixed on a single drop of moisture, like mother-of-pearl on a bed of dark silk. He watched the liquid as it drip-dropped, gliding down her creamy skin to disappear between her legs.

Desire clawed at his belly and a bitter smile twisted his lips. He was an idiot. He'd hoped that once would be enough to slake his hunger and get her out of his system, off his mind. Just once . . .

It wasn't nearly enough. Even now, only minutes after the best sex he'd ever had in his life, he wanted more. More of the sweet heat between her legs. More of her soft panting echoing in his ears. More of her warmth seeping into him, thawing the ice around his heart.

More . . .

"Jesse?" Her lazy eyes drifted open and she stared up at him.

Their gazes locked, her eyes widened in shock, and Jesse knew even before he chanced a glance in the dresser mirror what had caused her reaction.

His eyes gleamed with a fierce white light. Hot, consuming, and so damned revealing.

He whirled away from her and snatched up his jeans. He slid them on with lightning speed, grabbed his shirt, and headed for the door before she could force her passion-lazy limbs into motion.

"Jesse, wait! Are you all right?"

Wood creaked, hinges groaned; then he was through the living room, off the front porch. Outside, he shrugged into his shirt, not bothering with the buttons, and straddled the motorcycle. The engine rumbled to life.

Then he fled.

Away from Faith.

Away from his conscience.

And away from the damnable truth that it wasn't just *her* feelings that locked them together. She wasn't the only one who cared. He did, as well. He really cared for her.

Damn.

"Damn," Faith said in a hiss, frustration and anger and something dangerously close to regret fueling her voice. She sat on the bed, unwilling to chase him. "Damn, damn, *damn* him!"

But more than Jesse, Faith damned herself.

For letting him touch her in the first place, and for wanting it more than she'd ever wanted anything before. The fierceness of her desire startled her. She'd never felt such hunger for a man. There was something unnatural about it, about him.

Jesse's headlight flicked on, sending a play of shadows across the room, and she remembered his eyes, the unusual brightness, the brilliant light. . . .

Yes, a play of shadows. That was all it had been. Just the reflection of a passing car's headlights. That explained what she'd seen when she'd gazed up into his eyes, but what about what she'd felt?

The heat . . . A delicious heat calling her forward, hypnotizing her, promising so much, everything, if she would just reach out to that light—

A screech cut into her thoughts as a car skidded to a stop at a nearby intersection. She slumped against the pillows and strained her ears to hear the fading roar of Jesse's motorcycle. But it was too late. He was too far away. Gone. As always.

She blinked against the sudden stinging at the backs of her eyelids. If only she didn't care that he'd rushed away, turned his back, and left her cold and lonely.

Ah, but she wasn't cold. A lingering warmth gripped her senses, her nipples still erect, her insides still clenching and unclenching as if he were still deep inside her.

Her eyes burned with renewed vigor. She ached to touch him, to absorb his warmth, as if she knew on an instinctive level that he could rekindle the fire of life inside her that had dwindled.

As he'd done only moments ago, before he'd left her.

She dashed away a traitorous tear and hugged the pillow against her aching breasts. It wasn't as if he'd promised her anything. No tomorrows, he'd said.

She could live with that, she told herself, forcing away her tears. No tomorrows. No soft words, no tender kisses, no promises. Just down-and-dirty sex. Two people satisfying their basic instincts. Two mutually consenting adults.

No tomorrows.

With that thought in mind, Faith closed her eyes and concentrated on sleep. Instead, she tossed and turned until the first rays of dawn crept over the windowsill and the shrill ring of the telephone saved her from her misery.

She snatched up the receiver on the second ring.
"Hello?"

"Ms. Jansen?"

"Speaking."

"This is Dr. Stevens, Daniel's doctor. I hate to call you so early in the morning, but I needed to speak with you before I leave my office for my hospital rounds."

"Uh-huh." She struggled to her elbows and blinked her tear-swollen eyes.

"I needed to speak with you," the doctor went on, "regarding my early therapy session with Daniel. Let's see, it's five-forty-five right now . . . Can you be here by nine this morning?"

"I'm sorry. I'm not participating in Daniel's therapy. You'll have to talk to Bradley Winters. He's acting as Daniel's guardian right now."

"Actually, he's not," the doctor informed her. "My paperwork shows you as acting guardian."

Faith closed her eyes, picturing the blue-bound documents lying on the bookshelf in her living room. *Unsigned* documents.

"I've had a very hard time trying to get past Daniel's shell," the doctor went on. "To be honest, I've had no luck at all. He won't even talk to me, or anyone, for that matter, including Mr. Winters, who has attended each session. We're up against the wall and frankly, Miss Jansen, we need a bulldozer. An emotional bulldozer," the doctor added. "You've got quite a reputation with troubled kids. I could certainly use your expertise on this."

"I'm sure there are people much more qualified. Besides, I doubt Daniel will open up to me." She remembered the hatred simmering in the boy's eyes. Not pain, but hatred, directed straight at her. "The last time I saw him, he told me to get lost."

"But at least he told you *something*. He hasn't said a word in the five days he's been here. Please, Miss Jansen. I really think you could help. He's a very troubled boy."

Get out of here. Leave me alone. Daniel's words echoed in Faith's head, tugging at the heart she'd buried so deeply she'd thought no one could unearth it ever again.

235

"I . . ." *can't* was there on the tip of her tongue, but it would go no farther. It just sat there, stubborn. Immovable.

"For Daniel," the doctor added.

The boy's image pushed into her mind, and Faith heard the words coming out of her mouth before she could stop them.

"All right. I'll be there." She hung up and cradled her pounding head in her hands, her heart beating double time.

What had she just done?

"What do you want me to do?" Faith's gaze swept the therapy room, from the desk sitting off to one side, to the circle of chairs at the center. Cracked linoleum supported her feet as she stepped deeper into the room, all the while ignoring the urge to bolt back down the corridor, through the double doors, and out into the morning sunshine.

What was she doing? The thought pounded through her head just as the doctor captured her elbow and led her to the circle of chairs.

"Just make yourself comfortable." He abandoned her to retrieve a clipboard from the desk. "I want to thank you so much for coming, Ms. Jansen. I hope today's session will be the breakthrough we need."

Faith sank down in one of the chairs while Dr. Stevens, a fifty-something professional dressed in khaki slacks and a matching polo shirt, sat in a chair across from her. He looked like he should be holding a nine iron instead of a medical chart. His casual dress soothed her nerves a little and she unclenched her fingers from the straps of her purse. She smoothed the edges of her skirt down over her knees.

"I've read Daniel's case history with CPS and I have to say I'm not surprised at his behavior.

Mother committed suicide when he was only four years old, and he was abandoned by his father shortly after. He grew up on the streets, in and out of juvenile homes, arrested on a number of drug and theft charges." He shook his head. "And a family history of substance abuse. My first guess when he was brought here was that he was high on something, but blood tests have revealed absolutely nothing in his bloodstream. He's clean as a whistle, but . . ." He scratched his temple. "It's the damnedest thing."

"What is?"

"Well, we've been giving him a prescribed medication to help his depression, but routine blood work reveals no trace of it. I have someone monitoring him twenty-four hours a day, so we know he's swallowing it. I mean, he has to be, but if he were, then we'd find some trace of it in his bloodstream. Right?"

"Sounds reasonable."

"Zilch," he said. "Not a trace. He has to be ditching the medication, but my staff and I can't figure out how or where."

"Kids like Daniel are smart, Dr. Stevens. If there's one thing I've learned over the past five years at Faith's House, it's never to underestimate them, no matter what they look or act like. Just because they lack formal education doesn't mean they aren't as streetwise as they come."

"Amen." Bradley's voice carried from the doorway, and Faith turned to see the counselor as he walked into the room. Worry had deepened the lines around his eyes. Responsibility had furrowed his forehead. He looked tired, drawn.

A sliver of guilt worked its way through Faith, and her gaze dropped to her purse and the papers folded inside. Her reason for being here, she reminded herself. She'd convinced herself of that as she'd stood in the doorway at home watching Trudy sleep. The girl had seemed so young and helpless. So needy.

She was needy, but she would just have to need someone other than Faith. So would Daniel. They all would. She couldn't do it anymore. Rather than call and cancel with Dr. Stevens, she'd decided this would be the perfect opportunity to break ties altogether. She intended to get Bradley's signature once and for all, and be done with Faith's House.

She stiffened and took a deep breath. Bradley was tired and drawn by choice. He could walk away if he wanted to. No one was forcing him to stay or to care.

"It's good to see you." Bradley dropped into the seat next to Faith. "A real surprise, but then you've been surprising me a lot lately. I almost dropped my punch when I saw you at the dance. You and Jesse are getting to be . . . pretty close."

Heat crept through Faith to settle in all the wrong places and she stared down at her hands. "We get along."

"Just get along? This is Bradley you're talking to, Faith. I know you better than that. You don't just 'get along,' not when it comes to men. In fact, I've never seen you with a man. You turned down all Mike's dinner invitations."

"He's younger than me."

"By three years, and that's nothing. And you don't so much as glance sideways at Mitch Walker, Estelle's assistant, and he's had the hots for you since you faced off with him about getting Ricky's probation reduced. Admit it, you and Jesse are getting along pretty darn well."

"Look, Bradley—"

"Speak of the devil," Bradley cut in, staring over his shoulder.

Faith knew it was Jesse even before she turned around.

The hairs on the back of her neck stood at attention and an answering wave of heat rolled across her.

"What are you doing here?" she asked as he came up beside her.

"I invited him," the doctor offered. "Daniel needs all the help he can get." He motioned everybody into their seats while three orderlies ushered Daniel into the room.

The boy jerked to a dead stop when he saw Faith. He stared at her; then his gaze dropped to her neck and he smiled—a slow, evil smile meant to intimidate, to frighten.

Sympathy plucked at Faith's heart, but she stiffened, fixing her mind on the papers. She would sit through this session, then talk to Bradley. Period. No participation. No involvement. No risk.

"That's fine," the doctor said when the orderlies had steered Daniel to a vacant chair. The doctor sat next to the boy, Bradley on Daniel's other side. "Now, Daniel. We're all here today because we care about you." He patted the boy's hand, which protruded from the white cast on his broken arm. "You have a lot of problems, but we want you to know that we understand. That we can help you, if you let us . . ."

He went on for the next half hour in a monotonous droning that was wasted on Daniel. The boy sat in stony, belligerent silence, his unblinking gaze fixed up on his lap, his wiry body slumped in the chair.

He didn't change position, didn't shift his pale blue gaze, nothing.

"We need to share our thoughts. Why don't you go first, Bradley."

Bradley's voice echoed through the room as he talked about his job at Faith's House, what he liked and didn't like. Then he passed the gauntlet to Jesse.

Jesse talked about Ricky and Emily and the others at Faith's House, and how Daniel would fit in if he just gave the place a chance.

It wasn't so much what he said that struck a chord inside Faith. It was the way he said it. His deep voice resonated with so much sincerity that Faith felt her eyes burn.

She blinked frantically, counting the lines in the wallpaper. No attachment, no risk. *No tomorrows.*

It was better this way. She couldn't have a future with a man as committed to the kids as she used to be. It would only remind her of the past. Of Jane—

"Faith? Are you with us?"

She blinked. "Uh, Yes."

"It's your turn. Share your thoughts with us. Tell us about Faith. What makes her tick?"

"I . . . Let's see . . . I like pizza, Mel Gibson movies. I hate to exercise . . ." She went on about likes and dislikes in a superficial speech that lasted all of forty-five seconds.

"Deep, Faith. Really deep," Bradley muttered for Faith's ears only. Then he glared.

She chanced a peek at Jesse and wished she'd kept her eyes glued to the wallpaper. He looked . . . murderous.

So her answers hadn't been exactly what the doctor had had in mind. They would just have to do. She couldn't begin to verbalize the turmoil inside her, nor did she want to. She felt too many things.

The realization brought a hysterical laugh to her

lips. How had she gone from feeling nothing to feeling so much in such a short time?

She wanted to feel again; that wasn't the problem. She just didn't want to hurt. She wanted only good feelings. Safe ones.

No attachment. No risk.

"Well, now, Ms. Jansen," the doctor remarked after a thoughtful second. "That was very . . . insightful." He turned to Daniel. "We're all friends here, Daniel," he went on. "We've trusted you with our feelings; now you need to do the same."

Silence closed in as they waited. And waited.

The urge to reach out, to take his bony hands in hers and warm them hit her like a Mack truck. One minute she was watching the clock, and the next she felt a pull, a desperation stirring inside her, looking for an outlet. For Daniel.

He was cold. And scared. She knew on a gut level and every instinct screamed for her to lean forward. She could reach him so easily. Just a shift in her seat, a stretch of her arms, and she could ease his fear and his chill.

"Come on, Daniel," came the doctor's voice, like a dousing of cold reality.

Then as quickly as it had stirred, the urge to comfort fell silent. Unanswered. *Thank goodness.*

Faith forced her attention from Daniel and concentrated on breathing slowly, evenly, which wasn't very easy to do with Jesse right beside her. It wasn't enough that his jean-covered thigh rested so close to her. To make matters worse, he glanced at her every few minutes. She felt his gaze, a caressing pass of warmth that heated her cheeks, her shoulders, the hands she clasped tightly in her lap—everywhere that he looked.

Even more disturbing images fought their way

into her head, only to be quickly shoved out. She had to relax. Like a bad visit to the dentist, this would all be over in a matter of minutes.

"We all want to help you, Daniel. We want to be your friends, if you'll just let us. But you have to talk to us. Let us inside," the doctor was saying, all the while Faith stared at the clock. Five more minutes.

Then she could corner Bradley, get his signature.

Five . . . Four . . .

". . . Bradley and the other kids will be there for you once you leave the hospital, if you want them to be. You have to give a little, Daniel. Talk to us. Tell us what you're thinking."

Three.

"There's an entire world waiting for you. I know your past, Daniel, where and what you come from, but you'll be surrounded by kids who know what it's like. You're not alone, son . . ." The doctor's voice droned on and Faith watched the second hand ticking away. Anything to keep from looking at Daniel.

From feeling Jesse's presence.

Two.

"Come on, Daniel. I want to help you, man." It was Bradley's voice, so worried. So eager. So . . .

So much like Faith used to be.

She cut herself off from the thought, watched the skinny black arm wind down.

One.

"I can see you're still not ready," the doctor said. "We'll try again tomorrow. Think about what we've said, Daniel. That's all for today."

Zero.

The orderlies moved forward and Faith reached for her purse. It was over. Now to corner Bradley—

"I told *you* to leave me the hell alone." The venomous words sizzled across the distance to Faith.

Her head jerked to attention and she stared directly into Daniel's eyes. Where there had been nothing throughout the session, just pale blue pools of emptiness, now hatred and anger and deadly intent glittered there in full brilliance.

The orderlies moved toward him, but it was too late. He lunged across the two-foot radius of the circle.

"I told you, bitch! I told you!" His good arm swung and his fist smashed into her right temple. Jagged streaks of pain splintered through her skull, and the floor tilted.

Chaos erupted around her. Bradley and Jesse and the doctor's voices blended into the shrill ringing in her ears. The orderlies were a white blur closing in on a kicking and screaming Daniel. He'd caught everyone off guard.

Especially Faith.

Then the noise faded.

The images blurred.

Faith crumbled to the floor.

Chapter Fourteen

"Faith? Can you hear me?"

Faith blinked and found herself staring up into Jesse's concerned face. He knelt beside her, his large form blocking the overhead fluorescent lights, making him more shadow than man. Cold linoleum seeped through her skirt and bit into her backside.

"What—" The word faded into a groan when she moved her jaw.

"Daniel," he reminded her, anger simmering in his gaze, mingling with the concern that glittered back at her like twin beacons of light. "Think you can stand up?"

She nodded and he helped her to a sitting position.

The room shimmied and swirled for a few seconds. She swayed.

"Dammit, you do need a doctor." Jesse touched tender fingertips to the small lump at her temple.

"No, no," Faith murmured. "It hardly hurts at all."

"But you're dizzy."

"I'm just a little stunned."

Jesse wasn't convinced. "I'm going to find a doctor anyway. Just to be sure. Now don't move." When he seemed certain she was going to hold her sitting position, he stood and strode from the therapy room.

Voices carried from outside as a team of doctors, nurses, and orderlies tried to subdue Daniel. Faith glimpsed the chaos as Jesse left the room. Then the door shut and she was left sitting on the floor, her mind frantically trying to grasp what had just happened.

Daniel had knocked the living daylights out of her.

Faith tested the lump, mentally readying herself for a burst of pain. Instead, she felt only a dull ache when she pressed her fingers to the sore spot. It didn't make sense. She should have a full-blown concussion after the punch he'd given her. Not a measly headache.

"Are you all right?" Bradley rushed into the room, giving her another glimpse of the crowded hallway.

Faith abandoned her thoughts and struggled to see through the maze of bodies. She couldn't quite make out Daniel, but she knew he was there. Fighting.

Something tightened in her chest.

She fought for a breath and ignored the strange feeling. Now was her chance. She struggled to her feet, swayed a dangerous moment; then the dizziness passed.

"You ought to stay put. Jesse's hunting for the doctor. Someone really should take a look at you before you do so much moving around."

"I'm fine. Daniel just knocked the wind out of me."

She took a deep breath, located her purse, and retrieved the papers.

"I still think you ought to stay put."

She thrust the papers at him and rummaged inside her purse for a pen.

"What's this?"

"You know good and well what they are. Sign them."

He shook his head. "I can't."

"Please." She blinked at a sudden onslaught of tears. "Just do this for me, Bradley. I've never asked anything from you."

"Liar. You always ask for the moon."

"Then I'm asking again. The kids need you; you need them. This is the right thing."

"They need *you*."

She shook her head. "They need me the way I used to be, but not now . . . I've changed. I'm different. I'm no good for them." And they're no good for me, she added silently.

Nobody's savior.

He stared long and hard at her and she resisted the urge to snatch back the papers and rip them into tiny little shreds.

"You're sure this is what you want?"

She nodded and reluctantly, Bradley put pen to paper.

"The doctor's tied up, but he said to give you this ice pack and he'll be here in a few minutes—" Jesse burst through the door, his words falling short when he saw the documents in Faith's hands. "What the hell are you doing?"

She stuffed the signed papers in her purse, took the ice pack from Jesse, and held it to her head. "Leaving, if one of you will give me a ride. I don't feel like waiting for the bus. Bradley, how about it?"

"I—" he started, but his voice was quickly drowned by Jesse's furious growl.

"I'm talking about the papers. He signed them, didn't he?"

"I think I'll go check on Daniel." Bradley beat a hasty retreat to the door. "I'll be down the hall if you need that ride."

"I do—"

"Answer me, Faith," Jesse cut in. "Bradley signed the papers, the ones assuming responsibility for Faith's House, didn't he?"

The door rocked shut and silence pressed in, disrupted only by her quick breaths and the furious thudding of her heart.

"Yes." She stared up at him. "Not that it's any of your business."

He ran frustrated hands over his face, looking as if she'd just confessed to murder. "Like hell . . . This *is* my business. You're my business. Haven't you figured that out by now?" Before she could answer, his expression hardened. "I won't let you do this." He held out his hand. "Give me those papers."

"Excuse me?" She held her ground, barely resisting the urge to turn tail and run. But she wouldn't. She had her own anger to contend with, and it was all directed at him. "For your information, you're not my father, and you can't tell me what to do."

"I'm the next-best thing," he said in a growl, his eyes gleaming with a predatory light. And for the space of a heartbeat she was standing in her bedroom, staring at his reflection in the window, seeing his pain and heartache and hunger. Then . . .

Then nothing, because last night Jesse Savage had walked away. But this was now and he seemed braced for a fight.

"The next-best thing is a husband," she countered. "Not a one-night stand."

"I mean it, Faith. Hand them over." He looked ready to throttle her, but she wasn't intimidated. The hurt and anger of a night spent alone boiled inside her. It didn't matter that he'd warned her against getting too close to him. *No tomorrows.* Or that she knew she'd be better off without him, since he was as committed to Faith's House and the kids as she'd once been.

Nothing mattered except the frustration, indignation, resentment—the feelings swirling like a tempest inside her.

"I *said*, hand them over," he said.

"And I said no. N-O." She enunciated each letter. "What part don't you understand?"

He threw up his hands. "I'm already in hell. *You're* my hell. And here I thought I was trying to escape the future, when all along I'm smack-dab in the middle of it."

She frowned, her anger momentarily forgotten. "What are you talking about?"

"No, I won't let you do it," he went on, ignoring her question as he delivered his final ultimatum. "Either give me those papers, or I'll take them off you. Your choice."

"Well, then." She laughed harshly. "At least I get a choice. Let me see . . ." She feigned a thoughtful expression. "How about I choose to walk out of here?"

"That's not one of the choices." He reached for her and she dodged his grip.

"Then how about this?" Her palm hit the stubbled warmth of his jaw in a stinging slap that sent an echoing wave of pain clear to her shoulder. Then she whirled and stormed from the room, purse and papers firmly in hand.

Her bravado fled the minute she reached the hallway and the reality of what she'd done hit her like a blow to her own face. She'd actually hit him! She, Faith Jansen, who had never hit anyone or harmed anything in her life, had hit another human being out of anger.

Granted, justified anger, but anger nonetheless.

Shame rolled through her, and a strange sense of urgency. She needed escape. Space to collect her thoughts, to sort through the emotions distorting her brain.

She started walking. A door opened somewhere behind her and she knew it was Jesse. The unmistakable thud of his boots rang in her ears, urging her to walk faster.

She wouldn't make it outside before he caught up. She knew it. Her steps weren't quick enough and his were long and swift, determined. She rounded the corner and darted into the ladies' room. Just let him try to follow her in here—

The door slammed open and Jesse stood there, murder in his dark eyes.

"Nice try. Now give me those papers."

"No."

The stall behind Faith creaked open and she turned to see a frightened old lady peering through the handspan of space.

"You're insane," Faith told Jesse. "Could you try to show a little decency and leave me alone? You're not getting the damned papers."

"That's a matter of opinion." He stepped inside, held the door open, and motioned to the sole member of their audience.

The old lady swished open the stall door and

darted for the exit. The bathroom door shut behind her. Jesse flipped the lock and Faith found herself alone, trapped, with Jesse Savage.

"You can't do this," he told her, desperation creeping across his features.

"And just who are you to tell me what to do?"

"I'm somebody . . ." He paused to swallow, as if the words were getting caught in the sudden tightness of his throat. "I'm somebody who cares about you."

Joy leaped through her, only to die a quick death. He'd left her. He'd loved her, then left her, and the emptiness of last night refused to be consoled by words. Especially when she knew they were just that. Words. A statement meant to get her to hand over the papers.

"You'll have to come up with a better reason than that. The back of your head told a different story last night."

He loomed closer, a dangerous light in his eyes. "You think I left last night because I didn't care about you?"

"That's the way most people would take it. Let's see, breakfast in bed usually means things went well, but you didn't stick around long enough for even a midnight snack."

"And you're an expert when it comes to the morning after?" He raised an eyebrow at her and a wave of heat crept into her cheeks, sabotaging her forced control.

"No," she admitted, and the one word brought a smile to his lips.

"I'm sorry," he finally said, his expression serious once again. "I couldn't stay."

"Because you didn't want to."

"Because there was no point to it. Last night never

should have happened in the first place. It was a mistake."

Mistake. The word pounded through her head, fueling her anger and bringing fresh tears to her eyes.

Tears, of all things.

She was the insane one. Last night *was* a mistake. He'd never once made her any promises. He'd even warned her, and she'd been foolish not to listen. It was her mistake. She knew what sort of a man he was—the commitment-fearing, love-'em-and-leave-'em type. Yet, a part of her had hoped to change all that. Not at first. At first she'd meant what she'd said. She didn't want more. No tomorrows, just one night. But now, she realized in a heartbreaking moment that she wanted him to want her for more than one night.

Forever.

Insane.

She turned away from him, but it was useless. His reflection stared at her from the bathroom mirror, gazing into her, searching. . . . "Last night is over and done with. We both had our fun, and now we'll go our separate ways." She said the words he wanted to hear, hoping, praying, he would get out before she lost her last bit of control. She swallowed. "Simple."

"Don't I wish." He came up behind her, slid his hands around her waist. He turned her to face him and pulled her tight against his chest. His lips claimed hers in a slow discovery that sucked the air from her body and left her wanting more of him. So much more.

She tore her mouth from his. "Stop it." She gasped. "Just stop playing me."

His arms dropped away from her, his gaze catching and holding hers. "What are you talking about?"

"You're either all over me or pulling away. Advance, retreat, like last night." She leaned back, gaining a blessed few inches of distance between them. Swallowing, she rubbed the back of her hand across her passion-swollen lips. "It's a game to you. You like the pursuit, but once you catch whoever you're after, the fun is over. You lose interest."

"That's what you think happened last night? I lost interest?" He shook his head, an incredulous look on his face.

"I don't think. I know. You reached the finish line, found winning wasn't all it's cracked up to be, so you left." She felt the tear slide down her cheek. He reached out, but she turned away from him. "Don't mind me. I'm just under a lot of stress."

"I hurt you last night."

She tried to sound nonchalant as she dashed the tear away. "Don't delude yourself. Last night didn't mean any more to me than it did to you." Another traitorous tear slid free.

He leaned into her then, closing the scant distance between them. The gold flecks in his eyes burned brighter. "I was afraid of that."

His words caught her off guard even more than the sudden jolt of electricity when his chest brushed her nipples. "Go, Jesse. Just go. It's over. No tomorrow, just like you said. No sense dwelling on one meaningless night."

"Dammit." He forced her gaze to meet his, his fingers biting into her chin when she tried to look away. "Last night *did* mean something to me. I didn't want it to, but it did. Don't you understand? That's the problem."

"The problem is I actually thought last night that you . . . that maybe we . . ." She shook her head. "I guess I figured it would mean enough to keep you there a little longer than it did, instead of a wham-bam-thank-you-ma'am kind of thing."

"It wasn't like that," he said, as if the very notion left a bad taste in his mouth and he had to convince her otherwise. "It was more than sex, more than being inside you, more than sating the lust burning through me—"

"I can't listen to this." She pushed against him with her hands. "Don't do this to me. Let's just chalk last night up to mutual attraction and overactive hormones. The heat of the moment. You don't want me, and I don't want you. You don't care for me and I don't care for you—" His mouth silenced the rest of her words.

He kissed her, his tongue pushing inside to tangle with hers in a delicious dance that had her breathless by the time he pulled away.

His hands stole around her, slipped beneath her buttocks to cup them. He ground his hardness against the soft cradle of her and she gasped. He was hard and throbbing and she wanted to feel him inside her more than she wanted her next breath.

"It isn't just overactive hormones between us. There's more and you know it. I wish it weren't so, but it is. Heaven help me," he ground out, as if the admission were dredged from his very soul, "it is, and there's nothing I can do to change it."

He lifted her, sitting her on the marble vanity and parting her thighs. He slid her skirt up until his fingers stroked the silk-covered spot between her legs.

"I didn't want to leave you." His voice was ragged as he devoured her lips and pushed aside her panties. One finger touched her heated inner flesh and she gasped. "Dammit, Faith. I didn't. You have to believe that."

"But you did," she said, more to remind herself than him. She had to remember this was just lust to him. Nothing more, no matter what he said. He wanted the papers. Wanted her weak and pliable, and this was his way to get to her.

She knew that, yet when he touched her, she arched against him anyway, a night of longing still raw and unfulfilled inside her.

He worked at his zipper; then his length sprang hot and heavy into her hands. She stroked him from tip to root and caught his moan in her mouth.

Then he moved her hands, positioned himself, gripped her buttocks, and pulled her tight against him. His entry was quick and deep and her insides exploded at the first moment of contact.

A cry broke past her lips. Then she melted against him, shudders racking through her, the blood humming in her ears, drowning out the voice of her conscience telling her what a fool she'd been. Not once, but twice now.

It was a long moment before a pounding on the door penetrated the hazy bliss that wrapped around her as tightly, as protectively as his arms. Someone was outside.

"Is anyone in there?"

"Go down the hall," Jesse called out, and Faith realized he stood stock-still, not moving, just breathing. Surrounding her. Filling her. Buried so deep she could feel the slight pulse of his arousal—still hot and unspent.

Footsteps sounded and embarrassment flooded Faith as she realized what they'd just done a few feet away from a complete stranger. In a public restroom.

What they were *still* doing.

"I—we can't do this." She summoned her control

and tried to push him away, ashamed of herself and angry that she'd let him put her in such a compromising situation, that she'd practically jumped up on the counter and welcomed him.

"It seems like we can, and you already have." His deep voice sent a wave of heat to her cheeks.

"Please, Jesse." She struggled against his chest. "We have to stop. Someone else might come."

"Admit it first. There's more than just overactive hormones between us. You want me and I want you. You care about me and I care about—"

"And this was supposed to show me that you care, right? Seducing me in a public restroom?"

"No," he said, withdrawing from her. She had a momentary glimpse of his flesh, still swollen and wet from her climax, before it disappeared into his jeans. "This was supposed to show how much I want you." He fastened the zipper, wincing as the teeth closed over his very prominent arousal. "The caring part," he said, leaning forward to touch a tender kiss to her forehead, "you'll have to take my word on."

She was so close to believing him, so very close. Then he turned, grabbed the papers from her purse, and ripped them clear in two, and she knew that had been his objective all along. They hit the trash can with a soft *thunk* that echoed through her head like the flat-line *beeping* of a heart monitor.

Then he was gone, and Faith was left alone.

Faith walked into her kitchen later that afternoon with a major headache to rival the ache in her chest.

She came to a dead stop in the doorway, her gaze riveted on the girl sitting at the table. She knew she shouldn't be surprised to see Trudy. She'd left her sound asleep that morning. Still, she'd been so worried over Jesse and last night, Daniel and Faith's

House and the shredded papers, that she'd completely forgotten about the girl. Otherwise she could have prepared herself for the strange sense of melancholy that now gripped her.

How many times had she stood in the kitchen at Faith's House and watched the kids fight and eat and laugh and argue?

How many times had she stood in this very spot, watching Jane or Emily make chaos out of her kitchen with their enthusiasm for baking?

Never again, she told herself, but the vow didn't ring with half as much determination as she would have liked.

Trudy still wore the giant T-shirt Faith had given her last night, but she'd slipped on her baggy jeans, and her pale hair was pulled back in a sloppy ponytail. If not for the bruises mottling her young face, she would have looked like anyone's daughter or sister or niece just hanging out on a Saturday morning.

She *was* someone's daughter or sister or niece, Faith realized, no matter that she came from the streets. She deserved an adolescence filled with football games and slumber parties and prom nights, rather than an existence centered solely on survival. She was just a kid. Just a young, innocent kid who'd had a little hard luck and a great big dose of reality much too soon.

"Hey." Trudy glanced up from her task of pouring milk into a bowl of cereal. She stopped, carton paused in midair. "What happened to your face?"

Faith ignored the question and studied the girl. "Your eyes are better. Still swollen, but not so badly."

Trudy smiled. "Nearly as good as before. I guess no doctors, huh?"

"As long as no infection sets in."

Trudy's smile disappeared. "What about your face?"

"An accident. I walked into a door."

Trudy gave her a skeptical glance. "Did the door happen to be shaped like a fist?"

"As a matter of fact," Faith said, tossing her purse onto the counter and slipping out of her shoes, "it did."

"Figures." Trudy finished pouring the milk, then cast a wary glance at Faith, who stood flexing her toes near the sink. "I woke up and I was starving. I sort of helped myself. I hope you don't mind." She put her spoon down. "I could leave if you want—"

"No, I didn't mean to stare at you. It's just . . . I guess this is going to sound crazy, but you remind me of someone. A lot of someones." Faith touched the half-circle medallion hanging around her neck and a warmth spread through her.

"That doesn't sound so crazy. You remind me of someone, too."

"Oh, yeah? Who?"

Trudy opened her mouth, then snapped it shut. She shook her head. "Never mind."

Faith's curiosity inched higher. "Come on. Who?"

The girl looked undecided for a full minute. "Don't get mad."

"Maybe I don't want to hear this." Faith took a deep breath and braced herself. "Okay, shoot."

"Swear first that you won't get mad."

"Now I know I don't want to hear this." At Trudy's expectant look, she crossed her heart. "I swear."

"Mother Goose."

Faith smiled. "Mother Goose? Here I was hoping for Cindy Crawford, or Elizabeth Hurley, and all the while I was several levels off on the food chain."

Trudy studied her through smiling eyes. "You do

look a little like that Hurley chick. Same eyes." Her expression grew serious. "I was talking about the way you act. All that fussing over me last night. No one's done that in a long time. Hell, no one's ever done it."

Faith sank down into the chair across from Trudy. "Everyone should be fussed over once in a while."

"Not me," Trudy said, but the words were half-hearted.

"Do you like Mother Goose?"

"Sure. She's cool."

Faith wasn't sure why the answer pleased her so much, especially since she shouldn't care one way or another. She *didn't* care.

She smiled anyway. "How about some orange juice to go with those Cheerios?"

At Trudy's nod, Faith retrieved two glasses, poured some juice, and sat across from the girl, who busied herself gulping down spoonfuls of cereal.

"Uh, I'm sorry," the girl said, wiping at a dribble of milk that ran down her chin. "I'm sort of used to eating by myself."

Faith rested her chin on her hand. "So, tell Mother Goose where your folks are."

She shrugged and stared at the near-empty cereal bowl. "I never knew my dad. Last time I saw my ma, she was hanging out at some crackhouse off of Montrose."

"Where does she live?"

Trudy plunked her spoon down and pushed her chair back. "This has been nice and all, but I really got a lot of stuff to do."

"You don't have to tell me if you don't want to. In fact, I'd rather not know." At Trudy's questioning look, Faith added, "I have this bad habit of getting involved in other people's lives. You said yourself I reminded you of Mother Goose." She took a sip of her juice. "But no more. That's why it's better if I don't know. The less we relate, the better."

"Sounds good to me."

"You can stay here a few days, and in the meantime I'll contact somebody who can help you."

"I don't need any help." At Faith's pointed stare, Trudy added, "Okay, so maybe I do need some help. I can see better, but my eyes hurt like hell—heck, I mean. But once I'm better, I'm out of here."

Faith opened her mouth to argue, to give Trudy the dozens of reasons why a life on the street was a life thrown away. She knew the words by heart, she'd said them so many times.

I'm nobody's savior.

"If that's what you want," she said, her throat tight.

"Of course it's what I want. I ain't no welfare case. I can take care of myself just fine." The last words were loud and Faith knew Trudy was trying desperately to convince herself.

That was the trouble. Faith knew way too much. She could see inside Trudy, see the small girl begging for help, for guidance.

"So you're not a welfare case, but you still need a place to rest up, and I don't mind if you do it here. You stay a few days, then if you want to leave and go back to the streets, fine."

"Really?"

Faith nodded. "But if you decide you want something more for yourself, I know a really great lady; her name's Estelle. She could help you out."

Trudy looked ready to refuse, but then her gaze dropped and she stared at the near-empty cereal bowl. "I'll think about it," she finally said, and Faith barely resisted the urge to lean forward just a few inches and stroke Trudy's soft blond hair.

She stiffened, her fingers tightening around her orange juice glass. "Well, while you're thinking, you can help out around here." She glanced down at the puppy sniffing her ankles. "Grubby eats around four to five times a day. And he goes out at least once an hour, or whenever you see him sniffing. His leash is hanging by the door."

"You want me to feed and walk your dog?"

"You said you weren't a welfare case. This way you'll be earning your keep."

Trudy looked thoughtful for a long moment before her gaze went to Grubby, who licked excitedly at her bare toes peeking from the cuffs of her worn jeans. A smile tugged at her lips. "Earning my keep." She seemed to test the words on her lips. "I can do that. Yeah, I can do that. You got yourself a deal."

"Good." Faith downed the rest of her juice and stood up. "Now help yourself to another bowl while I go and change into my gardening shorts. I've got rosebushes to tend and Grubby will be expecting his lunch. Later on I'll clean those cuts around your eyes."

"Thanks." Trudy's small voice followed Faith to the kitchen doorway, stopping her at the threshold. "Jesse said you were all right and you are. No wonder he likes you."

Faith turned. "He doesn't like me."

Trudy looked dubious. "Sure he does. He's got that love-starved-puppy look. Anybody with half a brain can see that. How long you two been together?"

Together. The word sent a wave of heat from Faith's head to the tips of her toes, pausing at every place in between that Jesse had touched or kissed, or both.

Sure they'd been together for a few moments, but they weren't really *together*. No promises. No tomorrows. No future.

"We're not together. He's just a friend." And with that, she turned and hurried off to change.

Together. The word echoed through her head and haunted her for the rest of the day. And the strange emptiness she'd felt since he'd walked away battled with the anger brewing inside of her.

She kept her eyes on the rosebushes and her ears attuned to the sound of a motorcycle. Not that he would come, not after all that had happened between them.

Not if he knew what was good for him, she thought, snipping a wayward weed with a savage clip of her gardening shears, while Trudy sat on the back lawn playing with Grubby. Just who the hell did he think he was, to tear up her papers?

Somebody who cares about you.

No. If he really cared, he would have turned the papers over to Estelle and let Faith crawl away from Faith's House, from the kids. He would let her keep hiding.

Wait a second. Hiding? She wasn't hiding. She was simply making a choice to walk away and not look back. *Hiding.*

Maybe so, but it was her business. Not his. He hadn't stood idly by on the side of the street, heard the screech of brakes, seen Jane run down right in front of him. Faith had been the lucky witness to that, the guilty bystander. She had every right to hide, and damn him for butting in.

The trouble was, Faith wasn't simply damning him for butting into her business. She was damning him for butting out. For walking away, for whipping her emotions into a frenzy, then leaving her to deal with the chaos all by herself.

That truth kept her snipping away at anything remotely resembling a weed. Even a few leaves here and there, a small blossom—

"Hey!" Trudy walked up next to Faith. "You're getting a little carried away, aren't you? I don't know much about gardening, but I don't think you're supposed to whack the actual flower."

Faith stared down at the scattering of velvety pink petals at her feet. She shrugged. "I guess I'm a little preoccupied. I didn't get much sleep last night."

"Then I don't think you ought to be holding these right now." Trudy pulled the sharp shears from Faith's hands and plopped them on the porch steps.

Faith rubbed stiff fingers over her tired eyes. She needed a hot bath, some solid sleep, and a few good hours *not* thinking about Jesse or her feelings or . . . anything.

Faith shot Trudy a sideways glance. "What do you say we order a pizza and watch some TV?"

"Pizza?" Trudy's eyes lit up and Faith realized the girl probably hadn't had a pizza in a long, long time. "With pepperoni and hamburger?"

"And extra cheese if you want." Her suggestion met with an enthusiastic nod. "We'll order some sodas, too. And I've got ice cream and hot fudge. We can have a party. Just us girls."

Trudy grinned, tweaking Grubby's ears. "Us homeys."

"Yeah," Faith agreed, smiling. Jesse Savage could take a hike tonight, as far as she was concerned. She was hanging out with her homey.

Hell, Jesse thought later that night as he lay stretched out in his bed. He was definitely already smack-dab in the middle of hell. He was hot. Hard. Frustrated.

And mad.

He had no control when it came to Faith. He acted on impulse. Last night had proven that. Then again this morning at the hospital.

He could still see her, feel her when she'd come apart in his arms. It hadn't mattered that he hadn't reached a climax of his own. Just giving her pleasure had been fulfilling enough for him. Then.

But not now. He ached to storm her house, pull her into his arms, under him, to drive fast and sure and deep inside her, and finish what they'd started.

It wouldn't be enough. One encounter would only make him crave more. More of her surrounding him, more of the ecstasy rippling through his body, more of the rapture on her face.

I'm somebody who cares about you. The words haunted his conscience and he damned himself for speaking them. But she'd stared at him in such hurt and betrayal, and the truth had simply come out. That was what she did to him. She overrode his common sense, made him do and say things he would never even contemplate in a million years.

No more, he told himself. The physical part of their relationship was over. Done. He wouldn't think about her, or them. Just himself. His own future. Eternity. Forgiveness. Salvation.

A different approach. That was what he needed. Obviously growing closer to Faith wasn't getting him anywhere except into her pants, and that wasn't what he wanted.

Okay, so he wanted it, he admitted, his groin throbbing with its own answer. But it wasn't what he *needed*.

He needed to uncover that one all-important

thing he could do for her that would renew her faith in herself, in life, and draw her back to Faith's House. Just one special, monumental desire worthy of a miracle.

The kids. Maybe the answer lay with them. Faith had loved and cared for each of them as if they were her own. Surely they knew a great deal more about the woman than Jesse did. He could talk to them and maybe come up with an answer to his problem.

It was worth a shot. He needed to concentrate on his mission, and if nothing else, the distance from Faith would help him keep his priorities straight. He had all of four days until the anniversary of his death. He either delivered the miracle by then and went on to eternity, or . . .

He didn't want to think about the *or*—the rest of his life in this flesh-and-blood body, the rage and guilt eating away at his soul.

No. He forced the notion away. He would succeed, despite his flaws, and Faith herself.

There would be no hell on earth for him.

Only peace and serenity and an eternity of warmth to make up for the rotten hand Fate had dealt him.

He wanted to believe that. If only he didn't hear the soft tinkle of Faith's laughter when he closed his eyes, or smell the flowery fresh scent of her when he inhaled . . .

Chapter Fifteen

"So tell me about Faith's House," Trudy said two days later. It was early afternoon and she and Faith had just started preparing spaghetti for dinner.

Faith smiled and added a touch of garlic to the sauce and resumed stirring. "It's a nice place. Really clean. And the kids are great. There's Ricky. He's a sophomore in high school. And Emily, she's about your age. There's Melba and Drew and Pedro—he's the eight-year-old baby of the bunch—and Phillip and Jennifer and Cindy and . . ." She ticked off the names.

"And you take care of all of them?"

"I used to."

"What happened?"

"One of my kids was killed. I guess I took it pretty hard."

"You seem all right now."

Faith shrugged. "I'm working on it."

"So that's where you know Jesse from?"

Faith nodded. "He's the assistant to my head counselor." A smile touched her lips. Two days hadn't eased the bitterness over her situation with Jesse, but she found herself remembering other things about him. Like the tenderness in his eyes when he'd talked during Daniel's counseling session, or the gentle way he'd tended her roses, or rubbed Grubby's stomach, or—

"You got it bad for him, don't you?" Trudy asked, jarring Faith from her thoughts.

"Of course not. We're just colleagues."

"Sure." Trudy finished dicing a small bulb of garlic and handed the pieces to Faith. "I can see why you like him. He's a great guy. Not just good-looking, but nice, too. I cussed his ear off that night when he found me in the alley, but he helped me anyway." A blush crept over Trudy's face, making the bruises seem darker even though they'd healed considerably over the past two days. "I wanted him to leave me in that alley, but he wouldn't. I even hit him."

"I doubt you hurt him."

"Still, he didn't deserve that. Not after all he did, bringing me food and a blanket and some cash. Told me I should get help before something happened to me." She pushed the hair away from her bruised face and concentrated on slicing the sweet red pepper Faith handed her. "Not that he was right. I woulda been just fine if I had stayed put." She finished slicing, scooped up the slivers, and tossed them into the sauce. "But that money Jesse gave me was burning a hole in my pocket. I hadn't had a Coke in a long time."

"You were on your way to buy a soda when you got jumped?"

Trudy shook her head. "I was on my way home. I bought a whole six-pack and I couldn't wait. I popped one in the alley back behind the store and before you know it, I was on my third one. Then here come these guys." Fear creased the girl's forehead and something twisted inside Faith.

Turn away, she told herself. *Don't listen. Don't get involved, Mother Goose.*

"What happened?" she asked, her voice soft and tremulous.

"They took what was left of my six-pack, my money, and my shoes and jacket, and hightailed it out of the alley. Then Jesse found me. More?" she asked, reaching for another pepper.

Faith nodded, and the girl went to work slicing and dicing.

"How long have you known Jesse?" Trudy asked after a silent moment.

The sauce bubbled and Faith lowered the burner a notch. "Not too long."

"I just met him myself about a week and a half ago. He was poking around the abandoned building where I've been staying. Nearly scared me half to death, too, because not many people go nosing around up on the third floor, not after what happened."

At Faith's blank look, she added, "Two guys and a girl were murdered up there about a year ago. A cop and his younger brother and sister, Jesse said. It seems this cop's younger brother had been dealing and holding out on somebody. The cop came home early one night and walked in on his brother getting roughed up. The dealers turned on the cop. They sliced him up real good. The brother and the sister, too. Seems she walked in while everything was happening. They stabbed her in the right shoulder, and

here"—she indicated an area just below her elbow—
"and here"—she touched a spot just inches shy of
her heart—"two times in the chest, like a giant *X*."

The description blared in Faith's head and she
gripped the edge of the stove to keep from falling.
Right shoulder. Arm. Chest. *X marks the spot.*

"I know it sounds awful," Trudy went on, noticing
Faith's reaction. She dumped a handful of sliced
peppers into the simmering sauce. "It shook me up,
too, when I heard about it. But the place where it
happened ain't so bad. I been in worse holes, that's
for sure. It's quiet up there, and dry. . . ."

The words faded into the thunder of Faith's heart.

". . . Jesse knew the cop or something like that.
Said he knew the brother. The sister, too."

"Jane," Faith whispered, her own chest tight,
throbbing in the exact spot Trudy had indicated.
"Her name was Jane."

"We need to talk." Faith's voice echoed through the
kitchen at Faith's House, where Jesse stood making
sandwiches for the after-school rush.

He went rigid, every muscle instantly attuned to
her presence. A wave of longing swept through him.
So much for distance helping him keep his focus.
He'd been consistently aroused for the past forty-
eight hours, and he was no closer to giving Faith her
miracle than he'd been at the hospital.

Talking to the kids had netted him zero prospects
in the miracle department. According to them, Faith
already had everything—a content life, a successful
job. She wanted for nothing, except maybe a Led
Zeppelin commemorative *Black Dog* CD. That had
been Ricky's suggestion, and more his heart's desire
than Faith's.

Jesse had missed her, he admitted to himself, the

ache in his body undeniable. But as potent as his physical reaction was, her absence drew an even stronger emotional response from him. It was as if she'd chipped past the wall surrounding his heart, his soul even, and captured the few soft emotions Jesse Savage had left. The compassion, the kindness, the protectiveness.

The softness in her eyes when she looked at one of the kids; the gentle touch of her hands as she tended her rose garden; the way she laughed and smiled and snuggled into her pillow when she slept; all had fed those few precious feelings, nurtured them, until Jesse had one hell of a dilemma on his hands.

He had to walk away from her in the end, but with each moment that passed, he wondered how in the hell he would ever find the strength to do it. *If* he managed to deliver her miracle.

He had to. It was the only way for him to free himself of his guilt. However much Faith distracted him, she couldn't soothe his conscience. Only one thing—asking his brother and sister's forgiveness—could do that.

"You're right," he said, taking a deep breath, resigning himself to the inevitable. He would confront Faith. Come out and ask her, whether she thought he was crazy or not. He had all of forty-eight hours left and he'd passed the point of subtlety.

"We do need to talk," he told her. "I've got something to ask you—"

"Who *are* you?" she cut in, her gaze glittering with anger and suspicion.

Jesse all but stopped breathing. She knew the truth already. She *knew*.

No, she couldn't know! She'd gazed into his eyes when they'd made love, but only for a few seconds.

She couldn't have figured out the truth in such a short time, not as incredible as it was.

"You knew her," Faith said accusingly. "Didn't you? You knew her, and you never said a word."

His panic gave way to confusion. "What are you talking about?"

"Trudy told me where you found her," she said, as if that explained everything.

"I told you where I found her, and I've only known her a little over a week." He reached for a dishtowel and busied himself wiping his hands, anything to keep from reaching for her, pulling her into his arms. "How is she?"

The question seemed to distract her for a few seconds. She shrugged. "Better. I think I've convinced her to talk to Estelle, maybe get some help. She's meeting with her in the morning."

"Good." Tossing the towel on the counter, he reached into an overhead cabinet for a bag of chips.

"This isn't about Trudy. It's about Jane," she said, coming up behind him. "Talk to me, Jesse. I want to know who you are, who you *really* are. You didn't just wander into this job. You knew Jane, her family, and now you're here. Coincidence? I don't think so."

"That's crazy. I didn't know Jane." He plopped a bag of chips onto the counter and turned away from her, toward the refrigerator.

Distance, his sanity screamed. Just a few inches and he could breathe. His chest wouldn't feel so tight. His arms wouldn't feel so empty.

Her hand closed over his shoulder and she pulled, forcing him to face her.

"Come off it, Jesse. Trudy told me. You knew

Jane, what happened to her family. You told her you knew!"

"Relax, Faith." He shrugged free of her grip and yanked open the refrigerator door. "I never knew Jane, and the only thing I told Trudy about was my—" His hand stalled in midair and the air lodged in his lungs.

You knew Jane, what happened to her family. You knew Jane. You knew Jane . . . Rachel?

No! The word thundered through his head, beating down the realization like a hammer smacking a stubborn nail. It couldn't be. Impossible!

The trouble was, Jesse knew firsthand that nothing was impossible. He was alive and breathing when he should be six feet under. Everything else paled in comparison.

"How did you know her and why didn't you say something sooner?" Faith prodded. "Why didn't you come forward right when it happened? You could have told the authorities her real name. Something about her background. Instead she had no family. No past. Nothing."

He slammed the refrigerator door shut and leaned his forehead against the cool surface. "I—I didn't realize. . . ." His throat closed around the words and he did his damnedest to swallow. "I never knew your Jane was my . . ." *Sister.* The word was there, blaring through his head, but it wouldn't pass his lips.

"You didn't know she was your friend's sister? And I'm supposed to believe that?" she rushed on, mindless that his world was spinning out of control. "Out of all the foster homes in Houston, you wind up coming to mine, and you just happen to be the only person who actually knew Jane before she lost her memory."

"I didn't realize. . . ." He shrugged away from

271

Faith, stumbling toward the table, needing some space to comprehend what she was saying.

You knew her.

"Why are you here?" Faith demanded. "What do you want from me? Why didn't you tell me the truth? Why?"

He clamped his eyes shut against the accusing light in Faith's eyes. But the accusation was there inside him, gripping his chest until breathing was nearly impossible. "Dammit, I didn't even think. . . ." He gripped the edge of the table and sank down into a chair, his legs buckling from the reality pressing down on him.

Jane . . . Rachel . . . Jane . . . *Rachel.*

He buried his head in his hands, visions of his sister spinning in his mind, her voice echoing in his ears.

I love you, Jesse.

I wish you didn't have to work tonight.

Not tonight . . .

"But she died," he said in a voice that was barely a croak. "I saw her." He shook his head, the scene replaying in his mind. "I *saw* her!"

And he truly did see her. He closed his eyes and the past rushed to the surface; Jesse was back in apartment 3B, seeing death, hearing Rachel's pained voice.

"Jesse!" Rachel screamed, rushing into the room. But her warning came too late. The knife sliced into him, over and over.

He sank to his knees, her horrified expression clear in his mind. Then he could only watch as they turned on his brother and his sister.

Jason went down with the first slash of the knife. Then the blade lashed out, plunged into Rachel's shoulder, then her arm. She twisted. The knife slashed into her chest, once, twice, and it was over. Done. Dead.

"No!" *Jesse wasn't sure if he actually said the word, or if it just echoed in his head. But it didn't matter. It wasn't enough to save her.*

Wide eyed, she sank to the floor, her mouth open. Blood trickled from the corner. Then her eyes closed for good. Forever.

"Jesse?" Faith's soft voice pushed into his thoughts. She knelt in front of him, her hands grasping his. "Can you hear me?"

"She died," he said, his voice raw and open. "They stabbed her. She died."

"You *didn't* know, did you?" Her gaze probed his, searching for the truth, looking past his defenses to the emotion that lay beyond. "Sweet heaven, you really didn't know." Her voice caught and her eyes filled with tears. "Oh, Jesse." She gripped his hands, her fingers warm and soothing. "I'm so sorry. I thought you knew all along and you stayed silent on purpose while I went on and on about her. I thought it was some sort of sham or something. I thought . . ." Her gaze collided with his. "I don't know what I thought. It just hurt to think you'd lied to me after all that's happened between us."

"They stabbed her," he repeated, as if saying the words out loud could help him sort through the past. "In the chest. Twice. A deadly wound. *Fatal.*"

Faith shook her head. "The knife barely missed her heart and spinal cord. It was nasty, but it wasn't fatal." She stroked the back of his clenched fist. "She suffered a collapsed lung, some damage that required emergency surgery, but she pulled through."

"But I thought she bled to death." *I heard her,* he added silently.

Had that been his own life he heard slipping away into nothingness?

No heaven, no hell. Just a void surrounding him, making the regret and guilt unbearable. Focusing his rage.

She'd lived.

"You were a close friend of her older brother, right? Did you know her well?" She stroked the knuckles of his clenched fist and forced the hand open. Her fingers laced with his, and through his own pain, he felt her desperation. "You have to tell me about her. What was her name? Did she always like chocolate? Was she always good in math but terrible in science? Something, Jesse. Just tell me something real about her. Please."

He didn't want to answer, but in the face of her pleading gaze, he could no more resist her questions than he could turn his back on her pain.

Linked. Connected.

No! He didn't want to be linked to anyone, least of all this woman. He couldn't give her a tomorrow, a future. There would be nothing but heartache for her, while he moved on to an eternity of peace. And he *would* move on. He had to.

"Please," she begged. His gaze met hers and he could no more staunch the words that spewed from his lips than he could his own blood on that fateful night.

"She—" He swallowed. "She was my—"

The door crashed open and a breathless Ricky barreled into the room. "I've got fifteen minutes before I have to head back for after-school practice, and I'm starved—" His words stumbled as he stared at Faith. "Ms. Jansen." A smile lit his face. "You're here. Hey, everybody," he called over his shoulder. "Ms. Jansen's here!"

The room was filled with children in a matter of seconds. Schoolbooks and backpacks piled on top of the table, the counters, and Faith became the center of attention.

Jesse slipped away, eager to flee the chaos and put as much space as he could between Faith and himself.

Holy hell, he was losing it! He'd been about to blurt out his identity, and all because she'd looked at him with those tear-filled eyes. Her gaze had pushed inside his mind to see everything, even his dark, stained, guilt-corroded soul, and he'd been powerless to resist her.

Even in the face of the truth.

Jane had been Rachel. His sister.

He closed his eyes, seeing Faith's memories, the dark form huddled in the corner, and he knew. He might have known the first time he'd journeyed into her thoughts. Certainly he'd felt the strange familiarity, recognized the soft, whimpering voice. Perhaps he'd known all along.

She'd lived. . . .

Faith's laughter rose above the steady chatter of voices, to drift inside him and soothe the ache that gripped his insides. To remind him that his sister hadn't been alone. She'd been cared for and loved.

But it wasn't enough to salve his conscience.

Rachel had survived that night, only to spend the next year fighting her nightmares. She'd had no family, no memories. No big brother to tuck her in at night, to whisper reassurances to see her through the dark times.

No "I *love* you, Rachel. I'm here for you. I'm sorry."

Nothing but fear and hopelessness, and it had all been Jesse's fault. He should have listened to her that night and stayed home. But he hadn't. He'd left her and his brother, and in doing so, he'd killed them.

The truth shook him and he stumbled, coming up hard against the wall. He braced himself, desperate to keep from sinking to his knees and raging at whatever power had sent him on this mission. He didn't deserve a second chance. He deserved the endless drifting, the guilt. The scar on the back of his hand burned with renewed vigor, but it was small penance, not nearly enough for what he'd done.

Yet at the same time, he desired salvation, craved release from the turmoil raging inside him, and fulfilling this mission could give him that. Worthy or not, he had a shot at redemption, a chance to see his brother and sister again and beg their forgiveness. A chance he wouldn't screw up.

He had to give Faith her miracle. Soon.

The shrill ring of the phone penetrated the drumming in his ears, the sound like a foghorn guiding him through a murky night. He focused on the noise, refusing to listen to Faith's laughter, the soft, soothing calm of her voice as she spoke with the children. He had to bide his time and uncover what she truly needed, all the while keeping as much emotional distance as he could. No more sating his lust, giving in to his body's demands—or his heart's.

Just the mission, he told himself, reaching for the telephone. *Deliver the miracle and move on. Simple.*

"Jesse speaking. Can I help you?"

"Mr. Savage, this is Dr. Stevens at the hospital. I'm calling about Daniel. We have a serious problem."

* * *

". . . and there's this new boy in my English class who's been writing me notes."

"She doesn't want to hear about your stupid love life, Em," Ricky cut in, giving the girl a jealous glance. He turned back to Faith. "I broke my track record. Ran the twenty-yard sprint in under five."

"Like she really cares about your stupid track record," Jennifer chimed in. "The choir's going to Regionals and I'm singing a solo."

"I'm starting my first job this weekend," Drew said. "Concession stand at Theater Sixteen. Bradley helped me get the job."

"And I aced my chemistry test last week," Melba added.

The updates went on and on, the voices surrounding Faith, swamping her thoughts about Jane and Jesse.

"Are you ever coming back?" Jennifer asked.

"We really miss you," said Cindy.

"Bradley's killing us with his lasagna," declared Phillip. "Jesse makes a mean bologna and cheese, but we're getting sick of that, too."

"We need you, Ms. Jansen," Emily said. "Please come back."

"Yeah." Pedro, the youngest of the bunch, pushed his way in between Emily and Ricky. He was already eight years old but he didn't look a day over six with his small frame and huge brown eyes. "Em's been reading *Goosebumps* to me at night like you used to, but it's not the same." He leaned toward Faith and whispered, "She doesn't do the scary parts the way you do."

"Please come back," another voice added.

Faith smiled. "I . . . I don't know." Since when had *never* turned to *I don't know*?

Since Jesse, she realized, her gaze going to the

hallway where he'd retreated only moments ago. Since he'd come into her life and forced her to face the anger, the grief. He'd talked, listened, prodded, even pushed, and shown her that the memories didn't have to hurt or cripple.

The revelation washed through her as she sat there, surrounded by love and eager faces. Maybe she couldn't prevent death, or even sway a belligerent child from returning to the streets, but she could make a difference. She *had* made a difference, to each and every child in this room. She'd touched their lives, brought smiles to their faces and comfort to their troubled souls. She'd given them a warm place to stay and food in their stomachs. Maybe it only seemed that none of that amounted to much in the big picture. Maybe, however small, however trivial, each gesture meant something more than was evident.

She clutched the friendship locket suspended around her neck and smiled. Yes, everything she did, every life she touched, did mean something. It was the small things in life, the day-to-day living and sharing and caring, that shaped a person, that saved them from the evil of the world.

Faith knew in a crystalline moment that she could no longer live in fear of the future, of what might happen, of the pain and tragedy awaiting her. She had to live for today. Now.

No tomorrow. Jesse's words echoed in her head, and as much as they disappointed her because she wanted more with him, she also realized that she needed to put her anger aside and appreciate the time she'd shared with him, because for all the heartache, he'd also shown her more happiness in just a few moments than she'd known in her entire life. And if that was all they would ever share, she would cherish that time.

"Please come back," came the unison of voices surrounding her. "Please, please, *please* . . . "

"I'll see—"

"Faith." As if her thoughts had conjured him, Jesse appeared in the doorway. "We have to get to the hospital." A frown drew his lips into a grimace. His dark eyes sparkled with worry.

Her peace shattered and dread coiled in her stomach. "What's wrong?"

"Daniel ran away."

"I think this is a big mistake," Bradley said later that afternoon as he watched Faith load a stack of yellow paper into the copy machine at a nearby office supply store. "I talked to Estelle and her advice is for you to relinquish custody of Daniel back to the state. She won't insist because frankly, they've got their hands full as it is, but that's her recomendation."

Faith shook her head and fought with the paper tray.

"I'm serious. It's obvious Daniel doesn't want help. He traded a warm bed, medical care, and people who care about him for the streets. He's an incurable runaway. A lost cause."

"Nobody is a lost cause," she told him.

His expression shifted from a frown to a smile, then back again, and he shook his head. "I'm glad to see you back to your old self, but not over this kid. He's too far gone. You can't reach him."

"Maybe not, but I can try." She replaced the paper tray and stabbed a button. With a monotonous whir, the machine started spitting out flyers bearing Daniel's picture.

"You're setting yourself up, and to be honest, it

scares me. There's a whole houseful of kids who need you right now. Your time would be better spent with them than out chasing after some runaway."

"I'm his foster mother. I can't just turn my back. I already let him down by not being there from the beginning. He needs help, and he's scared."

"Are you forgetting that he slugged you the last time you saw him? I'd say he's more dangerous than scared."

"He slugged me because he's scared. I saw it in his eyes, Bradley." She gave him a pointed stare. "I saw it and I felt it, and I was this close to reaching out to him. He knew it and he lashed out to push me away." She took a deep breath. "I know Daniel's way out there, maybe too far, but I won't know how far unless I try to reach him."

"And what if you can't? I don't want to see you fall apart again if you fail."

"I won't," she told him. "Fall apart, I mean, even if I don't reach him. The only real failure is not trying." She handed him a stack of flyers. "Now distribute these to the kids and start combing the neighborhoods around Faith's House. Jesse and I will start at the hospital and work our way from there. Oh, and can you pick up Trudy and take her with you? I really don't want her sitting at home by herself."

He caught her hand, his concerned gaze drawing hers. "Don't worry about Trudy. The kids and I will look out for her. I'm more concerned about you. Are you sure about this?"

She nodded and he released her. Grabbing an extra handful of flyers, Bradley headed for the doorway, where Jesse waited near the cash register.

"This is your fault," the counselor told him. "I

don't know whether to pat you on the back or take a punch at you. This could be really bad, you know?"

Jesse nodded.

Bradley cast one last look at Faith and his frown turned into a smile. "Then again, it could be pretty damn good. At least she's back in action for the time being."

"Yeah," Jesse said as Bradley left. But there was no satisfaction in the word. Instead, he felt almost . . . sad. Faith's return to the land of the living marked the beginning of the end. This was her first major step back on the path to hope, faith, and charity. She was bound to hit a roadblock, but Jesse would be there to deliver his miracle and see her on her way—then his time here would be over—in less than forty-eight hours.

His guilty conscience rejoiced at that fact, but he quickly realized as he stared at Faith, saw the determination in her movements, the compassion in her eyes, that his heart didn't share the enthusiasm.

"Here," she said, coming up to him and handing him a stack of flyers. "Let's get to work."

Jesse threw himself into the chore, grateful to have something to think about besides Faith. He fixed his brain on finding Daniel, pushing away the images of Faith in her garden, Faith snuggling into her pillow, Faith sitting next to him on the back porch. He couldn't afford to remember their time together, how it felt to love her, to be loved.

It should have been easy, especially considering Faith seemed to have forgotten altogether about any intimacy between them. Engrossed in her work, she barely spared him a glance.

Good, he told himself.

If only he felt that way.

They started at the hospital and worked their way

through the surrounding neighborhoods, handing out flyers, talking to people, and asking questions. It was a tedious job and most of their inquiries met with no success.

Jesse had to admire her. She didn't give up, even when the sun started to set and dusky shadows closed in on them. She kept walking, tacking up flyers and asking questions until finally they found someone who'd seen Daniel. It was a few blocks over from the hospital, in one of the ghettos that surrounded the outskirts of downtown Houston. That person led to another, more questions, and then yet another person.

They followed the trail of leads to a sleazy bar on the outskirts of Jesse's old neighborhood. He'd been too wrapped up in questioning witnesses to realize where they were headed until they actually reached their destination.

He jerked to a halt outside the bar, his gaze riveted to the neon sign above. The name The Dungeon glared back at him in bloodred letters. Someone had to be having a huge laugh at his expense, he thought grimly.

"What's wrong?"

He shook his head. "Nothing." He took a deep breath, gripped her elbow, and ushered her inside.

"What can I do you for?" The man behind the bar wore his black hair long and unkempt, and a flowing beard to match. A miniature silver dagger earring dangled from his left ear. "A cold beer? Shot of tequila? What?"

"We're not here to drink," Jesse told him.

"We're looking for this boy." Faith slid a flyer across the scarred counter. "Have you seen him?"

The guy studied the picture, then cast a suspicious gaze at Jesse. "You a cop?"

"We're concerned citizens," Faith chimed in. "I'm the boy's foster mother. Have you seen him?"

The guy shrugged. "Foster mother, huh? So why'd he run away?"

"He's a young kid, lots of troubles," Jesse explained.

"I'm trying to help him," Faith added.

"Seems to me he don't want your help; otherwise he wouldn't be on the run."

"Have you seen him or not?" Jesse snapped.

The guy shrugged, and Faith let out an exasperated sigh. "Well, if you do, call the number on the flyer." She turned to Jesse. "I guess this was a dead end."

"Maybe." He eyed the guy behind the bar, then told Faith, "You go on outside. I'll be along shortly."

Faith cast a look at the bartender, then looked back at Jesse. "But why? He already said he didn't know anything—"

"Just trust me on this. Okay?"

She stared at him long and hard before finally nodding and heading for the door.

"So what's the deal?" Jesse said, turning back to the bartender.

"You tell me."

"You've seen the kid. He's been in here."

The bartender shrugged. "Maybe."

Jesse smirked. "There isn't any *maybe* about it. He's been here, all right, and your ass is going to be sitting in jail before the night is over if you don't come clean right now."

The bartender narrowed his eyes. "I thought you wasn't no cop."

"I'm not. Not anymore. But I've got friends in high places, and they wouldn't be too happy to find out you've been allowing minors in your establishment.

That violates at least four laws I can think of, and I'm sure they could make up a couple of others by the time you reach the station." Jesse leaned over the counter, his arm shooting out to grab the guy by the collar and haul him forward. "Understand what I'm saying?"

The guy gave a jerky nod.

"Good." Jesse stared deep into the bartender's eyes until the man started to shake.

"What the hell are you?"

"Like the lady said, a concerned citizen," Jesse replied. He eased his grip on the man. "Now, what gives?"

"He was in here earlier today, asked for a smoke and something to drink." The bartender shook his head. "But I didn't sell him either, I swear."

"Sure you didn't."

"Anyhow, then he asks me if I know somebody who might be looking to hire any run—er, salespeople. Said he had experience and could move just about anything, even with a broken arm."

"And what did you tell him?"

"I told him sure. There's always people interested in good movers. I know this guy over off Montrose who's always on the lookout."

"Who's the guy?"

The bartender shrugged and held out his hands. "Come on, man. You know I can't tell you that. I like breathing, if you know what I mean."

Jesse stared at him long and hard again, until the guy visibly paled.

"Uh, Kirk, man. That's not his real name, just what the street kids call him. I don't know his real name. Honest."

"Call," Jesse said, tapping the flyer. "If the kid comes in again. You got that?"

The guy nodded enthusiastically and Jesse turned away, his gaze sweeping the dim interior of the bar. A couple sat in the far corner, heads tilted toward one another, sipping bottles of beer. Smoke spiraled from a fifty-something biker who puffed on a cigarette and staggered around a pool table, cue stick in hand. Otherwise the place was empty. No familiar faces.

His name's Bryan. Jesse forced the voice from his head. He needed to concentrate. To get the hell away from here.

He started walking.

"Hey, mister, you ain't gonna tell the cops he was in here, are you? I could lose my license. Not that I sold him anything. I don't cater to friggin' minors."

Jesse didn't answer. He couldn't. The reply stuck in his throat when his stare riveted on Faith, who stood inside the doorway, watching him.

"I told you to wait outside," he ground out, coming up to her.

"What was all that about?"

"Getting information."

"You looked right at home. Like you've done this sort of thing before."

"I have," he said, gripping her arm and ushering her through the door.

"Before your wandering days?"

"Yes, now walk." He steered her down the sidewalk.

"You were a cop, weren't you?"

He didn't answer. Instead he urged her forward, his long strides eating up the pavement. He needed distance. From this place. From the past. From the damned voice blaring in his head. *His name's Bryan. His name's Bryan. . . . Bryan.*

"You were." Faith's voice cut into his thoughts.

She shrugged free and whirled on him. "That's why you handled the bartender that way. Why you said what you said. That's how you knew Jane's brother. He was a cop, too. That's it," she said as if she'd just figured out a puzzle. "You were a cop, weren't you?"

He rubbed at his eyes to keep from looking at her. She grabbed his arm and he muttered, "Yes, dammit. I was. I went through the police academy in a nearby town while I was still living in Restoration."

"That's why you left. There's no advancement in a small town like that."

Jesse nodded. "They had a two-man police force. The chief and his assistant."

"You," she said. "You were the assistant."

"And the chief wasn't anywhere near retirement so I came here."

"You were with HPD?"

"For a few months."

"What happened? Why did you give it up?"

"Leave it alone, Faith."

"You were a cop," she prodded, seemingly oblivious to the warning in his voice. "Then something happened. Something that took you away from the force and put you out on the street, aimlessly wandering. . . . Your brother and sister," she said. "You gave up the force because of what happened to them."

This ain't none of your business, Savage.

Her fingers gripped his forearm. "Tell me, Jesse. You never said how they died."

It's your brother we want.

"Please," Faith begged. "I want to know."

Your brother . . .

"Yo, Bryan."

The voice thundered through Jesse's head. At first he thought it came from inside, from his memories, but then he turned to see two men approaching The Dungeon from the opposite direction.

One he recognized as the guy he'd cornered in the alley a few nights ago, Bryan's murdering accomplice.

And the other . . .

It was him.

His heart lurched, then thundered forward as rage stirred to life, like a living, breathing devil inside. And where Jesse had fought so hard to ignore the hatred burning inside him, to stay focused on Faith and his mission, his control vanished in the blink of an eye.

It was his murderer.

He was on the pair before he took his next breath, his hands reaching for Bryan's throat, his conscience suddenly as eager for vengeance as his soul was for peace.

Maybe more so . . .

Chapter Sixteen

Jesse slammed Bryan up against a brick wall, lifting him higher, higher, his fingers tight, unyielding, crushing both beard and flesh.

"I told you, man. It's him. *Him!*" came the frenzied voice of Bryan's accomplice. "Man, I told you I saw him the other night. I told you!"

"But I cut you," Bryan gurgled. "I . . . cut . . . you."

Jesse's hands trembled, the scar burning with the vengeance boiling inside him. Hotter, hotter.

He squeezed harder, harder.

"You cut me, and you cut my brother," Jesse spat, "and my sister, and left us for dead. *Dead*," he said in a hiss.

"No," Bryan said with a gasp, the word little more than a frantic rush of air. "You and your brother were dead, but not"—he swallowed against Jesse's grip—"the girl. We—we left her outside the hospital."

"Like hell. She could've fingered both of you."

"She was close to dead," he explained in a rush of breathless words. "I didn't think she'd make it. Didn't even want to go to all the trouble, but Little J there"—he gestured to the other man—"he's got a kid sister. Wouldn't let us leave her." He struggled for air. "Your brother held out on us, and you got in the way. But the girl didn't have nothing to do with it, and Little J had to clear his damned conscience."

I tried to help her. The accomplice's words whispered through Jesse's head. *I tried.*

"*You* had the knife," Jesse said, the words meant for Bryan's ears only. "You killed my brother, and now you're going to see what it feels like."

A roar beat at Jesse's senses, a thundering tempo that drowned out all right and wrong. Bryan's mouth moved, but no words pierced the rage holding Jesse prisoner. Then the man's face blurred into a red haze and Jesse's entire world centered on his own hands, the tightening of fingers and the hatred gripping him as fiercely as death had that night.

"Jesse!" Faith's cry pierced the rage enough to return him to reality, to the bite of brick against his knuckles, the bulging Adam's apple and frantic pulse beneath his hands.

He glanced over his shoulder to see her several feet away, a silver blade pressed to her throat. Bryan's accomplice held her prisoner, one arm wrapped about her chest, the other holding the weapon.

"Let him loose," Little J said, his voice shaky with false bravado. "Or I'll cut your lady here."

Visions of Faith hurt and bleeding and gasping for air blinded Jesse for what seemed like an eternity. His hands shook and he remembered the pain of the blade. Again, he felt his life slip away. And Faith would know the same agony if he didn't let go of Bryan's throat.

Or would she? For all of Little J's threats, there was no heart in his words. He wasn't a killer, not like his friend.

Still, Jesse fought to loosen his fingers. He couldn't take any chances where Faith was concerned. He willed his hand to unclench, but it wouldn't obey. The blood pounded through his body, pumping as frantically as his heart, and he knew he had to bury his demons once and for all. He'd done his best to resist, to subdue the hatred inside, but fate had gone too far now, throwing obstacles in his path, forcing him to face what he wanted only to forget. This was a test, he knew. But it was one he was doomed to fail.

Maybe Little J wasn't a killer, but Bryan was. Jesse had to set things right. Avenge his brother and sister. Himself. A life for a life—justice.

"I'll cut her, man," Little J said nervously. "I will."

"In your dreams, buddy." Faith jerked an elbow backward. The blade fell away and her abductor doubled over. "I've faced worse than that at the hands of kids who love me, buster. Who *love* me, you got that?" She shoved away from him and turned pleading eyes on Jesse. "Don't do this, Jesse. Please don't." Her voice joined with the guttural plea of the man Jesse held captive.

"Don't . . ." Bryan gulped, eyes bulging with fear, "Please. Sorry," he rasped. "Forgive me."

Forgiveness . . . The word beat at Jesse's conscience, demanding attention, and he could no more ignore the plea than he could resist Faith's desperate voice. That was what he himself sought.

"No, Jesse. No." He felt her hand on his shoulder. The anger drained away, as if someone had pulled the stopper on a sink full of dirty dishwater. Then the faucet seemed to come on, relief rinsing away the dirt and grime, cleansing his conscience.

He loosened his grip. Bryan regained his feet and scrambled away. His face, barely visible through the overgrown black beard, pulsed a mottled purple, his eyes wide with shock and disbelief.

"You're dead," Bryan said incredulously. He backed away and rubbed a hand at his throat. Then his features hardened. "You're dead," he said again, the words a promise this time. "I ain't no coward like Little J, you got that? You're history, man," he said before bolting. "*Dead.*"

"No," Jesse whispered, watching him scramble down the street, Little J hot on his heels. "I'm alive." Then he turned and strode toward his motorcycle.

Faith followed, so warm and close, and confused. She wanted so much to understand what had just happened. To understand him.

"Would you like to tell me why you attacked that guy?"

He shook his head, straddled the motorcycle, and shoved the key into the switch.

"So that's it?" She planted her hands on her hips and stared at him. "I'm just supposed to ignore all of that and pretend everything is fine? You almost killed a man, for heaven's sake."

She seemed unaware of the danger she herself had faced. Then again, Jesse amended as he replayed the scene in his head, Faith had been anything but helpless. She'd known exactly how to respond, how to deal with an aggressor. She was something else—

He cut himself off midthought and gripped the handlebars.

"That guy was talking to you, saying something

while you were choking him. What?" When he didn't answer, she added, "Don't do this, Jesse. I deserve an explanation."

"You do," he finally said, his gaze meeting hers. "But I can't give you one."

"You mean you won't give me one." She touched his arm. "Why? What are you afraid of?"

He stared at her then, his dark eyes drilling into hers, and Faith heard his deep, unmistakable voice echo through her head.

You. The word was so deep, so real, yet he hadn't moved his lips.

Faith shook away the disturbing thought. "Who was that guy? Did you arrest him before?"

"I never had the chance."

"But that's how you knew him? From the streets, right?"

He shook his head, tension rolling off him in waves, pushing her further away. "He was a bad guy, and I chased bad guys. End of story."

She stiffened. "So that's how it is? I spill my guts to you, my feelings, say things I never would have said to anyone else, and you don't reciprocate."

"Get on." He revved the engine, the roar killing any more talk. Faith climbed on, barely resisting the urge to pound some sense into him.

As if that would make any difference. He'd closed himself off, shut her out, and that was that.

She clenched her fists and wrapped her arms around his waist. He was rigid in her embrace, so solid and unbendable. The ride home was short and silent and filled with an unsettling tension that infused Faith and held her body rigid.

"I'll be back tomorrow morning and we'll follow up on that bartender's lead," he said after he'd parked the motorcycle and walked her to the front door. "I'll call the cops, too, and let them know. Maybe they can come up with something—"

"Jesse." She turned to face him, her gaze slicing through the shadows of her front porch to collide with his. "Don't leave."

He shook his head. "I have to, Faith. It's for the best."

"And how is that? Because there's no future for us?"

He nodded.

"But I don't want a future. I'm talking now. Right now. This moment. I don't want you to leave." She gripped his hand, half expecting him to resist her, but he didn't. "You can at least see me safely inside. I didn't know how late I'd be tonight. Trudy's bunking with Emily at Faith's House." At her words, he let her pull him into the house. The door creaked shut behind him.

Moonlight coupled with the flickering burn of a street lamp pushed past the drapes. Soft shadows floated through the living room. The air-conditioning hummed from the corner. Cold air swirled around her, but she wasn't cold. She was hot. The tense ride home had seen to that. He'd been so close, his body's warmth infusing her despite his silence.

She wiped away a drop of sweat sliding down her temple. Yes, she was burning up, all right, and now Jesse was the only thing that could cool her.

"I'd better go," he said, as if reading the hungry gaze she fixed on him. "You're inside. Safe and sound."

"But I'm not," she replied. "I'm not sound at all. I'm this close to going out of my mind. I can't stop thinking about us."

"Don't."

"And about you tearing up my papers," she went on as if he hadn't said a word. "I was so mad, and so relieved. I'm not sure why you did it. There's more to you, Jesse. I know it, but if you don't want to talk to me, fine. It can wait until later."

"There won't be a later," he said, shoving his hands through his hair. "I've told you before. There's no future for us. There can't be."

"Why?" she insisted. "Give me one reason."

The question seemed to tear at him. His expression shifted from stubborn resolve to heartbreaking sadness. "We're too different." His voice was low and rough, as if saying the words hurt. "Your soul is pure and untouched and mine . . ." He shook his head. "There's so much about me you don't know. Bad things, Faith. Things you would never approve of, or accept, or overlook."

"People make mistakes. I know that. If this is about that guy, if you were into some seedy things in the past—"

"It's not that simple," he cut in. "Not for me." He rubbed at his weary eyes. "Things are too confusing right now."

"Stay anyway," she said, her body aching as fiercely as her heart. "I know you want to, and I need you to. I need to touch you, Jesse. To feel your arms around me, to feel you inside me. I need it more than I've ever needed anything." And before she could change her mind, she reached down, grasped the edge of her shirt, and lifted it over her head.

He wouldn't give his heart to her, so Faith would settle for his body. She could scale the wall separating them, close the distance yawning between them, if only for a few blissful moments. She could touch him, if not emotionally, then physically.

But you've touched more than my body, sweet Faith. Much more.

Jesse's familiar voice rumbled through her mind, and Faith's hands froze on the latch to her bra. Her fingers trembled, ice against the fiery skin of her chest. She'd heard the words distinctly. *His* words, yet his lips hadn't moved.

I'm not talking with my mouth. I'm speaking from the heart. Your heart.

"I . . . How did you do that?"

"You wanted me to talk to you," he said out loud, his lips hinting at a grin. "So I did." There was no humor in his gaze, however. Only hunger. A deep-seated, desperate hunger. The confusion, the pain of a moment ago had disappeared, fading into the dark ebony pools that seemed to reflect her every thought.

"Talk usually implies moving your mouth." The words stumbled past her trembling lips. Fear streaked through her, but then his voice whispered through her thoughts and the feeling subsided. It was so strange, and yet it seemed so natural for him to speak like this.

Not when it comes to us. We're linked, Faith. You and I. Connected. Can't you feel it? Just put aside your skepticism and feel.

She did. She closed her eyes, breaking the mesmerizing pull of his gaze and concentrating on the thrumming of her own blood within her body. It was *her* body, yet . . . She didn't feel alone. She felt an energy inside her, pulsing through her veins, filling up all the empty spaces.

It's me you feel.

Her eyes snapped open and found his. Turmoil raged in the dark depths and she knew he fought himself. He wanted to leave; at the same time he wanted to stay. With her. Inside her.

You feel me, Faith, and I feel you just as strongly. You were so worried about touching me emotionally, but you don't realize that you already have. You might not know all my secrets, but you know me. You can feel my heart beat, my blood pump. You can feel me, inside yourself.

Her heart beat faster and her palm pressed to her chest. Denial streaked through her as she felt the frantic double thump. Not one heartbeat, but two. Side by side. Hers and his . . .

She shook her head, her passion on hold in the face of the shock swamping her. "This is impossible."

Nothing is impossible.

The heartbeats increased in tempo, demanding to be recognized. Believed.

She shook her head. "I—I don't understand this. How? Why?"

Put aside your questions, Faith, and just let yourself believe. For tonight. And finish what you started. His gaze riveted on her breasts, still concealed beneath the lace of her bra.

"A few minutes ago you said this was a bad idea. That we shouldn't. That you didn't want to."

"I never said that last part," he said out loud. "I do want it. I want you, but I can't make any promises. For us there's just one night. This night. No talk. Just the two of us, touching, loving."

His eyes sparkled in the darkness, like a velvet sky filled with stars, and Faith found herself mesmerized for a long second. Gone were the turmoil and indecision at staying with her. He'd made up his mind.

For now. Tonight.

Faith's own niggling doubts faded away. So many things stood unanswered between them, but at that moment none of them mattered.

She needed him and he needed her. Everything else—his secrets, his past, this strange connection between them—all faded in the desire swamping her—*their*—senses.

The bra unsnapped and Faith let the silk straps slide down her arms.

His gaze reached across the distance to her, stroking her skin, following the curve of her breasts, tracing her aching nipples.

More . . . She wasn't sure if it was his command or her own, or maybe both. She only knew she needed to comply. Her fingers went to the snap on her jeans. Then the zipper hissed and Faith slid the denim down her legs. Cool air swept over her bare skin, turning it to gooseflesh. Then his gaze chased away the sudden chill as quickly as it had come, heating her body, her blood, until she felt a bead of sweat glide down her temple. It was so hot. Blistering . . .

More.

With the word came another wave of heat, until even the skimpy silk of her panties felt stifling against her skin. She hooked her fingers through the lace and slid the material down.

Righting herself, she stood before him, her skin bathed in moonlight, her nipples hard and throbbing, so desperate for him that it was all she could do to keep from sinking to her knees from the incredible need.

"So beautiful," he said. "You're so beautiful." He stared at her, his eyes burning over her, through her. Tension held his body tight; his muscles bunched beneath his T-shirt. Taut lines carved his face, making his features seem harsh, fierce, predatory.

The specks of gold in his eyes flared, gleamed, scorching her when fear might have cooled the desire searing her senses. He stepped closer, blocking out the play of light through her living room window.

Pale silver light shimmered around him, making him seem dark and sinister by comparison. A man of deep secrets and forbidden dreams. Yet the light didn't just outline him; it enveloped him.

He pulled the T-shirt over his head and dropped it at his feet. Where Faith had felt his strength before, now she saw it with her own eyes. Muscles carved his torso, from his bulging biceps and shoulders to the rippled plane of his abdomen. Dark, silky hair sprinkled his chest, narrowing to a tiny whorl of silk that disappeared beneath the waistband of his jeans.

Her gaze swept down to the prominent bulge beneath his zipper, and a memory rushed at her—his arousal pressing into her buttocks, so strong and insistent. She swallowed.

He reached out and crooked a finger under her chin, forcing her attention to his face. "There's nothing to be scared of. We've done this before."

"We weren't face-to-face then."

"We were that day at the hospital."

"That was different. You . . ." Her words tripped and she blushed.

"Don't be embarrassed, Faith. Not with me, not ever."

"I've never really seen you before."

"But you've felt me." His fingertip trailed down the column of her throat to linger at the base, where her pulse pounded a furious drumbeat against the pad of his thumb. He caressed the spot and the tempo increased. Faster, faster . . .

She swallowed, gathering the remnants of control, and caught his hand. "I felt you, all right. But not all of you. You were hiding from me. Last night and today."

"I was hilt-deep inside you."

His gravelly voice conjured a vivid image and her insides tightened. Want speared through her and she forced a calming breath. "You were still hiding. You were surrounding me, inside of me, but you were holding back." She touched the shadowed plane of his jaw, felt the sting of stubble and ached to rub her face against it, her body.

She stiffened, fighting the urge. "No more," she went on. "I want all of you tonight. Everything you have to give. No hiding. Please." The last word came out as a desperate plea, and Faith cursed herself for sounding so needy.

But God help her, she was. She needed him. All of him.

A moment of silence passed between them and she could feel his indecision, his turmoil as it raged to the surface for a frightening moment in which she feared he would refuse her.

And if he did? Would she meet him on his terms?

Before she could contemplate the answer, a single word sighed through her head. . . . *Tonight*. Then he reached out.

He touched her nipples, just the soft rasp of his palms, and pleasure bolted through her. His strokes were featherlight, reverent as he brought the sensitive peaks to a throbbing, tingling, swollen awareness. Then he slid his hands under her breasts, grazed her rib cage as he moved to cup her buttocks.

He lifted her, sweeping her legs up on either side

of him and around, to lock her ankles at the small of his back. Then he settled her firmly against the rock-hard length barely contained within his jeans.

She wrapped her arms around his neck and lost herself to the delicious friction as he rocked her. The coarse material of his jeans rasped against her sensitive flesh, and pleasure prickled through her, igniting every nerve ending until her body fairly glowed from the feel of his.

A day's growth of beard rubbed against the tender flesh of her neck, the slope of her breasts, chafing her in a motion that was so exquisite—a white-hot pleasure simmering with tender pain—that it brought tears to her eyes. He was so gentle, and at the same time fierce, as if she were a treasure to be protected, cherished.

He arched her backward, drew one swollen nipple into his mouth, and suckled as gently as a babe. Sensation spread through her, like thick honey pooling over a warm surface. It was just a hint of things to come, a subtle stirring of feeling that marked the beginning of a leisurely seduction, and Faith realized that he'd meant what he'd said.

Tonight. All night. He intended to take his time. To drive her to the brink, only to pull her back. Again and again and—

"Again," he added, moving his mouth away from her pouting nipple to stare into her eyes. "We've had it fast and furious, and now I want it slow."

"And sweet?" She raised an eyebrow at him, feeling wicked and wild and incredibly sexy. He made her feel that way. He shattered her inhibitions until there was nothing but the two of them. No world waiting to pass judgment. No expectations to meet. Just them. Jesse and Faith. Man and woman.

"Not exactly." He trailed his tongue over his bottom lip, and her nipple, still damp from the moist heat of his mouth, seemed to tingle. "More like slow and *thorough*. But since you brought it up . . ." His eyes gleamed brighter, a lazy grin tilting his sensuous lips. "I bet you taste every bit as sweet as you look."

Before she could respond, he captured her lips in a kiss that sent her thoughts spinning. His tongue tangled with hers, delving and tasting until she could barely breathe. And when she did, it was his breath that filled her lungs, just as his desire flowed into her, pumped through her, mingling with her own in a storm of need that raged fiercer than the nastiest typhoon.

She didn't feel the motion as he carried her. He could have floated into the bedroom, for all she knew. She was suddenly aware only of the soft mattress at her back, and of his body—dark and hot— towering over her.

He straddled her, his knees planted firmly on either side of hers. The faded material of his jeans hugged his hard thighs, showing every ripple of muscle. His bare torso gleamed with a fine sheen of perspiration that caught flickers of light from passing cars, like the twinkle of stars reflecting off a dark, mysterious lake. Faith couldn't help herself. She reached up, trailed her hands along his slick muscled flesh, felt the bulge and ripple of his shoulders. She splayed her fingers in the hair covering his chest, her touch tentative, exploratory, as she followed the path of silk that narrowed as it descended his abdomen. She stopped just shy of the waistband to his jeans, suddenly wary.

His eyes burned like midnight fire, his muscles tight with raw energy. He balled his hands into fists at his sides, and she knew it took everything he had not to cover her hand with his and urge her on.

Touch me. His deep voice echoed through her mind, yet she couldn't seem to make herself follow the command.

She'd felt his body's strength, but this was different. This was . . . *looking,* and for all her determination and bravado, heat crept up her neck. Her fingers trembled.

He leaned down, his tongue flicking a ripe nipple, and she gasped. His mouth was hot and wet, his tongue tormenting the stiff peak until she arched against him.

"Unzip me," he finally said, his voice ragged, and there was no hesitation in her movements this time.

The zipper hissed and he sprang hot and eager into her hands. He pulled away from her then and stared down as she held him. Her attention riveted on his hot, pulsing flesh. She'd known he was huge. She'd felt him, glimpsed him, but the reality was more than she'd bargained for. Bigger. More beautiful.

He was smooth as satin and as hard as an iron spike, she realized as she trailed her fingers over him, touching the ripe head of his desire. He jumped in her hands and she smiled, feeling a surge of feminine power she'd never experienced before.

But then she'd never touched a man like this. Never held him in her hands and stroked him the way she now stroked Jesse.

In a way, just this—this holding and stroking and exploring—seemed more intimate than anything she'd experienced in her past. Her encounters with her college boyfriend had been hollow. There had been a couple of tender kisses, some groping in the dark to remove boxers and panties, a few moments of heavy panting; then it had been over.

But this . . . This was surely the way it was meant to be between a man and a woman.

"Between us," he said. He stilled her movements then and placed her arms above her head. "Now it's my turn."

He kissed her then, slowly and deeply before his mouth moved to her jaw, sweeping a trail of fire down her neck to her tender breasts. He cupped and licked and suckled until Faith thrashed her head on the pillow and her hips rotated, searching for him. She came so close to falling apart. He suckled her hard, exerting just the right amount of pressure to have her moaning his name, clutching at the bed-sheets. She reached for him time after time, but he forced her hands back above her head, the motion lifting her breasts in silent invitation. And he suckled her harder, greedier. Only when she nearly burst into a thousand pieces did he pull away. The distance cooled her feverish skin for a rational moment, until she became acutely aware of his hands.

They slid down her belly, fingers ruffling her pubic hair with gentle tugs that sent tingles of electricity dancing up her spine. Then his attention moved lower, to the insides of her thighs. Fingers rasped lazy circles against her tender flesh, moving so close to her heat, her heart. So dangerously close.

"More," she begged shamelessly. She was past the point of modesty. She needed him inside her. *Now*.

"Soon," Jesse promised, aching to fill her as much as she ached to be filled. But he wanted to watch her. Like her, he'd been deprived of that pleasure their first night together, and the time at the hospital had been sweet, yet unfulfilling. Tonight he intended to satisfy them both. Completely. No holding back, he'd promised her, and he meant to keep his word.

He cupped her heat and she arched into his palm. Every muscle in his body went rigid as he fought for control. His gaze riveted on her face and he touched her slickness, rubbing her sensitive nub with his index finger.

The friction of his callused fingertip against the delicate tissue wrung a gasp from her. He repeated the motion, exerting just the tiniest bit more pressure.

She came up off the bed, her body bowing toward him. A pink flush spread over her breasts, up her neck, to gather in her cheekbones. Her kiss-swollen lips parted on a breathless moan that filled his ears and sent an ache straight to his already straining flesh.

He wanted her like this every night. Wanted to wake her up with his kisses in the morning, share breakfast, lunch, and dinner with her, wrap his arms around her and watch the sun set from her back porch. He wanted . . . her. Every moment of every day, from here until—

No! He clamped his eyes shut. He had only this moment. This night. Now.

He opened his eyes to find her staring up at him, her gaze bright with desire despite her fierce culmination only moments before. He stood, stripped away his jeans and underwear, then joined her on the bed.

She opened her legs, welcoming him, and he slid between them. He wanted to warm her up, to stir her senses again before he entered her, but she would have none of it. She grasped his buttocks and pulled him to her.

He slid inside in one deft motion that sucked the

air from his lungs and sent the blood roaring through his veins. Before he could catch his breath, she started to move, rotating her hips, her inner muscles contracting, sucking at him, the internal caress nearly making him spill himself right then and there.

She was so hot, so welcoming, and she was killing him. But this death was sweet and Jesse followed her willingly into the unknown.

He started to thrust, strong and sure and deep in a motion that sent them both hurtling into oblivion. Eyes clamped tight, he pumped into her over and over.

And in those last few moments, as they teetered on the edge of climax, he felt her soft fingertips on his face.

"Look at me," she commanded in a breathy whisper. "I want to see you."

Their gazes locked, and though Jesse knew he was about to make the biggest mistake of all—and he'd made many where Faith was concerned—he couldn't refuse her. He thrust deep, watched her beautiful neck arch, her lips part, her eyes glaze, and never so much as blinked.

Even when he felt his control slip and saw the frightened expression that gripped her face.

"What . . . ? Your eyes . . . your"—she gasped—"*eyessss.*" The word trailed off into a deep moan of pleasure.

He simply pumped harder, loving her with his body and lulling her with his gaze until her fear disappeared and wonder took its place. A few more strokes and he exploded. His back arched, his teeth ground together, and he spilled himself deep inside of her.

She followed his climax with one of her own, calling his name and clinging to him as if he were her last hope on earth.

The action would be repeated again and again before sleep finally overwhelmed them and *tonight* dwindled to a bittersweet close.

A pale pink glow softened the horizon when Jesse finally opened his eyes. He stared down at Faith curled against his side, the sheet bunched at her waist, her beautiful breasts gleaming white in the semidarkness. He leaned over and placed a tender kiss on her chest, felt the beat of her heart against his lips. His own heart thudded in response.

His eyes burned and he blinked against the sudden realization.

What the hell had he done?

He'd thrown all thoughts about the future to the wind and loved her as he'd wanted to from the beginning. No holding back. No hiding.

His mind replayed visions of the night before, the fear when she'd stared into his eyes and seen the truth. . . .

For the length of two seconds, he'd thought he'd fouled things up royally; then their lovemaking had overwhelmed her and he'd been safe, his identity still a carefully guarded secret.

But she was sure to remember and want an explanation.

I'm not really a man. I mean, I am a man, but I'm not. I'm an angel—a spirit who looks and feels like a man, and I've got a miracle for you before I say goodbye.

Dread washed over him. There was no way she would believe the truth. She would think he'd lied to her, manipulated her feelings to get her to open up to him, then duped her into bed for a quick lay before going on his merry way.

And what if she did believe him?

It still wouldn't change the fact that he *had* lied to her, manipulated her feelings to get her to open up to him, then duped her into a quick lay—or a couple of them—only to say *adios*. Good-bye . . .

A knifelike pain sliced through him and buried its blade in his heart. Had he really thought he could push everything aside, have one terrific night with her, then turn his back? Had they snatched his common sense when they'd been handing out miracles?

He took another deep breath and the scent of her—roses and fresh rainwater—filled his senses. He had to get away. To think. To calm his raging hormones, he realized when he glanced down at his already pulsing flesh.

But at that moment, the throbbing in his groin was nothing compared to the pain gripping his heart.

He didn't want one night. He wanted every night with Faith Jansen. Every tomorrow.

"Dammit," he muttered, sliding from the bed to yank on his jeans.

His hand paused at his pocket, his fingers diving inside to pull out the scrap of lacy silk. Faith's panties. He'd carried them around since that night in the restaurant. They'd tormented him, tantalized him almost as fiercely as the woman herself.

Almost, but not quite.

He forced his fingers open, letting the panties fall to her dresser. He'd never meant to get this close, to fall this hard, to *love* her. . . .

Holy hell, what *had* he done?

Chapter Seventeen

"Have you heard anything about Daniel?" Faith asked Bradley early the next morning as she sat on the edge of the bed, the phone clutched in her hand.

"Not a word, but the police seem to think he'll turn up. I thought Mike and I would hit the streets in a little while. Trudy knows the area pretty well and she said she'd be glad to help us out after she meets with Estelle this morning."

"Thanks for looking out for her yesterday and last night."

"No trouble. She and Emily took to each other right away. They talked about everything, mostly you. Emily and the others were really glad to see you yesterday."

Faith smiled. "I was glad to see them."

"Good, because I expect you to be even more glad in the weeks to come. Even with Jesse around, I need help over here, especially with summer break just days away."

"I'll be back," she promised, almost amazed at how easily the words came. But then they'd always been there inside her, buried beneath the pain and grief. The fear.

And though she was still afraid, it wasn't the paralyzing fear she'd felt only a few short weeks ago. Jesse had seen to that. He'd helped her overcome the emotion to see what really mattered in her life. Her kids.

Him.

"Daniel's one tough kid." Bradley's voice drew her away from her thoughts. "Did you and Jesse find out anything last night?"

Too much, Faith thought, her gaze going to the empty space on the bed next to her, the indentation still warm and smelling of Jesse.

"We came up with a couple of leads." She picked up the pillow and lifted it to her nose, drinking in the scent. The musky mingling of raw male and soap drifted through her senses and fed her determination. "I'm going to hit the pavement again and start passing out flyers this afternoon, as soon as I take care of something," she told Bradley. She said goodbye, slid the receiver into place, and sat there for a few minutes, the pillow cradled in her lap.

She'd found out something last night, all right, but it had nothing to do with Daniel and everything to do with the man who'd run out on her this morning. Again.

Her gaze shot to the dresser, to the silky panties she hadn't seen since Jesse had stuffed them into his pocket that night at Flaco's. He'd left them behind, a memento to say what he didn't have the courage to.

Good-bye.

It shouldn't have surprised her. He'd made no promises last night. *No tomorrows.* But while his mouth had been warning her away, she'd seen a future in his eyes.

Those incredible eyes. She closed her own, seeing the brilliant white of his, so warm and mesmerizing. So . . . out of this world. There'd been no play of light, no overactive imagination—nothing to dismiss the impossibility of what she'd seen.

It had been real. He'd been real.

She could still hear his thoughts, feel the double heartbeats thumping away in her chest.

Jesse wasn't merely a man. She knew it in her heart, and perhaps she'd known it all along. The signs had been there—the faint glimpses of that unnatural light in his eyes, the strange coincidence of his presence at Faith's House, his knowledge of Jane—yet Faith's head hadn't wanted to acknowledge them, to believe.

She did believe now, but in what?

Moving the pillow aside, she headed for the closet. She didn't have a clue at the moment, but she intended to find out.

"Jesse," Faith said softly as she sat in a downtown branch of the Houston Public Library later that afternoon and stared at the result of hours of research on the microfiche screen in front of her.

She wasn't sure what she'd expected to find when she'd started researching Jane's brother. Maybe a link as to Jesse's identity—the mention of his name as a friend, a co-worker of the murdered cop. She hadn't thought to find Jesse, himself.

His image, so handsome in a police uniform, glared back at her. But it wasn't the sight of his handsome face, his dark, intense eyes that froze the air in her lungs. It was the front-page headline printed above the picture. LOCAL POLICE OFFICER MURDERED.

She swallowed against the sudden tightness and went on to read the story about a rookie cop who'd only been with the Houston Police Department for a few months when the tragedy had happened. He'd had no friends, no family other than his brother.

Or so the authorities had thought, because no one really knew Jesse Savage. He was a loner, a new kid in town. The authorities had known only what they'd found in the house. Two bodies. Two brothers. Surely someone, somewhere had known there was a sister. Jesse had more than likely signed insurance papers, or listed her as his beneficiary in case of death. But the knowledge had slipped through the cracks.

And so no one had realized that the wounded girl who'd been anonymously dropped outside a hospital across town had been Jesse Savage's sister. No family had come forth to claim her. In a city the size of Houston, there'd been no way to link Jane with Jesse. But she'd been the sister he'd mentioned. Faith knew it in a heartbeat.

Rachel.

Faith clutched the friendship medallion and whispered the name, feeling the syllables on her lips, and a warmth spread through her, a temporary reprieve from the turmoil raging inside her. Rachel lived on. Inside of her.

But Jesse?

The warmth faded into a chill that seeped into her bones, causing her to tremble. Jesse was dead. *Dead.*

Denial raged through her, sending the blood pounding through her veins. She'd been prepared for something odd, but this was insane. It couldn't be! She'd talked to him, touched him, loved him only last night, and he'd been very much alive.

The papers had made a mistake. A terrible, terrible mistake. He'd survived. . . .

Only to abandon his sister?

As fiercely as her conscience ranted against the notion of his being dead, the facts were too clear to ignore.

Most compelling was Jane's continued anonymity. Faith remembered the softness in Jesse's eyes when he'd mentioned Rachel's name, the affection in his voice. He'd loved her. He wouldn't have abandoned her to the foster-care system. Never in a million years. She knew it in her heart. He would have found her and nothing short of death would have kept him away.

Death.

Her gaze flicked to the closed casket in the far corner of the photo, the American flag draped atop, and she knew, despite logic and reason that denied the possibility, that Jesse *had* died that night. He'd been buried alongside his younger brother. He'd gone on to the hereafter.

No, he hadn't gone on. Somehow, some way, he was here now.

And Faith had fallen in love with him.

Tears filled her eyes, spilling over. *Love? No way!* She didn't want to be in love with a man full of secrets and lies and—

Goodness, strength, and warmth.

She'd seen the goodness in the way he treated the kids at Faith's House, felt his strength as he'd drawn her out of her grieving shell and helped her stand up to her own fears. She'd reveled in his warmth when he'd looked at her, into her, to see past the barricade she'd built around her heart.

He was *dead*. The truth was there, in front of her, inside of her, yet it wasn't enough. She needed more—the how and why and where.

She flicked off the screen. The newspapers had told her all they could. There was only one man who could fill in the blanks and turn the impossible into the possible, or tell her that the papers had, indeed, been wrong.

He was a man who'd walked into her life under false pretenses, telling lies and weaving some kind of magic spell she'd been unable to resist.

A man who'd loved her so fiercely, only to turn his back on her, not once or twice, but three times now.

A man who was more than a man . . . or less.

And he was the man she loved, despite everything.

In the garage apartment at Faith's House, Jesse stepped into a cold shower. He grimaced, feeling the water prickle his aching muscles.

He really was a man again. Flesh and bone. Muscle and tissue. The knowledge still overwhelmed him. One minute he'd been drifting; trapped in a black void with only his damned conscience for company, and the next he'd been knocking on Faith's door. She'd opened her door to him, and her life.

Faith's vision filled his mind, and he saw her as she'd been that morning, sleeping next to him amid a tangle of sheets. As he watched her chest move in a steady rise and fall, felt each soft breath she took, he wasn't sure which was more beautiful: the warm, encompassing light, or this woman. *His* woman. The woman he loved.

313

Who was he kidding? He knew. Hell, he'd known from the beginning, he just hadn't allowed himself to recognize it. He'd needed to fulfill his mission, to move on to an afterlife of forgiveness.

Yet leaving no longer held the same promise as before, because Jesse Savage had already found forgiveness.

He'd realized it the moment he'd kicked the motorcycle into gear and roared out of Faith's driveway that morning. As he was running, hiding.

In a crystal-clear second, the stormy turmoil inside him had given way to a clear, cloudless sky, and Jesse had understood what had happened to him with his murderer outside of The Dungeon last night.

Why he hadn't killed the man and avenged his own and his brother's deaths.

He leaned against the cool tile of the shower. Cold water hammered at him as his mind replayed the scene—the desperation in Bryan's eyes, the terrified apology bursting from his lips. Of course it didn't make up for what had happened to Jesse and his family. Words meant absolutely zero. Actions carried the only real weight.

And Jesse knew now in his heart—his beating, flesh-and-blood heart, that it didn't matter that he'd never said the words to his brother and sister.

I love you.

They had known. He'd given up his own life to make theirs better—forfeited a chance at a football scholarship to quit school and get a job; he'd sacrificed his own time and energy to work two, sometimes three jobs to keep clothes on their backs and food in their stomachs. Perhaps he hadn't been the

314

best brother in the world, but he'd always done his utmost.

And they had known that.

He felt it in his gut, a knowledge that had been with him since that last breath, but he'd been too bitter, too busy villifying himself to acknowledge it.

Always blaming himself . . .

If only he'd been more obedient, more helpful, better at sports or cards or fishing, maybe his father wouldn't have left in the first place. And if he'd been bigger, stronger, more handsome . . . more like his father, then maybe his mother wouldn't have drunk herself to death. And if he'd been a better listener, a stronger role model, then maybe his brother wouldn't have fallen in with those drug dealers. And if he'd kept his brother and sister in Restoration, away from Houston, then maybe Death never would have paid them a visit. And . . .

The *and*s were endless. Pointless, he saw now.

His father had left because he'd wanted to, his mother had died because she'd given up, and that fateful night had been beyond his control. He couldn't control everything. There was a predetermined time to come into this world, and a time to leave. Everything in between was left up to chance. Even if Jesse had done things differently that night, his brother would still be gone. It had been his time.

But it hadn't been Jesse's time. He'd died too soon, and so he'd been given a chance for salvation—before Judgment Day—a chance to ease his troubled conscience and find forgiveness.

But he'd found forgiveness here on earth, inside himself. Last night. He'd faced his past—the man who'd robbed him of his family and his future—and the tight leash of rage had snapped.

He'd realized then that speaking the words to his

brother and sister wouldn't gain him forgiveness any more than killing his murderer would soothe the anger festering inside him. Jesse had to forgive himself, make peace with his conscience. And now he had. The moment he'd let go of Bryan, he had. Bryan and Little J would pay for their crimes sooner or later—everyone did—but not by Jesse's hand. Vengeance wasn't his objective, or his duty.

Last night had brought another revelation, as well. Jesse wasn't ready for heaven, for an eternity of light. He wanted a lifetime with Faith, and there was only one way for him to have that.

He'd never considered it before, because he'd been haunted, but now . . . Now he was at peace with himself, and Faith no longer needed a miracle to restore her hope in life. He'd seen the proof yesterday when she'd searched so diligently for Daniel. Her faith had already been renewed. She was returning to her old self, her responsibilities. She didn't need a miracle to urge her on the right path. She was already there.

He shut off the water, pulled the shower curtain aside, and reached for a towel. Dripping, he crossed the tiled floor, stopping in front of the bathroom mirror. His eyes flickered. Light. Although clothed in flesh and blood, he still wasn't an ordinary man. Not completely. Not yet.

But he could fix that, he thought, glancing through the open doorway at the alarm clock sitting on the nightstand. It was already late afternoon, today was the day. The anniversary of his death. He either delivered the miracle before midnight, or forfeited his chance at heaven and lived out his remaining days here on earth.

Gone was the urgency Jesse had always felt, the internal clock ticking his chance away. He wasn't anxious because he knew what he was going to do, or rather what he wasn't going to do. As warm and comforting as heaven had felt, it paled in comparison to the warmth in Faith's eyes. The hunger. The tenderness. The love.

Dammit, he couldn't leave her. He wouldn't. He would stay with her, love her with all his heart, make her happy and hopeful and all the things she should be. He could do it himself, without a miracle.

At least he told himself that, swore it with every bit of determination he had. He would be everything to her—friend, lover, pillar of strength—and it would be enough. *He* would be enough.

With that vow firmly in mind, Jesse Savage dropped to his knees one final time.

"Jesse!" Faith stood at the top of the stairs leading to the garage apartment and pounded on the door. "I know you're in there! Open up!" She pounded harder. "Dammit, I said open up—"

The door swung wide. Clad only in a fluffy white towel draped around his waist, Jesse filled the doorway. Water trickled down his bare torso through the dark hair covering his chest.

In the bright light of day he seemed even darker, more mysterious. . . .

Dead.

She swallowed. "I know about that night." Her voice was shaky. "About what happened to you. You're . . . You're supposed to be . . ." She couldn't make herself say the word. But she didn't have to.

He knew.

His gaze caught hers, and his dark eyes were shuttered. The specks of gold that always flared whenever he looked at her had dimmed.

He wore no expression, his face a collection of

sharp angles and planes. A day's growth of beard covered his jaw, crept down his neck. His wet hair had been slicked back, curling down his neck, just above his shoulders. He adjusted his grip on the door handle, the movement rippling the muscles in his arm and shoulder.

He's just a man, she told herself. *A powerful, attractive, sinfully sexy man. But just a man.*

Suddenly an entire day of searching at the library, staring at microfiche records, seemed like a hazy dream, and a smile tugged at her lips. "This is crazy. I can't believe I'm standing here about to say what I'm going to say. I mean, it's so impossible."

"Anything is possible if you believe."

She gave him a pointed stare. "And if you don't?"

"I'm here, Faith. Real, whether you believe it or not."

She tried to swallow past the sudden lump in her throat. "But you can't be. You're . . ." She swallowed again. "You were murdered."

He didn't deny the fact. He merely held her gaze, his dark eyes probing into hers. "I'm not dead."

She gave a quivering smile. "Of course not. I mean, I know that. You're standing right in front of me." She touched him then, as if to reassure herself that he was real. Warm muscle met her palm. So warm and . . . *alive.*

Hysterical laughter bubbled on her lips. To think she'd actually come here to confront him and accuse him of dying. Of being dead. *Dead*, for heaven's sake!

But the evidence stayed rooted in her mind, and even while she tried to dismiss the thoughts as bogus, she couldn't. Not until Jesse reassured her with his own mouth. Then she would trust him. She would believe. When she heard the truth straight from him.

"I've been doing some research."

He nodded.

"I was looking at old newspapers. After last night . . ." She licked her suddenly dry lips. Her gaze caught his. "Jesse, I went to City Hall, and to the library, to try to find some record of you."

"I was born in Restoration."

"I know that. City Hall didn't have a birth certificate, but they had . . ." She swallowed and tried again. "They had a death certificate." Her gaze collided with his and the words poured from her lips. "You died from several stab wounds exactly one year ago today."

"It wasn't my time to go."

She shook her head, trying to clear it. She'd expected him to say the account was wrong, the death certificate forged. That he was part of the Witness Protection Program and had assumed the real Jesse Savage's identity. Or that maybe he really was Jesse Savage, now a criminal running from the law, who'd needed to fake his death to evade justice. Or . . .

"What are you telling me? You didn't die that night? The newspapers were wrong? The death certificate is a fake?"

"I didn't say that."

She threw up her hands. "You're not *saying* anything. Yes or no. Did you die?" She couldn't believe the words were coming out of her mouth. Obviously he hadn't died. He was alive and well and standing right in front of her.

"Yes."

The word thundered through her head, shaking her sanity and sending her reality into a tailspin. This wasn't happening.

"You mean yes, the newspapers and death certificate were wrong?"

"No, I mean I did die that night."

He grabbed her hands, but she pulled away, afraid that if she touched him, she might want to believe his ridiculous explanation. She pushed past him into the apartment and crossed the room to gaze out the window. "This is crazy. It can't be for real."

"It is," he said, shutting the door and coming up behind her. But he didn't touch her. He simply stood there, so close, so warm, so . . . alive.

"You remember that guy we met up with last night outside the bar?"

She nodded, her attention fixed on the window. She stared at the roof of the shelter, while her mind flashed back to the rage she'd seen in Jesse's eyes, the anger holding his body tight.

"He was the one."

She whirled. "What do you mean?"

"You know what I mean."

She backed away from him, her mouth open, soundless for several seconds. "He—he was the one? The . . . the one who *killed* you?" She closed her eyes and shook her head. "I don't understand this. If he killed you then how can you still be here? What are you? My imagination? Some sort of ghost? A devil? An—"

"—angel," he finished for her. "Sort of."

She blinked. "Sort of?"

He stared at her. "Do you believe in Fate?"

She shrugged, clasping her trembling hands in front of her. "I guess so. I never really thought about it."

"Not it. Her. I did die that night, but it wasn't my time to go. It was an accident of Fate. She made a mistake, took me too soon; so here I am now, flesh and blood, with another chance to live out my life. I didn't want that chance at first, but now I do."

"Let me get this straight. There's a preordained time to die, and you died too soon?" He nodded. "You were shortchanged?" He nodded again. "So God—"

"It's a bright light," he cut in. "I don't know exactly what it is. . . ."

"Okay, so this light gave you a second chance to live here until your time does come?"

He nodded.

She shook her head. "You really expect me to believe all this?"

"You already do." He stared deep into her eyes, into her soul, and saw the truth.

You already do. The words whispered through her head. His words. Their words. They were linked, connected by some invisible force. The same force that had brought him back here. To her.

"To save you," he said, reading the frantic thoughts racing through her head. "You're a good person, Faith, and that's rare in this day and age. They couldn't stand to lose you."

"They?"

"The voices in the light. They didn't want to lose you. Fate had to correct her mistake, so I was sent to you. You were lost, Faith, and I was to help you find your way."

She inched to the side and backward, and came up against the wall. Leaning back, she splayed her fingers against the cool wood, needing to feel something real. Jesse wasn't real, and this couldn't be happening.

"Faith, trust me." His fingertips forced her chin up and her gaze met his. "I am real. I'm flesh and blood." He touched her hand to his chest. "You felt me with your hands, your body. I'm a man now."

"And the past year?"

"I told you the truth before. I was wandering . . . in the nothingness. And then I knew what I was to do, and what my reward would be. I never understood why I was chosen. There were many who would have jumped at the chance to come back. But now I realize it was because of Rachel—Jane. My sister." His eyes brightened and he swallowed. "Thank you, Faith," he said in a quiet voice that wrenched at her heart. "Thank you for being there for her, for helping her find her way out of the nightmares, and for all you did."

"I . . ." Her throat tightened and hot tears spilled down her cheeks. She closed her eyes as memories rushed at her—visions of Jane's smiling face and dark eyes—Jesse's eyes. Denial waged one last battle inside her. It was all too incredible. Unbelievable. *Impossible.*

"I know it sounds wild and crazy," he went on. "Hell, a year ago I wouldn't have believed it myself. The afterlife, angels and devils and all that hoopla, was just a lot of bunk, a nice explanation to give people hope in a hopeless world. But it isn't a crock. It's real. I've seen it." He stared past her, and for the first time since she'd come into the room, she saw the specks in his eyes twinkle and flare. "You die, but that's not the end of it. Afterward, there's this light," he said, wonder in his voice. "And it's so bright, so warm. . . . I've never seen anything like it."

"I have," she said. She touched his jaw and drew his gaze to her own. "Every time I look at you."

The last niggling doubt slipped away as she stared at him, into him. Some things weren't meant to be explained logically or rationally. Some things simply *were*.

Jesse had come to her, had saved her, loved her,

and she refused to question the how and why. It was enough that he was here now, in front of her, with her.

She smiled, and for the first time in a long time Faith Jansen started to believe in a happily ever after.

Then she heard the shout coming from downstairs, the pounding of footsteps, and her happiness shattered.

"Faith! Jesse!" Bradley called out, his fists pounding the door. "They found Daniel! He's on top of the old Marbury Building, and he's getting ready to jump!"

Chapter Eighteen

Ten minutes later, Faith and Jesse swerved to a stop in front of the Marbury Building, a six-story structure that had once housed Marbury Savings and Loan. The savings and loan had gone under, the building closed up to await sale. That had been nearly six years ago and the property still stood vacant. Once neatly trimmed shrubs sat neglected, now a tangled mass of overgrown vegetation partially concealing the broken first-floor windows. The NO TRESPASSING sign shone like a red-and-white beacon against the crumbling brick.

There were many trespassers now. Patrol cars littered the parking lot, along with an ambulance and a fire truck. A police barricade blocked the front of the building. A group of uniformed officers held a buzzing crowd of onlookers in check.

Jesse killed the motorcycle's engine, climbed off, and reached for Faith.

She hesitated, her gaze sweeping the front of the building, her neck craning up as she directed her attention to the small figure peering over the edge of the roof. Daniel.

Her heart stopped beating for a long second and fear iced her insides.

"This is too intense." She shook her head, a swirl of doubt gripping her body, refusing to let her budge. "I—I don't see what I can do to help."

"Just being here will help, Faith. You're his foster mother." Then Jesse's warm hand covered hers. "Come on. It'll be all right."

She gathered her courage and managed a nod. A few seconds later, she was following him through the crowd to the front of the barricade, where Bradley waited for them. There an officer ushered the three toward the building.

Faith wasn't quite sure how she managed each step. She'd covered many blocks over the past two days, beating the pavement to find Daniel, and now that she had, she could barely manage the short walk to the front door.

The minute she and Jesse and Bradley stepped inside, they found themselves in the middle of a monstrous room that had once been the bank lobby. The floors had been stripped of carpet, and an old Cupid fountain was now a decapitated block of chipped concrete. Police officers, firemen, and paramedics overflowed the room. Jesse stopped to answer background questions about Daniel, while Bradley went to use a nearby cellular phone to call Estelle.

"The name's Miller. Detective in charge," said a middle-aged man in a suit, who gripped Faith's elbow and led her toward the stairwell at the back of the building.

"This is the only way up or down," the detective said when Faith hesitated, her hand on the banister. "I'd offer you the elevator, but those things are in sorry shape, even if we could get the power turned on. Besides, they don't reach the roof, and that's where we're headed."

She stared up into the impenetrable blackness, and panic swamped her senses. Her fingers tightened. This was different, she told herself. This wasn't just searching for a missing teen. This was life and death. Life *or* death.

Oddly enough, as much as the notion frightened her, it was the very thing that forced her to take a step, then another and another. It was the one thing that kept her going when her fears and the endless chant—*Nobody's savior*—threatened to turn her around and send her running home.

"There's a rusted-out fire escape on the east side," the detective went on, his steps a steady clang on the metal steps. "We were hoping to send a surprise team up there, maybe get somebody behind him before he could realize what was happening, but my men have checked it out and it's very creaky. He would hear us coming a mile away."

"What about the fire department? They have ladders, don't they?"

"That would make too much noise, too. We don't want to spook him. They're busy setting up a tarp right now, in case he does jump. But that's about all they can do, especially considering the circumstances."

"What circumstances?"

The detective stopped two steps shy of the top and stared down at her. Softer shadows pushed from the door leading to the roof, outlining his shape. His features were indistinguishable, but where she couldn't see the serious set of his eyebrows, or the thin lines creasing his mouth, she could hear the strain in his voice.

"An old couple who lives up the street was driving by and saw Daniel up here about three hours ago. They're the ones who reported him. They wouldn't have thought anything about it—kids routinely hang out in this building—but the woman saw him holding a gun."

"A gun?"

The detective nodded. "Maybe he figures if he can't get up the nerve to jump, he can use a bullet. Or vice versa. Anyhow, the gun is what makes this situation all the more volatile. With his record, if things don't go his way, he could easily turn that gun on one of my men, or a civilian. Which brings me to my next point. I've agreed to let you talk to him, but you keep your distance, and under no circumstances move away from the shelter of this doorway. Understand?"

"Yes."

"I have to warn you. I doubt you'll have much luck. We had the staff shrink up here and she couldn't even get him to look at her. He just stands there, that gun in his hand . . ." His words trailed off and a shiver crept through Faith. Her fingers tightened on the banister.

"If you can't talk him down, I've got a team busy setting up a tarp out front. If he jumps from where he's standing now, we should get him. If he doesn't turn the gun on himself first."

Nobody's savior.

The phrase haunted Faith, making her legs tremble as she mounted the last two steps. She couldn't do this, she thought as she reached the doorway, the detective right in front of her. She couldn't save

Daniel. Just as she hadn't been able to save Jane. Not when it really mattered. Not when it came down to life or death.

Jane.

The girl's image flashed in Faith's mind, the way she'd been those last few moments before the accident. Laughing and smiling and talking nonstop. They'd just walked out of the movie theater after seeing *Sleepless in Seattle*, and Jane had been set on walking back to Faith's House rather than taking the bus. It had been a warm night. Clear. Perfect for an evening stroll.

Faith braced a hand against the stairwell wall and took a deep breath, but she didn't smell the sour stench of garbage and air pollution. Instead, the warm, buttery scent of popcorn filled her nostrils, and brought tears to her eyes.

I'm nobody's savior.. . . .

Faith saw the flashing DON'T WALK *sign as she and Jane approached the intersection. She was about to reach out, to remind the girl to hold up when a little old lady to Faith's right dropped her purse.*

"Let me," Faith said, bending to help the woman retrieve her belongings. She glanced away for just a few seconds. Two blinks of an eye, but that was all it took.

The squeal of tires filled her eardrums, and her gaze shot up to see the car whirl around the corner. So fast. So wild. Then she saw Jane halfway through the intersection.

"Nooooooooooo!" The scream tore from her lips, but it was too late. Jane's body smashed against the grille, flipped into the air, then crashed facedown near the opposite curb while Faith stood motionless. Powerless.

Nobody's savior . . .

* * *

"I—I can't do this," Faith mumbled, turning to go back down the stairs. Then the detective moved aside, giving Faith an unobstructed view of the roof, and Daniel.

A two-foot tall construction of raised concrete bordered the edge. Daniel stood on the short wall, staring off into a blue night sky that seemed to beckon him forward. Stars twinkled unspoken promises. *Salvation*, they whispered. *Comfort. Safety. Home.* And the nasty-looking gun cradled in his good hand was his one-way ticket to everything life had deprived him of.

At least that was the way he saw it. Faith knew it even before he turned and his gaze caught hers.

Hatred glittered in his pale eyes, but there was something else, as well. Fear. She'd read the emotion so many times in so many other kids. Kids she'd watched walk away from her. And kids she'd helped.

Every child at Faith's House had had the same look at one time. The same desolation. The same sense of hopelessness.

But no more.

Nobody's savior.

The truth rushed at her as frenzied as the sudden gust of wind that lashed at her face.

She hadn't been able to save Jane because what had happened, the accident, had been just that: an *accident*, no rhyme or reason to it. Faith had had no control of the driver or the car, no way of foreseeing or preventing the tragedy.

But this . . . This situation was entirely different. This was why she'd sat through four years of college. Why she'd volunteered hours on end at every shelter in the city that would have her. Why she'd spent nights with a telephone glued to one ear, answering phones for the local crisis hot line. To help troubled kids.

Here was a troubled kid, and he needed help.

His life or death wasn't going to be predetermined by a freak twist of fate. The outcome rested in his own hands. And hers.

Nobody's savior.

Not in Jane's case, but maybe for Daniel . . .

Please, she silently begged. *For Daniel.*

Fear slipped away as she stepped across the threshold. Police officers clustered just inside the doorway, none daring to venture out onto the roof, into Daniel's line of fire.

"Daniel," she called his name, her gaze as desperate as her voice. She stepped just outside the doorway.

"Hold it there," the detective ordered. "Not an inch farther, Ms. Jansen."

She heard the words and she knew of the danger. Daniel had a *gun,* for heaven's sake. She knew, yet she stepped forward anyway, against all reason and logic, as if the softly gusting summer wind changed direction and reached out for her, hauling her forward rather than pushing her away.

"Dammit!" the detective swore, reaching out for her, but Daniel waved his gun.

"Get back!" the barrel pointed wildly in their direction and the detective froze.

"You!" Daniel said to Faith. "You go back home." For all the viciousness in his words, he didn't point the gun at her. He kept it trained on the doorway behind her, on the cops who muttered and cursed at Faith's foolishness.

And they were right. What she was doing was foolish—and had never felt more right—as if all her training had led up to this one moment. This final test.

"You ain't wanted here," Daniel told her.

She shrugged. "Maybe not, but I'm here anyway." She held up her hands. "So why don't we talk?"

"You don't want to talk to me," he said, as if he'd crawled inside her head and read every past doubt she'd ever had. "I'm just another responsibility to you, another messed-up kid. Another burden."

"That's not true."

"Ain't it? You walked away from Faith's House that first day, away from me. 'Cause you had enough problems already, right?"

"I . . ." She shook her head, feeling suddenly like a bug under a microscope. "I had to go then, but I'm here now. I want to be here." As if he sensed the sincerity in her voice, his gun hand dropped to his side, and Faith took the opportunity to inch forward, step by slow step. "I want to help you, to be your friend."

As if Detective Miller had the same idea, she heard the squeak of his boots, the soft thud somewhere behind her, just to her left.

"Hold it!" Daniel jerked his hand up. The gun streaked through the air to aim at the roof door again.

The detective let loose another string of curses, echoing through the small group clustered at the top of the stairwell.

"And I don't need any friends," Daniel said, turning to Faith, yet he didn't point the gun at her. He kept it trained over her shoulder. "I don't need not one stinking friend."

"I do." Another step, then another. "I need all the friends I can get. Life is tough, even tougher without

331

somebody to share it with." She took another step. Then another.

He shook his head. "I ain't into sharing, and I don't like people nosing into my business. I don't want any friends."

"But what about needing them? There's a big difference. I don't necessarily want to be a foster mother, but I need to. It's something inside me that I can't control." The words came on their own, from deep inside her, and Faith marveled at the ease with which she said them. It was the truth, a truth she'd ignored for so long. Yet it was there, no matter how she tried to bury it. It was there, defining who she was, her actions.

And so she was here now. Trying her hand at salvation.

One more time.

One last time. The thought drifted through her head at the same time Daniel laughed.

"Get off it, lady. You don't *have* to be anything. None of us do. Ain't you ever heard of freedom of choice? That's what we got here in America." He laughed again, a sad, bitter sound that drifted across the distance to her. "Land of the free and all that crap."

"Then I'm free to come out here and talk to you, right?"

He shrugged. "And I'm free so's I don't have to listen."

"But I can still talk."

He didn't say anything. He just tilted his head upward and stared into the sky for all of five heartbeats. Enough time for her to move even closer.

"Are you crazy?"

"He's got a gun!"

"Don't be foolish!"

"This is suicide!"

The phrases echoed behind her. Far away, it seemed. So far, and Daniel was so close. No more than five or six steps.

"You should listen to them." He motioned toward the doorway. "Playing the hero ain't worth your life, lady."

"That's right, it isn't. My life is worth more than that gun in your hand, and so is yours." Another step. "It is, Daniel. I know it seems like such an easy way out, a solution, but it's not. There's no answer in giving up."

"You oughta know that." He smirked. "Given up a couple of times yourself, huh?"

"Yes," she said, the word trembling on her lips. "But here I am anyway."

"You don't have to be," he told her seriously, and the way he said the words shifted something inside her. "You could walk away. I'll let you walk away. Just turn around."

"Why are you doing this?" she asked.

"Haven't you figured it out by now?"

"You've obviously got a death wish. But why?" She took another step forward. "Are things that bad?"

"Damn straight. I ain't got no home. No family. Nobody."

"You've got me."

"You and your pity, right? I don't want it. I don't want anything. I just want to be left alone."

"I can't do that. You're my responsibility. I signed papers promising to look out for you. I know things seem bleak right now, but they'll get better if you just step down off that ledge, put the gun down, and talk to me."

He shook his head. "It's too late for talk. I need

this. This is what I deserve." He turned tortured eyes on her. "My ma killed herself, did you know that? Took one of these babies"—he held up the gun and pointed the barrel at his forehead—"and put a bullet right here. Bam!"

Faith flinched.

"Then it was over," he went on. "So quick. So final. I was standing right there and I didn't even have time to grab her hand. She was my ma, the only person I had. Then she was gone and I had nothing. Story of my life. A kid from nowhere with nothing but a foul mouth and a bad attitude."

"You've got more than that."

"You're right," he said, scratching his temple with the gun barrel, his finger resting on the trigger. "I've got this baby here."

"I was talking about me. You've got me, Daniel. I want to be your friend, if you'll give me a chance." She swallowed, fighting back the chill that chased down her arms as he tested the weight of the barrel near his temple. "Don't do this now. If things are really that bad, you can always end it later. Tomorrow. What's one more day?"

"No use putting it off."

"Maybe not, but you've made it this long. Another twenty-four hours isn't going to make that much of a difference. Just step down and talk to me." She reached him then, no more than an arm's length away, and stopped. She held out her hand. "Put down the gun, step down off the ledge, and we'll both walk away and go someplace to talk."

He stared at the gun in his hand, and for all his harsh words a moment before, his hands trembled. He shook his head. "I can't," he said, his voice suddenly small. "I have to do it this time. Things keep getting worse and I can't stop it."

"Faith!" Jesse's voice rushed at her and she glanced over her shoulder to see him in the roof doorway, struggling between the detective and a uniformed officer who fought to hold him back.

What the hell are you doing? The words exploded in her head like a loud boom of thunder.

It's okay, she thought, praying with all her might he could hear her. *Everything's going to be okay. Trust me.*

She turned back to Daniel. "Things don't have to get worse. You can help yourself, Daniel. You can let me help you. No more foster homes, no more detention centers. Just trust me, Daniel. Work with me, and things will be better." His gaze collided with hers and she saw the desperation. He wanted so much to believe. "Things don't have to be bad. You can have a good life, a home."

"A home . . ." He echoed her words, wonder in his voice. "A real home." The words were so soft they might have been her imagination. But then he leaned down. The gun clunked against the concrete.

"Yes," she said, her pulse leaping. She reached forward and held out her hand. "Now step down off the ledge. Take my hand and step down."

He stared at her, indecision in his eyes. Then it was like seeing an eraser wipe the trouble from his gaze. His features smoothed and he actually smiled.

And Faith's heart stopped beating altogether. Because she knew that smile—so warm and soft and familiar. His eyes sparkled, so rich and *brown*—She blinked. The color brightened into an undeniable blue and she shook her head to clear it.

This wasn't Jane. This was Daniel.

Nobody's savior.

This time she was. This time.

He leaned forward, his fingers brushing hers, and

Faith's heart thudded a victorious rhythm. Her fingers twitched, then closed, but it wasn't Daniel's hand she held. She held nothing.

She stared at her empty palm, which still tingled from his brief touch; then her gaze jerked up to capture his.

"Home," he whispered a heartbeat before he turned and stepped off into thin air.

"Nooooooooooo!" She lunged forward, grabbing for him, but it was too late.

"Faith." Jesse's arms closed around her, pulling her down off the ledge where she now stood. "I'm sorry. I'm so sorry."

But it was too late for sorry. Too late.

Daniel was—

"He's still alive!" Jesse said, staring down. "I saw him move."

Faith took off running then, Jesse on her heels. She flew down the stairs, out front to where the paramedics were looming over Daniel's body.

"I don't understand," a fireman was saying. "The tarp was right below him. He shoulda hit smack-dab in the middle."

But he'd missed it by a precious few inches, his body broken and bleeding on the pavement.

"The pulse is jumpy, but it's there," a paramedic said excitedly. "Let's get him loaded up. Radio Ben Taub that we've got a critical one."

"I need to go with him," Faith said, her gaze fixed on Daniel's bruised and bloodied face, as if, if she stared hard enough, she could will his eyes open.

"I'll take you." Jesse stood behind her, his hands on her shoulders, so warm and comforting. But she felt neither. She felt cold and isolated. Desperate.

"I want to ride with him," she said. "Please."

The paramedics nodded and motioned Faith inside once they had Daniel loaded.

"I'll be right behind you," Jesse promised, and Faith nodded at him, her gaze meeting his for the two seconds before the doors swung shut.

You did all you could, the reassurance echoed through her head, Jesse's gaze drilling into hers. *You tried. That's all anyone can ask of themselves.*

She nodded and a tingle of warmth rippled through her, thawing the ice that had settled into her bones. She took her seat near Daniel, careful to stay out of the way of the three paramedics who rushed here and there, turning on machines, hooking up IVs, each of them desperate to sustain this boy's life for those few precious minutes to the hospital.

And afterward?

She tried to focus on what Jesse had said. *You did all you could. You tried. That's all anyone can ask. . . .*

But his deep voice still couldn't keep the memories at bay, or soften the dreaded truth that Faith Jansen had failed again.

I'm sorry, Ms. Jansen.

Massive trauma.

We did all we could.

Faith reached for Daniel's bloody hand, closed her eyes, and did the only thing she could. She prayed.

Please! Faith's soft voice whispered in Jesse's head, and tears burned his eyes, blurring the fast-disappearing ambulance.

He turned and climbed onto his motorcycle. He needed to get to the hospital. To be with her, talk her through this—

But that wasn't the reason Jesse followed the racing ambulance. He knew there was nothing he could

337

say to ease her grief or restore her hope. His dream of a life here with her had been just that. A dream.

He'd wanted to be all things to her—the answer to every problem, the hope that opened her eyes in the morning, the strength that lulled her to sleep every night—and he could be, but not in this life.

His comforting words and embraces couldn't help her now, but his actions could. One final action that would separate them forever.

One miracle.

And as much as that scared him, it drove him on, her image, her sadness so heavy inside him that he felt it as his own. It *was* his own, because he loved Faith Jansen with all his heart, the emotion stronger than any he'd ever known.

Nobody's savior. She'd been wrong on that count. She was everybody's savior, especially his. And he was hers.

And his time here was finished.

Chapter Nineteen

"He's dying." Faith's heartbreaking voice filled Jesse's ears as she stood at Daniel's bedside and held his hand. "Th-they said he has massive internal injuries. . . ." The words trailed off into a strangled sob that reached inside Jesse and chipped away at his heart.

He came up beside her and slid his arms around her waist, pulling her close. She seemed so cold, so alone as he cradled her, stroked her hair, and what was left of his heart crumbled.

It made what he had to do all the harder.

And also that much easier.

After a long, heartbreaking moment, he pulled away from her and turned his attention to Daniel. The boy lay unconscious, the steady *whoosh* of air from a respirator lifting his small chest in a labored, artificial rhythm.

"Daniel," he whispered, taking the boy's hand.

There was no response; not that he'd expected any. Daniel would be dead soon by all accounts. Comatose, the doctor had said. Brain-dead. The machines were keeping his body alive, but there was little hope.

He closed his eyes and concentrated on the fire burning deep inside him, the blessed soul-saving light he'd carried back with him from the other side. It burned hotter, brighter, like a growing tidal wave that finally broke, washing through him, surging through his fingertips into the near-lifeless teenage boy.

Then it was done.

Jesse opened his eyes to see Daniel's chest rise with the pump of the respirator. His eyes remained closed, his body limp, but there was life in him now. Jesse could hear the steady beat of Daniel's heart echoed in the pulsing red lights of a heart monitor. He could feel the steady thump in his own chest, just as he felt the anguish gripping Faith, the tightening around her heart, the coldness seeping through her. Her hope was dying. As she watched Daniel waste away, she was doing the same. Dying herself. Inside.

Not for long, he told himself. Not for long.

"It'll be all right." He drew her into his arms, soaking up the soft, warm feel of her, the fresh scent of roses and rainwater that made his eyes burn and his chest ache.

After a few precious seconds, he forced himself away. His fingertips touched her chin and urged her gaze to his. "Don't lose hope, Faith. I know it's tough, but hang in there."

Her lips trembled in answer. Her eyes glittered, mirroring the unshed tears stinging Jesse's own eyes.

Tears, of all things, from a man who'd never cried for anyone or anything. Not when his father had left, or his mother had died. Not even when he'd lain crumpled on the floor next to his brother and sister, dying. The tears had been there, burning the backs of his lids, threatening to overwhelm him, but then he'd closed his eyes, and . . . death. Then it had been too late to shed even one.

He shut his eyes now, felt a drop of moisture squeeze past his lashes to blaze a trail down his cheek, and he relished the sensation. This was life. His last sweet taste.

Faith's hand cupped his jaw, catching the drop, as if it were the most natural thing in the world for him to cry, for her to comfort him. Her soft voice rang in his ears. "I'm so scared."

He opened his eyes then and smiled. "Everything will be all right this time." He trailed a fingertip down the side of her cheek, memorizing the delicate curve, feeling her heat and her vulnerability and her soul-eating fear. "I promise."

And for the next instant, her anguish eased just the tiniest bit. Hope flared, and Jesse knew that Faith Jansen was going to be all right.

Then he turned and walked away from her.

For the very last time.

"Doctor!" The nurse's frantic cry filled the hospital room a few minutes after Jesse left.

Faith had pulled a chair up next to Daniel to rest her cheek against his cold hand. At the noise, she jerked upright, blinking her tear-filled eyes.

"What's wrong?" Her gaze darted frantically from nurse to nurse as the hospital room quickly filled with medical personnel. Faith quickly found herself hustled out of the way as the medical team crowded around Daniel, blocking him from her view.

"I told you," one nurse rushed on. "One minute I'm sitting at the nurse's station, I glance up, and then I see his heart monitor, and this."

"It can't be right." The doctor leaned forward to get a closer look. "This *can't* be right."

The doctor ended his examination of the machine with a final check on the leads attached to Daniel's body, a puzzled glance at the green-and-black monitor, and a shake of his head. "I don't get it." He hooked the stethoscope into his ears and leaned over Daniel, disappearing from Faith's view.

She stood on the sidelines, tears streaming down her face, her breath shallow and pained.

We're sorry. There's nothing we can do.

Massive trauma.

Internal bleeding.

"Is he . . . Oh, my God, is he—." She swallowed, the word sticking in her throat. "Is he . . . getting worse?"

"I don't believe this!" the doctor exclaimed. "Look at him. Look at his eyes. I just don't believe it."

"What?" Her voice was a strained whisper. While she didn't want to hear the worst, she also hated not knowing. "Just go on and tell me."

"I've been treating trauma cases for twenty years and I've never seen anything like this."

"*What?*" she blurted, and a half dozen heads finally swiveled in her direction.

"This," the doctor said, a bewildered expression on his face as he motioned her forward.

The crowd parted, leaving her a clear trail to Daniel's bedside. She stared between two nurses to see Daniel, his eyes wide open, alert. The bruises mottling his face seemed pale now, the swelling that had distorted his features not as pronounced, almost as if the healing process had already begun.

Impossible.

"By all rights this boy should be dead. And even if he was hanging on by a thread, under no circumstances, I repeat, *no* circumstances, should he be wide-awake. He had a massive brain hemorrhage, and," the doctor said, checking several switches and knobs on the respirator, "two collapsed lungs. Or at least he *did*. . . . This just isn't possible."

Murmurs echoed the doctor's denial, yet no one could ignore the teenage boy who lay wide-awake on the bed before them.

Daniel lifted his hand then, to everyone's astonishment, and reached out. "Faith," he rasped, despite the respirator tube that hindered his speech.

Hot tears spilled past her lashes as she stepped forward and took his hand, felt his chilled fingers curl around hers.

"I need another CAT scan, an MRI, new blood cultures. . . ." The doctor barked out orders to the shocked medical team.

But Faith didn't need new tests to prove what lay right in front of her. Daniel was alive. *Alive*.

"It's a miracle," one of the nurses said, crossing herself as she held on to a small crucifix dangling from around her neck.

The doctor simply shook his head and hustled everyone off to carry out his orders. "I'm not saying anything one way or the other," he told her when she raised questioning eyes to him. "I want test results first." Then he turned on his heel and disappeared.

"You're going to be okay," she told Daniel, stroking the hair back from his bruised face, all the while holding his hand. "I promise."

He nodded, a peaceful look creeping across his features. His eyes closed then and he fell asleep. The heart monitor pulsed with a steady beat. His chest rose and fell in a relaxed rhythm, and Faith knew that she'd told him the truth.

He *was* going to be all right.

I promise. Jesse's words echoed through her head, her heart, and she knew that somehow, some way, he was responsible for Daniel's quick recovery.

The reality of all that they'd shared in the moments before Daniel had been spotted on the roof came rushing back to her. Jesse had *died*, and he'd come back.

But how? The possibilities whirled in her brain, but none of them made any sense. She needed to talk to him, to understand what had happened.

She found Bradley asleep on the sofa in the waiting room, surrounded by a half dozen slumbering kids. A light tap on his shoulder and he started.

"What's wrong?"

"Nothing," she told him. "Absolutely nothing." Then she went on to explain Daniel's seemingly miraculous recovery.

"So he's out of the woods for sure?"

Faith nodded and gave him a quick hug before sweeping another gaze around the room crowded with sleeping kids. "Where's Jesse?"

Bradley shrugged. "I saw him take off maybe five or ten minutes ago. Right after he looked in on you."

"I thought he was coming out here to sit with you and the kids."

Bradley shook his head. "No. I figured he told you he was leaving."

"He didn't say a word, not even good-bye." As the last word slid past her lips, the truth hit her like a two-by-four. She sank down to the sofa and buried her face in her hands.

And she knew then that Jesse had, indeed, said good-bye to her.

Everything will be all right. . . . I promise. . . . , he'd said. And he'd kept his promise.

It's a miracle.

Her mind rifled back through their last conversation, to the glittering in his eyes. The light . . .

I've been sent here to renew your faith in life. To make you love and care again. I've been sent. . . .

An angel.

Images flashed through her mind from the past two weeks—Jesse arriving on her doorstep out of the blue; Jesse with eyes that flickered with such an intense light; Jesse, who climbed into her head and knew her thoughts; Jesse, who felt her emotions. Jesse.

More than a man. An angel.

"I think I know where he went."

Faith glanced down through tear-filled eyes to see Trudy standing beside her.

"You do?" She dashed away several tears, hope blossoming.

Trudy nodded. "I mean, I don't know exactly, but I've got a pretty good idea. I saw him take off. He seemed sort of upset, kind of out of it, you know? He had this look in his eyes. . . . I saw it once before back at my place when he came there the first time."

"That old apartment building he found you in?"

Even before the girl nodded, Faith knew the answer. It was Jesse's building. The place where he and his brother and Jane had been attacked. The place where Jesse and his brother had died.

And though Faith didn't know for sure what was about to happen, she had a good hunch. Jesse had called himself a messenger. A delivery boy. An angel packing a miracle.

Tonight he'd delivered that life-renewing, faith-reviving, hope-inspiring miracle. And now . . .

"No!" The word slid past her trembling lips at the same time she bolted to her feet. She all but ripped the Suburban keys out of Bradley's pocket before rushing out of the hospital, Trudy beside her.

Jesse was leaving her. And though she had no clue as to what she could do to stop him, to hold on to him, she had to try.

Climbing behind the wheel, she slid the key into the ignition, gunned the engine, and gripped the steering wheel for a long, desperate moment.

And for the second time that night, Faith closed her eyes and did the only thing she could. She prayed.

When Faith rolled to a stop in front of the old building, she saw Jesse's motorcycle parked a few feet away, and her breathing all but stopped. Before the engine could rumble and die, she told Trudy to stay put, and rushed up the front steps into the vacant shell that reeked of death and desperation and hopelessness.

But Faith wasn't hopeless. Not yet. Not until she could see with her own eyes what waited inside.

Then . . .

She wouldn't think about *then*. Only now. This moment. She hurried up the decaying staircase to the third floor, down a darkened hallway, past strips of wilted yellow crime-scene tape. Her heart grew heavy with each step, and all but stopped beating the moment she reached the threshold of apartment 3B.

Jesse knelt in the far corner, his face tilted heavenward, and it was nothing short of heaven that opened before him.

A white hole gaped through the blackness, sending shimmers of cascading light down around him, a bright halo that surrounded his entire body, cradling him, calling him home.

The realization sent a burst of fear through her and she lunged into the room, to come up short only inches away from the circle of light, as if an invisible wall separated them, keeping her from reaching out, from grasping his hand. From keeping him here with her.

And Faith knew then that this was truly good-bye. His mission was over, his miracle delivered, and he was on his way home.

Her mouth opened and a keening wail exploded from deep inside her. A cry for mercy. For life. For Jesse.

"Please!"

Jesse barely heard Faith's anguished voice through the heat that consumed his senses. At first he thought it was his imagination, but then he heard it again, like a desperate, fervent prayer slicing through the encompassing silence to shatter the peace inside of him.

"Don't leave me, Jesse! Please!"

But he had to go. Even though his heart begged him to turn away from the light, he couldn't. It was stronger, so consuming, and so promising.

Peace. The brilliance whispered the first of its heavenly offerings. *An eternity of peace.*

But Jesse had found peace on earth. Inside of

himself. In the warm comfort of Faith's arms, in her smile, in her soft voice.

Forgiveness, the light offered. *A chance to see your brother and sister again, to speak the words and ask their forgiveness.*

But he'd already found forgiveness, too. Inside himself.

Love. The light played its trump card. *A never-ending love that doesn't walk away, turn its back, die. A love that lasts forever.*

But Jesse had already found that, as well. A love greater than any he'd ever known. The emotion burned as fiercely as the light, as brightly, but it wasn't on the outside, surrounding him; it was inside, filling him, gaining in intensity with every moment that passed.

"Please!" He heard the frantic plea again, but it wasn't Faith. It was his own voice, his own heart pleading for mercy, for life. "*Please!*"

The light seemed to dance in a million points of dazzling heat, as if gathering energy, ready to envelop Jesse and take him forever.

But Faith was ready for a fight. She gathered her courage, her strength, and threw herself forward. "I won't let you take him. You can't just send him to me and take him back. I need him. I *need* him!"

As if the invisible barrier couldn't hold up under her words, it crumbled into nothingness and she fell forward onto her hands and knees. Then she started to crawl, tears streaming down her cheeks.

"Stay with me," she cried with trembling lips, and the sound of her voice finally drew Jesse's gaze. Their eyes locked and the white-hot light of his stare flickered, dimmed, faded into a familiar brown, and she knew he was still a part of this life. For now.

"Please," she begged, reaching out into the shimmering circle of white brilliance.

It was like thrusting her hand into an oven. Fire licked over her skin, searing her for all of five seconds. Then it was as if she became accustomed to the blazing onslaught, drank in the heat, craved it.

Warmth surged through her whole body, pushing away the chill of mortality, sending fear and pain and sadness scurrying for their lives. A wave of happiness swept through her, followed by peace and serenity, and Faith longed to close her eyes and give herself up to the incredible sensations.

Yet she didn't so much as blink. She kept her gaze fixed on Jesse's, begging him to resist the light, as she was.

It wasn't their time, she thought fiercely. She had a lot of living left in her, a lot of kids to save, and she wanted Jesse by her side, living and sharing and caring. The two of them.

"Please," she begged again, but the word wasn't directed at Jesse. She begged the light. Fate. The powers that be. "I love him," she whispered, tears splashing down her face. "I love him."

As if the words triggered something, Jesse's eyes darkened even more and he leaned forward, closing the few inches that separated them. His fingertips touched hers, and the light faded to a pinpoint that winked once, twice, then vanished into the blackness overhead.

But the warmth remained. The inner heat that had touched her soul. It coursed through Faith, into Jesse, and back, like an invisible current connecting them, binding them together as one.

They *were* one, she realized, crawling forward, collapsing in Jesse's arms.

He was hers and she was his.

"I love you," she whispered against the hard wall of his chest. "I love you."

"And I love you." Jesse stared down at the woman snuggled in his arms. A man's arms. That was all he was now. A man. He felt it in the pulse of blood through his veins, the frantic thud of his heart—his own, not hers. There was no more emotional link with her, other than their love.

His gaze snagged on his right hand, the skin now smooth and tanned, sprinkled with dark hair. For a moment, to Jesse, all was right with the universe. The scar was gone. Faith was in his arms, her love mingling with his own, filling his heart.

And as he held her, he knew with an unwavering certainty that no afterlife could be better than what he held right here in his hands. His woman, his love, his . . . heaven.

The hospital was buzzing with excitement when Faith and Jesse walked into the intensive-care unit a half hour later. The news of Daniel's miraculous recovery had spread like wildfire. The doctor had been forced to post a NO VISITORS ALLOWED sign on Daniel's door to cut down on the number of well-wishers and Curious Georges who kept disturbing his rest.

"He's sleeping, but you can look in on him," the doctor told Faith when she found him in his office several minutes later, perusing the previous results of Daniel's initial tests. "Just keep it short." He wiped a hand over his tired eyes as he drank in page after page. "I still don't understand. . . ."

Jesse smiled, his fingers tightening around Faith's as they headed down the hall to the boy's room.

"Daniel—" The words choked in her throat as she

stared at the empty hospital bed, the covers thrown back. *Empty*.

"Maybe he's out having some of those tests the doctor ordered," Jesse offered.

She shook her head, dread churning in her stomach. "It's the middle of the night, and you heard the doctor say he was here asleep. Unless . . ." *Dead*. The word pushed into her conscience and accelerated her heartbeat.

It couldn't be. Not after all this. But then maybe that was the price for Jesse's return to humanity. Maybe that rendered the miracle null and void—

"No." As if he'd read her thoughts, Jesse's denial rumbled in her ears. "I'm sure there's another explanation. Stay here while I get the nurse."

Faith leaned over the bed railing and rested her hand in the indentation where Daniel's head had been. Warmth seeped into her fingertips and her eyes burned.

"Daniel," she said softly, the name a prayer on her lips.

But it was too late for any more prayers. Faith knew in her heart what had happened. She had been given Jesse, but at a price. Daniel's life.

A movement outside the window caught Faith's attention and she moved around the bed to stare through the thick glass, out into the fog-shrouded night.

She saw him then, and the sight made her blink her eyes.

Once, twice, but he was still there.

Daniel stood outside on the ledge, a ghostly apparition in the white hospital gown that trailed down past his knees. His head was tilted back, his gaze fixed on the sky.

Déjà vu washed over Faith and she saw him as

351

he'd been on top of the Marbury Building, a hairbreadth from jumping.

Panic swamped her and she searched the glass, looking for a way to open the window. Nothing. There was no latch. No way out. Her gaze skittered to the left and she spotted the intercom. She reached for the button to call the nurse, a heartbroken whisper passing her lips.

"No!"

She saw him turn then, as if he'd heard her through the thick glass. Her hand stalled in midair halfway to the nurse's button, the light in Daniel's eyes freezing her to the spot. She'd seen the same light in Jesse's eyes. The same light surrounding him only a short time ago: A heavenly light.

As that thought dawned on her, Daniel smiled, then turned his gaze back heavenward. The mist seemed to come alive then, swirling around him, embracing him. He blended into the fuzzy grayness as if he'd always been a part of it.

"No!" Jesse's voice echoed her own and she felt him behind her, staring over her shoulder at the empty spot where Daniel had been standing.

Faith blinked frantically, but the boy didn't reappear. Surely he'd jumped. He couldn't be here one minute, gone the next.

Yet deep inside she knew he hadn't jumped. He hadn't so much as moved a muscle. He'd simply stood there, then poof! Nothing.

Her gaze caught a twinkling reflection in the window. She turned to see her friendship charm lying on the wrinkled sheets covering the hospital bed.

Immediately, her hand went to her throat. She must have dropped it earlier—

The thought stalled as she found the warm metal

of her own charm. With trembling fingers, she picked up the charm from the bed and cradled it in her palm. It was identical to the one she wore, down to the familiar initials engraved on the back. *J and F . . . Friends forever*. Jane and Faith. She was staring at Jane's charm.

Impossible!

Jane had been buried with her half of the friendship circle. Faith had placed it in the coffin herself.

She blinked the tears away and gazed into the gold half circle. Reflected in the charm was Daniel's smiling face as she'd seen him a moment ago. His eyes twinkled blue fire, then faded.

The image blurred and Faith found herself staring at a girl's image. *Jane . . .*

Tears blurred her eyes, blurring the image, but Faith didn't need to see any more. As if she'd fit the missing piece into a puzzle, she stood back and surveyed the final picture. As crazy as it was, it made perfect sense.

All along Jesse had thought *he'd* been the one sent to renew Faith's hope, but Daniel had really been sent to save them both. To make them feel again, care, share, believe, and most important, to show them how precious life was.

Faith had earned a miracle with all her nurturing, and apparently Jesse Savage had earned his own miracle as well. Daniel had been the delivery boy, the Cupid to bring two lonely people together and show them the meaning of love.

She knew the truth now, and so did Jesse, she realized when she turned to find his dark eyes as bright as hers. He drew her into his arms and they hugged each other, sharing their incredulity, their sorrow, their joy, while a pinpoint of light, no bigger than a twinkling star, broke through the clouds outside the window.

And a young girl's soft voice carried on the breeze.

Be happy, Faith and Jesse. Be happy. . . .

Epilogue

"And what is this little angel's name?" the nurse asked as she placed the newborn infant into Faith's arms.

"Jane."

"Rachel."

Faith and Jesse spoke the names at the same time, their full attention on the tiny baby girl bundled in a soft pink blanket. Their gazes shifted, colliding with one another's, and the nurse chuckled.

"I won't even ask about this one." She handed Jesse a second child wrapped in a blue blanket. "I'll just give you proud parents a moment alone; then I'll be back to collect these two for the nursery. Maybe you can decide on their names by then. Oh." She paused in the doorway. "Should I tell the gentleman waiting outside the good news? He's been here all night. We tried to get him to go home, but he said he intended to be here until you squeezed this puppy out."

"Squeezed this puppy out?" Faith stared at Jesse, a grin tugging at her lips. "And we picked him to be the godfather?"

The nurse laughed. "Oh, give him a chance. The way he's been nagging, he'll make a great godparent."

"And he won't be going it alone," Jesse reminded Faith, giving her a wink. "Trudy and Emily are sharing godmother responsibilities. What with the way they've been reading all your baby books, I'm sure they'll keep Bradley in line."

A gleam lit the nurse's eyes. "So what do you say? Can I break the news?"

Faith and Jesse exchanged glances, then nodded. "Make sure you sit him down first. We didn't tell anybody we were having twins, so he's only expecting one."

The nurse smiled. "Oh, I'll sit him down, all right. Him and every one of those kids packed into the waiting room."

"How many kids?"

"At least two dozen, and all as anxious as that Bradley."

Faith and Jesse exchanged glances. "I guess he brought everybody at Faith's House and the shelter, too." The shelter referred to Salvation House, a new temporary refuge for homeless teens now located in Jesse's old apartment building. With the help of several private investors, the building had been bought, renovated, and now served as a beacon to the community. Jesse ran Salvation House, while Faith remained the foster mother to her kids at Faith's House. She had just finalized adopting Trudy.

Based on his past history of fleeing foster homes

and county agencies, CPS had classified Daniel's sudden disappearance from the hospital as another runaway attempt. His case remained open, and authorities were still on the lookout for him. Not that anyone would ever find him, Faith thought. Daniel had simply vanished, as abruptly, as mysteriously as all records of Jesse's untimely death.

Estelle's background check on Jesse had finally come through a few days after Daniel's disappearance, and oddly enough, records showed Jesse alive and well and living in Houston.

A miracle, Faith and Jesse had concluded.

Now only the small headstone next to his younger brother's grave stood as a reminder to them. But oddly enough there were no engraved words, as if someone had wiped the marble clean. It was enough that they remembered, and were grateful for all that they had been given.

Faith stared down at the tiny baby girl with dark hair and dark eyes so much like Jesse's; then her gaze shifted to the little boy cradled in his daddy's arms. Nine months of worrying and wondering surged through Faith and wiped the smile from her face.

"Jesse?"

"Mmmm," he said, trailing a fingertip down his son's cheek.

"What if . . ." Her words trailed off and his gaze lifted to meet hers. "I mean, we've never had a real baby before. The kids at Faith's House and the shelter are different: They aren't babies. And we don't just have one. We have two, and I don't know how to handle one, much less both of them. What if they start crying and I can't comfort them—"

Jesse touched his fingertips to her lips. *"We'll* comfort them. The two of us. Together."

She tamped down her fears and summoned a smile. "I forgot you raised your brother and sister from diapers. You're practically an expert."

"Not yet. But after five or six more . . ."

Her eyes widened in shock. "Five or six?"

He grinned. "Maybe seven."

She started to protest, battle-weary after fourteen hours of excruciating labor. Then the baby girl sighed and snuggled deeper into Faith's arms, and warmth surged through her. "Okay, maybe seven." She touched the baby's tiny nose, her mouth. The small lips parted, suckling the tip of her finger. "You're so beautiful," she cooed. "Just like your aunt."

The boy chose that moment to let loose a loud wail, obviously displeased to be left out of the compliment.

"And this one's got a set of lungs to match his uncle's." Jesse grinned as if his new son had just been named a first-draft pick by the NFL. "He's just as loud as Jason," he said, remembering his brother. But there was no sadness in his voice. He'd come to terms with his grief. Now all that remained were fond memories. "I swear I didn't sleep for the first six months after he was born."

Tears spilled past Faith's lashes as she watched her husband cuddle the tiny baby boy and shush his crying, and with each soft word he whispered, each rock of his strong arms, Faith felt her heart swell.

Soon the boy quieted and both babies settled into a safe sleep, nestled in the arms of their mommy and daddy.

"Rachel Jane Savage," Faith finally murmured. "That's her name."

"And this is Jason," Jesse added. "Jason Savage."

"Rachel and Jason." Faith stared down at the precious children born of the love she and Jesse shared, and smiled. A boy and a girl. *Rachel and Jason.* "I wonder if your aunt and uncle would like that?"

Far, far away, beyond the hospital room and the storm clouds, in the vast diamond-studded blackness of heaven, two stars twinkled in answer.

They liked it. Very, very much.

Something Wild

Kimberly Raye

Dependent only upon twentieth-century conveniences, Tara Martin seeks to make a name for herself as a top-notch photojournalist. But when a plea from her best friend sends her off into the Smoky Mountains to snap a sasquatch, a twisted ankle leaves her in a precarious position—and when she looks up, she sees the biggest foot she's ever seen. Tara learns that the big foot belongs to an even bigger man—with a colossal heart and a body to die for. And that man, who was raised alone in the wilds of Appalachia, will teach Tara that what she needs is something wild.

___52272-1 $5.50 US/$6.50 CAN

Dorchester Publishing Co., Inc.
P.O. Box 6640
Wayne, PA 19087-8640

Please add $1.75 for shipping and handling for the first book and $.50 for each book thereafter. NY, NYC, and PA residents, please add appropriate sales tax. No cash, stamps, or C.O.D.s. All orders shipped within 6 weeks via postal service book rate. Canadian orders require $2.00 extra postage and must be paid in U.S. dollars through a U.S. banking facility.

Name_____
Address_____
City_____ State_____ Zip_____
I have enclosed $_____ in payment for the checked book(s).
Payment <u>must</u> accompany all orders. ❑ Please send a free catalog.
CHECK OUT OUR WEBSITE! www.dorchesterpub.com

Bestselling Author of *Hand & Heart of a Soldier*

With a name that belies his true nature, Joshua Angell was born for deception. So when sophisticated and proper Ava Moreland first sees the sexy drifter in a desolate Missouri jail, she knows he is the one to save her sister from a ruined reputation and a fatherless child. But she will need Angell to fool New York society into thinking he is the ideal husband—and only Ava can teach him how. But what start as simple lessons in etiquette and speech soon become smoldering lessons in love. And as the beautiful socialite's feelings for Angell deepen, so does her passion—and finally she knows she will never be satisfied until she, and no other, claims him as her very own...untamed angel.

___4274-6 $4.99 US/$5.99 CAN

Dorchester Publishing Co., Inc.
P.O. Box 6640
Wayne, PA 19087-8640

Please add $1.75 for shipping and handling for the first book and $.50 for each book thereafter. NY, NYC, and PA residents, please add appropriate sales tax. No cash, stamps, or C.O.D.s. All orders shipped within 6 weeks via postal service book rate. Canadian orders require $2.00 extra postage and must be paid in U.S. dollars through a U.S. banking facility.

Name_____
Address_____
City_____State_____Zip_____
I have enclosed $_____ in payment for the checked book(s).
Payment <u>must</u> accompany all orders. ❑ Please send a free catalog.

An Angel's Touch

Heavenly Persuasion

LORRAINE HENDERSON

Lovely Jessica McAllister vows to honor her dying sister's final request. Determined to raise orphaned Maria as if she were her own daughter, Jessica never thinks she'll run into trouble in the form of the child's uncle, handsome winery-owner Benjamin Whittacker.

Benjamin is all man, and as headstrong as Jessica when it comes to deciding what is best for Maria. As sparks fly between the two, their fight for custody turns into a struggle to deny their own burning attraction.

Left to their own devices, the willful twosome may never discover their blossoming love. But Benjamin and Jessica are not alone. With one determined little girl—and her very special angelic helper—the stubborn duo just might be forced to acknowledge a love truly made in heaven.

_52069-9 $5.99 US/$7.99 CAN

HOUSE OF FOUR SEASONS

Abigail McDaniels

Subject of myth and legend, the wisteria-shrouded mansion stands derelict, crumbling into the Louisiana bayou until architect Lauren Hamilton rescues it from the encroaching swamps.

Then things begin to appear and disappear...lights flicker on and off...and a deep phantom voice that Lauren knows can't be real seems to call to her from the secret shadows and dark recesses of the wood-paneled rooms.

Lauren knows she should be frightened, but there is something soothing in the voice, something familiar that promises a long-forgotten joy that she knew in another time, another place.

_52061-3 $4.99 US/$6.99 CAN

FOREVER & A DAY

VICTORIA CHANCELLOR

When Linda O'Rourke returns to her grandmother's South Carolina beach house, it is for a quiet summer of tying up loose ends. And although the lovely dwelling charms her, she can't help but remember the evil presence that threatened her there so many years ago. Plagued by her fear, and tormented by visions of a virile Englishman tempting her with his every caress, she is unprepared for reality in the form of the mysterious and handsome Gifford Knight. His kisses evoke memories of the man in her dreams, but his sensual demands are all too real. Linda longs to surrender to Giff's masterful touch, but is it a safe haven she finds in his arms, or the beginning of her worst nightmare?

__52063-X $5.50 US/$7.50 CAN

BAD COMPANY

CAROL CARSON

Trixianna Lawless is furious when the ruggedly handsome sheriff arrests her for bank robbery. But when she finds herself in Chance's house instead of jail, she begins to wish that he would look at her with his piercing blue eyes . . . and take her into his well-muscled arms.

___4448-X $4.99 US/$5.99 CAN

Dorchester Publishing Co., Inc.
P.O. Box 6640
Wayne, PA 19087-8640

Please add $1.75 for shipping and handling for the first book and $.50 for each book thereafter. NY, NYC, and PA residents, please add appropriate sales tax. No cash, stamps, or C.O.D.s. All orders shipped within 6 weeks via postal service book rate. Canadian orders require $2.00 extra postage and must be paid in U.S. dollars through a U.S. banking facility.

Name_____
Address_____
City_____State_____Zip_____
I have enclosed $_____ in payment for the checked book(s).
Payment <u>must</u> accompany all orders. ☐ Please send a free catalog.